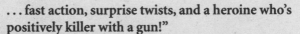

"The Assassin delivers the goods

... fast action, surprise twists, and a heroine who's positively killer with a gun!"
—Lisa Gardner, *New York Times* bestselling author of *Alone*

"Wow! fast-paced, sexy suspense: *The Assassin* is a thrill ride I didn't want to end."
—Karen Robards, *New York Times* bestselling author of *Bait*

"Gritty and sexually charged. The cop and the killer are a dynamite duo."
—Andrea Kane, *New York Times* bestselling author of *I'll Be Watching You*

"Selena McCaffrey is the coolest, sexiest, most compelling heroine to come along since *Buffy*, *Xena*, and *Alias* set the standards for kick-ass female suspense/adventure. Combine Selena with a villain who will raise your goose bumps, a sexy cop who will raise your temperature, and a secondary cast that definitely raises the bar for excellence, and what you have is a must-read new suspense series that will keep you turning pages all night long. I can't wait for the next dose of Rachel Butler!"
—Lynda Sandoval, former cop and award-winning author of *Unsettling*

"Taut, fast-paced suspense with a twist at every turn, *The Assassin* delivers one surprise after another all the way to the explosive ending—great characters, great fun, and a great read."
—Tara Janzen, author of *Crazy Hot*

The Assassin

RACHEL BUTLER

A Dell Book

THE ASSASSIN
A Dell Book / April 2005

Published by Bantam Dell
A Division of Random House, Inc.
New York, New York

Dell is a registered trademark of Random House, Inc., and the colophon is a trademark of Random House, Inc.

ISBN 0-440-24120-0

Printed in the United States of America
Published simultaneously in Canada

www.bantamdell.com

OPM 10 9 8 7 6 5 4 3 2 1

The
Assassin

Prologue

The attack came from behind, a muscular forearm across her throat, diminishing the oxygen supply to her lungs. Before Selena McCaffrey could react, she was lifted from her feet, then slammed to the ground. What little air she'd had left rushed out in a grunt as pain vibrated through her midsection. She pushed it out of her mind, though, and let instinct take over. As her attacker's weight came down on her, she slashed at his face with her nails and was rewarded with a sound that was half groan, half growl. He eased his hold for one instant, all she needed to arch her back and throw him off balance. With another heave, she was free of him.

As she scrambled to her feet, his fingers wrapped around her right ankle in a grip so brutal her vision turned shadowy. Clamping her jaw tight, she shifted her weight and kicked him with her left foot, a sharp jab to the ribs. He swore, yanked her leg out from under her, then rolled on top of her the instant she landed.

His face inches from hers, he laughed. "What are you gonna do, sweet pea? Huh? I'm on top. I can do whatever I want, and there's nothing you can do to stop me. You're all out of tricks, aren't you?"

Adrenaline pumped through her, along with fear and excitement. Her chest heaving, she stared at him, locking gazes. As the muscles in her right arm flexed, she eased her left hand toward the waistband of her shorts, her fingers closing around the handle of the knife tucked there. Without breaking eye contact, she raised her right hand as if to claw at his face. Laughing, he caught her wrist and forced it to the ground at her side. But before he could get out the first word about such a predictable response, she whipped the knife up in her free hand and pressed the razor-sharp blade to his throat.

He froze. Barely breathing, he murmured, "Fuck me."

"Get off me."

He hesitated. She pressed just hard enough to pierce his skin with the knife point, bringing a drop of crimson blood to the surface. His curse was vicious, but he backed away carefully.

Once he was out of her space, she easily got to her feet, folded the knife, and returned it to her waistband.

Jimmy Montoya clamped his fingers to his throat, then stared at the blood smeared across them. "You could have hurt me!"

"I *could* have killed you."

"Bitch."

"Loser." She removed the band that held back her hair—at least, what hadn't fallen loose in their struggle—then gathered the long thick curls and corralled them with the elastic once more.

"Weapons aren't fair."

"You weigh fifty pounds more than me. I'm just evening the odds."

"What would you have done without the knife?"

She picked up a water bottle from the nearby patio table and took a long drink. "I wouldn't *be* without it."

"Humor me. Assume you were. What would you have done in that situation if you hadn't had the knife?"

Gazing out over the ocean, she considered it a moment before replying. "I suppose I would have broken your neck."

He grinned, but the amusement didn't reach his eyes. He didn't know whether she was teasing . . . or meant every word.

Fair enough. Neither did she.

"See you next time."

Leaning one hip against the table, Selena watched as Montoya walked inside. Through tall arched windows, she saw him stop to correct a student's posture in the ongoing yoga class, then offer encouragement to another struggling on a weight bench.

For two years she'd been coming to his gym. The word hardly did justice to the structure, or to the elaborate grounds surrounding it. Self-defense, yoga, and tai chi were taught on the lush lawn, and a jogging trail wound along the perimeter of the property. She ran five miles there every day, lifted weights three times a week, and took tae kwon do, kickboxing, and aikido classes regularly. She held a first-degree black belt in tae kwon do and could break any bone in the human body with one kick. She could have broken Montoya's ribs, and if he were an attacker, she would have.

And if that failed to get her out of the jam, well, there was always the knife.

Her own ribs ached when she pushed away from the table. She would be bruised and stiff the next day, but she'd suffered worse and survived. She was tough. She would always survive.

Instead of showering in the locker room, she grabbed her backpack and started walking the three blocks home. She should have been gone hours ago, but she'd needed one last workout with Montoya for good luck . . . or was it confidence?

The June sun was warm, the air heavy with the scents of the sea and the flowers that bloomed in profusion along the sidewalk—bougainvillea, jasmine, plumeria. Selena made a conscious effort not to think as she walked—to simply breathe and relax while remaining aware of her surroundings. It didn't pay to let your guard down—*ever*. That had been a painful lesson to learn.

Her house was on the ocean side of the street, though she lacked Montoya's gorgeous view except from the second floor. The structure was more than a hundred years old and had survived tropical storms, hurricane-force winds, and decades of neglect. The white paint on the boards and the dark green on the shutters had been her spring project. The new shingles on the roof, completed over the winter. The small green lawn, bordered on all sides by a cutting garden gone wild, cultivated over the past eighteen months. The picket fence that circled the lot, repaired and whitewashed last summer. The handpainted sign swinging from a post near the gate, last week's accomplishment. *Island Dreams Art Gallery.*

She had moved into the house the day she'd signed the papers, and she loved everything about it. The high ceilings, tall windows, and oversized rooms. The wide veranda wrapping around three sides, the stairs climbing straight and true to the second floor, the butler's pantry, the louvered shutters, and the dusty chandeliers. The cypress floors, the porcelain sinks, the claw-foot tub, the marble fireplaces. The age. The history. The welcome. The security.

And the fact that it was hers. The only home she'd ever had. The only thing of value she'd ever possessed. One of only two things she could *not* afford to lose. Her home. Her freedom. Everything she was, everything she might ever be, depended on those two things. Protecting them protected *her*.

An older couple, white-haired and tanned, was coming down the steps as she approached. She greeted them, then opened the screen door with a creak. What had originally been the formal living and dining rooms was now home to her gallery. The library had become the gallery office, leaving only the kitchen and pantry to their original purposes. A mere half dozen of her own paintings were currently exhibited, along with bins of signed and numbered prints. Of all the artists represented in Island Dreams, her own work was most popular with her clientele. But that stood to reason. If they didn't like Selena McCaffrey's paintings, they wouldn't shop at Selena McCaffrey's gallery.

Asha Beauregard, her only employee, was chatting with another customer. She gave Selena a wave behind the man's back. Asha liked to say that she couldn't draw a straight line to save her life, but she knew talent when she saw it. The gallery was in good hands.

Selena detoured through the kitchen to get another bottle of water, then took the back stairs to her bedroom. Originally there had been four rooms and a bath upstairs. Now there were two—a large living room at the front of the house, with enough space for a workout when Montoya's seemed too far to go, and an airy bed/bath combination. She'd lived too much of her life in cramped, dark places. Now she liked large spaces, lots of glass, a sense of openness.

After showering, she dressed in a silk outfit, the top crimson and fitted, the color repeated in the tropical print of the skirt. The hem fluttered around her ankles except on the left side, where it was slit halfway up her thigh. Her suitcases were already packed, with just one bag left. She laid it open on the plantation-style bed, unlocked the small safe in the back of the closet, then began transferring the necessary items.

A Smith & Wesson .40 caliber pistol, illegally modified to fully automatic.

A compact Beretta .22 automatic, small enough to fit in her pocket or her smallest handbag.

A dagger, sheathed to protect the double-edged blade. The switchblade she carried had been chosen as much for concealability as function. The dagger had been chosen strictly for function.

She added extra clips for each of the guns, a change of IDs, and a stash of cash. It wasn't a lot, but in an emergency, she didn't need a lot.

Not that she was planning on having any emergencies.

She closed and locked the bag, then slid it inside the suitcase she'd left half empty for just that purpose. After securing the key on the chain around her neck so that it rested out of sight between her breasts, she picked up the suitcases and started for the stairs. She probably looked like any young woman setting off on vacation.

In fact, she was going to kill a man.

1

A triple homicide was a hell of a way to start a Monday morning, Tony Ceola thought as he eased his Chevy Impala to the side of the street. A patrol unit was parked in front of the house, blocking the driveway. The officer who'd caught the call leaned against the back fender, yellow-and-black crime-scene tape fluttering in the light breeze, his face mottled shades of green.

Fat leather attaché slung over one shoulder, Tony greeted him with a nod. He glanced at the Cadillac in the driveway, then checked out the piss-yellow Ford across the street. It belonged to Frank Simmons, fellow detective and general goofball, but not a bad guy. There were worse guys to work a triple homicide with.

As he started up the driveway, Simmons stepped out onto the porch and took a deep breath. "You know, Chee, there oughta be a law against killing people in the middle of a heat wave."

"There's laws against a lot of shit. Some people just don't obey them."

"Imagine that." Simmons gestured toward the Caddy. "Look familiar?"

"Make my day and tell me it belongs to Mykle Moore."

"Who else you know drives a fuckin' tank like gas ain't nearly two bucks a gallon? He's inside, and his partners in crime are with him. I already got a call in to the M.E. and the crime-scene unit."

"Banks and Washington? They just got arrested the other day. I thought they were in jail awaiting trial."

"Ain't you heard?" Simmons snorted. "The district attorney installed revolving doors down there to speed up the process of getting these poor misguided souls back out on the street. Let's get started, son. They're already swellin' and smellin', and it ain't gonna get any better."

Taking one last deep clean breath, Tony followed Simmons inside. The stench of death was strong, but not yet overpowering. Grover Washington, lucky to have lived long enough to see thirty-two, five-feet-nine-inches tall and about that across, sporting a shiny gold ring in his left ear and a shinier gold tooth, lay sprawled in the middle of the floor, looking for all the world like a rag doll tossed aside, except for the large-caliber holes in his chest and the blood pooled around his torso.

The second corpse was Walter Banks, twenty-seven, guilty of at least four murders, but too slick to get convicted even once. He was seated on a ratty old couch, his head tilted back. He could have been asleep if not for the fact that he was wearing most of his blood on his clothes.

The third victim, on the floor in front of the side window, was the youngest at eighteen. Mykle Moore had been lean and wiry, with a baby face that couldn't even sprout a decent mustache, but he'd beaten his sister to death with a baseball bat for doing the nasty with one of his competitors. Now that face bore a gunshot wound in the forehead, and an exit wound from a second shot dead center in the chest.

Next to each body was a calling card with a one-word message: *Repent*. They would bag them, of course, but Tony already knew what the lab would find—standard playing-card size, printed on common index cards by the best-selling brand of printer in America. No fingerprints, no smudges, no clues.

"Maybe somebody should explain to this guy that it's real hard to repent with a bullet in your brain."

Simmons snorted again. "I hope not. He might stop putting those bullets there, and then where would we be?"

"Not so bogged down in cases is where," Tony retorted.

"Hey, you and me, we do our best to take this scum off the streets, and the *justice system*"—Simmons said it as an epitaph—"puts 'em right back out there. Our vigilante is taking 'em off the street permanently. Any way you look at it, that's justice."

"Any way you look at it, that's murder." Tony set his bag down on the floor, pulled on a pair of powder-free latex gloves, then took out a camera. CSU would photograph everything, but he liked taking his own pictures, as well, to ensure he got every shot he wanted, at the angles he wanted. He snapped off long shots of the room and close-ups of the bodies, the windowsill, and the calling cards, then crouched near Washington's body.

Considering all the misery Grover had caused—the drugs he'd dealt, the people he'd killed, the assaults and intimidation and rapes—lying dead on the floor of an abandoned house was as much justice as anyone could hope for. Too easy a death, some would say, but in the end, dead was dead.

A card lay faceup on the torn linoleum, its top edge just touching the pool of congealed blood. *Repent.* Had he? Had he known what was coming and had time to say a prayer?

Tony doubted it. The only way to take out these guys was by surprise. They were always armed—*MasterGun,*

Grover had frequently joked. *Never leave home without it.* No weapons were visible on any of the bodies, but no doubt they would turn up once the M.E.'s guy was ready to tag 'em and bag 'em.

"What do you say, man?" Simmons looked up from his own examination of Walter Banks. "Let's call it 'death due to natural causes' and go get some breakfast."

It didn't get much more natural for people like these, Tony thought. Those who lived by the sword died by it.

"Looks like a .45, maybe a .357," he remarked as he stood up.

"I'm surprised the guy didn't need an elephant gun to bring down ol' Grover here. He's a big mamou." Simmons grimaced. "You know we're gonna have to help load him up."

Tony straightened. His muscles were already protesting in anticipation as he backtracked to the door.

Presumably, the killer had been standing in the vicinity of the doorway when he'd opened fire. None of the victims had expected trouble, or they would have had their weapons drawn, and surely one of them would have gotten off at least one shot. Had the shooter walked in on them without warning? Or had they been expecting him, if not the gunshots? Banks hadn't had time or, just guessing, reason to rise from the couch, and Grover had been on his feet, facing the door. Looking at someone who had just come in?

"What about the brass?" he asked, turning his gaze to the floor in search of shell casings. "You see any?"

"Not a one. But a .357 wouldn't eject 'em, and a .45 . . . a pro would take 'em."

"Anyone who watches *C.S.I.* would take 'em." TV had taught people more than they needed to know about criminal investigations. Fortunately, crooks didn't tend to be quick learners.

Switching the camera to his left hand, Tony flipped on a flashlight and played the beam over the floor to his right. Rubbish was piled against the wall—beer cans, fast-food wrappers, used rubbers, a couple hypodermic needles. Punks came here to get drunk, get laid, and get high in relative comfort.

He'd never been that horny or that desperate in his life.

Before he faced the task of sorting through the trash, he turned a hundred and eighty degrees, then crouched, lighting up the floor in the opposite corner. The angled beam highlighted a half-dozen faint shoeprints in the dust. Maybe their shooter hadn't walked in on his victims, but had been here waiting for them. Standing in the corner of the darkened room, a person could go unobserved by anyone who entered. Then it would have been a simple matter of stepping out, gun in hand, and blowing the bastards away.

He finished off the roll of film, then studied the clearest footprint while reloading the camera. It looked to be about a size eleven—his own size—and unremarkable. A dress shoe, probably, with no markings or obvious defects. Too bad it wasn't a running shoe with the fancy tread patterns common to that type. That would make it easy to identify the brand and style.

On the other hand, probably ninety percent of the population in northeast Oklahoma wore running shoes, including all three victims. The size-eleven-dress-shoe group was significantly smaller.

"I'm gonna talk to the kid outside," he said, peeling off his gloves and trading the camera for a notebook and pen as Simmons raised a hand in acknowledgment.

As soon as he stepped off the porch and took a breath, Tony realized just how bad the air inside was. His rough guess was that the bodies had been closed up in the house a day or so. With the temperature expected to hit the mid-nineties, after another twenty-four hours, they probably would have been able to catch a whiff of the stench at the station downtown.

The patrol officer had regained some color. Tony leaned against the car next to him. "First homicide?"

The kid nodded.

"I'm Tony Ceola." He stuck out his hand, and the kid shook it, mumbling his own name. "What brought you here, Petry?"

"A neighbor reported a suspicious vehicle parked in front of the house. Said the place has been empty for years. Kids use it to party, but they usually don't stick around during the day."

Tony was surprised anyone had bothered. This was a rough neighborhood in a tough part of town, the houses so shabby that it was hard to tell the abandoned ones from those still occupied. It *wasn't* an area where it paid to show too much interest in what went on.

"So you came over and . . . ?"

"Walked up on the porch. The door was partly open. I called out, but no one answered, and I was about to go inside when I smelled . . ." His face took on that puke-sick tinge again, and his Adam's apple bobbed. "Anyway, I decided to look in the window instead, and I saw . . ." He finished with a limp gesture.

"You didn't go inside?"

"No, sir."

"Have you touched anything inside or out?"

"No."

"Talked to anyone? Seen anyone?"

Petry shook his head.

"Okay. If we need anything else, we know where to find you. You can clear and go 10-8."

Grateful, the kid pushed away from the car, got in, and drove away. A white van pulled into the space he'd vacated and the driver jumped out. Pete Wolenska was an investigator for the M.E.'s office—tall, lanky, with a cast-iron stomach and thick glasses that gave him a bug-eyed look. He'd made it as far as the second year of medical school before deciding the doctor route wasn't the way he wanted to go. He'd taken a temporary job with the medical examiner while he figured out what he did want, and had been there ever since. "Hey, Chee. We got three D.B.s?"

"Yeah. Small, medium, and super-jumbo size."

"Shit." Wolenska pulled a gurney from the back of the van, tossed three body bags and a tackle box on top of it, then started pushing it toward the driveway. "I should've let the geek take this one. I've already met my quota this month."

"The geek" was the M.E.'s newest investigator, and it was an apt description. The guy was short, scrawny, and personality-free. It was like the pot calling the kettle black, though, when Wolenska was nothing but a taller version himself.

They hadn't made it halfway up the drive when the crime-scene unit arrived. Tony would have preferred to let them all go inside while he started canvassing the neighborhood, but pronouncing the victims would take about ten seconds, CSU would take their pictures, and then it would be time to move the bodies. Everyone would be royally pissed if he was off chatting up the neighbors instead of helping.

Wolenska left the gurney at the bottom of the steps, walked through the door, and stopped to sniff the air. "Yup, they're dead."

"And it took you six years of college to figure that out?" Simmons called from the living room.

"Fuck you."

"Sorry, Wo, you're not my type," Simmons retorted.

"Who is?" That came from a crime-scene tech, a cute little blonde named Marla.

As Tony stepped into the room once more, the stench struck him anew, making his throat tighten and his breathing go shallow. He forced himself to ignore it and began filling out evidence tags while Wolenska bent over the first body.

"Definitely dead. Twenty-four hours maybe, no more than forty-eight. You want the hands bagged, Chee? The way he's starting to putrefy, we might not get anything, but it's your call."

"Yeah, bag 'em." The M.E. could test for gunshot residue, which would tell them if any of the victims had fired a weapon recently. These three had liked guns and their ability to frighten, intimidate, and destroy.

"Grover Washington, Mykle Moore, and Walter Banks." Marla stood beside Tony and took the evidence tags from him to slap on the paper bags Wolenska was securing over the victims' hands. "Can you think of three more deserving victims?"

"Not offhand." He filled out the last set of tags—case number, victim's name, left hand, right hand—then glanced at Marla. She barely reached five-feet-six on her tiptoes and hardly cast a shadow in the bright June sun, but she was tough, tenacious, dedicated, and smart as hell—all the qualities he admired in a woman. Too bad it took more than good times and great sex to satisfy her.

"When are you and What's-his-name getting married?"

"His name is Richard."

"Oh, yeah. Dickless."

"The wedding's at the end of the month." She tilted her head. "Why? You want to make a better offer?"

"We couldn't agree on what constituted 'better' two years ago. What makes you think anything's changed?"

"Because in the future you'll be thinking of me longingly as the one who got away." Neither her tone nor manner changed as she gestured around the room. "What do you want pictures of?" she asked, then chimed in with him. "Everything."

"Smart-ass," he added.

"Anything in particular you want us to pay attention to?"

"Footprints in the dust over there. I think the shooter was hiding in the corner and surprised them. Here're the pictures I took. I'll stop by and pick them up later." He handed over the film. "Also, check the window frames for prints. If he was waiting inside, he might have looked out to watch for them."

"Our vigilante's been a busy boy," the other crime-scene tech, Flint, remarked. "How many does this make?"

"Six," Wolenska said at the same time Tony answered, "Seven."

Silence settled in the room as everyone looked at him. It was no secret that he was the only one in the department who thought Bryan Hayes's murder was also the vigilante's handiwork. Hayes had been the fourth to die, killed the week before, but beyond his involvement in the drug trade, the circumstances were completely different. The others had been killed in locations like this—empty buildings, abandoned houses—while Hayes had died at home in midtown Tulsa. Calling cards had been left with the other bodies, but not with Hayes's. The others had been shot with a large caliber weapon while Hayes's wounds had come from a .22. The other crime scenes were short on evidence, while they had a witness and a possible partial tag number in the Hayes case.

Despite all that, Tony's instincts said Hayes was another of the vigilante's kills, even if everyone from the chief on down thought he was wrong.

With a shrug, Flint turned away and focused his camera on Mykle Moore. "At the rate he's going, no one's gonna need you Homicide guys anymore."

"Speak for yourself." Marla made sure everyone saw the big smile and wink she gave Tony. "*I* have a lot of needs."

Tony ignored the laughter and lewd comments from the other guys as he studied the scene. Who was their shooter, and why had he taken to murdering drug dealers in the past two months? The obvious theory was also the popular one—that the killer was cleaning up the streets, taking care of the scum the police couldn't keep under control. Most cops thought he'd lost someone he loved to drugs, probably a kid, maybe a sibling, and was using his grief to ensure it didn't happen to anyone else. Some thought he was a fanatic, out to punish wrongdoers, obeying orders sent straight from God—an idea that tied in neatly with the cards calling for repentance.

Tony didn't buy either theory. Each time one of these lowlifes died, his share of the drug business went up for grabs. There had been no shortage of drugs coming through Tulsa in the past two months, so *someone* was doing the grabbing. There was a lot of money in the drug trade, and it stood to reason that people would kill to get a share of those profits.

The room was too small for five people—eight, if he counted the bodies. Tony removed his suit coat, loosened his tie, pulled on a pair of gloves, and went to work in the least crowded area, the rubbish heap in the corner.

They didn't need every piece of trash, but anything that appeared to have been dumped fairly recently would go to the lab. If his guess was right and the killer had been waiting for his victims to arrive, he might have brought food, had a drink, or smoked a cigarette to pass the time. Tony discarded the condoms—it wasn't likely the killer had brought a woman, as well—and the wrappers and cans coated with dust, leaving him with a small pile. He was tagging the last item when Wolenska spoke.

"Did everyone have their Wheaties this morning? 'Cause it's time to gift wrap Chubs here and carry him outside."

Everyone groaned except Marla, who flashed a simpering smile. "I'm a girl. I don't lift bodies."

"Bullshit," Flint retorted. "I've seen you bench-press your own weight."

Marla turned. "Honey, I can bench-press *your* weight, but that doesn't mean I'm gonna help."

"Isn't it enough we have to look at him and smell him? Now you want us to touch him, too?" Simmons scowled as he laid his clipboard aside and removed his jacket. "Man, getting ol' Grover here into a body bag is gonna be like stuffing five pounds of sausage into a one-pound casing. Three-hundred-plus pounds of dead weight. Shit."

Just getting Washington onto his side took a hell of a lot of work, and they had to hold him there while Marla retrieved the pistol holstered in the small of his back. With a maximum of effort and obscene complaints, they got the body bagged, zipped, and outside to the gurney. It was sweaty, messy work, and for a time they just stood there, recovering from the exertion.

"Man, why couldn't our vigilante be a firebug, too?" Simmons grumbled from his seat on the top step. "This place would have gone up in a flash, and we still would've known who the bodies were without having to go through any of this hassle. I didn't sign up for this kind of shit."

"What did you sign up for?" Wolenska asked. "The shiny badge, the cool gun, and all the doughnuts you could eat?"

"Hey, at least I don't spend my days with dead bodies like you do."

"No, just your nights."

Turning out the insults, Tony fixed his gaze on the scene ahead. Farther down the block, houses lined both sides of the street, but here there was a wide stretch of overgrown grass, separated from another street that curved past beyond a steel guardrail. The killer could have parked around the bend and walked back to the house. Easy access and, in the middle of the night, the neighbors wouldn't notice a thing.

In the middle of the night in an area like this, it didn't pay for the neighbors to notice a parade of elephants dancing down the block.

"In this hot weather, you really should wear short sleeves." While the others continued their banter, Marla came to stand beside him, touching a dark smear of blood on his sleeve with her gloved hand.

"I'd rather have Grover's blood on my sleeve than on my skin. I'm not sure there's a disinfectant powerful enough to make me feel clean again. Besides, I don't like short-sleeved dress shirts."

"And you don't mind sweating."

Not for the right reasons. In their months together, the reasons had always been right.

"Will you come to my wedding?"

"Will I get to kiss the bride?"

"You don't have to come to the wedding for that."

He studied her for a moment—sleek blond hair, golden tan, blue eyes, and full mouth. Excellent for smart talk and kissing and other, more carnal activities. Did she look like a woman in love, a flirt, a tease, or someone seriously looking for a little premarital fun? Fine detective that he was, he didn't have a clue.

"You know, Marla, if I thought you were serious, I'd—"

"What?" she asked. "Take me up on it? Or run the other way?"

"Maybe both." But that wasn't true. He didn't have a lot of rules—no, that wasn't true, either. He did, and not screwing around with married or almost-married women was at the top of the list.

She opened her mouth to reply, but Wolenska interrupted. "Hey, you two, break it up. I can't leave Chubs sitting here or he'll pop before I get him to the lab. Let's get the others so I can get out of here and get them under refrigeration."

Gesturing for Marla to lead, Tony climbed the steps and headed back inside the house. Bagging the other two corpses was easy. Any one of them, even Marla, could have carried Moore without help, and Banks wasn't much heavier. Once the bodies were gone, the smell of decay dissipated a little, but it was still enough to give Tony a headache. Spending the next two hours talking to neighbors who *didn't know nothin' 'bout no killin's* didn't help any.

After getting the door slammed in their faces for the

fifth time in as many houses, Simmons gave Tony a sour smile. "Sometimes this job is just too much fun, isn't it?"

William Davis stood at the window in his second-floor study and gazed across the vast expanse of lawn to the west. Riverside Drive fronted the property that had been in his family since the early years of Oklahoma's oil boom. A few yards from the far side of the street flowed the Arkansas River, and occupying the narrow strip of land in between was the city's River Parks. Though the temperature didn't reflect the fact that the sun was setting, there was no shortage of people in the park—joggers, cyclists, walkers, neighbors taking a stroll with their dogs and parents doing the same with their children. With its amphitheater, open grassy spaces, and the Pedestrian Bridge—an old railroad trestle bridge converted when the tracks were rerouted— the park was a popular spot.

Shifting his gaze from the peaceful scene, William studied the cigar he'd taken from the inlaid teak box on his desk. There was no better way to relax on a quiet evening than with a Cuban and a glass of fine old cognac. The cognac waited on the desk, but the cigar remained in its protective wrapper. It had been a week since he'd lit up and savored the rich aroma and the smooth, sweet flavor. A week marred by doctors' visits, tests, and—yes, he could admit it, now that it was over—fear.

The physical had been purely routine, nothing more than official confirmation of what he already knew—that he was as healthy as a man half his age. But instead of the usual banter—*I'd wish all my patients were this healthy, but then I'd go broke*—the doctor might as well have lapsed into a foreign language. Hilar nodes, parenchyma, adenoma, sarcoidosis . . .

The fear had been foreign, as well. In all his life, William had never been afraid of anything . . . except dying as his father had, slowly, the pain excruciating, the cancer destroying his lungs and his body before taking his life.

But this afternoon, after yet another round of tests, the doctor had given him a clean bill of health. The thickening in his lungs was likely due to aging, smoking, or everyday pollution. It wasn't cancer. He'd even given the okay for an occasional cigar.

It *wasn't* cancer. Amazing how powerful those three words were.

But it *was* a wake-up call. He had let important issues slide, had put off certain goals. He didn't have unlimited time. He was sixty-two years old. Old enough to be thinking about retirement. To start planning for the future. To deal with any problems that might interfere with those plans.

He heard the sound of a board creaking, a hand turning the doorknob, moments before he saw movement reflected in the window. Footsteps crossed the room, louder on the marble tile than the faded Aubusson rug. They stopped on the opposite side of the desk he'd brought back from a long-ago trip to France, but still he waited, one minute, two, before turning.

Damon Long was his right-hand man—thirty-five years old, a few inches under six feet, muscular, and solidly built. Presently his hair was blond, his eyes blue. Dressed in the proper clothes, he could pass as the most well-bred and aristocratic of men. In truth, he came from the toughest, most lawless neighborhood in a tough and lawless town south of the Mexican border. The only child of a crack-addicted whore, he'd had an extensive criminal record by the time he'd gone to work for William. It had been a profitable twenty years for both of them.

Crossing to the desk, William returned the cigar to its box, then settled into the luxurious leather chair before speaking. "She'll be here on Thursday. Is everything ready?"

Damon shifted his weight but didn't move toward the twin chairs that fronted the desk. He wouldn't do so without an invitation, and William chose not to offer one yet.

"Christine has a cleaning crew coming in tomorrow morning. The utilities are on, and the phone company is scheduled for tomorrow afternoon."

"What about the package?"

"She'll deliver it herself."

Christine Evans was the owner of a small but successful real-estate agency. She specialized in top-dollar properties, like his own, and understood the value of discretion. Her price was hefty, but her services, according to Damon, were worth it.

"Can she be trusted not to open it?"

"Yes." Damon's answer was neither rushed by guilt nor delayed by uncertainty. Not that it mattered if the realtor's curiosity got the better of her. The leather folio didn't hold anything that could cause problems for him later—just a prepaid cell phone, virtually untraceable, and five thousand dollars in cash for Selena McCaffrey, the newest resident of Princeton Court.

That wasn't the name she'd been born with—merely the one she was using these days. For all he cared, she could call herself Sheena, Queen of the Jungle . . . as long as she did what he asked.

Damon opened his mouth to speak, apparently thought better of it, and closed it again.

William gestured casually. "Go ahead. If you have something to say, say it."

"You're taking a big risk bringing her in. The stakes are too high. She could screw up everything."

William studied him. The hostility underlying his words was faint, but not surprising. Damon liked being the number two man in William's global business venture. He liked handling William's problems and being the only one William turned to for assistance or advice. He liked having Selena tucked away in Key West, painting pretty pictures and staying out of their business.

But what Damon liked didn't particularly matter.

"She knows what she's doing." William waved his hand again, signaling the end of the conversation.

"You knew what *you* were doing last week, but you still screwed up." Realizing what he'd said, Damon clamped his mouth shut, as twin spots of color reddened his face.

William didn't tolerate criticism from anyone, especially the hired help. He fixed a frigid stare on Damon. "And what was I doing, Damon?" he asked, keeping his voice soft, almost gentle. "I was cleaning up after *you.* I was correcting *your* mistakes. Thanks to me, we're safe. And Selena will make sure of that."

The young man's reaction was tedious in its predictability—relief that William hadn't flayed him, accompanied by eagerness to make amends. "We don't need her. I can take care of it."

"If I wanted you to take care of it, I would have asked you. And while you might not need Selena, I do. She's family."

And you're not. William didn't say the words aloud, but the clenching of Damon's jaw proved he'd heard them just the same. He knew the young man thought of him as a father figure, knew he wanted William to think of him as a son.

He didn't. Damon had been loyal, trustworthy, and committed from the beginning, true, but he'd also been easy. Selena was a challenge. Breathtakingly beautiful, elegant, and graceful, and yet there was something terribly flawed about her. She was, at the same time, the strongest and the most fragile woman he'd ever known. She loved him and hated him and owed him.

That was the bottom line—she *owed* him. Had owed him for fourteen years and counting. The time had arrived for repayment of her debt . . . with interest.

2

Tony's first stop Tuesday morning was the forensics lab located on the ground floor of the police station, where he found Marla bent over a microscope. When he was still several feet away, she remarked without raising her head, "I wondered when you'd show up. Usually you pester us to work faster."

"I've had plenty to keep me busy—and I don't pester."

She straightened and gave him a level look. "Right. What do you want first?"

"Whatever you've got handy."

"Okay. The shoeprint was a man's dress shoe, maker unknown. It's a size eleven, and it shows uneven wear on the outside of the sole, so your shooter supinates, or rolls to the outside of his foot when he walks. So does about half the population. There's a nick here"—she reached for a black-and-white photo, then pointed to a spot on the leading edge of the heel—"and there's heavy wear near the toes. Either he scuffs when he walks, or he likes to pivot sharply. The stitching's worn down here, but there's no significance to that, other than if you find this particular shoe, it'll help us identify it."

"Jeez, that's a lot of help. You have any better luck on the fingerprints?"

"The place was used as a hangout by the neighborhood kids. We got more prints than Simmons has freckles. It's gonna take some time. Same with the trash you picked up. Oodles of prints, probably not any that are gonna help. On the other hand, there is some positive news. Ballistics matched the bullets taken from these three to those taken from the first three victims, so it's definitely the same gun and presumably the same shooter."

"Of course, we don't have a clue where that gun is or who that shooter is." He leaned against the counter, hands resting on the cool surface. "What about the GSR?"

"There was plenty of powder stippling on Mykle Moore—that shot in the forehead was from a distance of less than eighteen inches—but no gunshot residue on any of the victims' hands. It was a .45, which means that the shooter policed his brass . . . though anyone smart enough to pick up the shell casings is probably smart enough to wear gloves while handling the bullets and magazine." She returned to the microscope. "Jog my memory. Weren't these three considered suspects in the first three murders?"

"Yeah."

"So you have three fewer suspects in those cases."

"Yeah, that must bring the list down to somewhere around a hundred thousand."

She smiled. "Be grateful for what you can get. What's on your agenda today?"

"Talking to a lot of people who don't like cops and keep suggesting that the vigilante is a cop."

"Have you considered that possibility?"

"I consider all the possibilities," he replied dryly. He didn't like the idea that a cop could be committing the murders, but he hadn't ruled it out. Cops were people, and like all people, some were good and some weren't. Putting on a badge and a gun didn't automatically place a man above suspicion. That said, just as there was nothing to rule out a cop as their killer, there was nothing to suggest it, either.

"Well . . ." She reached past him for a clipboard. "If you're free around twelve-thirty, give me a call. We can have lunch."

"Sure." *Like hell*, he thought as he left. Maybe his ego was reading something more into what were merely friendly gestures, but until she spelled it out for him, he would do well to keep his distance. The guy she was going to marry was a lieutenant in Uniform Division Southwest, and the last thing Tony wanted was to get on the wrong side of a supervisor who carried a gun.

Simmons was waiting for him in the garage, leaning against Tony's Impala. He held a cup of coffee in one hand, a bag of cookies and a fast-food bag in the other. "You ready to go visit Mama Washington again?"

After leaving the crime scene the morning before, they had made death notification calls to the families. Tony hadn't gotten out more than "I'm sorry" and Grover's name before Mae Washington had collapsed in tears, unable to answer any questions. They'd left her with a neighbor and the promise that they would come back today.

"I can think of a few hundred things I'd rather do." Like playing chicken with a speeding bullet, or facing up to Marla's lieutenant. "You planning on eating that in my car?"

"Get over it, Chee. It's nothing a little vacuuming can't clean up."

"Like you would know. You've never touched a vacuum in your life."

"That's women's work."

"Yeah, right. I'd pay money to see you tell your wife that. She'd kick your ass into next week." He unlocked the car, tossed his notebook into the backseat, then slid behind the wheel and buckled up. Juggling his breakfast, Simmons settled in the passenger seat and, right off the bat, sloshed coffee between the seats. With a scowl, Tony handed him a stack of napkins from the door pocket, then backed out of the parking space.

Simmons mopped up the coffee and tossed the napkins onto the back floorboard. "Where are we going?"

"North," Tony replied as he turned in that direction.

"Jeez, why do I have to work with all the smart-asses?"

"Before we start interviewing the other families, we may as well check out Grover Washington's place. They're all in the same area." And searching an unoccupied house was a far more pleasant prospect than asking difficult questions of grieving relatives.

"Great. I like comparing lifestyles of the corrupt and lawless with my own."

Grover's house was located a few blocks off North Peoria. As Tony cut the engine in the driveway, Simmons muttered, "Home, sweet fucking home. Christ, can you believe this?"

No one would have given the house a second glance if it had been located on Tulsa's south side, but here, in a neighborhood of shabby houses that could be improved only by leveling them, the place stood out. It was large, probably four thousand square feet, and was built of a combination of brick and native stone. Fat white columns stretched up two stories, and tall arched windows lined the front.

There were no vehicles parked in front of the four-car garage, and the in-ground pool out back was as smooth as glass. The grass was damp, courtesy of an automatic sprinkler system, and its rich green provided a sharp contrast to the yellowing yards that neighbored the lot.

Returning to the front of the house, Tony pulled on a pair of latex gloves, then took out the keys he'd picked up from the medical examiner's office once he'd secured a warrant to search the house. While he undid the multiple locks on the front door, Simmons looked on disgustedly. "You know how much I make? Of course you do—same as you. And you've seen my house. This bozo, who never worked a day in his life, has a place like this, and he don't even have the sense to build it where it matters."

"It matters here," Tony said as he opened the final lock, then the door. "He grew up less than a mile from here. These people knew him when he was just one more poor kid from the wrong side of the tracks. They're the ones he wanted to impress."

The entry opened into a foyer tiled in black and red. The windows were bracketed with heavy red drapes, and an elaborate staircase curved around a niche that held a grossly disproportional marble statue of a nude. Water trickled from the urn she held to fill the pool below, where fat koi swam lethargically.

"Jesus," Simmons said. "Wonder where he keeps the velvet paintings."

"In here." Tony gestured to the living room on the left. To be fair, there was only one velvet painting, but it was enough.

The living room looked as if it was rarely used, so after a cursory examination, he followed Simmons across the hall to the formal dining room. Heavily gilded furniture, a chandelier with rose-colored prisms, and more bordello-red fabric at the windows made it look like something out of a French provincial whorehouse.

Simmons snorted. "Okay, this proves it. Money can buy

a lot, but it can't buy you class. Even I know this shit's tacky, and Suz says all my taste is in my mouth."

Tony grunted in agreement as he quickly searched the drawers in the buffet and china cabinet, finding nothing but layers of dust.

Off the kitchen, they found the first room that looked lived in. Glass doors exited to the patio and the pool. Inside was every toy a man could want—a well-stocked bar, a pool table, a plasma TV, a stereo system, and a selection of CDs, DVDs, and video games that would compete with any electronics store.

And, sitting in the middle of a table, a notebook computer.

"Leopard-skin sofas and tiger-skin rugs." Simmons sounded torn between amusement and disgust as he headed back toward the hall. "I can't wait to see what he did with his bedroom. If you find anything, give a holler."

Tony nodded absently as he waited for the computer to boot up. What were the odds of finding anything useful on it? A traceable E-mail from the killer would be nice, but he would be happy with details of some of Grover's own crimes. Clearing old cases always counted for something. But he'd never yet met the crook who kept incriminating records where they were easily accessible, and Grover wasn't likely to be the first.

The first icon he clicked on was a day-planner program. He couldn't imagine going to the trouble of keeping his schedule on the computer—his reminders were penciled in the margins of a legal pad or tacked to the bulletin board at home—and Grover hadn't seemed the type, either. But he *had* liked gadgets. The novelty of computerizing his life had probably appealed to him, at least for a while.

Tony called up the preceding weekend and found *Mom*

scheduled for Saturday evening, along with *dinner* and, in the early morning hours of Sunday, the address of the house where he'd died. No mention of who he was meeting or why. No phone number in case it became necessary to reschedule.

Other appointments were listed, as well, all in abbreviated form—D.B. at ten A.M. Wednesday, T. with a question mark on Friday. Series of numbers appeared by some dates—deals, transactions, shipping info . . . Tony didn't know, but someone in Narcotics might.

He'd closed the day planner and was about to check Grover's E-mail when an angry voice from the doorway stopped him. "Who are you and what the hell are you doing?"

Slowly he turned to face a woman somewhere between twenty-five and thirty-five, maybe five feet six, and twenty pounds past pleasingly plump. She was clutching a canister of pepper spray in one hand.

"I wouldn't recommend using that," he said with a nod to the spray. "You've got the nozzle pointing the wrong way." As she checked, then adjusted her aim, he withdrew his badge from his pocket and held it up. "Detective Ceola, Tulsa P.D. Who are you?"

She came close enough to study the badge, then returned the spray to her purse. "LaShandra Banks."

"You must be Walter Banks's . . . ?"

"Cousin. Grover's fiancée . . . more or less."

Tony leaned against the table and watched as she walked to the bar, poured herself a drink, then circled around to sit on one of the stools that fronted it. " 'More or less'?"

She shrugged. "Some days we were getting married. Some days we weren't."

"How long had you been seeing him?"

"A couple years, off and on."

If she'd cried any tears, it hadn't been recently. It made Tony wonder about the true nature of their relationship . . . though he would wonder about *any* woman who voluntarily got intimate with scum like Grover. Had she found something in him to care about or—his gaze flickered across the expensive dress, the flashy gold and diamond jewelry—had theirs been more of a business arrangement?

"When was the last time you saw Grover?"

"Saturday night. After he went over to his mama's, we had dinner at this Thai place he liked on Memorial, then stopped by a club on Admiral. We got back here around one, and he went out again a few hours later. He never came back."

"Did he say where he was going?"

"He had a meeting."

"In the middle of the night?"

"His business"—she said the word delicately—"required odd hours."

"Who was the meeting with?"

"I don't know. I don't think he knew." Before Tony could say anything, she raised one hand. "I know. You're thinking only an idiot would meet someone he didn't know at four in the morning in an empty house. Grover wasn't an idiot. The guy was referred to him by a . . . an associate."

"Who?"

"A man named Marcell. I don't know his last name." She shrugged. "He was before my time."

"What was the meeting about?"

"The guy said he had a business proposition, one too good to turn down. Grover was curious. He liked money— liked spending it on his house, his mama, his woman." The look that entered her dark eyes made it clear that she knew what Tony had been thinking.

"Where can we find Marcell?"

She shrugged. "Like I said, he was before my time."

If Marcell was a business associate of Grover's—one he trusted enough to meet with a stranger on his referral—it shouldn't be too hard to track him down.

Tony shifted the direction of his questions. "Do you live here?"

"Sometimes. I have keys." She proved it by dangling them from one manicured finger before dropping them on the bar.

"Is your name on the deed?"

"No."

"Do you know if Grover had a will?" It led to the most important question in a homicide: Who would benefit from the victim's death? They always took a good look at spouses and business partners, though in this case it was more likely a competitor. After all, Grover's partners had died with him.

"Are you thinking maybe I killed him?" A smile spread across her face. "If he had a will, I'm sure it leaves everything to his mama. I got mine while he was alive, Detective—a regular allowance, a car, clothes, jewelry. That all stops now."

So he was worth more to her alive than dead. She might be the only person who could truthfully make such a claim. Now all Tony had to do was weed through the multitudes who *had* wanted Grover dead.

Two years after swearing she would never return, Selena found herself back in the heart of Tulsa. After exiting I-44, she stopped at a convenience store, where she picked up a city map. At the Braum's next door, she studied it over a late lunch of a hamburger and fries.

Considering how brief her previous visit had been, she remembered quite a bit about the city. A short distance west, then north of where she sat, was William's Riverside Drive home, and she was sure she could still find her way to the museums—Philbrook just a mile or two away, Gilcrease in west Tulsa, and the Fenster Museum of Jewish Art. Admiring their collections remained one of her few pleasant memories from that trip.

After folding the map, she threw away the wrappers from her lunch and walked outside to her car. The bright afternoon was uncomfortably warm. Having spent much of her life in Puerto Rico, Jamaica, and Florida, she was accustomed to heat and humidity, but it was the ocean with its cooling breezes and fresh scent that made it bearable. The only water here was the Arkansas River a few blocks away. It lacked any breeze at all, and its strongest scents came from the oil refinery on the west bank.

She took Peoria north to Twenty-first, drove a short distance east, then turned back south to follow a winding street to the parking lot of the Marlowe Mansion. In a neighborhood of lovely, gracious old homes, this one was particularly so—three stories of native sandstone, with a tiled roof and an even two dozen Palladian windows on the front facade alone. The varying shades of the stone blocks and the graceful lines of the windows appealed to the artist in her, along with the golf-course–perfect lawn and the lush gardens. If she had the chance while she was in town, she would sketch it and tour the exhibits it housed. But at the moment, art was the least of her interests.

The lawn had once been twenty acres or more. Now a

stretch of only two hundred feet remained on each side of the house. Elaborate iron-and-brick fences opened onto neighboring houses on two sides. A wooded area sheltered the third, and the parking lot occupied most of the space on the fourth side. Leaving her car in the lot, she grabbed a camera from the bag in the passenger floorboard and headed toward the trees.

As she strolled across the grass, she contemplated her actions. She had been instructed to call the real-estate agent as soon as she arrived on Thursday, and she was expected to follow those instructions to the letter. She *wasn't* expected to put in an appearance forty-eight hours early. She intended to put that extra time to good use.

When she reached the edge of the lawn, she snapped off a few shots of the mansion, in case anyone was watching, then continued into the woods at a leisurely pace. The air seemed heavier there, though the dense foliage blocked the afternoon sun. She couldn't identify much of the growth. There were oaks of an indeterminate variety. Sumac grew in thick clusters. Cedar trees sprouted wherever they could take root. Leaves crackled underfoot as she walked roughly north, sending up a scent of dry decay.

The woods ended abruptly, as if someone had drawn a line and decreed nothing but grass could grow on the opposite side. Selena crouched behind a massive hedge of forsythia that would be breathtaking when it bloomed next spring—not that she would be there to see it.

The house ahead on her left was unoccupied for the time being. The house to its left belonged to Harold and Mardelle Watson. Once Harold had retired from various jobs in the aerospace industry, they had downsized from their Maple Ridge mansion to a luxury RV and this home, merely a stopover between trips. Their children were grown and living elsewhere, but the Watsons still had strong ties to the city.

Across the street from them were the Franklins. Aaron was a recent graduate of the University of Tulsa Law School, and Dina, born and raised in Guadalajara, was a partner in a family practice clinic a few miles away. Childless, they traveled as much as their careers allowed.

It was amazing—or appalling, depending on your point of view—how much information was available for the asking on the Internet, Selena thought as she shifted her gaze to the final house in the cul-de-sac. It belonged to Anthony Ceola, who answered to Tony and Chee, but not to Anthony. He was thirty-four, single, and a detective investigator with the Tulsa Police Department.

He could be a problem. But every problem, her uncle was fond of saying, had a solution.

She intended to find the solution to hers.

By the time Tony and Simmons got back to the office, their shift was almost over and all Tony wanted was a cold shower, a handful of aspirin, and a beer to wash them down with. They hadn't found anything at Grover's beyond the day planner and the name of his associate. There had been no stash of drugs. No list of customers, suppliers, or distributors. Nothing that even hinted at his drug business, unless it was hidden on the laptop, and certainly nothing that pointed to his killer.

Mae Washington hadn't been any help, either. All she'd known was that her son was a good boy who hadn't deserved to die. It amazed Tony how blind a mother could be to her child's failings. His mother had never cut *him* that kind of slack, and his failings had nothing on Grover's. But maybe that was part of the difference between him and Grover. Anna Ceola had certain expectations of her children, while all Mae had were excuses for hers.

Tony was finishing his notes when the phone rang. Another detective bellowed his name. "Chee, you're wanted in the chief's office."

"Must be nice to have an in with the head honcho," someone else remarked.

"We'll probably be taking orders from him before long," Simmons chimed in.

"Hell, Frankie, *someone* has to tell you what to do." Tony picked up his jacket from the back of the desk chair, made an obscene gesture to the room in general, then headed out of the squad room and down the hall. He'd been a cop twelve years, following in the footsteps of his father, Joe, who'd retired from the department, and his uncles, John and Vincent, who would both be hanging up their guns this year, but none of that stopped the jokes that had started when Henry Daniels had taken the chief's job a few years earlier.

On the surface, no one would have pegged Henry Daniels and Joe Ceola for friendship potential. They were as different as two people could be—Henry, a blue-blood WASP, born with not just a silver spoon but the whole freakin' service, and Joe, the son of working-class immigrant Catholic Italians. But they had become friends in the academy and remained so forty years later. Even when Henry had left Tulsa to work his way through the ranks in other departments, they'd stayed in close touch. He was godfather to the Ceola kids and joined them for all their family events. His birthdays and accomplishments were treated no differently from any Ceola's.

In the eyes of the people Tony worked with, Henry was

family first and Tony's boss second. Tony tried hard to make sure they knew it was the other way around.

The secretary waved Tony into the inner office, where Henry stood gazing at a photograph on the wall. He was in uniform, which meant he'd had a public function to attend or the press to deal with. Considering the way Tony had spent *his* day, it was probably the latter.

"Chief," he said.

Henry turned. "Detective. Come on in and close the door."

After doing so, Tony turned back to Henry with a grin. "Been rousted on any suspicious-persons calls lately?"

Henry grinned, too. "No, thank you. Once was enough."

The previous week, following a rash of armed robberies at the same midtown convenience store, the antsy clerk had called the police to report a man behaving suspiciously outside. When a patrol officer had investigated, he'd found himself questioning none other than the chief of police, who was checking out the situation for himself. It wasn't the first time Henry had taken a hands-on approach to his job as chief, but it was, he'd joked, the first time he'd been treated as a suspect instead of one of the good guys.

Henry sat down and gestured for Tony to do the same. "You've been busy the last few days. Bring me up to speed."

Tony settled in the chair and gave the short version of everything he and Simmons had learned. When he was finished, Henry steepled his fingers. "Sounds like you've got enough to keep you going for a while. You aren't still working the Hayes case, too, are you?"

His tone was mild, but Tony wasn't fooled. Henry might have been as good as family, and he might even have cut Tony some slack because of it, but he was still chief of police and Tony was still his subordinate. The morning after the murder, he had suggested that Tony hand the Hayes case off to another detective. A few days later he had asked him point-blank to do so. The time was coming when the request would become an order, no matter how hard Tony argued.

"Yes, I am." Before Henry could say anything, he raised one hand. "I know you don't believe the cases are connected. No one does but me. But I *do* believe it, and it's not like seven murders are so much harder to investigate than six, especially when I'm looking for the same guy."

Henry's smile came quickly. "Ah, we're talking the famous Ceola instincts. Your father used to get these ideas from out of the blue with absolutely nothing to support them, and damned if he wasn't always right." He paused a beat, then quietly asked, "But what if you're not right? You know better than to go into an investigation with preconceived notions. You find what you expect to find, and you dismiss evidence that leads in a different direction."

"I've never dismissed evidence," Tony said levelly. He was a better cop than that, and the chief, of all people, should know it. "Whatever direction the evidence in this case leads, I'll follow it. At least I *have* evidence in the Hayes case—a partial tag number and a witness."

Henry's gesture was dismissive. "That boy? Hell, Tony, his description was so vague it fits you, me, and damn near every white man in this city."

"So I'll concentrate on the white men whose license plates match our partial."

"You can't base a murder investigation on the word of a five-year-old."

Tony resisted the urge to point out the Prinz kid was six, not five, and young, not stupid. Yeah, to a kid who was short for his age, anyone over five feet was tall, and sure, he'd been able to offer nothing else beyond "white," but that ruled out the black, Latino, Asian, and Indian communities. That was a start.

"You've already got a full caseload—"

"Everyone in the division has a full caseload. Homicide is a growth industry in Tulsa." Tony hesitated. He was sure he was right—enough that he was willing to break his own rule and deliberately blur the line between his personal and professional relationships. "Trust me on this, Uncle Henry. I won't screw up. I won't embarrass you or the department. I'll keep an open mind, and if I'm wrong and this isn't a vigilante case, I'll be the first to admit it. Just give me a chance to find out."

Henry studied him a few moments, then shook his head. "You are so damn much like your father. Okay. Keep the Hayes case. Whether you're right or the rest of us are, find me a killer."

"I intend to."

"Speaking of your father . . ." Henry's voice dropped and became cautious. "How is he?"

Tony would rather discuss the fallibility of his instincts all day than talk about his dad. "Some days are better than others." On his good days, Joe was the man they'd always known—smart, funny, quick with a joke, as sharp as the proverbial tack. On his bad days . . . he wasn't—and the last time Henry had seen him had been one of the bad days.

"And your mother?"

Tony shrugged. All his life his mother had been the strongest, most capable woman he'd ever met. Raising seven kids on a cop's salary, keeping the house spotless and all seven kids out of trouble, and supporting every worthy cause to come along—Anna had done it all and made it look easy. But his father's diagnosis last month had knocked her for a loop. She didn't know how to deal with it, so she didn't. Tony couldn't even take issue with her. He'd rather ignore it, too, than face the fact that Alzheimer's was destroying his father's mind and would eventually claim his life.

Henry sighed. "Tell Anna if there's anything I can do, anything at all, all she has to do is call."

"I will."

"Well . . . it's past time for you to be out of here. You have any plans for this evening?"

"Just the usual."

"Supper, television, bed?" Henry laughed as he stood up, then came around the desk to clap him on the shoulder. "Those are my plans, too. That's no way for a man like you to live."

"But it's okay for you?"

"My life is winding down. Yours is still stretched out in front of you. You should be going out, seeing a beautiful woman or three, thinking about settling down and giving Anna some grandchildren to dote over."

"Nick, Julie, and J.J. have already given her seven. How many more does she need?"

"She did have seven of her own. If each of you matches that . . ."

Tony snorted. "I'd be lucky to manage one on what I'm paid."

"I'll take it up with the city council. I'd hate to see Anna suffer because my officers are underpaid." Hand still on Tony's shoulder, Henry walked with him to the door. "Go out and have some fun. Don't put yourself out too much over this vigilante case. It's not as if the victims matter so much, considering who they are."

"They *all* matter, Henry," Tony said as he grasped the

doorknob. "They may have been scum, but that doesn't give this guy the right to blow them away."

"You really believe that, don't you?" Henry stroked his chin. "In theory, so do I. But it's a lot easier to get worked up over the *real* victims, the innocent ones, than trash like them. I'd have a hard time knowing which way to vote if *I* was on the vigilante's jury."

Tony smiled thinly as he opened the door. "You and half the city, Chief. An awful lot of people only want this guy found so they can pin a medal on him."

"And you can't condone that any more than you can condone what he's doing." Henry didn't wait for a response. "You're a good cop, Tony, and a good man. But I wouldn't expect anything less from Joe's son. Go. Relax. Find some female companionship. Concentrate on bodies of another sort, at least for tonight. If you see your folks before I do, give them my best."

"I will, sir."

After leaving the office, Tony bypassed the elevator and took the stairs to the ground floor, then went outside into the heavy, radiant heat. His footsteps echoed in the garage as he walked to his car. A plain blue Impala bearing multiple antennas, it was obviously a cop car and was about as personality-free as the lab geeks he dealt with. He hadn't washed it since the last rain, so a thin coat of dust covered it from top to bottom. It was clean inside, though, without the layer of fast-food trash that filled Simmons's car.

Though the command visit to Henry's office had kept him past his three o'clock quitting time, he was still out in plenty of time to miss the evening rush. He took Sixth Street to Denver, then headed for Twenty-first, driving through a neighborhood of half-million-dollar houses before reaching his own street. When Buck Marlowe had struck it rich over in the Osage County oil fields eighty or ninety years ago, he'd built his mansion, then added four small brick-and-wood houses as an incentive to keep his most valued employees in his employ. Ol' Buck was long gone from the mansion, but the social status of the residents of Princeton Court hadn't changed much. They were the poor relations to their richer neighbors.

He pulled into the driveway and parked next to his own car, a '57 'Vette that ran only when it wanted to. He regularly threatened to sell it, and two of his brothers regularly pestered him to carry through with it, but so far he'd held off. After all, the city gave him a car for work, so he wasn't without transportation . . . at least, not often.

As he walked around the car, he gave the house next door his usual once-over. It had stood empty since Mrs. Howell died back in the winter. The old woman hadn't had any family, so he'd taken in her dog and cats. He got along fine with the dog, and had come to tolerate the cats. Once they'd agreed upon one basic rule—he fed them, and they left him alone—they'd managed to coexist peacefully in the same space.

He let himself in the front door, where he got as much of a greeting as he ever did from the felines—the calico swishing its tail on the way from the living-room sofa to the floor under the guest-room bed, and a hiss from the fat black cat. The coonhound, on the other hand, was banging the back door with his tail, unable to wait one more minute to get inside and sniff Tony from head to toe.

Ten minutes later, his suit traded for running shorts and a T-shirt, and Mutt finished with his welcome-home, Tony sat down at a dining-room table that saw far more paperwork than food and settled in to work.

The chief was right, he thought sometime later as he

chowed down on a frozen dinner, surrounded by glossy eight by tens and case notes. This was no way for a man to live.

Then he looked at a long shot of the front room of the abandoned house, at Grover Washington, Walter Banks, and Mykle Moore, and at the multiple wounds, any one of which was enough to be fatal. No matter who they were, no matter what they'd done, *that* was no way to die.

3

If anyone had asked Damon at fourteen what he wanted to do with his life—if anyone had cared—his answer would have been simple: live it. In the neighborhood where he'd grown up, dying young, whether by drugs, homicide, or suicide, was a fact of life. He'd witnessed his first murder when he was five, and had become so used to gunshots and screams that he could sleep right through them. He'd grown up surrounded by misery and hopelessness that could sap the soul right out of a person.

Like his mother. Pregnant at fifteen, abandoned by her boyfriend and her rigid parents, she'd tried to make it, but every disappointment had destroyed a part of her. She'd gone from high school to waiting tables to welfare to prostitution, from a pretty girl who'd made a mistake to a crack addict who didn't care whether she lived or died. She *had* died, emaciated, gaunt, her body so abused that it had worn out at thirty-one. Sometimes he missed her, pitied her, wished she'd held on long enough to get a taste of the new life he could have given her. Other times he scorned her. It was the first lesson he'd learned: only the strong survive. His mother had been weak. He was strong.

Almost as strong as William, the old man liked to say. Bullshit. William had never had to fight for a thing. Had never known hunger or poverty or fear. Had been given every advantage a person could have, and had still managed to become as twisted and ruthless as someone who'd never had anything to lose. The money had a lot to do with that. Life had taught him that anything was his for the asking— or the taking—and he'd embraced that notion wholeheartedly.

The beauty of it was, he hid it so well. He could, and did, present himself as the most generous, upstanding man on the face of the earth. It wasn't even entirely an act. Some part of him *was* generous and upstanding, just as some part of him had always been deadly. At one time the balance had tilted the other way, but over the years, it had shifted. That was why he'd rescued Damon from his pathetic life. He'd had plans, and needed someone with Damon's particular skills to put them into motion.

Damon smiled faintly. *Plans*. He had plans of his own— plans that would make William regret that rescue twenty years ago.

He parked his motorcycle near a little red Miata in the lot at the Tulsa campus of Oklahoma State University. He'd learned a lot from William, not only about business but also about himself. Such as how to compartmentalize himself, to show people only the aspects of his personality that would help him achieve his goals. This meeting might be the most important test of that he would ever face.

The workday was over, as were most of the classes, so the lot was nearing empty and the steady flow of employees and students streaming out had slowed to a trickle. As he passed the Miata, he dropped his keys, crouched to pick them up, then continued to the nearest building to wait.

It wasn't a long wait. As his target passed, he stepped out of the alcove and followed a half-dozen feet behind her to the parking lot.

She would have been easy to pick out of a crowd and

was impossible to miss alone. Even in heels she barely topped five and a half feet, and she was so slender that a good breeze might get her airborne. Her hair was pulled back in a fancy braid, and her ivory suit looked good against the olive tones of her skin. Give her a pair of wings and she could pass for a delicate little fairy. There was nothing delicate, though, about the words that came out of her mouth when she saw her car.

"Fuck me. Aw, shit. I can't believe . . ."

She stopped ten feet from the Miata, scowling at the right rear tire. Damon walked up beside her, looked from her to the tire, then back again. "You've got a flat."

"Brilliant observa—" She glanced at him, and the scathing retort faded away. So did her scowl, replaced by a chagrined smile. "Sorry. I've had a lousy day, and I was really looking forward to getting home and putting it all behind me."

"If you have a spare, I'd be happy to change it for you. It wouldn't cost you more than . . . oh, an hour or so of your time for dinner or a drink."

Her eyes twinkled. She was accustomed to men coming on to her, and why shouldn't she be? She was twenty-five, single, and beautiful. She liked herself, liked men, and it showed. "You change my tire, and I'll be happy to give you two hours or even more." She practically purred the words, obviously a ploy that had taken her far with other men.

He held out his hand for her keys and went to work. She leaned against the lamppost next to the car, one slender ankle crossed over the other, her arms folded underneath her breasts. She was a woman he would have looked twice at even if he hadn't known who she was.

Changing a tire was about the extent of his mechanical ability. After stowing the flat in her trunk, he cleaned his hands with the wet-wipe she offered from her purse. She looked up at him, dark eyes screened by long lashes, and smiled seductively. "How can I thank you?"

"Dinner?"

"Where?"

"Wherever you want."

He expected her to choose something upscale, expensive—in his experience, women liked *expensive*—but she surprised him. "How about Billy Ray's Barbecue? Do you know where it is?"

Though he did, he shook his head.

With a smile that promised all sorts of wicked things, she slid behind the wheel, started the engine, then lowered the car's ragtop. "Follow me."

She drove exactly the way he expected an easy woman in a red convertible to drive—fast. He kept the Ducati mere feet off her rear bumper the whole way, then roared into a space beside her in the restaurant parking lot.

As she got out, she removed the band that held her hair, combed her fingers through to loosen the braid, then shook it free. Thick, black, it reached just past her shoulders and looked soft as silk. Thanks to William, he knew just how soft that was.

No—thanks to *himself*. William had given him opportunities, but he was the one who'd taken them, who'd done the work, who'd repaid every chance a hundred times over. He was grateful to his boss . . . but gratitude took a man only so far.

"We forgot to introduce ourselves," she said as they started toward the door.

He hadn't forgotten. He'd just been waiting for the right time. "I'm Damon."

"And I'm Lucia Ceola."

He knew that.

Truth was, he knew everything about her.

Shortly before midnight, Selena pulled into the River Parks lot just off Thirty-first Street, parked in the shadow of a tall oak, and stepped out of the car. It was past curfew for the park, and her lemon-yellow Thunderbird was the only car in the lot. Resting her hand on the hardtop for balance, she bent her right knee and brought her foot up behind her in a slow stretch. The night was too warm for the clothing she wore—black warm-up pants, a long-sleeved black T-shirt, and a black ball cap—but she was expert at ignoring minor discomforts.

She'd spent three hours in the park the night before, hunkered down in the shadows, watching William's house, timing the guards' activities. Earlier that morning, she'd familiarized herself with the neighborhood, had walked and run the trail that curved from the river and behind the house on its way north. She'd learned all she could learn from this side of the fence. It was time to see what was on the other side.

Pulling on a backpack, she walked to the west end of the lot, climbed the stairs to the bridge that crossed Riverside, then stopped on the far side to study the house. An iron fence encircled the entire estate, with only two ways in: the main gate at the northwest corner of the property, an elaborate arch set in massive stone pillars and guarded at all times by armed men, and the service entrance at the rear of the property. The gate there was smaller, purely functional, and security was limited to a fixed camera sighted on vehicles entering or exiting the estate.

On her visit two years ago, that was the gate she had been instructed to use. It had been William's way of reminding her of her place in his world.

Shivering, Selena concentrated on the task ahead of her. The house, big enough for a half-dozen families, gleamed white in the night. If William's description did it justice, it was every bit the mansion the Marlowe place was. She couldn't say, since she hadn't been allowed inside the main-house to see for herself.

At the distant corner of the estate, lights shone in the guard shack located just inside the main gate. There were two guards on duty during the day and three at night, two of whom patrolled the grounds every hour. Between that and the alarms on the house and the guest cottage, William apparently felt secure enough. There were no motion sensors on the grounds, no surveillance cameras along the fence, no dogs to ferret out intruders.

Drawing a penlight from her pocket, Selena jogged back the way she'd come. After the trail entered the wooded area, she flicked the flashlight on and kept it pointed at the path, not to light her way, but to search for the marker she'd left alongside the trail earlier that day—a small pile of stones, none bigger than a golf ball. The weeds behind them showed only faint signs of her passage that morning, and she was careful to make a new path as she headed through the underbrush once more.

Once she reached the heavy shadows at the bottom of the hill, she shut off the flashlight, keeping one hand on the fence to guide her. When she arrived at the point she'd chosen that morning, a glance at her watch showed the guards should be returning to their command post. It would be another fifty minutes before their next rounds, probably another hour before they reached this location. Plenty of time for what she planned.

It was poor judgment on the part of William's security people to let a tree grow in such proximity to the fence, but perhaps that had been his decision. He liked pretty things, and among the many unremarkable trees that surrounded her, the mimosa was, indeed, pretty. It was a massive specimen, its feathery-tipped branches extending gracefully in all directions, and it was well suited for climbing, each limb leading easily to the next.

She quickly reached the branch she'd targeted, a thick limb extending over the top of the fence. Carefully she edged away from the trunk until the branch began to dip beneath her weight. Then she pulled a rope from her backpack, knotted one end around the limb, and studied the area.

There was no sign of life on the grounds, and only one light was visible in the house—a dim bulb in what she presumed was the kitchen. During her visit two years ago, William had warned her to avoid his live-in staff, an elderly couple who worked as housekeeper and butler. They were likely snoring in their quarters at the north end of the house, and William was probably sleeping, as well, arrogant in his certainty that he was safe from all danger.

All except her. But he didn't consider her a danger, did he?

He should know better. After all, as he constantly reminded her, he'd made her what she was.

She let the rope drop, its free end hitting the ground with a soft thud. She would need it to make her escape, but she chose an easier route in. Wrapping both hands securely around the branch, she let herself slide off into thin air. For a moment, she hung there, swinging slightly, then she let go. As the ground rushed to meet her, she drew her knees to her chest, landing with a harsh grunt. Instinctively, she rolled, letting her body absorb the shock before rising to her feet.

She stayed close to the fence and the shadows that enveloped it as she approached the guesthouse. Her first impulse was to hurry past, to pretend she didn't see it, but she forced herself to maintain a steady pace, to give up the security of the shadows in order to inspect it more closely. If she pressed her face to the dark windows, she would see through the sheer curtains to a lovely space, decorated in soothing tones and textures, as homey and welcoming as anyone could ever want. And yet the worst night of her life had taken place in there. The night that had, ultimately, forced her back here again.

The pool between the guest cottage and the house was still, as well, illuminated by a few weak lights. The patio furniture was in pristine condition, as if a party might begin at any moment. William liked parties and was a consummate host, or so he said. She couldn't agree from experience. She had never been invited to any of his social affairs.

But he'd thought of her when he needed a man killed.

Selena crept around the house, making a mental note of every entrance, locating the electric meter and the point where the phone lines entered the house. There were keypads for the alarm inside every door, and there were likely motion sensors in every room, at least on the ground floor. There was an intercom system, as well, and probably a panic button that sounded in the guard shack.

Moving stealthily through the quiet night, she approached the guard shack next. Two men sat watching television, while a third dozed on a cot beneath the window she peered through. A bank of monitors, their screens displaying the service gate, the front of the detached garage, and the patio, sat on the opposite side of the room from the TV. Another poor decision on security's part.

She ducked out of sight and headed for the garage. She'd already proven that the perimeter could be breached. The guards could be disarmed almost as easily, and with a little advice from Montoya, the camera signals blocked, power and phone service disrupted, and alarms bypassed. She could gain access to William and escape with no one the wiser.

If she found it necessary.

When he'd called a week ago and threatened to destroy her life, he hadn't been so crass as to do it outright. No, he'd hinted, implied, his voice rich with avuncular concern. *It would be a shame if the authorities found out what happened two years ago. You would lose your lovely home, the gallery you've worked so hard for, everything. The best you could hope for is deportation, the worst . . .*

She'd frozen at the threat. The worst was life in prison, or possibly death. She'd spent half her life fighting to survive, and she wasn't ready to give up. But prison—spending the rest of her days locked away in a small cell, never having the freedom to walk outside in the sun, never being able to take a single breath that didn't hurt . . . That just might be a fate worse than death.

And how would the authorities find out? she had asked. Whispered. Only William knew what she had done. He had cleaned up after her, had destroyed the evidence—

And then she'd known. He hadn't destroyed anything. He had merely been biding his time until he could use the proof of her crime to blackmail her, to bend her to his will.

Her uncle was not an honorable man, but he *was* a man of his word. If he said he would destroy her, he would. So she had agreed to come to Oklahoma to do what he asked. Yet despite all he'd done for her, despite all he'd given her, if she had no other choice . . .

A shudder rocked through her as she bypassed the front of the garage and went to a small door on the side. She pulled a lockpick set from her pack. Her hands were shaking badly, but she soon had the door open and was slipping into the dark cavernous space.

Know your enemy, William often preached. How ironic that now the enemy was him.

The beam of her flashlight played over the garden equipment that filled the first bay of the garage. A Mercedes was parked in the next, a Cadillac beyond that. Holding the light between her teeth, she dug out a small notebook and ink pen and scrawled the Mercedes' tag number on the first page. She didn't know if she could even get any information from the number, but if she couldn't, Jimmy Montoya could. He knew people who could find out *anything,* he'd once told her, and she believed him.

She was straightening, intending to copy the same information from the second car, when a hand grasped her shoulder from behind. Before she could do more than stiffen, a bright light spilled over her shoulder to illuminate the car's trunk. The notebook and pen slipped from her fingers and the penlight clattered to the concrete.

"Well, well, what have we here?" The voice was male, with a strong twang. Her first impression was "redneck"; her second, "arrogant redneck." "Looks like you took a wrong turn while you was out for your midnight stroll. Get those hands in the air and come on back here where I can get a good look at you before I handcuff you."

His fingers bit into her skin as she slowly raised both hands to her shoulders, and he began pulling her back. As soon as they cleared the cramped quarters behind the car, no doubt he would turn her around and shine that light in her face, and she would be in a world of trouble. Even the most basic of descriptions—a half-black woman—would be enough for William.

"You must be some kind of stupid, breaking in here. Hell, boy, do you have any idea—"

Clear of the car, Selena jabbed her right elbow into his stomach, then wrenched free. Doubling over with a yelp of pain, he dropped his flashlight but managed to key the microphone attached to his uniform collar. "Webster, get in—"

Grabbing a handful of hair, she shoved him, head first, against the Mercedes' rear door. He sank bonelessly to the floor. For a moment she just looked at him. She had trained with Montoya for two years, had sparred and fought and attacked and defended, but this was the first time she'd ever used what she'd learned for real. It had come surprisingly naturally.

"Brodie? What the hell's going on?" The shout came from both the radio and from outside, accompanied by the pounding of footsteps on the driveway. The man was headed for the door both she and Brodie had used, standing open in invitation. Selena snatched up her penlight, then crouched to locate the notebook and ink pen. Dropping them into the pack, she squeezed past the Mercedes, then the Cadillac, into the empty fourth bay and punched the button for the overhead door.

The guard named Webster charged into the garage as the door ground its way up, the beam from his flashlight bouncing crazily around the space. "Brodie— *Hey! Stop!*"

She ducked under the door and set off at a full run for the southeast corner of the estate. She didn't need to look to know he was following her. His boots thudded heavily as he slowly gained ground, but his breathing was growing heavier, too. He would be winded before they reached the tree, but how much wind did he need to tackle her—or to shoot her? The thought spurred her to push harder, to lengthen her stride by a few precious inches, to ignore the demands placed on her own lungs.

The moonlight gleamed silver on the outer layer of the mimosa's delicate leaves, but the rope hanging underneath remained in shadow. Sweat dampening her face, she took a flying leap, caught hold, and was shimmying up its length when the unmistakable click of a revolver being cocked, sounded behind her.

"H-h-hold it right—right there," Webster panted.

She froze in midair, hands gripping the rope, legs dangling, body swaying.

"C-come on down here. Don't make me—" He dragged in a wheezing breath. "Don't make me shoot . . ."

Giving up wasn't an option. Neither was getting shot. She remained motionless, surveying the distance to the ground. Eight, ten feet, tops. Opting for the element of surprise, she let go of the rope, hit the ground, rolled, and came up in a kick that knocked the guard's feet out from under him. Another kick, this one to the chin, snapped his head back against the ground with a solid thud.

She quickly grabbed his pistol and the radio, throwing both into the distance, then returned to the rope, climbing hand over fist to the branch that was her bridge over the fence. Catching her breath, she cut the rope, crammed it into her pack, then slid the knife back into her waistband as she shimmied down the tree on the opposite side of the fence.

By the time Selena reached the running trail above,

she'd stripped down to the tank top and running shorts she wore as a second layer. She stuffed the gloves in her pack, wadded the rest together, and jogged back to her car. As soon as she reached the motel, the clothes went into the Dumpster and she went to her room, where she undressed and climbed into the shower.

Know your enemy, William said. Good advice.

Maybe he would live to regret not getting to know *her.*

Or maybe he would regret that he'd ever known her at all.

Dwayne Samuels brought his SUV to a stop in front of the brick ranch house and climbed out, scowling at the dust that settled on the bright red paint job. He'd rented this place out here off Coyote Trail because it was fucking hard to find and nobody lived close by, but damned if he wasn't tired of having to wash his truck every goddamn time he came out here.

The house was looking shabby, the grass needed mowing, and the trash had been scattered everywhere by dogs or possums or, shit, maybe even coyotes. He didn't care about any of that, though, as he walked around the house to the barn that sat a hundred feet behind it. When he was twenty feet from the door, it opened and his cousin, Lewis, stepped into view, a sawed-off twelve-gauge shotgun cradled in his arms.

"You call that standing guard?" Dwayne groused.

"Hell, I heard you drive up, and nobody can do that without the code for the gate. Since Bucky and I are already here, it had to be you."

Dwayne slapped Lewis on the back of the head, then stepped inside the barn. The building looked rickety from the outside, but this was no fly-by-night meth lab. Barring any fuckups with the chemicals, he figured this just might be his permanent base of operations.

Lewis closed the door and cool air slowly replaced the afternoon heat. Dwayne walked back to the counter where Bucky was measuring out chemicals. "How's it going?"

Bucky didn't even glance up. "It would go better if you'd stick his skinny ass outside where he wouldn't drive me nuts."

Yeah, Lewis was real good at driving people nuts. Lazy, whiny, shiftless, too stupid for his own good—that was Aunt Louella's pride and joy. He'd already settled in front of the tube with a cold beer, the shotgun forgotten by the door.

"Hey, Lewis, why don't you drive into Mannford and get us some food?"

"Nah, I'm not hungry."

Dwayne saw Bucky smirk. "Goddammit, Lewis—" He crossed the room in three strides and thumped him on the head again, this time hard enough to make the wooden chair teeter. He tossed a couple of twenties in his cousin's direction, then shut off the TV. "Get us some Sonic or something. Go on."

"Jesus H., Dwayne, we ain't kids no more and you can't order me around like we was. You are *not* the boss of me."

Dwayne jerked him to his feet and gave him an ugly smile. "Who runs this operation, Lewis?"

"You do."

"And who do you work for?"

"You."

"So what does that make me?"

Lewis's chin sank to his chest as he mumbled, "The boss."

"Go on. Get outa here." Dwayne gave him a shove toward the door, then went back to the counter.

"It's a shame what inbreeding does to a man," Bucky said, still wearing that smirk.

Dwayne would like nothing more than to smack him the way he had Lewis, but Bucky was six five and tipped the scales at more than three hundred pounds. He'd been meaner than a snake before he'd gone down for ten years at the state pen in McAlester, and he'd learned a lot while in the system. Dwayne had seen him interrupt his dinner to break a man's neck, then finish eating like nothing had happened. He wasn't about to get crossways with Bucky.

He got two beers from the refrigerator, gave one to Bucky, then leaned against the counter. "I got a call this morning from a friend of a friend who's looking to invest a little cash in our growing enterprise."

"He tell you who the friend was?"

"A guy by the name of Arias. Says you knew him down in Big Mac."

Bucky nodded. "I knew a guy. Wouldn't trust him as far as I could throw him."

"You don't trust anyone."

"Not even you." Bucky grinned, sort of crazylike. "You gonna meet with this 'friend of a friend'?"

"I don't know."

"What if it's the vigilante? I heard that fucker, Washington, got a call to meet with someone just before he got popped."

"Where'd you hear that?"

Bucky shrugged. "Somewhere."

Bullshit, *somewhere*. Dwayne had no doubt Bucky knew exactly who had told him, and when and where they were and what they were doing at the time. "So somebody called

Washington up, arranged a meet, then blew him away. Damn, if I'd known it was that easy, I'd've got rid of the competition years ago."

Bucky's snort said it all. Dwayne didn't have the stomach for cold-blooded murder. Where he came from, that was a good thing. Not so in Bucky's world. "So what are you gonna do?"

Dwayne didn't like the idea that somebody might be out there looking to kill him. But he couldn't stop doing business just because some nut job had taken it on himself to clean up the streets. If he got too chickenshit to do his job, somebody else would step in and do it for him.

"I'll have to think about it," he decided, ignoring Bucky's grin.

Think about it a *lot* . . . and maybe take out a little insurance with a Street Crimes cop he used to know.

At three P.M. on Thursday, Selena was waiting on the small front porch of her new house on Princeton Court when a silver Jaguar turned into the driveway. The driver was female, a well-preserved early forties, with short red hair, killer nails, and a practiced smile. "Selena," she greeted, extending her hand long before she reached the porch. "I'm Christine Evans. Welcome to Tulsa. Did you have any problem finding the place?"

"No, not at all. Your directions were good." Selena stood up, then shook hands while taking stock. The other woman was only five six in heels. Her perfume was Chanel, and her dress was Vera Wang. Very flattering, very expensive.

Christine unlocked the door, shut off the alarm, then stepped back so Selena could enter. She followed, stopping expectantly in the living-room doorway while Selena moved around the perimeter of the room. "What do you think?"

"It's lovely." And it was, with twelve-foot ceilings, plaster walls painted pale cream, and elaborate crown molding around the ceiling and the doors. The furniture was pricey reproductions of period-appropriate pieces, with a faded Persian rug covering a well-worn hardwood floor. A corner armoire, carved and painted in country French style, concealed a television and DVD setup.

The fireplace, complete with marble surround, took up most of the outside wall, with a matching one visible through the wide doorway into the dining room. Another broad door led into the kitchen, where black-and-white floor tile formed a diamond pattern. The cabinets were metal and looked original to the house, with their powder-green finish and chrome half-moon pulls, and the counter-tops were made of stone, coarse and cool beneath her fingers. The appliances were no-frills, basic pieces, lacking so much as one fingerprint or grimy smudge. They were temporary props and looked it.

She continued the tour, making the appropriate responses to Christine's chatter about the weather, the neighborhood, and shopping. The rest of the downstairs included a half bath, a laundry room and pantry, a sun-room addition, and a door off the kitchen that led to the basement. Barely concealing her shudder, she declined Christine's offer to examine the room. Upstairs were three bedrooms and a full bath.

It was all lovely . . . and small enough to be damn near claustrophobic.

"Let me show you the alarm," Christine said as they returned to the foyer, "then I've got to rush to my next appointment. There's a keypad at both the front and back doors. . . ."

Selena only half listened. She committed the code to memory, though changing it would be her first priority, then thanked the agent for her help and ushered her out the door.

Once the Jag was gone from sight, she returned to the kitchen. She had noticed the leather attaché on the counter, though Christine had pretended it wasn't there. Inside was the cell phone William had promised, along with some cash. She had her own cell phone, she had protested, and William had let out a long-suffering sigh. She had a lot to learn about his business, he'd announced.

But she already knew more than she wanted to know about his business.

She knew it involved murder.

There was nothing else in the attaché. No note saying *Thanks* or *I'm sorry* or *Let's get together*. Nothing to suggest that she was more than just another employee paid to do William's bidding. She knew better than to expect anything more, but that didn't stop the faint twinge of disappointment forming inside. Habit. She had wanted so much but been disappointed for so long that it had become second nature.

She'd taken only a few steps away from the counter when the silence was broken by the trill of the cell phone. The tune was "The Sting," no doubt William's idea of a joke. She answered with a cool "Hello."

"Selena, sweetheart. Did I disturb you?"

The sound of his voice brought its usual rush of emotions. She was overwhelmingly grateful for all he'd given her. Some part of the frightened little girl whose life he'd saved fourteen years ago in an Ocho Rios alley remained inside her, craving his attention, but the woman she'd become had learned to welcome his indifference. She despised the business he was in, the way he manipulated her, and that little girl's need for his affection. She sometimes thought she loved him and sometimes knew she hated him.

Did he disturb her? *All the time.* "Not at all. I'm unpacking."

"How was your trip?"

"Uneventful." Just as this conversation was destined to be. Would he mention last night's intruder at the estate or what action he had taken? Had he fired the guards? Beefed up security? Had the thought even crossed his mind that it could have been her?

"You could have flown and saved all those hours of driving."

His remark answered her last question. No, he hadn't suspected her for an instant. For their entire life together, he had given orders and she had followed them. *Learn to read, write, walk, and talk,* he'd said, and she had. *Go off to live among strangers thousands of miles from home,* and she had. *Transform yourself, educate yourself, become someone to make me proud,* and she had. *Come to Oklahoma to kill a man,* and there she was. No, it never would have occurred to him that she might do anything other than exactly what he told her.

"I enjoyed all those hours of driving," she said evenly.

"When did you get in?"

"A few hours ago. I had lunch, then called Christine Evans. She just left."

"Is the house satisfactory?"

"It's lovely."

"What did you think of Ms. Evans?"

She leaned against the island, her gaze on the scene

outside the window—a bit of lawn, the rear corner of the neighboring house, and a black-and-tan dog snoozing peacefully in its fenced-in yard. How many excruciatingly polite conversations had she and William shared over the years? Too many.

For a long time she had blamed herself for his distance—she wasn't polished enough, perfect enough, to be allowed close. As an adult she'd realized it was a means of control. She wanted a closer relationship, so he kept her at arm's length. If she gave him what *he* wanted—her working in his business—she suspected that would change. Some small part of her still wanted it to.

Showing no hint of her annoyance over the pointless conversation, she replied, "Ms. Evans seemed very nice."

William chuckled. "She grew up in Oakhurst, you know . . . but of course you don't. It wasn't on your list of places to see two years ago, and rightly so. Let's just say that, at one time, you would have felt very much at home there." The chuckle came again. "At *one* time, you would have felt very lucky to live there."

Closing her eyes, she let her mouth curve in a sardonic smile. She would never forget where she'd come from—it was as much a part of her as her black hair, her brown eyes, and her brown skin—but William damn well intended to make sure of it.

"Thankfully, you don't have to worry about where you live anymore. I took care of that little problem for good."

As regular as clockwork—first the dig, then the reminder of how *he* had saved her. It had been such a routine part of their conversations that for years she hadn't even noticed.

Deliberately she changed the subject. "Will I see you while I'm here, Uncle?"

"It's been a long time, hasn't it?"

"Two years." If pressed, she could narrow it down to the exact number of months, days, and even hours.

"A special dinner, perhaps. Remember when we celebrated your eighteenth birthday in Paris? The food was amazing. And that incredible seven-course meal at the castle in Germany?"

"Of course." She remembered virtually every moment she'd ever spent with him—every time he'd dropped in on her at school, every trip they'd taken, every visit he'd arranged in neutral territory. She had felt important at those times, special, and she'd been grateful for every one of them.

Did he have any idea that she was dangerously short on gratitude these days?

"It was easier then. We shared such a bright, promising future." Until she'd disappointed him by refusing to join his business. The sigh accompanying his words sounded genuinely regretful. "Well, perhaps we can have dinner next week. Of course, we'll have to keep a low profile, but I'm sure we can work something out."

She stood motionless. She truly hadn't expected time alone with him on this visit. "Low profile" didn't begin to cover his past behavior with her. On her previous visit, when there had been nothing at stake, she had been lucky to catch a glimpse of him as he left the house. Even on the trips to Europe he'd mentioned, they had traveled separately and stayed on different floors, sometimes in different hotels, all for the sake of his "low profile."

Before she had recovered enough to respond, the blast of a siren sounded over the phone, and she realized there had been a fair amount of traffic noise in the background from the beginning. He was calling on either a cell phone or a pay phone. Though regular cell-phone calls were easy to track, prepaid cells and pay phones, he had informed her, provided the ultimate in anonymity.

After the siren had faded, he asked, "What about your neighbors? Have you met any of them yet?"

"No, not yet. I imagine they're all at work. Perhaps this evening."

"My cell number is programmed into your phone. Once you've met them, I would be interested in hearing your impressions. In the meantime, I'll let you get back to your unpacking, sweetheart. If you need anything at all, you have Christine's number, right?"

It was so typical of him—surprise her into silence by suggesting they get together, then remind her to turn to a total stranger if she needed assistance. Typical or not, it sparked an ache inside.

"Right," she said, hearing the bitterness that eased into her voice despite her best efforts. "I'll talk to you soon, Uncle. Good-bye."

4

"I love cell phones."

Tony glanced up from the thick stack of pages in front of him to see Simmons grinning at his desk.

"Think about it. They're convenient as hell. Everybody has one, even my eighty-year-old grandmother. People use them all the time, and every single call is documented. What could be cooler than that?"

"You've been looking at those call records too long, Frankie. You're getting a little crazy." *He* sure as hell was. None of their three latest victims had had a home phone, which *was* a good thing for the cops. The phone company didn't track all outgoing and incoming calls in the local area, not without a warrant beforehand, but the cell providers did. On the records he and Simmons had divided between them, they had the phone numbers of every single person Grover and his boys had called, and everyone who'd called them, in the past three months. All their business and personal contacts, literally hundreds of them.

And he and Frankie had the pleasure of identifying them, questioning them, and cross-referencing the numbers with the other victims' records. As jobs went, this one topped the list headed "tedious," and would probably be unproductive, as well. It had been in the previous vigilante cases.

But Tony could put off the tedium until later. It was

after three o'clock, and he was planning to stop by his folks' house before he went home. After stuffing the records into his briefcase, he stood, stretched, then pulled his jacket on.

"Throwing in the towel already?" Simmons asked as he started packing up, too. "You're usually the last one out."

"I've got things to do."

"What? Go home, run, then work all night?" Simmons sorrowfully shook his head. "You need a life, Chee . . . and I've got just the woman to provide it. Her name's Mary Beth and she's got a body . . ." He gave a low whistle.

"Is she a friend of Suz's?"

"Yeah, but—"

"No, thanks."

"Hey, Suz has some really hot friends."

"Who are all looking to get married, and Suz has pledged her unrelenting assistance to the cause. Thanks, but no, thanks."

Simmons followed Tony to the stairs. "It's not natural for a man to turn his back on a beautiful woman, Chee. You got a problem? Tell Uncle Frankie about it and he'll fix it."

"Yeah, I've got a problem, Frank. I'm hot for you, but I couldn't bear to break up Suz's happy home."

"Asshole. Wanna get a beer before you go home?"

"No, thanks. I've got to stop at the dry cleaner's and the bank, then check in on my folks. If I time it right, Mom will feed me."

"If you'd join the rest of us suckers and get married, your wife would feed you."

"Yeah, right. That's why you bitch all the time that Suz's idea of cooking is McDonald's or Domino's."

"One of these days you'll take the leap, partner, and I'm gonna laugh my ass off. You won't be so smug about it then."

With a nod good-bye, Tony slid into the Impala, cranked the engine, turned the AC to high, and rolled down the windows. By the time he reached the dry cleaner's, the temperature inside the car had reached comfortable. He stashed the clothes in the backseat, rolled up the windows, then headed south.

His parents lived east of Yale and south of Fifty-first. When they'd bought the house nearly forty years earlier, it had been right at the edge of town. Now the city went on for miles in each direction and showed no sign of stopping.

He drove past LaFortune Park, admiring a jogger on the three-mile trail that circled the park. She wore tight shorts and a neon-pink bra, and her blond ponytail wasn't the only thing bouncing with each step. Maybe Simmons was right, he thought, taking one last look in the rear-view mirror. He did need a woman. He could hardly remember the last time he'd gotten laid, and didn't want to remember the last date he'd had. It had been that bad.

He turned off Fifty-first, drove two blocks, and took a left, then made a right after another block. He slowed, then stopped beside a familiar figure. In the last seconds, his chest had tightened until he could hardly breathe, and his fingers were knotted around the steering wheel. He rolled down the window, swallowed hard, then forced a smile. "Dad. Why don't you get in and let me give you a ride home?"

It was painful, facing the man he'd known all his life—the smart, funny, tough guy who wasn't the least bit ashamed of showing his emotions—and seeing no hint of recognition in his eyes. The face and body were thinner, but otherwise the same, and the eyes . . . hell, Tony faced those eyes every time he saw himself in the mirror. They were so damn familiar . . . and, at the moment, so damn blank.

"I'm going for a walk," his father said dully, and shuffled away.

Tony parked at the curb, then easily caught up, reaching out for Joe's arm. "Come on, Dad. It's too hot for a walk. Let me give you a ride. I'm going there anyway."

Joe stopped. "Do I know you?"

"Yeah, Dad, it's Tony. Your favorite son," he said with a weak grin. It had long been a family joke, with all seven kids claiming to be their dad's favorite and Joe agreeing, absolutely, yes.

There was nothing funny about it now.

"I've got to get home. It's almost time for work. I'm a police officer, you know."

"I know, Sarge. So am I—I'm in Homicide. How about I give you a lift so you won't be late?"

Joe gave him an appraising look as he allowed Tony to steer him to the passenger side of the car. "A detective, huh? I swear, you kids are getting younger every day. It makes me feel my age, you know." He stared out the window as Tony fastened the seat belt for him, then remained silent for the three-block drive to their house.

As Tony pulled into the driveway, his older sister, Julie, burst out the front door, cell phone in one hand, car keys in the other. She stopped abruptly, then rushed to the car and jerked open the door. "Daddy, what are you doing? Where did you go?"

Joe got out, gave her a distant look, then started toward the door. "Thanks for the ride, Detective. I've got to get changed now." Shoulders erect, he went inside the house without so much as a glance back.

Tony gazed at Julie over the roof of the car. "What happened?"

"I turned my back for a minute—just *one* minute—to

check on dinner and when I turned back around, he was gone. I don't know—I thought—"

"Where's Mom?"

"She's gone to the grocery store. I offered to go for her, but she said no, just keep an eye on Daddy, and I tried, but I *lost* him. My God, he could have been hit by a car or—or—"

Tony circled the car, slid his arm around her shoulders, and headed for the door. "It's not your fault. He got away from Mom last week, remember?" That time Joe had made it halfway across town to Henry's house, but when he'd gotten there, he hadn't had a clue who Henry was. By the time Tony arrived, Joe's agitation over the strangers living in Henry's house had been full-blown. Tony had needed Henry's help to get Joe into the car, and he'd ranted all the way home. Then, after a few hours' rest, he'd forgotten the incident and never mentioned it again.

Grimly shutting out the memory, Tony followed Julie inside. "You can't hog-tie him, you know."

For a moment her distress was replaced by the big-sister bossiness he knew so well. "You wanna bet?"

The house was cool and smelled of pot roast and citrus. The lights were off in the living room, the blinds drawn against the afternoon sun. Tony found his father in the master bedroom, meticulously removing his clothing. The bedcovers were folded back. "You taking a nap, Dad?"

"I had a hard day at work. It tires a man out." Stripped down to his boxers and T-shirt, and still wearing his shoes and socks, Joe sat down on the bed, slid his feet under the covers, then stretched out on his side. "Turn off the lights on your way out, would you?"

Tony glanced at the overhead light that wasn't on. "Sure." Three steps took him into the room. He lifted the sheet and blanket, unlaced and removed Joe's shoes, then spread the covers again. "Sleep tight. Don't let the bedbugs bite."

"Uh-huh."

Another childhood ritual, right down to the response. Only the roles were reversed.

He closed the door behind him, then returned to the front door to lock the double-keyed dead bolt. If Joe tried to wander off again, he would have to go through the patio or the garage doors, and to get to either, he would have to pass Tony and Julie in the kitchen.

He found his sister at the sink, scrubbing dishes as if someone's life depended on it. When he touched her shoulder, she stiffened and sniffled a time or two before glancing at him. "What are we going to do, Tony?"

He wanted to protest. He wasn't the oldest—that was J.J.—or the most responsible—that was Nick—or the most maternal. Julie won that one. He didn't have any suggestions or ideas. Hell, like their mother, he didn't even want to acknowledge that anything was wrong. He'd looked up to his father all his life, and damned if he wanted to accept that Joe was slipping away a little more every day.

"I know why Mom wanted to do her own grocery shopping," Julie went on. "She would never admit it, but she needed to get away from him. Watching him is like watching a hyperactive three-year-old, except you can reason with a kid better than you can with him, and a kid doesn't forget who you are every time he turns his back."

And you didn't have forty years of memories with a kid. You hadn't lived, loved, worked, and raised a family together. You hadn't planned and saved for retirement, hadn't sacrificed in anticipation of all the things you were going to do together someday—all the trips you were going to take, all the hobbies you'd never found time for, all the grandkids you were going to spoil.

"He still has good days," Tony pointed out.

"Yes, he does, but I'm not sure whether that's a blessing or a curse. I called yesterday and talked to him for half an hour, and it was just like old times. It was so wonderful that I found myself thinking maybe he can beat this. Maybe it's all a mistake; it'll go away, and he'll be all right. Then I came over this afternoon, and he didn't know who I was. It's so hard. Sometimes I think it would be easier if he just—" Clamping her mouth shut, she turned back to the dishes.

If he just died. That was what she'd been about to say. The thought shamed Tony, because no matter how desperately he wanted Joe to live a long, healthy life, there was a part of him that shared the sentiment. Sudden death must be easier than watching the disease destroy Joe's mind before it ended his life. Even though he couldn't imagine life without his father.

"We'll handle it," he said, bumping against Julie as he began rinsing the dishes and stacking them in the drainer. "We'll figure something out."

Though he was damned if he had a clue what.

By nightfall, the temperature had dropped to a comfortable level, made more so by the breeze blowing out of the west. Selena had finished unpacking—a few clothes in the closet, a few toiletries in the bathroom—and was in the process of fixing a late dinner. Etta James was on the stereo, her voice drifting through the open doors onto the small patio. Selena had set the CD player to repeat one particular song so she could learn the words, feel the emotion that gave them life, and wonder why it, of all the songs on the CD, struck a chord with her. It was bluesy, achy, about love and loss and fighting the inevitable. *I would rather go blind,* the refrain went, *than to see you walk away from me.*

She was standing next to the grill, basting the chicken, moving naturally, almost subconsciously, to the music, when a voice came out of the darkness.

"I would rather go deaf than hear that song one more time."

Alarm skittered down her spine, there, then gone—nothing more than the natural startle reflex. She didn't let it show, though, other than in the tightening of her fingers around the basting brush. Forcing a casual air, she rested the brush in the dish of marinade, then turned to face her visitor.

Tony Ceola stood in the weak illumination cast by the light above the back door. He wore running shorts, a T-shirt, and broken-down sneakers without socks, and his dark brown hair stood on end, as if he'd been trying to concentrate—or sleep—without much success. His skin was dark, too, though not as dark as her own, and his nose was straight, his mouth nicely formed, his jaw square. He topped six feet by an inch or two, with broad shoulders, narrow hips, and muscled arms and legs. He was . . .

Not particularly handsome. *Solid* was the first word to come to mind. Unremarkable, except for his eyes—dark brown with a luxurious sweep of thick lashes. Average, except for the smile that quirked his mouth. Still, there was something about him . . .

She mentally shook herself. "Sorry. I'm not accustomed to having neighbors so close they can hear my music. I'm Selena McCaffrey. And you're Anthony Ceola." Though she knew better, she pronounced his name the way it was spelled, with a soft *s*, just to see if he would correct her. He did.

"It's Tony. And while I'll answer to *see-OH-luh*, or *chee-OH-luh*, or just plain Chee, in the family we say *chay-OH-luh*."

"I'll remember that." It wasn't a meaningless nicety. Once she'd accomplished her uncle's orders and left Oklahoma, she had no doubt she would remember everything about this trip for the rest of her life.

He glanced through the open door into the kitchen, where the mess of her dinner preparations still covered the island, then through the tall windows into the sunroom, where canvasses and paint supplies were clearly visible. "You just moved in?"

She used tongs to remove the chicken from the grill to a plate, then gave him a sidelong look. "Can't put anything past you, can I, Detective?"

His grin carried even more of an impact than his smile. It made her hand unsteady, made the tongs clatter against the grill. "You've been talking to the neighbors."

"Actually, the real-estate agent," she lied. She wasn't looking to make friends. She wanted only to do the job she'd come for.

"I didn't even know this place was on the market."

She didn't comment as she transferred skewers of fruit and vegetables from the grill to the plate. The housing arrangements had been entirely William's responsibility. She didn't know whether he'd bought the house or was merely renting it. She did know he'd been smart enough to ensure his name wouldn't be associated with the deal. Though she'd handled the business end, Christine Evans probably didn't have a clue who she'd been handling it for.

No, when the detectives of the Tulsa Police Department

went looking for answers, the only name to cross Christine's lips would be Selena's. It would be up to her to create an airtight alibi or, failing that, to disappear and resurface in a new place with a new name. It wasn't difficult. She'd done it before.

"Have you had dinner?" she asked, extending the plate in offering. "I have plenty to share."

He shook his head. "I stopped by my mom's after work and she stuffed me with pasta, fresh bread, and tiramisu."

She gestured toward the small patio table covered with a cloth and holding a lighted candle, a bottle of wine, and silverware. "Would you like a glass of wine?"

He considered it a moment—thinking about the lateness of the hour or work the next day?—then shrugged. "Sure."

After setting the plate on the table, she went inside to get another wineglass from the cabinet. While there, she reset the CD player to continue to the next song.

When she returned, he was sitting at the table, one ankle crossed over the other knee, eyes closed, looking tired and relaxed, but not at ease. Was it work on his mind? Or something personal?

He'd mentioned his mother, a natural lead-in for questions that she didn't want to ask. She didn't ask many personal questions, didn't make many friends. She'd learned the hard way that life was safer alone. But thanks to William, what she wanted mattered little. "Does your mother live here in town?" she asked as she filled both glasses with wine, then set one in front of him.

"My mother, my father, four brothers and two sisters, various in-laws, nieces, nephews, aunts, uncles, and cousins. There's no shortage of Ceolas in northeastern Oklahoma."

He sipped the wine and made an appreciative gesture. "What about your parents? Where do they live?"

"They don't." Her answer was automatic, one she'd given for so long that sometimes she believed it. Truthfully, she knew nothing about her father, and what she remembered most about her mother was her shame. When Luisa had looked at Selena's coarse hair and coffee-colored skin, she hadn't seen a daughter, but a reminder of an affair that never should have happened. A mistake that couldn't be hidden or ignored when her father's black heritage was stamped so clearly on her features.

"I'm sorry," Tony said. "That's tough. So . . . what brings you to Oklahoma?"

"I needed a change of scene. I was feeling stifled."

"Where?"

"Florida. Key West."

"Oh, yeah, sure. I can see that. Ocean breezes, tropical weather, beautiful people . . . So much better to be in Oklahoma, landlocked, hot, and soon to be entering our annual summer drought."

"You like it enough that you haven't moved elsewhere," she pointed out. She couldn't imagine spending thirty-four years in the same place. The longest she'd ever stayed in one place had been as a child, when she'd lived with her mother, her mother's husband, Rodrigo, and their children in a tiny town in Puerto Rico. Nine years—that was all they'd been able to bear with her.

"It's home," he said with a shrug.

Home. Such a little word to stir such longing inside her. Her big white house in Key West was the only real home she'd ever had. If she succeeded here, she could go back to it. If she didn't . . .

She ate leisurely, as if her appetite weren't nonexistent,

as if she wouldn't rather be anyplace else. The artist in her appreciated the tenderness of the chicken, the sweet tang of the salsa, the dark smoky flavor of the peppers, pineapple, and onions, while the woman recognized them for what they were—required sustenance, no more.

"Tell me about the neighborhood."

He extended both arms to encompass the area. "This is it. Small, quiet, no excitement. The people next door are hardly ever home. The ones across the street work long hours and travel a lot on weekends. Through the woods here is the Marlowe Mansion. Used to be home to one of Oklahoma's richest oilmen, but now it's an art museum. I try to avoid it, but you would probably appreciate it."

She followed his gaze once again to the canvasses in the sunroom. Most of them were blank, though the faint outlines of a sketch were visible on one. The only real work-in-progress was tucked out of sight, a self-portrait she'd started months ago but had never been able to finish.

Common sense had decreed that she leave the supplies at home—after all, she had no idea how long she would be in Tulsa or how quickly she might have to leave. But need had overridden it. Her art grounded her, gave her purpose and control. She grew unsettled when her canvasses and paints weren't at hand, and since coming here had already unsettled her, she'd opted to bring the supplies for balance. If she had to leave them behind to make a quick getaway . . . well, nothing was irreplaceable. Not even the self-portrait.

"You think it takes an artist to appreciate art?" she asked as she pushed her plate away, then settled back in her chair.

"Not necessarily. Well, sometimes. I'm one of the unsophisticated masses who wants paintings to look like what they're supposed to be. Don't slap a smudge here, a splatter there, and a blob elsewhere, then tell me it's anything other than a smudge, a splatter, and a blob."

"My paintings always look like what they're supposed to be." Usually even better. She painted houses with rambling verandas and inviting wicker chairs, gardens filled with emerald grass and lush tropical flowers, idyllic villages spread along the beach like jewels dropped from the sky. There was no disrepair in her paintings, no poverty, no misfortune or betrayal or disappointment. Just perfect little slices of paradise.

But no one knew better than she that even paradise was never perfect.

"Do you sell them?"

She nodded once. "I have a place in Key West. Island Dreams Art Gallery."

"Can I see some of your work?"

"Sometime." She ran one fingertip along the choker around her neck, lifting it so the breeze could cool her skin, and saw his gaze follow. The narrowing of his eyes meant he'd noticed the bruises on her throat, fainter now, the colors muted, but still difficult to miss. Similar marks on her arm and rib cage—souvenirs of her last workout with Montoya—as well as the bruise on her shoulder from her run-in with William's guard, were hidden by her clothes, while the one on her ankle could be mistaken for a trick of the light. The ones on her throat, though, like her paintings, looked exactly like what they were. Would he ask about them like a good cop, or opt for discretion and ignore them?

"So you've always lived in Oklahoma," she remarked, letting the choker's wooden beads settle back against her skin. "Does that mean you have a Stetson, a pair of boots, and a horse tucked away somewhere?"

"Hardly. I'm more likely to wear a ball cap than a cowboy hat, and horses and I don't get along." He drained the last of his wine and set the glass on the table, then shook his head when she offered the bottle. "As for other Oklahoma stereotypes, I'm that rarity among native Okies—no Indian blood. I don't listen to country music, I don't own a single oil well, and I don't live and breathe football."

"But you *are* an Italian-American cop. That's a stereotype."

He grinned. "If there wasn't some truth to stereotypes, they wouldn't last long enough to *become* stereotypes. How long do you plan to stay here?"

"I don't know. As long as it takes."

"You're not married." When she raised one brow in question, he matched her with one shoulder lifted in a negligible shrug. "Most men don't like it when their wives move away for indefinite periods of time."

"No," she agreed. "I'm not married." She'd seen little to recommend the institution. Luisa had grown old before her time, caring for a new baby every year, struggling to make ends meet, giving to her fat, lazy husband until there was nothing left for her children or herself. Selena's teachers, her acquaintances, even Asha, who ran the gallery for her— all had been married, unhappily so, subservient to the men who controlled their lives. She had enough male domination in her life because of William. She didn't intend to seek out more elsewhere.

"Any brothers or sisters?"

Nine half siblings at last count. Luisa had still had a few childbearing years left when Rodrigo had sent Selena away. Who knew how many babies she'd produced before nature had intervened? As for siblings on her father's side, that was impossible to know. Not that it mattered. Unless he'd made a habit of choosing women of other races, she would have been as much an outcast with his family as she'd been with her mother's.

"None," she lied.

"A lonely only," he teased. "Or is that a spoiled only?"

"A little of both." Another lie. William was the only person who'd come close to spoiling her, and his indulgences were financial in nature, not emotional. As for loneliness . . . Breathing deeply, she pushed the thought away. Indulging in self-pity served no purpose.

The faint wail of a siren sounded in the distance, growing louder as it came closer. Detective Ceola perked up, his gaze shifting in that direction. She smiled as she murmured, "Like Pavlov's dog."

Once more he grinned, and once more she was struck by how it changed his appearance—or rather, her perception of it. Though portraits weren't her strength, she would like to capture the transformation on canvas.

"I'm not drooling," he pointed out.

"You're also not denying that your ears pricked up, your heart rate increased a beat or two, and your curiosity was piqued."

He brushed one hand over the hair that barely touched his right ear. "My ears don't prick up. Besides, that's a fire engine."

"How can you tell?"

He gestured toward the house. "You can recognize Etta James by hearing her voice. I can recognize a Federal Q siren by hearing it."

So he was an Etta James fan, as well. The idea of sharing interests with him made her uncomfortable.

The siren soared to its loudest, accompanied by the growl of the engine, as the vehicle sped past on a nearby street. In the quiet that followed, she covered a fake yawn with her fingers. "It's late."

"Yeah." Detective Ceola pushed his chair back, the metal feet scraping the brick, then stood up. "Thanks for the wine, and welcome to the neighborhood." Waving, he stepped from the patio into the shadows, then headed toward the rear of his house.

Rising from her chair, Selena carried the dishes inside, locked up, set the kitchen to rights, then shut off the lights. For a moment she lingered at the kitchen window, gazing at the neighboring house, dark now. Detective Ceola was an interesting man. Given the opportunity . . .

With a scowl, she turned away from the window and walked down the hall and up the stairs. She couldn't afford any distractions, no matter how interesting.

Light spilled out at the end of the hallway from the frilly beaded lamp next to her bed, along with the sweet fragrance of the jasmine blooming on the nightstand. She dressed for bed, then sat in a wingback chair, chosen more for its style than comfort. Spine straight, nerves taut, she picked up the cell phone next to the lamp and dialed the only number in its directory.

William answered on the second ring, his tone curt. That would change, she knew, once he heard what she had to say.

"Hello, Uncle," she said coolly. "Sorry to call you so late, but I've just finished having dinner with the detective who lives next door."

Selena rose before dawn Friday. Dressed in shorts and a tank top, she sat cross-legged on a mat on the living-room floor, spine straight, eyes closed, breathing in deeply as if a balloon were expanding inside her rib cage, then exhaling slowly, slowly, as the balloon deflated.

Her yoga instructor's soothing voice murmured inside her head, calming and guiding her attention inward, but another part of her mind remained attuned to the external—the coolness of the wood through the rug. The pendulum tick-tick of the grandfather clock in the hallway. A dog barking somewhere in the distance.

When a door closed nearby, she expelled the breath she'd been holding, got to her feet, and moved to the window, staying well back from the glass. Detective Ceola was striding along the sidewalk that connected his front stoop to the driveway, a black bag over one shoulder. He wore a dark suit with a white shirt and patterned burgundy tie. Conservative, as a good detective should be. As he passed the 'Vette, he gave it a pat.

She turned away to check the clock. Six-forty. Dr. Franklin, down the block, left five minutes later. Her husband followed half an hour after that. Once he was gone, Selena picked up the canvas bag she'd left beside the door, took her keys from the hall table, and went outside to the car. There was no sign of life on the street. She could pick the lock at any one of the houses, walk right in the front door and make herself at home, and no one would know the difference.

Instead, she drove west to River Parks, parking in the narrow lot nearest William's estate. After pulling her braid through the back of a ball cap and adding an oversize pair of sunglasses, she carried the canvas bag to a shady spot halfway between the main gate and her car, settled down, and took a sketch pad and pen from the bag.

The morning sun bathed the house in a soft glow. In front a gardener tended the flower beds and, closer, two men stood outside the guard shack, one holding a coffee mug while the other ate a fast-food breakfast sandwich. Other than that, everything was still.

She sketched absently, not caring whether she captured the house's grace and elegance. Though she earned a living painting beautiful houses, this one left her cold. Once this trip was over, she would be happy never to see it again.

The breakfasting guard was on his third sandwich when he abruptly went into the guard shack, then returned, hands empty. The other guard set his coffee cup inside and came back out, smoothing his shirt, adjusting his gun belt. A moment later she saw why. A Cadillac glided around from the garage at the back of the house and slowly approached the gate. One of the guards hit the button that swung the gate open, then they both stood practically at attention as William drove through with a smile and a wave.

Selena's breath caught in her chest. This was her first glimpse of him in two years. He was a handsome man— tall, tanned, with thick hair that had gradually turned white. His eyes were blue—usually cool and distant, though at times they were fired with passion. Business inspired him; so did the prospect of her joining him in that business.

She had come to believe that was the reason he'd rescued her. Not because it was the decent thing to do. Not because he was kind and generous, but because a man wanted to leave something behind, and wanted someone to leave it to. He'd had the *something* in his business, but, divorced and childless, he'd lacked the *someone*.

Until he'd found her. He'd groomed her, pushed her, tantalized her with images of the two of them working together, like a real father and daughter. In the beginning she had been willing, but then she'd learned the truth about his business.

Her dignified, elegant Uncle William was nothing more than a drug dealer.

And no matter how grateful she was to him, she couldn't allow herself to become one, too.

At the first break in traffic, he turned north on Riverside. Quickly she stowed her supplies in the bag, then jogged back to her car. He'd traveled nearly a mile by the time she sighted him again, heading toward downtown Tulsa. What kind of career did he dabble in to create a front for his criminal activities? she wondered as she settled in four cars behind him. Business of some sort, no doubt, dealing with money. Money and the power it brought were his gods; wheeling and dealing, his idea of entertainment.

He turned onto Sixth Street, then into the Civic Center parking lot. She couldn't follow, not without the risk of discovery, so she circled the area. Besides the Civic Center itself, the lot provided parking for the complex of government buildings located there—city hall, the police department, the courthouse, and, across the street to the north, the federal courthouse.

He wasn't likely to have an office in any of those buildings, so perhaps he'd merely been making a visit, she admitted a short time later when she'd driven through the lot twice without finding his car. While she'd been dallying to ensure he wouldn't see her, apparently he'd left again. Maybe he hadn't even stopped. Maybe he'd suspected he was being followed and had merely pulled through the lot to exit on the opposite side.

But that was all right. She was nothing if not patient.

5

Friday found Tony in a north Tulsa cemetery in ninety-degree heat to see Grover Washington laid to rest—or, more accurately, to see who else came to see him laid to rest.

The family had forgone the church service for graveside rites. Most of the mourners were gathered under the big green tent erected by the cemetery. He and Simmons had taken shelter in the shade of a scraggly cedar, near enough to see and hear the proceedings, far enough away to give the mourners some privacy. Cars lined the narrow road behind them, including the surveillance van off to the west, where another detective, Darnell Garry, was set up with a camera.

Tony wondered if one of the three dozen or so men was Marcell. The computer had given him a last name—Napier—and an old booking photo that could have matched any number of people. His last known address was an overgrown lot littered with debris from a house fire four years ago. The utility companies had no accounts in his name, his driver's license showed another no-good address, and there was no current vehicle registration under that name in the state. Tony had even tried Voter Registration—as if Grover's type bothered being responsible citizens—but had come up blank.

None of which meant Napier wasn't living and doing

business right there in town, and quite possibly standing across the cemetery from them.

"Is that the flowers smelling, or Fat Grover?" Simmons whispered as the breeze carried a sickly sweet odor their way.

"Hard to tell." The flowers were wilting fast under the midday sun, as were many of the mourners.

"If I go before you, have me cremated," Simmons said. "Don't let Suz lay me out in the sun for two hours of wailing and moaning."

"Suz doesn't have two hours of wailing and moaning in her, at least not for you."

"Jeez, how long can this go on?"

Tony's narrow look was lost on Simmons because of his sunglasses. "You're not Catholic, are you, Frankie?" he asked dryly. "A funeral mass can last long enough to make you wish *you* were dead."

He scanned the crowd again. He'd already picked out Mae Washington in the front row, flanked by LaShandra Banks and another woman, all three dressed in black and wearing elaborate hats. There were plenty of other familiar faces—people he'd interviewed with regard to the murders, people he'd arrested, people he'd taken reports from as victims. He had a great memory for faces and names, dates and circumstances, crimes and punishments. Some of them ignored him and Simmons. Others watched them as steadily as they were being watched.

"You ever see that movie *The Big Easy*?" Simmons asked.

"Several times."

"You know the scene where they go to investigate the triple homicide, and everybody in the neighborhood is stirred up outside the house? One of 'em says, 'Don't be lookin' at us, 'cause you did it,' or something like that. That's what they're thinking every time one of them looks over here."

Have you considered the possibility that the vigilante could be a cop? Marla had asked. How could he not, when everyone else was considering it? But it wasn't him, or Frank, or anyone else he worked with. He couldn't do anything about the uneasy relations between the police and the black community, other than what he'd always done—his job, as professionally and fairly as he knew how—but he knew one thing for sure: He was just as willing to put away a dirty cop as any other bad guy.

Finally the last prayers were said and the mourners began to gather around Mae to express their sympathies. The pastor stood at her side, one arm around her waist.

"Looky who's over there," Simmons said, pointing toward the far side of the grave. "Jerome Little."

Tony's gaze went straight to the man Grover Washington had once beaten into a coma. Thin, wiry, the guy didn't weigh a hundred and fifty pounds soaking wet, but he had a mouth on him that would do an eight-hundred-pound gorilla proud. "What do you wanna bet he's none too broken up over Grover's passing?"

"Don't you know it. I think I'll amble over and say 'Hello.' You gonna look for Marcell?"

"Yeah." But what were the odds, Tony wondered, heading for the family as Simmons angled off toward Little, of a white cop walking up to a bunch of black men at a black drug-dealer's funeral and getting a straight answer about anyone's identity?

LaShandra was standing near Grover's mother, gold and diamonds glinting brightly in the sun. She looked neither pleased nor displeased to see him, merely resigned. "That's some job you've got, Detective, hanging out at graveyards and intruding on people's grief."

"I'm only here because it's part of the investigation. I try my best not to intrude."

She studied him a moment before pulling a pair of sunglasses from her purse. "Okay. Let's say you're trying to find whoever killed Grover. What do you want from me?"

"Marcell Napier. Is he here?"

"I told you the other day, I don't know him."

"Maybe some of these other people do."

"Then ask them."

He smiled faintly. "You know they'll be more likely to answer if you ask."

She smiled, too. "People tend to get evasive when you come around with your badge and your gun, don't they?" After looking around for a moment, she brought her gaze back to him. "You want to tag along or wait here?"

"I'll wait. Tell them I just want to ask Marcell a few questions."

"Oh, yeah, that'll reassure them."

He took shelter again under a tree and watched her move from group to group. He got a lot of stares, saw some heads shaking no, and caught a few reactions that could only be considered hostile. When LaShandra returned, perspiration dotted her face and made him aware of the sweat trickling down his own spine.

"Marcell wasn't here. Tiny says he's staying with a cousin in south Tulsa. Deion says he's moved out West. Kendra says she saw him last week and might see him again. She says she'll let me know if she does."

"And you'll let me know?"

The look she gave him could have melted ice in January. "The boy isn't of any interest to *me*. Now, unless you have any other errands you'd like me to do for you, I'm going to get out of this heat."

"Thanks, LaShandra. I appreciate it."

He headed toward his car and the surveillance van parked where the road curved back around to the cemetery exit. Halfway there he spotted a familiar figure, out of sight of the mourners, behind a big oak. Thinking longingly of air-conditioning, Tony turned in his direction.

Javier Perkins was thin in that painful way caused by too much booze and drugs and too little of anything good for him—food, sleep, a clear conscience. He wore a long-sleeved shirt that covered the needle tracks, and shifted his weight from side to side. "Hey, Chee," he greeted Tony, his voice raspy.

"Javier. You paying your respects to the Washington family or looking for me?"

"Looking for you." Javier took a drag from his cigarette, then blew out a thin plume of acrid smoke. "I figured you'd be here."

"You know if you want to talk to me, you can call." Back when Tony had worked Burglary, he'd cultivated Javier as an informant. In spite of his addictions, his information was generally reliable, but he offered it only when he was short on cash and needed a fix.

Javier shuffled his feet, his gaze darting around the area. "Yeah, well, I don't like to call if I can avoid it."

Tony leaned one shoulder against the tree. Everyone else was heading for their cars while, off in the distance, the cemetery crew waited to finish their job. "You have some information for me?"

"Y-yeah, I do." Drawing a handkerchief from his pants pocket, Javier wiped the sweat that beaded his forehead. When Tony had first turned him, he'd figured he was an old guy—late fifties, early sixties. It had been a shock to discover that the man wasn't even forty yet. "It's about Washington."

"What about him?"

"I, uh, I was over there—in that area—the night . . . the night him and them others was killed. I, uh, s-s-saw . . ." Realizing his cigarette had burned to the filter, Javier dropped it to the ground, shook another from the package, and stuck it between his lips, but his hands were too unsteady to light it.

Tony took the matchbook from him, lit the cigarette, then ground out the butt in the grass. "What did you see?"

"Them." He jerked his head in the direction of the grave. "At that house. The one where everyone hangs out, you know? Where they was killed. And—and—and the man. The man what did it."

A quiver of anticipation skipped down Tony's spine— the same quiver he'd felt the week before when he'd found out the Prinz kid had witnessed Bryan Hayes's murder. Removing a notebook and pen from his jacket, he flipped open to a clean page. "Did you get a good look at him?"

Javier's head bobbed. He swiped his forehead with his shirtsleeve, then took another anxious look around at the surveillance van and the cemetery crew, now working at the grave. "G-good enough. He was tall, taller than me. Heavier, too. Maybe—maybe about *his* size." He gestured toward Simmons, who was now waiting at the car. "He come to the house after they"—another jerk toward the grave—"got there, and there was gunshots, and then he left."

"Was he black, white, Hispanic, Asian?"

"Black." His head bobbed again. "Black as me. And bald. Balder than me." With a nervous grin, he combed his fingers through his thinning hair, then seemed to realize for the first time how bad the shakes were. He stuck the cigarette between his lips, then folded his arms tightly across his chest as if he could hold himself steady that way.

A black man. The Prinz kid was just as certain that Hayes's killer had been white. Maybe Henry was right, and Hayes's murder had nothing to do with the vigilante. Tony felt oddly disappointed—and stubbornly disbelieving.

"You're sure he was black?"

"Come on, Chee. I been black all my life. You think I can't recognize a black man when I see him?"

So maybe the Prinz kid was wrong. It had been late for a six-year-old—nearly midnight. He had been awakened by a dog barking outside his open window, then a knock at Hayes's apartment across the sidewalk, and had rolled over in time to watch a tall man shoot Hayes when he opened the door. Maybe he'd gotten confused, or had been so traumatized by what he'd seen that he didn't really *know* what he'd seen.

But Tony had interviewed the kid a short time later, and he hadn't seemed at all traumatized. In fact, Tony would have bet he didn't even understand what death really was. People died on TV and in movies and video games all the time, and then they showed up again, just fine, in other TV shows and movies or when the video game was restarted.

"That neighborhood's three miles from where you live. What were you doing there in the middle of the night?"

"Wasn't the middle of the night. It was almost morning—about four o'clock." That uneasy grin came again. "Time don't matter when a man has certain needs. I was lookin' to—to fulfill those needs."

"Your dealer live in that area?"

Nervous energy damn near vibrated through Javier. "Aw, Chee, don't ask me about that. I can't tell you nothin' about nothin' if you're gonna be like that."

"Okay. Tell me everything from the beginning."

Javier rolled back on his heels. "I been trying to cut back, you know, but I had a tough night Saturday. I couldn't get by on my own, so I went to score. I was waitin' over by that house when them boys came. They went inside, and a little bit later, the other guy showed up."

So much for his theory that the shooter had been waiting for the other three to arrive. "How much later? Five minutes? Ten?"

"I don't know. I don't wear no watch. But, yeah, somethin' like that."

When he didn't go on, Tony prodded. "Then what happened?"

"For a minute, nothin'. Then all of a sudden, there was six gunshots, real quicklike. *Bam, bam, bam.* Then the fourth man come out, got in his truck—a red one, like a Bronco or something—and he drove off. He wasn't in no hurry at all, just takin' his own sweet time."

"And then?"

"I didn't stick around no longer. I scored someplace else," Javier said with that shaky grin. "Today's the first chance I had to talk to you."

Something nagged at Tony—the unwillingness to admit that his instincts had been wrong?—but he pushed away from the tree. "Thanks, Javier. I'll be in touch, okay?"

"Yeah, sure. Mind if I get out of here before you leave? Wouldn't want people to see me talking to cops." At Tony's nod, Javier darted away, hands in his pockets, head down.

Before he'd gone ten feet, Tony called, "Hey, Javier, you know a guy by the name of Marcell Napier?"

He didn't slow his steps, but just replied over his shoulder. "Nope. Sorry." As soon as he reached the gate, he trotted across the street and ducked into a waiting car. The driver made a U-turn, then headed off in the opposite direction.

Tony headed for his own car, where Simmons was munching on a cookie and talking with Darnell Garry. He'd discarded his suit jacket, revealing sweat stains on his too-tight shirt.

"Crank up the AC on this thing," he said, straightening as Tony opened the door. He affected a bad Southern accent. "I'm about to wilt in this hot summer sun."

Garry snorted. " 'Wilt'? I always thought you were a little light in the loafers, Frankie."

Simmons made kissing noises at him as he gave him the finger.

Garry turned to Tony. "The lab'll have these pictures ready for you in a few hours. They'll give you a call."

Tony nodded as he slid behind the wheel. The car had been in the shade when he'd parked it there nearly three hours earlier, but now the sun shone down on it full blast. He started the engine, rolled down the windows, and flipped the AC to high, then fastened his seat belt as Simmons hunkered down in the passenger seat, juggling cookies, suit coat, and seat belt.

"Wasn't that ol' Javier? What'd he want?"

After Tony repeated the gist of the conversation, Simmons frowned. "So now we're looking for a tall black man *and* a tall white man. Hell, that oughta cut our suspect list down to no more than fifty thousand." He stuffed the cookie bag onto the dash and ignored the shower of crumbs that spilled to the floor. "Hey, Chee, have you ever noticed when we work together that everyone always has information for *you*? Like I'm not even workin' the same case? I wonder why that is."

"Because they know I'll do something with it?" Tony

responded dryly as he followed the van along the winding road to the nearest gate.

"Hey, I'd do something with it."

"Yeah. Put it away until Monday morning."

"The city don't pay me enough as it is. They're damn sure not gettin' overtime from me. Besides, is it my fault that I have a life?"

"I have a life."

"Yeah, sure. What're you gonna do tonight? No, wait. Let me guess. Have a frozen dinner while you study those photographs and all the other evidence, then go to bed. Am I right, or am I right?"

He was closer than Tony wanted to admit.

"No answer, huh?" Simmons shook his head mournfully. "Just say the word, and I'll set you up with one of Suz's friends."

"I told you, I'm not interested. They're all looking to get married."

"Not all of them. There's one or two who're just looking to get laid. They're not the hottest ones in the bunch, but hey, in the dark who's gonna notice?"

The hottest one in *any* bunch was temporarily living next door. If Tony was looking for anything, that was probably where he'd look first. Not that it mattered. The only thing he wanted to find right now was a killer.

And if that said something pathetic about his life, so what?

The thud of his footsteps on the asphalt Saturday morning seemed to echo the thud of Tony's heart as he matched his pace to Marla Johnson's. Given a choice when he'd met the crime-scene tech jogging on the trail, he would have said

"Hello," then continued along his usual route, but she'd asked him to join her.

"Anything new on the case?" she asked, her breathing labored.

"We might have a witness to the last three deaths."

"Reliable?"

"Usually. He says the killer was a black man."

"What does that do to your theory that the same guy killed Hayes?"

"Blows it to hell." *Maybe.* Something still nagged him about Javier's version of events. He hadn't figured out what yet, but it would come to him. Sooner or later, it always did.

"Anything else?"

"Jerome Little showed up at Grover's funeral."

"Those months he spent in the hospital might be a pretty good motive for murder."

"Uh-huh. But that was more than a year ago. Why wait until now?"

"Revenge is a dish best served cold, or so they say."

"Maybe." Jerome had been busy in the past year, relearning things like how to walk again. He'd made a pretty good recovery, though his gait was stilted, his speech slurred.

But it was tough to see him as an avenger. He was small-time—a petty thief, a petty human being. He didn't take big risks or expect big payoffs, and he didn't have what it took to commit cold-blooded murder. Tony was sure of it.

"Maybe," Marla repeated sarcastically. "Richard uses the same tone when he thinks I'm totally wrong but doesn't have the nerve to say so. So what's your theory?"

"I'm not sure I have one."

"You think the guy's a vigilante?"

"Could be."

"Or maybe another dealer looking to take over the business for this area?"

"Could be that, too. Maybe they shared an unhappy customer. Or maybe only one of these guys was really a target and the rest were meant to throw us off the trail." He didn't put much weight in either possibility, though. If forced to choose at that very moment, he would opt for a power grab. If one person controlled all the drug trade for northeastern Oklahoma, he could make a hell of a lot of money . . . and a hell of a lot of enemies. But dead enemies weren't a problem, were they?

As they approached the Twenty-first Street crossing, Marla slowed to a walk, then stopped, bending over, forearms resting on her knees. The position pulled her nylon shorts snug over her butt and drew a whistle from a teenage boy whizzing past on in-line skates. She flashed the kid a grin, then slowly straightened.

"I don't suppose you'd want to skip the rest of your run and have breakfast with me."

For the hundredth time, Tony wasn't sure exactly what she was offering. Her words said "just breakfast," but the sly look in her eyes hinted at more, and the seductive smile suggested a hell of a lot more. He was tempted to say yes just to find out. But he didn't know how much temptation he could withstand this early on a warm Saturday morning, and he wasn't willing to find out.

"Sorry," he said, and saw she'd expected his refusal. "Go home and have breakfast with your lieutenant."

"I'm having lunch and dinner with him. Can you blame a girl for liking a little variety now and then?"

Tony used the sound of approaching footsteps as an excuse to shift his attention away—and found he couldn't look back. The woman who'd just turned the corner onto the trail was tall and slender, and wore bright blue shorts that made her legs look a mile long. Her sports bra was blue, too, partially hidden beneath a crimson tank top that clung, jeez, the way clothes should. Her black curls were pulled off her neck with a big clip, and her eyes were covered by mirrored lenses that reflected the scenery back at him. She smiled faintly as she passed, and neither noticed nor cared that he turned to watch her go.

He was still staring, mouth dry, when Marla's voice drifted through the fog around him. "And here I've thought all my life that being blonde and petite was the way to get a man's attention. Catch up to her. Get her number."

"I've got her number," he murmured. Not literally, but even better, he had her name and address. Finally he managed to look away. "She's my neighbor. Moved up here temporarily from Florida. She's living in Mrs. Howell's house."

"That's convenient—though it makes it hard to cheat."

"I don't cheat," he said automatically, then frowned. "Did you cheat on me when we were together?"

"Don't take it personally. I cheat on everyone," she said matter-of-factly. Then she patted him on the arm. "Go on. At the rate she's going, she'll be at the river before you catch up. See you around work."

He watched Marla jog off to the north, then pivoted and headed back along the trail. Selena had been moving pretty quickly—and why shouldn't she? She was only a few inches shorter than him, and was all legs. But he wasn't following her. He was just running the same route, and it had been his route years before it had become hers.

He zoned out all the distractions around him—the skaters, the cyclists, the runners, the walkers—and concentrated instead on his cases. He'd spent so much time studying the evidence that he could call it all to mind—photos, fingerprints, ballistics, autopsies, financial records, phone records. Seven homicides—because he was still counting Hayes until he had solid reason not to—with the victims all male. Three black, two white, one Hispanic, one Asian, all involved in the drug trade. The last three killed in north Tulsa, one each in midtown, east, west, and south neighborhoods. One partial license plate number that led to hundreds of cars, and two conflicting eyewitness descriptions that matched thousands of men in the city.

Not much to go on.

When he'd returned to the office after the funeral the previous day, he'd met with Henry and Captain Billings, the chief of detectives, and filled them in on what little he and Simmons had learned, including Javier Perkins's story. *So you were wrong about Hayes,* Henry had said. *It isn't a vigilante case. Now you can hand it over to someone else.*

Not yet, Tony had argued. He'd talked his way into keeping the case, though Henry had made it clear his patience was wearing thin. Once that was settled, Tony had asked permission to form a task force, which was pretty routine for a case like this. They could put together some Homicide detectives, some guys from Narcotics and Street Crimes, maybe even someone from the DEA, and have a better shot at finding the killer before he found his next victim.

The chief of detectives had looked to Henry for guidance on how to respond, and when Henry had shown no enthusiasm, neither had Billings. There wasn't enough manpower, he'd said—a difficult point to argue considering the budget cuts in preceding years. Tony and Simmons could handle it just fine.

Tony scowled. If seven students at the University of Tulsa had been murdered, there damn well would have been a task force. If seven bankers or seven nurses or seven teachers had been shot to death, he and Simmons would have had all the help they could use and then some.

Which led to the dirty little truth—none of the people charged with stopping the vigilante, or whatever the hell he was, cared. He was cleaning up the streets, making the city a safer place. As for the fact that he was breaking the law . . . well, the ends justified the means, right?

The tenor of his footsteps changed as he started across the Pedestrian Bridge. People fished below the dam, kids peered between the rails into the river, and one teenage couple made out beside a massive beam. The closer he got to the west side, the stronger the odor from the refinery became. *The smell of money,* Henry often said. Oil had built the state in general and Tulsa in particular. All the great oilmen of the twentieth century were long gone—Phillips, Gilcrease, Skelly, and Henry's own grandfather—but their legacy lived on.

Tony had gone back north, then turned east across the Twenty-first Street bridge when a flash of bright blue and crimson caught his attention at the far end. He picked up his pace until he'd caught up with Selena, then matched his stride to hers. Her coffee-colored skin glistened with sweat, and her sunglasses sat on top of her head, anchored in all that thick hair. When she glanced at him, her dark gaze suggested she'd been aware all along that he was behind her.

"It's a little warm this morning." The mark of a true conversationalist—open with the weather, he thought scornfully.

"Come to south Florida. We'll show you warm." Her breathing was measured, even, as if she hadn't run several miles already.

"This is a poor substitute for the ocean, tropical breezes, and palm trees." His gesture took in the muddy brown of the river, the still air, and the growth of blackjacks, river birches, and post oaks. He could easily imagine her in a Caribbean hideaway, spacious and airy, with verandas and French doors opening off every room, a lush lawn and flowers growing wild right to the edge of a white sand beach. Steel drums would play in the background, a subdued accompaniment to the regular ebb and flow of the waves lapping against the shore, and the fragrant breezes and steady supply of tropical drinks would be enough to make a man forget the heat, the world, everything but her, dressed in flowing white clothes, feet bare, curls tumbling down her back . . .

Scowling again, he swiped the sweat from his face. He didn't get poetic over women, and this wasn't the woman to start with. Not that she wasn't beautiful. Exotic. Just reticent enough to be mysterious.

But she was temporary. When her stifled feeling went away, she would leave, going back to the islands where an exotic beauty belonged.

And there was that reticence. He liked mysteries, liked finding clues and solving puzzles—at work. But in his personal life, he preferred openness and honesty.

When they reached a drinking fountain in the shade of a tree, she stopped to take a drink. In spite of the heat and her activity, she wore a wooden necklace, thin medallions of gleaming mahogany separated by matching beads and strung together on a leather thong. It fell forward when she bent, giving him a glimpse of the fading bruises that marked her throat.

He'd wanted to ask about them Thursday night. The cop in him had been all ready, but the part of him that was off-duty, that had been on her patio in the capacity of neighbor, had stifled the questions. It hadn't been easy, turning off his protect-and-serve side, especially when any rookie could recognize the source of the bruises.

"Who choked you?" He kept his voice soft, not making accusations, trying not to intimidate, but to himself he sounded both accusatory and intimidating.

She straightened abruptly. As she wiped a stray drop of water from her chin, the necklace fell back against her skin. "Who—?" Her hand reached toward her throat, then, as if catching herself, she folded her arms over her chest instead. It was a poor attempt at nonchalance, particularly since it brought another set of black-and-blues on her right upper arm into prominence. "It's not what you think."

"Bruises caused by choking are pretty consistent. So are the bruises you get when someone grabs your arm." Stepping closer, he matched his fingers to the shadows that marked her arm, four on the outside, the thumb on the inside. "Is that why you ran away to Tulsa?"

"No." She shrugged away from him and started walking.

He caught up with her, stopping her again. "If someone's hurting you—"

The muscles beneath his fingers tightened, then slowly eased. Her movements controlled and deliberate, she removed his hand from her arm and started walking again, heading for the stairs so she could cross Riverside. "It's no big secret. I got the bruises in my last workout at home. I study tae kwon do, and we do full-contact sparring. That's all."

Tony dodged a mother with stroller-bound twins, then broke into a jog as Selena did the same. "Why?"

She glanced his way. "Why what?"

"Why tae kwon do? Why full-contact sparring?"

"It's good exercise and a great stress reducer. It teaches discipline. And I practice full-contact sparring because that's what my instructor teaches. Besides, for a single woman who lives and travels alone, a little knowledge of self-defense can mean the difference between life and death. You should understand that better than most, Detective."

Having worked his share of crimes against women, he couldn't argue the point. "Are you good?"

A faint smile curved her lips. "I'm very good in the gym. In the real world, I haven't had a chance to find out."

"I hope you never do."

She gave him another of those long, steady looks before agreeing. "Wouldn't that be nice?"

The knife blade clicked against the wood of the cutting board, providing a subtle accompaniment to the music spilling from the CD player as Selena methodically chopped onions and peppers. It was a hot, sunny Sunday, perfect for heading to the nearest beach, for lying back in the sun and forgetting that she had a care in the world . . . but some cares couldn't be forgotten.

The knife stilled as the banging of a door drew her gaze to the window overlooking her neighbor's backyard. The dog came into view first, trotting eagerly to the grill at the edge of the small patio, followed by his master. Detective Ceola was dressed casually in shorts, T-shirt, and no shoes, and a growth of beard darkened his jaw. He carried a plate of burgers in one hand, a pancake turner in the other, and was accompanied by two men who looked a great deal like him. Brothers, she assumed. As soon as he got the burgers on the grill, one of his guests handed him a bottle of beer, and the three of them talked and laughed while the dog kept a watchful eye out for the tidbits of meat Ceola occasionally dropped to him.

The homey scene filled her with wistfulness. Because she'd never had friends to invite over for a cookout? Or because she wouldn't mind being the friend Detective Ceola invited over?

It was foolish. This was the worst time in her life to develop an interest in any man, and Ceola was the worst choice. It would be nothing less than disastrous . . . and she'd learned two years ago just how bad that could be.

Still, he crept into her thoughts every time she relaxed. She wondered why he wasn't married and raising a houseful of kids. What his relationship was with the pretty little blonde who'd looked at him as if he were a hot fudge sundae and she'd just come off a diet. If he was as nice as he seemed. If all women felt a sense of security when he was around.

Because *she* did. Oh, there was caution and suspicion and wariness, but underneath . . . he could make her feel safe.

All her life she'd wanted to feel safe.

He used the pancake turner to flip the burgers onto a plate, shut off the grill, then followed his guests to the house, the dog on his heels. When the door closed behind them, Selena gave herself a shake and set to work again. She had far more important things to worry about than her neighbor and her response to him.

Such as what she was going to do about William. She'd idolized him most of her life, but she didn't want to go to prison for him. Didn't want to be controlled by him any longer. Didn't want to live at the mercy of a merciless man.

If she followed his bidding, she would never escape his control. Just as he'd blackmailed her this time, he would do so the next time, and the next, until she had no choice but to surrender and become the puppet he wanted her to be.

She could run away . . . and live the rest of her life in

fear of getting caught, for there was no doubt William would search for her. He wasn't the sort of man who took kindly to losing what belonged to him, and in his mind, *she* most surely belonged to him.

She could turn the tables on him—blackmail him into leaving her alone. Not an easy task, considering how very little she knew about him. He had been as miserly with the details of his life as he'd been generous with his financial support.

Or she could silence his demands.

Not many choices, and none of them good.

Laying the knife aside, she added the vegetables to the skillet on the stove, then stirred the noodles on the back burner. At the moment, she was leaning toward choice number three—trying a little blackmail of her own. To that end, she'd spent most of the afternoon on the Internet. Her search for "William Davis" had brought tens of thousands of hits, and not one of the hundreds she'd checked had been the right man. Finally she'd gone to a website that promised, for a fee, to find out anything about anyone. She had filled out the form, though she didn't hope for much. After all, if she'd had the information they'd requested— full name, date of birth, Social Security number—she wouldn't need them.

If they didn't come through, she could ask Montoya for help. That was a last resort, though. If worse came to worst—and she believed in being prepared—she didn't want to connect him, even remotely, to murder.

No more than she wanted to be connected to it. But experience had taught her that too often, worse did come to worst. If there was no other way out, if someone did have to die . . .

She wanted it to be a death she could live with.

6

Mondays were a bitch, and in Tony's opinion, this one was no exception.

"Oklahoma must be the only freakin' state in the union that doesn't list vehicle color on DMV records," Simmons groused as he pulled out of the police-department garage. "How many cars you got left on that list?"

"Too many." The partial license plate number had come from a suspicious-vehicle report in the area of Bryan Hayes's apartment at the time of his death—a dark car, no make, no model, no two-door or four-door. The computer had spit out a list of all vehicles matching the partial number, leaving it up to him and Frank to weed them out. They'd spent hours the week before doing just that before the next three homicides had doubled their workload.

Tony loosened his tie, then adjusted the AC vents. When he shifted his feet, he swore they stuck to the carpet—a reminder why he usually refused to ride in Simmons's car. Bits and pieces of at least six months' worth of snacks were sticking to everything he touched.

"You're awfully quiet."

He glanced across at his partner. "Just wondering when you last cleaned this shitbox."

"The city don't pay me enough to clean their car."

"They don't pay me enough to ride in it. Next time, I drive."

"Hey, not everyone's as anal as you about their vehicles. Some of us have more important things to do, like solve crimes."

"You go out and solve a crime without telling me?" Tony asked sourly.

Simmons made an obscene gesture before asking, "What's the next address?"

Tony studied the printout. They'd started the week before with the addresses south of Interstate 244. Their only witness at the time had said their suspect was white, and the ratio of whites to nonwhites south of 244 was much higher than north of that line. After his talk with Javier on Friday, though, this morning they'd started in short north—the area of the city immediately north of downtown—and worked their way deeper in.

Setting the printout aside, he pulled a notebook from his jacket pocket, flipped through the pages until he found the address he wanted, and read it out loud.

"Who's that?" Simmons asked as he started in that direction.

"Javier Perkins."

"You think he remembered somethin' new, or do you just want to see if he still remembers what he already told you?"

Tony responded with a shrug. Not everyone considered Javier a good candidate for a confidential informant, but as some movie character had once said, bankers and ministers rarely witnessed crimes. But that nagging feeling was still there, and Tony just wanted to see if an additional interview would make it go away.

Halfway there, Simmons stopped at a red light and started drumming his fingers on the steering wheel. "Hey, Chee."

He grunted absently.

"Why are we bothering with this?"

Tony looked at him.

"Seriously. We've been identifying phone numbers, hanging out at funerals, and hunting down a vehicle with a shit-for-nothin' description that ain't gonna get us anywhere. And for what? To lock up the guy who did what we couldn't?"

"We were trying to arrest them, not kill them."

"We were trying to take 'em off the street. Well, they're off the street, and it ain't costin' the taxpayers six figures a year to make them comfy down at McAlester. Why don't we just say we tried and get on with something that matters?"

"This matters."

"Oh, come on . . . you can't tell me that at least once you haven't been glad these guys are dead. That when you walked into the scene and saw *their* bodies, you weren't just a little relieved."

"No," Tony admitted. "I can't."

"You're bustin' your balls—and mine—over these skanks, just like you do over all your other cases, when any one of them wouldn't have thought twice about offing you if he had the chance. Why?"

"My job is to find their killer. Not judge or condemn them."

Shaking his head, Simmons made one last turn, then parked in front of a tiny shotgun house. Over the years, all the color had leached from the paint, leaving a dull shade of nothing behind. For every window that was intact, two were held together by duct tape or covered with cardboard, and the rotting porch was tilting away from the house. A good wind might tumble it right down.

Notebook still in hand, Tony knocked at the door, heard

shuffling inside, then knocked again. "Hey, Javier, it's me—Ceola. Open up."

"Jus' a minute." After more shuffling, the lock turned, then the door opened with a creak and Javier's sleepy face appeared. He stuck his head out to look in both directions, then backed up so Tony could step in. "What you coming 'round here for? You know I don't like people to know I'm talkin' to the police."

"I know. This won't take long. I just wanted to ask a few questions about what you told me the other day."

Javier was steadier than he'd been Friday, which probably meant he'd spent the weekend higher than a kite. He wore the same dark trousers, but in place of the long-sleeve shirt was a grimy undershirt. "What I told you . . . oh. About them boys that got killed."

"You said you saw the man who killed them. Can you describe him for me again?"

Javier glanced around the room, picked up an armload of clothes from the only chair, and gestured for Tony to have a seat, then sat there himself when Tony declined. "Let's see . . . He was tall, taller than me. Heavier, too."

"And he was black?" Tony prompted.

"Black as me. And bald." A quick grin, a hand through his hair. "Balder than me."

Tony looked at his notes. On both occasions, Javier had used exactly the same words to describe the killer. Not just similar, but word-for-word the same, which meant his delivery had been rehearsed. Someone had told him what to say, and being the jittery type, he'd practiced to be sure he got it right. *Too* right.

Tony put the notebook away, then looked around the room. There was a pillow and a pile of sheets on the sofa, a needle half hidden underneath a magazine on the coffee table, and a large, nearly empty bottle of Chivas next to it. "You're drinking the good stuff these days, Javier. What'd that set you back?"

Just like that, the unsteadiness returned. Javier couldn't hold his grin in place or keep his hands still long enough to light the cigarette he'd just removed from the pack. "Aw, s-somebody give that to-to me. You know me, Chee. I don't c-care about the g-g-good stuff. It's quantity that c-counts, not quality."

Tony picked up the bottle by the neck, read the price sticker still attached, then set it down again. "How long have we been working together?"

"Long, long time."

"Yeah. And you've always been straight with me, haven't you?"

Javier nodded vigorously. "I have, Chee. You know I have."

"So why do I get the feeling you're lying to me now?"

Now his head was shaking just as vigorously. "I-I-I w-wouldn't do-do that, Chee. N-not to you. I-I swear to God." But he couldn't look Tony in the eye. "I al-always been straight w-with you. You c-come to me, I go to-to you, either way we g-give each other what we need. Right, Chee? Right?"

"Right," Tony answered absently. And that, he realized, was the other thing bothering him. What Tony always needed was information. What Javier always needed was money. Every conversation between them had started the same way—*I've got some information you can use. How much is it worth to you?* Except this last one. Javier had never mentioned money—hadn't made a deal up front, hadn't asked for it after the fact.

Because he'd gotten it from someone else?

Before he could decide the best way to proceed, the cell phone in his pocket rang. He excused himself and turned toward the door to answer.

"Tony, it's Henry." The chief's voice was terse against the wail of a siren. "Are you busy?"

"Kind of. I'm re-interviewing the witness in the Washington case. There are a few things that don't quite add up."

"Can you finish up later? There's been an accident on I-44 at Forty-first. I need you to go to the scene."

Tony's gut clenched. It had been years since he'd worked Traffic, and accident investigations on the interstate were the highway patrol's jurisdiction. "Who?" It was all he could get out as he acknowledged Javier with a nod and headed out the door.

"It's Joe. I don't know how he is. The call just came in. I'm on my way."

"I'll see you there." As he buckled himself into the passenger seat, Tony repeated the information to Simmons.

"I thought you took his license away," Frankie said as he pulled into the street.

"I did, but hell, people drive without licenses all the time. You know that." And a license meant nothing to Joe. He'd been driving since he was fifteen and a half. He didn't need some piece of paper to continue doing it. That was why they'd sold his pickup and taken away his keys to Anna's car. Why she had become very vigilant about hiding her own keys.

For all the good it had done.

As soon as they reached the four-lane, Simmons turned on the light on the dash and the siren, then gunned the engine. The Ford really was a shitbox—piss yellow and smelling like the inside of a wino's mouth after a three-day binge—but there was nothing wrong with its engine. They were pushing a hundred before they'd gone a full block.

Emergency lights were flashing at the scene—two highway patrol units, the chief's car, an ambulance, and a wrecker. Simmons pulled onto the shoulder and parked at the end of the line.

Out the door before the car came to a complete stop, Tony covered the distance to the smashed-up vehicle in record time. He spotted Henry first, then his father, sitting on a gurney and fussing at the paramedic trying to bandage his head.

"Dad, are you all right?"

Joe looked at him, and his expression became one of chagrin. "Vincenzo. They called you off the job to handle a little fender bender?"

"Dad, it's me, Tony, not Uncle Vince . . ." He let the words trail away. Joe's gaze had that distant look that meant his mind had drifted off.

Henry laid his hand on Tony's shoulder, then guided him to the side of the road as the paramedic set to work again. "If it's any consolation, he didn't recognize me either. He thought I looked familiar. Other than that, though, he's fine. Just some scratches and a cut where he bumped his head. The car was reported stolen from a gas station about a mile from the house. The owner filled it up, then left the engine running while she went to pay." His tone turned sarcastic. "She didn't want it to get hot while she was inside."

Tony looked at the car, realizing for the first time that it wasn't his mother's Chrysler. The thought of the charges Joe could face—auto theft, driving without insurance or a license, destruction of personal property—was enough to make his head ache.

"Don't worry about it, Tony," Henry said. "There won't be any charges."

He glanced at the car again, a new Honda with at least a few grand in damages. "You sure about that?"

"She never should have left the keys in the ignition. If she's difficult, we'll make noises about the family maybe suing her. After all, he's . . ." His gaze shifted to Joe and turned sad. With a bleak shake of his head, he left the sentence unfinished.

Tony couldn't. Incapacitated. Impaired. Debilitated. Feeble-minded. Senile. He could think of a dozen ways of saying it, some polite, some not, all of them ugly. His father was losing his mind and his self. Before the disease was through, there would be nothing left of the Joe Ceola they both knew and loved.

Henry reached in his pocket for a handkerchief. When he pulled it out, a slip of paper fluttered to the ground. Before the breeze could carry it more than a few inches away, Tony stepped on it, then picked it up. It was the standard message form used by the department, and his name was scrawled across the *To* line. He didn't have a chance to read more, though, before Henry took it back and returned it to his pocket.

"I was leaving a note at your desk when the call came in about Joe. I didn't get to finish it." The smile that accompanied Henry's explanation was less than steady.

"A note about what?"

"Nothing import—" Henry's gaze skimmed over the banged-up vehicle and his denial stopped midword. When he looked back at Tony, his expression was grave. "Hell, under the circumstances, it's even more important. Lucia called this morning."

Mention of his younger sister made Tony scowl. Unlike

the teasing with Joe and Anna, Lucia really was Henry's favorite of the Ceola kids. *Princess,* he always called her, and he supported her in virtually everything. At the moment, there was only one thing she wanted, and it deepened Tony's scowl.

"She's on that kick about the old folks' home again, isn't she?" It was an argument that had started soon after Joe's diagnosis. Lucia thought Anna should sell the house and move with Joe into an extended-care facility, and Tony thought Lucia should mind her own damn business. Any decisions about moving would be Anna's, and Anna's alone.

"It's not an old folks' home, Tony," Henry said, his tone conciliatory. "It's a retirement community. Some of them are very nice."

"No."

"At some point you're going to have to consider it."

"No."

"I know it's tough. Christ, he's been my best friend my entire adult life. It kills me to see this happening to him. But it also kills me to see what it's doing to your mother, and to you. He walked over a mile from the house today, Tony, and took that car. He could have killed himself or someone else. The woman who left her keys in the car could have just as easily left a baby. He's becoming a danger to himself and to others." Henry laid his hand on Tony's shoulder again. "You have to think about it."

Jaw clenched, Tony watched as the paramedics prepared to roll the gurney to the ambulance. Joe was lying back, looking pale in spite of his olive skin. He opened his eyes as they drew near and offered a fierce grimace. "Sweet Mary, your ma*ma*," he said, putting the emphasis on the second syllable the way his Italian mother had taught him. "She's gonna kill me. When you break the news to her, Tony, tell her to take it easy on me until this headache is gone. Then she can yell all she wants. I deserve it."

Tony took his hand, remembering other times when he'd held on to his father—crossing streets or walking to the park, on the first day of school, going to Sunday mass. Not one of those times had he held as tightly as he did at that moment. "I'll tell her, Dad. You okay?"

Joe raised an unsteady hand to his temple, then lowered it again. "Yeah, I'm okay. I love you."

"I love you, too." The paramedics moved on, leaving Tony with no choice but to let go. Once he did, he faced Henry again. "No," he said flatly. "I don't have to think about it."

Not then. Not ever.

The smell of hot pizza filled Dwayne Samuels's SUV, making his mouth water even though he'd finished dinner not more than an hour before. He usually stayed away from the lab on Monday nights—that was Bucky's night off, and without a cooker, things got pretty slow—but his idiot cousin Lewis had called, whining that he wanted a pizza and wanted it now.

Usually he kept Lewis away from the lab on Mondays, too, but at the moment they were too well stocked on inventory to leave the place unguarded. It was a good thing most of it would be going out the next day. Then Dwayne would have a few days to disappoint his aunt and find someone to replace her moron son.

As he rounded a corner, headlights flashed some distance behind him. He kept one eye on the rearview mirror. There wasn't a lot of traffic on these dirt roads, and it made him uneasy . . . but most things did. That was one of the disadvantages of his chosen profession. When he turned onto his own road, he slowed down and watched as the other car drove past. Immediately the tension in his shoulders eased. By the time he turned into his driveway, he was back to feeling nothing more than pissed at his cousin.

After keying the code into the heavy-duty gate, he drove through and watched in the mirror until it was closed. He followed the road through the woods to the house and parked in front of the barn. When he got out, he could hear some late-night talk show on the television. Swearing, he let himself into the barn, tossed the pizza on a table, and thumped Lewis on the back of the head.

"Jesus H., Dwayne, what's that for?"

Dwayne grabbed the remote and muted the sound, then glared at him. "You have that fuckin' television turned so loud, a fuckin' tank could've driven in here and you never would've known it."

Lewis scowled at him. "I knew if anyone come, it would be you, bringing my supper."

"So just because you're expecting me, it couldn't possibly be anyone else? Christ, Lewis, you're a moron." Dwayne headed across the room to get a beer from the refrigerator, but it was empty. Turning back, he saw Lewis had settled back in his chair, his mouth full of pizza, and the table next to him littered with cans. Shit.

"The pizza's not hot," Lewis said even as he bit into a second piece. "What were you doing when I called?"

"I was on a date."

"With who?"

"No one you know." Or ever would. Dwayne couldn't think of much that would scare away a woman quicker than meeting Lewis. He didn't say much for the Samuels gene pool.

Lewis grinned. "Did you score?"

"I would have, if some retard hadn't called and made me leave early."

"Who?" Understanding was slow to cross his cousin's face. "I ain't no retard, Dwayne, and your mama said for you to stop calling me one."

"Yeah, yeah." Like a man his age was going to worry about what his mama said.

Washing down the last of the pizza with the last of Dwayne's beer, Lewis wiped his hands on his T-shirt, then stood up. "That was good, but, man, I gotta take a leak." Instead of heading for the bathroom at the back of the building, though, he walked to the front door, opened it, and unzipped.

"For Christ's sake, Lewis, what the fuck—!"

A deafening blast echoed through the barn, and Lewis tumbled back a dozen feet, landing on the concrete floor like a rag doll. Holes dotted his chest, seeping blood that quickly turned his shirt red.

Dwayne stared at his cousin in horror before raising his gaze to the man in the doorway, pointing a shotgun right at him. He tried to run, to duck and hide, but his feet wouldn't move. "Goddamn," he whispered, whimpered. "Goddamn, goddamn, God, please . . ."

The man reached in his pocket, pulled out a stack of white cards, and flipped them into the air. Most scattered outside, but a handful drifted in. Their message was the last thing Dwayne saw before another shotgun blast exploded into the room.

Repent.

• • •

Selena awoke with a start, her eyes popping open, her breathing loud in the quiet room. For an instant, she couldn't think what might have disturbed her, then she heard the sound of an engine turning over. Sliding from the bed, she reached the front window just as the headlights of Detective Ceola's car came on, and watched as he backed out of the drive. The white of his dress shirt seemed stark in the predawn light, and the tousled condition of his hair suggested he'd dressed so hastily he'd forgotten to comb it.

She watched until he'd passed from sight. Only then did she realize she'd been holding her breath. What had happened to call him out so early? Family emergency? Personal business with Saturday's blonde? Or work? Had some unfortunate soul lived his last hours?

She had wondered about death sometimes, about what it would be like to suddenly cease to be. A few times she'd thought she might find out for herself—when Rodrigo had hit her one too many times, in an alley in Ocho Rios, on her visit to Tulsa two summers ago. But she could only imagine how it felt to die.

She *knew* how it felt to kill.

Unable to go back to sleep, she dressed in running clothes, laced her shoes, slipped the switchblade into her waistband, and took the stairs two at a time. She could run anywhere in the city, but she automatically headed west toward River Parks and its miles of trails. Toward William, who was expecting her to kill again.

As he was quick to remind her, she owed him so much. In twenty-eight years, he was the only one who had ever protected her, who had ever thought her worth protecting. He'd given her all the necessities of life and more than a few luxuries. He'd cared.

And all he wanted in return was her soul. Was it such a terrible trade? She had a wonderful life. She wanted for nothing. Was killing a man such a high price to pay for that?

Yes. She wasn't a murderer. She owed William *her* life, but not someone else's.

But that was the price he'd set for her, and he would see that she paid one way or another. With his enemy's life or her own. From that perspective it wasn't cold-blooded murder but survival, and she'd learned at a very young age that she would do whatever it took to survive.

After jogging the circuit from Twenty-first to the Pedestrian Bridge and back again twice, she returned home, slowing to a walk when she reached Princeton Court. As she passed the Franklin house, a light came on inside and a woman's silhouette appeared in an upstairs window, joined a moment later by, presumably, her husband, merging into one indistinct shadow as they embraced. What was it like for Dina Franklin—sharing her life with someone special, waking up with him, making love with him, having a reasonable expectation that he would be there for her not just now but in the weeks and months and years ahead?

Selena *wasn't* envious. There was no one special to share her life with, but she neither wanted nor needed that. *She* would be there for herself, would be strong and capable. *She* was the only one she could count on. Luisa had taught her that lesson with her neglect, Rodrigo with his fists, William with his manipulation.

It was a lesson she would never forget.

When Tony turned off Highway 51 onto Coyote Trail, a sheriff's car was waiting. The deputy didn't look a day over eighteen, though he was trying, his manner self-important, his expression overly stern. They exchanged introductions, then the kid climbed back into his Crown Vic and took off. Without his lead, the only thing Tony would get out there was lost. He knew every square inch of Tulsa, but take him ten miles outside the city limits, and he could get into trouble real fast.

By the time the deputy slowed to turn off the road, Tony felt as if he'd been dropped in the middle of a maze. They'd bypassed the driveway, blocked with an elaborate iron gate, to drive through a wide hole in the barbed-wire fence. The Chevy bumped over the rough ground, scraping over rocks and bushes before he could turn onto the driveway.

Where the road ended there were three sheriff's cars, a pumper from the nearest fire department, a van from the medical examiner's office, a vehicle belonging to an investigator from the state fire marshal's office, and the sheriff's crime-scene unit. As he stepped out of his car, he caught the first acrid whiff coming from behind the house.

The crime scene was obvious. Where a structure had once stood, only rubble remained, and streaks of blackened earth stretched out in every direction from spreading flames, hungry for more fuel. In another six weeks, after the summer drought had started, such a fire would have taken out half the countryside, but everything was green enough now to slow the process.

The odors coming from the smoldering rubble were powerful—smoke mixed with the acidic residue of chemicals and burned flesh. *We got a meth lab blown to kingdom-fucking-come,* the sheriff's detective who'd caught the case had said when he'd called. *And there are fucking little white cards scattered everywhere. Wanna take a look?*

As he crossed the uneven ground, Tony spotted one such card, half buried in the damp soil and bearing the distinct impression of a tire tread. From one of the fire trucks? Or maybe the vigilante's vehicle?

He took a moment to mark it for the crime-scene guys, then joined the men gathered some distance from the scene, where deputies in Tychem protective suits were starting to gather evidence. Pete Wolenska was there to pronounce and claim the bodies, and Mike Collins, a detective with the sheriff's department, would be sharing the investigative duties with Ernest Pratt, an arson investigator for the state.

And, apparently, with Tony.

"Hey, Chee." Wolenska greeted him with a grin too cheery for sunrise. "A little out of your jurisdiction, aren't you?"

"Not by choice." He shook hands with the other two men, then scowled when Wo stuck out his own hand. "I know what you do with those hands. I'm not touchin' 'em."

"Get fucked," Wo retorted good-naturedly.

"In my dreams," Tony said with a snort. He shifted his attention to the other two men. "What happened?"

"Barn go boom," Pratt replied. He was in his late fifties and had been an arson investigator for the Tulsa Fire Department as well as the ATF for about as long as Tony had been alive. These days he worked part-time for the state and, apparently, spent too much time with his grandkids.

"Neighbors to the east reported hearing an explosion around midnight," Collins said. "The place was fully involved by the time the fire department got here."

A fireman leaning against a nearby pumper, standing by in case of flare-ups, responded to that. "It wouldn't have taken so long if we hadn't had to cut through the goddamn fence. Goddamn electronic gate."

Collins turned to look at him. "You got pusher bars

on the front of that thing. Why didn't you just drive through it?"

"And risk tearing up my rig? I don't fuckin' think so. 'Sides, even if we had, it wouldn't have made much difference. Them two would've just been well-done instead of extra crispy."

Wo and Pratt snickered, and Collins rolled his eyes. "Christ, three jokers this early in the morning. Who did I piss off to deserve this?"

"What can you tell us about them?" Tony asked Wo.

"They're dead."

This time the fireman snickered. "Like we needed an M.E.'s investigator to tell us that."

"Any sign of foul play?"

"Being roasted and toasted isn't enough?" Wo asked. "I think I can safely say they didn't set fire to themselves."

"Meth labs blow up all the time." The chemicals were volatile as hell, making the labs about as dangerous as the product itself.

Squinting his bug eyes against the rising sun, Wo peeled back the wrapper on a candy bar he'd pulled from one pocket. "Victim number one, who was found closest to the door, had a hole about the size of that sun right in his middle. A shotgun, up close and personal. Victim number two, who was across the room, was riddled with smaller holes. Also a shotgun, but from a greater distance."

"Somebody comes to the door," Collins said, starting toward the barn. "Number one opens it, the guy blows him away, then takes out number two before he can react."

Tony fell into step with him. "These guys aren't the trusting type. They're not going to open the door to anyone who comes knocking in the middle of the night unless they know him. If the gate was locked when the fire department got here, either he knew the code or he didn't go out that way." He glanced around, judging the distance to the house, the tree line, and the closest hiding spots. "Probably he didn't go to the door at all, but set down out here and waited for one of them to come out."

"Must have been a patient son of a bitch."

"Or a man with a mission." The calling cards—*Repent*— suggested that. Tony just wasn't ready to believe it. It was so obviously calculated to make the killer appear sympathetic. A vigilante dedicated to punishing drug dealers for their sins was so much easier to accept than another drug dealer eliminating his competition. For one, it was a crime of passion; for the other, it was greed. For one, retribution. For the other, murder.

"You have any ID?"

Collins opened his mouth, hesitated, then said with a straight face, "About what?"

Wishing for a cup of coffee—or, better yet, his bed and a sweet wet dream—Tony scowled at him. "You guys are sick fuckers."

"Sorry. I was reading my E-mail this morning and my brother-in-law down in Georgia sent me one of those 'You might be a redneck' things. The neighbors who reported the explosion didn't know the guys. Said they moved in a few months ago, installed that gate, and kept to themselves."

"They didn't find a five-thousand-dollar gate on a fifteen-thousand-dollar house unusual?"

"Son, they's times when it's best to mind your own bidness," Collins said, exaggerating his already-strong Oklahoma accent, then reverting to a normal voice. "We're checking property records to find out who owns the place. I ran a twenty-eight on that SUV over there. It comes back to a Tulsa address—guy by the name of . . ." He flipped back a page in his notebook, then frowned. "Damn. It was dark, I was walking, and I hadn't had my coffee. Looks like Dwight—no, Dwayne Sim—Sem—something."

Tony glanced toward the M.E.'s van, where the bodies had already been loaded. "Wouldn't be Samuels, would it?"

"Yeah, that's it. You know him?"

"I arrested him a time or two when I worked Street Crimes, until he became one of my C.I.s. After a while, we both moved on." Tony had transferred to Homicide, and apparently Samuels had graduated from confidential informant and small-time crack dealer to the big time. There was a hell of a lot of money to be made in meth, with the price in this part of the state running between fifteen hundred dollars and two thousand dollars an ounce.

Joining them, Pratt asked, "You guys ready to go in? Just watch where you step and don't touch anything."

Little of the structure was left standing—part of one corner post, a few slivered boards that had fallen out of reach of the flames. The skeleton of a metal table stood near the back of the large room, along with a soot-covered refrigerator and some metal shelving. Pratt identified lumpy messes that had once been chairs, a television, and a stereo, then gestured to a sink hanging precariously since the cabinet supporting it had been destroyed.

"The fire started here in the sink. Smell that?"

Tony smelled a hell of a lot of things, not one he could identify besides burned wood.

"That's acetone. Your guy soaked some rags in acetone in the sink here, then set 'em on fire. The flames caught the cabinet up above, where some of the chemicals were stored, and *voilà*—barbecued drug dealer."

Everybody brings something to a crime scene, and every-

body takes something away. That was one of the first lessons Tony had learned as a cop. Everything the vigilante had brought—fibers, hairs, fingerprints, footprints—had been destroyed in the fire, with the exception of the calling cards, left deliberately. The lab had already examined the previous ones, and they weren't likely to find anything different on these new ones.

So the guy had brought a shotgun and taken it away. Probably had a flashlight, too, if he'd come on foot through the woods. If the killer had waited for Samuels or the other guy to open the door, he would have made himself comfortable in his hiding place, leaving smashed grass, broken twigs, footprints, maybe a cigarette butt or gum wrapper.

Leaving the others talking, Tony walked outside, his gaze on the ground. Any prints that might have been left near the barn had been obliterated by the fire trucks and the footprints of everyone who'd been in and out, including his own. He picked a large oak about fifteen feet away as the most likely cover.

He wasn't surprised to find a couple of footprints in the dirt at the base of the tree—running shoes, probably. About an eleven, just like the last case. Someone who knew the fine art of tracking could probably find more prints and maybe even follow them to where the killer had left his car. Tony had done some reading on the subject, but he'd never actually tried it, and the scene of a double homicide wasn't the place to start.

"Find anything?" Collins asked, his shadow falling over the grass.

"Couple of prints. You any good at tracking?"

"What? White man think because me heap big Injun and smokum peace pipe, me also trackum wild buffalo?"

Giving him a long level look, Tony said dryly, "You're Indian? I never noticed."

Collins flipped him off. "Fine detective you are. I'm part Cherokee, part Creek, and part Osage, with a little Irish thrown in for good measure. And I don't know nothin' 'bout trackin'." He stretched, then pulled a package of mints from his pocket and shook a half dozen into his mouth. "Since it appears we're looking for the same guy, you got anything on your homicides you wanna share?"

"Yeah. A whole shitload of tags we're checking, looking for a dark car driven by a white guy who may or may not be involved, plus enough phone numbers and suspects to fill two phone books."

"Thanks, but you follow your leads and I'll follow mine. I was thinking more along the lines of a suspect who stands out in the crowd—a mutual friend or enemy."

Tony shook his head. "I don't have a clue."

Maybe Dwayne Samuels had.

But he'd taken it to his grave with him.

Selena had set up her supplies on the small patio behind her house and was painting when Detective Ceola came home from work. He parked beside the Corvette and walked out to the street to get his mail. With his gaze on the ground, his shoulders slumped, and his hair standing on end, he looked as if he'd had a tough day. Definitely a long one, she noted with a glance at her watch. He'd left two hours early that morning and was home an hour late.

His dog jumped to his feet and alternated barking with howling until the back door opened and he shot inside. Maybe she would get a dog when she returned home. Lazy as he was, the animal wiggled from head to tail with excitement every time his master came home. Never having been the recipient of such a wholehearted welcome, she thought she would like to try it.

Less than fifteen minutes had passed when Ceola's back door opened again. This time he came out, wearing broken-down running shoes, faded cutoffs, and nothing else. She watched as he unlocked the small storage shed in the back corner of the yard. It was nothing more than an artist's appreciation for the human form, she told herself, and even pretended to believe it.

He took out a lawn mower, filled the gas tank, then started it with one powerful jerk on the cord. As the engine broke the silence with its steady buzz, she forced her attention back to the painting before her. After dipping a fan brush in pink, then white, she filled a terra-cotta pot on the porch with flowers. She repeated the steps for the second and third pots, then switched to a clean brush. She didn't do anything with it, though. She merely held it and studied the canvas—pretended to study it—as she listened to the back-and-forth of the lawn mower.

Abruptly it went silent, then Ceola's voice filled the quiet from a few yards away. "Does this bother you?"

She looked up to see him pushing the mower through the gate. Sweat glistened on his face and arms, and tiny flecks of green clung to his arms and legs. "No. I like the smell of fresh-cut grass." Noise wasn't a distraction. She could concentrate in the middle of a gun battle if necessary. He, on the other hand, could make it difficult, indeed, to keep her thoughts focused.

He gestured toward the easel. "Can I see?"

With a shrug, she took a step back. He came onto the patio and circled around behind her. He smelled of grass, of hard work on a hot day and, more faintly, of cologne, spicy notes with a musky undertone. His jaw was stubbled with beard, and his eyes seemed darker, more tired than usual, as he studied the painting.

She waited, not caring what he thought, if he compared it to a greeting card or dismissed it entirely, as William did. He thought she was wasting her life and all her other talents, trying to re-create the home she'd never had, the person she'd never been. Maybe he was right.

"Is that your house?" Ceola asked after a time. When she nodded, so did he. "It looks like it."

"What do you mean?"

"It looks like the kind of place where I would expect you to live. On an island someplace, where the weather is always warm and life is always easy. Where you can go barefoot and wear flowers and never have a care."

She shifted one bare foot on top of the other, then folded her arms over the floral print of her silk top. "That island doesn't exist."

He glanced at her then, a hint of a smile turning up the corners of his mouth. "You can make it exist. I bet tourists love your work. They take it home with them and hang it on their walls as a reminder on long winter days of warmer places and vacations long past." His voice was quiet, soothing, almost hypnotic. He could keep talking, say anything, nothing, and she wouldn't care as long as she could listen. "If it were in her power, Johnson, this female detective I work with, would banish all slender, pretty women to a mythical island, where they could torment each other and people like her wouldn't have to look at them and feel inferior. 'Island girls,' she calls them." His gaze swept down her, then back up. "You certainly are. You should wear flowers in your hair and relax under an old paddle fan and sleep in a four-poster bed surrounded by filmy netting, with the

French doors open to let in the ocean breezes. You should dance under the stars and . . ."

His voice trailed off. Her throat dry, she looked at him. She couldn't turn away, couldn't think, couldn't fill her lungs with even one particle of air that didn't carry his scent, and so she just stood there and looked at him, and he looked back as if . . . as if . . .

The sound of a car horn blasted through the air, catching her so completely by surprise that she started. When was the last time that had happened? Two years ago, a voice inside her whispered. Two years since she'd let down her guard, and she'd paid dearly for it. Was still paying for it.

Heat flushed her skin as her gaze jerked to the street where the same two young men who had been over for hamburgers on Sunday were climbing out of a pickup. The trailer it towed bore a sign proclaiming "Summer Break Lawn Service," and was loaded with mowers, rakes, and other such devices. "I—" She swallowed, then moistened her lips. "I think you have company."

He glanced their way, too, giving her a moment's relief—or disappointment?—at being freed from his gaze. "Nah. They're just brothers."

She had suspected that Sunday. One was taller, one shorter, both were younger, and both had the Ceola eyes—dark brown, lush lashes, incredibly appealing.

"Yo, Tony, what're you—" The brother who'd spoken stopped short and stared. "Wow. She beats all hell out of old Mrs. Howell. Lucky bastard."

Selena's flinch was involuntary, and she thought she'd covered it well by turning to the side to pick up her sunglasses, but when she turned back, it was to find Ceola thumping him on the back of the head. "Watch your mouth. Dad taught you better than to swear in front of a woman."

His brother didn't look the slightest bit chagrined. "Oh, yeah. Sorry. I'm Dom." He stuck out his hand, then jerked his head in the third Ceola's direction. "He's Matt. And you're beautiful."

"Thank you. I'm Selena." She shook his hand, aware of warmth, strength, and calluses, and returned Matt's nod. At a loss for what to do next, she folded her arms across her middle again.

Matt came around to look at the canvas. "Pretty picture. You paint this?" When she nodded, he said, "You should do more and sell 'em. I bet people would like 'em a lot."

Detective Ceola responded for her. "People do like them a lot. Selena has her own gallery in Florida. She's an artist, and she would probably appreciate us getting out of her hair so she can get back to work." His gaze strayed to her hair, and she heard his earlier words repeated as surely as if he'd spoken them once more. *You should wear flowers in your hair . . .*

The heat returned, warming her a few degrees past comfortable.

As Tony shepherded the men toward his own house, Dom called over his shoulder, "Nice meeting you, Selena. Hope to see you again."

She lifted one hand in accompaniment to her faint smile.

Before they reached the back door, she heard his next words, not intended for her ears. "Shit, Tony, she's freakin' hot. Have you got something goin' on with her? 'Cause if you don't—"

The closing door blocked out the rest of his sentence, as well as Tony's response.

Tony. She wasn't sure she'd ever called him that, even in her thoughts. She *was* sure she shouldn't do it again. It was too friendly. Too intimate. Too right.

Too wrong.

Setting her jaw, she turned her attention back to the painting. She picked up a brush, touched the tip into the green paint, lifted it to the canvas, and watched as her hand trembled uncontrollably. Dropping the brush to the table, she squeezed her right hand tightly with her left, closed her eyes, and concentrated on her breathing. With each calming, cleansing breath, she repeated the mantra that had gotten her through every bad time in her life.

I will survive. I will survive. I will survive.

7

As he walked the halls of the old mansion, William found the sense of family impossible to escape. Their portraits gazed down from the walls; their voices whispered on the quiet air; their memories lingered in shadows. He had lived his first eighteen years in this house with his parents, his grandparents, and his sister. He'd given little thought at the time to the quality of his life. His family had been wealthy, and he'd been given everything he ever wanted. That was the way life was supposed to be.

The way it had continued . . . until the first time Selena had refused him. It had been a surprise—this woman who'd completely made herself over to please him, telling him no. The foolish girl thought she had that right, thought she could make her own decisions. One way or another, she would learn just how wrong she was. Whether the lesson was easy or painfully hard . . . that was the only choice she had.

Did she think he'd taken her in out of the goodness of his heart? Hardly. He'd turned her from an exotic little creature with quick hands, a furtive manner, and a knack for stealing in all its guises, into a beautiful, elegant woman who could reign over this mansion as if she'd been born to it. He'd seen to it that she'd gotten the proper education, the proper training to run a business, so that with his expert guidance, she could reign over his empire, as well. She just had to accept it as her fate.

Her visit two years earlier had provided him with the means to achieve acceptance. That last night her eyes had been swollen with tears and her face had borne the marks of an angry man intending to take what she wouldn't give, but unlike Ocho Rios, she hadn't needed William to rescue her—at least, not from her attacker. No, the only rescue she'd needed was from the nightmarish aftermath, and he'd handled it quite efficiently. He had disposed of the body, cleaned the blood, and destroyed the evidence . . . or so he'd told her. He'd known that someday it would be of use to him, and sure enough, the threat of exposing the incident was all he'd needed to get her back in Tulsa.

Realizing his aimless wandering had stopped, he found himself gazing out a window in the grand ballroom that filled the third floor. A few hundred yards away was the northeast corner of his property and the service entrance. Only invited guests came in the main entrance. Deliveries and hired help used the back gate. Selena's yellow Thunderbird was there now, its driver waiting for the gate to complete its slow swing open.

He descended the stairs to the main floor. His staff was gone for the day, and the security guards were in the guard shack near the main gate. They wouldn't start their nightly patrols until dusk fell, and Selena would be gone by then.

After circling the pool, he let himself into the guesthouse. He'd redecorated it a few years earlier with Selena in mind—had doubled the number of floor-to-ceiling windows, traded stuffy upholstery for wicker and pastel prints, replaced heavily ornate dark woods with elegantly simple pieces. In place of the original cold marble flooring, he'd put in wide wood planks the color of honey, and textured rugs in ivory, seafoam, and aqua.

He'd replicated the perfect little island paradise for her, and she had exclaimed how lovely, how nice, then turned down his offer to live there.

She was no longer in a position to turn down anything he asked. For the six years since her college graduation, she had put him off oh, so politely, with a smile and a *No, thank you, Uncle, I'm not interested.* But no more. After he'd killed for her in Ocho Rios, her heart had been his.

After she killed for him, her soul would be his.

As he lit the candles on the dining table, he felt a moment's regret for forcing her to return to the scene of her crime. Common sense told him it was best to avoid meeting with her, but sentimentality overrode it. It had been two years, and they'd parted under difficult circumstances. He'd missed her.

Stepping back, he was studying the setting when Selena walked through the door he'd left ajar. Sonja, the housekeeper, had prepared everything exactly the way he'd specified—a snowy linen cloth on the table, the antique china and silver he'd purchased on his last trip to London, fresh flowers, an excellent chardonnay chilling in the refrigerator, and dinner warming in the kitchen.

"Uncle." She stopped at the edge of the stone entry and glanced around. He could read nothing in her expression, no hint of the distress he knew she must feel at being back in the place that held such bad memories for her.

"Selena. You look lovelier than ever." He extended his arms, circled the table, and greeted her properly, with an embrace and a kiss first on the left cheek, then the right.

"Thank you. You look wonderful, as well."

Though the words were meaningless, they pleased him

nonetheless. At sixty-two, he liked to joke that he didn't look a day over sixty-one. "Have a seat, and I'll serve the excellent dinner Sonja prepared for us."

He expected her to move to the chair that would place her back to the room. She surprised him, though, walking instead to the opposite seat. When she'd fled this guest-house two years ago, she had sworn in her tearful good-bye that she would never return. Yet here she was, calm and controlled, pretending she didn't want to flee again.

But she hadn't yet looked around the room—hadn't let her gaze go anywhere near that patch of floor between the sofa and the fireplace, hadn't risked even the faintest of glances at the marble-and-bronze statue that stood on the table behind the sofa.

The meal started with a salad of greens, fruits, and nuts, drizzled with a sweet onion dressing. The entrée consisted of seafood, sprouts, peppers, and pineapple sautéed in a mango curry sauce, served with fire-roasted vegetables and a crunchy rice dish, and for dessert, fried bananas with caramel sauce and whipped cream.

"A little taste of the tropics," he said as he served the main course, "all for you. We wouldn't want you getting homesick while you're here."

"I was surprised to receive your invitation," she said after taking a few bites.

Of course she was. He'd waited until six-thirty to call, then had requested her presence for dinner at seven. She'd sounded pleased by the invitation. He'd been pleased by her acceptance.

"I hope you don't mind meeting here," he said, gesturing carelessly around the room with his wineglass. "I know it brings up a bad memory or two for you, but I couldn't invite you into the house. The staff, you know . . ."

Something flashed across her face in the instant it took her to regain control. Hurt? Sorrow? He couldn't say.

"I don't mind coming here."

Silently he applauded her excellent lie. If he hadn't known better, he would have believed her . . . but he knew how traumatic that night had been. Knew how it still affected every aspect of her life.

After that brief foray into the past, he directed the conversation to inconsequential things—the weather, her art, how the city had grown since her last visit. With dessert finished and the last of the wine poured into their glasses, she finally looked past him. "Nothing's changed."

"Actually, it has." He left the table, going to stand in front of the fireplace. "The rug that was here is gone, and a section of flooring was replaced." He hesitated a moment, then added, "Blood is so difficult to deal with."

Her gaze remained steadily fixed on him as she lifted her glass to her lips.

"Come. Have a seat. It's so much more comfortable than those wooden chairs." He lowered himself into the far corner of the sofa, resting one arm on the back in invitation.

She rose gracefully from her chair, crossed the room, and sat at the opposite end of the sofa. The pale hues were a perfect foil for her dark skin and hair, for the crimson and navy of her clothes.

"Tell me what you think of Detective Ceola."

She stroked one fingertip over the pattern etched into the wineglass. "He seems harmless."

"Part of the reason for his success as a detective, I'm sure. People tend to underestimate him, right up to the moment he slaps on the handcuffs." William would never make that mistake. His irritation suddenly flared at the mistakes that *had* been made. He was walking a razor-thin line. Detective Ceola had too many pieces of the puzzle and if anyone could tie the loose ends of the vigilante killings together, it was him. And the best way to stop him was Selena.

"It would help if I knew exactly what I'm looking for," she replied, gazing at the bare floor where an ancient Persian rug had once been. His grandfather had paid a substantial sum for it, but ultimately it had proven far more valuable to William than price could ever reflect.

"Details about his cases." He was deliberately vague.

"Which cases?"

"The vigilante killings." He doubted she knew much, if anything, about the recent rash of murdered drug dealers. She had little interest in politics, crime, and the like, but pretended instead that the world was perfect—probably because her world before him had been so *im*perfect. Ignorance, at times, really could be bliss.

"He has evidence against you?"

He shrugged. "His evidence very well might lead to me."

"Or it very well might not."

He gave another shrug.

"What kind of evidence?" she asked stubbornly. She kept all but the faintest hints of frustration from her voice, but he recognized it. Good. He wanted her a little on edge. She needed to learn that, unless she complied with his wishes, her easy life was over. He had given it to her; he could take it away.

"Anything. Everything. I want to know exactly what Detective Ceola knows, not just what's contained in his files and notes." And in the meantime, he wanted the good detective distracted from his investigation. William couldn't think of anyone more capable of distracting a man than Selena.

"And once I've picked his brain, then what?"

"Then you complete the job I've given you. When you've done that, you're free to go back to Key West, to your home and your art."

He delivered the lie so naturally. Did she suspect he would never let that happen? She was an intelligent woman, but she had a blind spot when it came to him. She'd been so very grateful for all he'd given her—not just the material things, but the affection. Security. Hope. A future. For years that gratitude had led her to ignore the true source of his income. It was only when she'd finished college, when he'd made the first of many job offers, that she'd been forced to face the truth.

Was she still wearing blinders? Still pretending he would honor his word and let her go? He liked to think she was, that she loved him enough to remain in denial, at least for a time. Soon enough, though, she would face facts.

Reaching across, he squeezed her fingers reassuringly. "Come now, Selena. Have you forgotten what I told you that night in Ocho Rios?"

I killed for you. Someday you may have to do the same for me.

"Of course I haven't."

"Did you think my words were meaningless? You know better. I don't indulge in idle chatter. For fourteen years I've warned you that someday I would require repayment from you. An eye for an eye—isn't that the way it goes?"

"You have other people who could do this."

No, not this. Oh, Damon would be happy to—he'd already said as much—and naturally there were numerous people on his payroll who would carry out the task without a qualm. William could even handle it himself. He was no stranger to killing. Just as he'd given life, he'd also taken it. But he wanted this particular job done by this particular woman. Her compliance would be the one act that would damn Detective Ceola and forever seal her fate with his. It would forge a bond between them that could never be severed.

"I want you to do it, Selena. Besides . . ." He let his gaze slide from her face to the statue situated between them on the sofa table, let his fingers trail over the cool marble and the unyielding bronze in a languorous caress. "It's not as if you haven't killed before."

It was past lunchtime on Wednesday, and Simmons wasn't about to forget it. Just one more interview, Tony had promised, and then they could eat. Simmons was satisfied with that until they pulled into a parking space next to Mike Collins's Crown Vic. "This is about that meth lab out on Coyote Road, isn't it? Jesus, don't we have enough to do without you goin' out into the county and drummin' up more ways to waste my time?"

Tony ignored him as he climbed out. The sheriff's detective was leaning against the front fender, mirrored glasses hiding his eyes, his expression impassive. He straightened, adjusted his jacket, then smoothed back his hair.

"Christ, it's the freakin' pretty boy," Simmons jeered. "If Chee had told me it was you we were meeting, I'd've dressed for the occasion. That's one fancy suit. They pay that much better over in the sheriff's department or are you on the take?"

"You know why they stuck you in Homicide, Frankie?"

Collins responded. "Because it's harder to piss off dead people . . . though if anyone could do it, it would be you."

"What can I say? It's a talent. What're we doing here?"

Here was on East Pine, outside a bar that every cop working Uniform Division North got to know well. The month without a shooting or stabbing on the premises was rare. On more than a few occasions, they'd had both.

"Did you hear we got definite IDs on last night's bodies?" Collins directed the question to Tony. "It was Dwayne Samuels's operation. Lewis McElroy was his cousin and was in charge of security. Obviously, he did a piss-poor job of it. That leaves the chief cook and bottle washer. You familiar with Albert Spradlin?"

Both Tony and Simmons shook their heads. Collins smiled smugly. "You're in for a treat. Albert's better known as Bucky. Every day he stops in here for a drink before going to work. Since he's out of a job at the moment, his usual one drink has likely turned into five or six."

"Everyone mourns in his own way," Simmons said.

Collins snorted. "Bucky doesn't mourn people's passing—he causes it. We're pretty sure he's responsible for at least a couple homicides, but we've never been able to make a case. People tend to clam up when you start asking questions about him."

"Are they that loyal?" Tony asked. "Or that scared?"

"Wait till you see him. You'll figure it out for yourself." Collins crossed the uneven sidewalk to the door. Early in Tony's career, there had been plate-glass windows across the front of the bar, painted black to match the door. After unruly patrons had thrown each other through the glass a few times, the owner had cinder-blocked the openings and opted for a heavy metal door. It had been dented, but so far it hadn't broken.

As Collins reached to open the door with one hand, he removed a can of pepper spray from his pocket with the other and gave it a good shake. Eyeing the canister suspiciously, Simmons blocked his way. "What else do we need to know about this guy?"

"Well . . . he did ten years down at McAlester."

"For what?"

"Possession of crack cocaine with intent to distribute. Trafficking. Manufacture and possession of methamphetamines with intent to distribute. And, uh, a couple assaults." He opened the door, stepped back so they could enter first, then stopped just inside. "There he is. Over by the bar."

"Where?" Simmons squinted against the dim light. "All I see is—holy shit."

Holy shit was right. Albert Spradlin stood at least six and a half feet tall, and probably tipped the scales somewhere around three-twenty. His hair hung in a brown, greasy ponytail, and at first glance it appeared he was wearing a long-sleeved shirt. But the T-shirt was sleeveless, Tony saw on closer inspection. It was the tattoos covering Spradlin's arms from shoulder to wrist that made it look otherwise.

"By the way," Collins added, "those assaults were on the cops who arrested him. He put four of them in the hospital."

Tony exchanged glances with Simmons before stating the obvious. "There's only three of us."

"Yeah, well, we're just gonna talk to him, not arrest him. I figure he'll be satisfied with cracking only one skull, and since Frankie's is already empty . . ."

"Fuckin' asshole's gonna get us killed," Simmons muttered as he straightened his shoulders. "Remember—I want to be cremated. Then sic Suz on this bastard."

Like every other bar Tony had ever been in, this one was

dimly lit, with smoky air and loud music. He had a bad feeling about this—a gut instinct that, as Collins had said, a skull or two might get cracked. He damn well didn't want it to be his.

They separated, approaching the guy from different angles. Spradlin spotted Simmons first and straightened, adding another couple inches to his height. When his gaze shifted to Tony, he grinned, and an unholy gleam came into his eyes.

"Looks like he made us," Simmons said from the opposite side of a table.

"You think?" As if the suits and ties weren't enough to give them away, they were the only ones in the place who'd recently bathed and weren't sporting prison tats out the ass.

Simmons pulled his badge from an inside coat pocket. "Albert Spradlin? Detectives Simmons, Ceola, and—"

For a big man, ol' Albert could move. One instant he was standing there grinning, and the next he was smashing a chair over Simmons's head. Before Tony could do more than think about reaching for his weapon, three-hundred-pounds-plus were flattening him into the floor. Spradlin bashed his head against the concrete twice before Tony managed to land a right jab that didn't faze him. The big son of a bitch just shook it off, kept on grinning, and wrapped one hand around Tony's throat as he landed a fist somewhere in the vicinity of his eye. Pain exploded and Tony's vision went hazy, along with his hearing. There was cursing nearby—Simmons—and taunts and yells of encouragement from the other side of the room, all muted and distant.

Tony clawed at the hand that was cutting off his windpipe, but the bastard seemed oblivious to the pain. He managed to shove one knee into Spradlin's balls, but all that did was make him grunt and squeeze even harder. "Collins," he croaked. "Shoot this fucker!"

A baton cracked over the back of Spradlin's head, and he reared back, easing his hold just enough that Tony could slide his hand into his jacket. When Spradlin looked back down, he found himself nose-to-nose with Tony's .40, the hammer cocked and his finger on the trigger.

"Don't fuck with me, Albert," he said, his voice hoarse, his breathing heavy. "I'm having a really shitty week. Get the fuck off me *now*."

Selena stood at the island in the kitchen, studying a Yellow Pages ad. She'd located a gym similar to Montoya's, with equipment and/or partners for all her needs, including full-contact sparring. Now she was looking for a shooting range. In the past two years she hadn't gone more than a week without a gun in her hand, until now. She felt the need to sight in on a silhouette target and blow the hell out of it—

The ring of the telephone broke the stillness and made her stiffen. It wasn't William—he would call only on the cell phone. After three rings, she leaned across the counter to answer.

"Hi, is this Selena?" It was a woman's voice, cheery and warm. "I'm calling from the emergency room at St. John. We have a patient here, Tony Ceola, who would like to ask—" A low murmur in the background interrupted her. When she continued, it was clear she was smiling. "Who would like to *nicely* ask you to pick him up and give him a ride home. I tried to convince him to wait until I get off in a couple hours, but . . . you know how men are." She punctuated the words with a melodramatic sigh.

At the mention of the emergency room, Selena's nerves had tightened and her fingers gripped the receiver hard—a natural response, she told herself, that had nothing to do with the fact that it involved Detective Ceola. She forced a deep breath to ease her lungs, to slow the sudden increase in her heart rate. "I'll be there in a few minutes."

"Thanks." Ms. Merry Sunshine hung up first. Selena slowly did the same.

Moving mechanically, she grabbed her purse from the living room and her keys from the crystal dish on the hall table. She had taken notice of the St. John Emergency Room on her daily runs. She knew the route well enough that she didn't have to think about it. Unfortunately, that gave her the freedom to think about other things instead.

Such as what had happened to him. How seriously was he hurt? And why had he called her? He had parents, siblings, in-laws, uncles, the pretty little blonde, and the whole police department at his disposal. And yet he'd chosen her.

"Because you live next door," she said aloud, injecting a scathing tone into her voice. "Because you're five minutes from the hospital, and you don't have a job or anything else that might make you unavailable."

He'd called her for convenience's sake. Expediency. Nothing more.

Though it would be nice to think it could be something more.

When she turned into the ER entrance, an ambulance was idling in front of the doors. A pretty brunette wearing surgical scrubs stood nearby, and next to her, in a wheelchair, was Detective Ceola. A dark line of sutures ran just above one eye and his face was bruised and swollen, but other than that, he appeared to be all right.

Even with the injuries, he looked amazingly good.

The knot in Selena's gut suddenly dissolved. Relief that Ceola wasn't badly hurt? Though if she had any sense, she would regret that whatever incident had brought him to the ER hadn't also killed him. That would have taken her off the hook with William and she would have been free to go home, at least until the next problem arose.

The brunette wheeled the chair over to the T-bird, then gave Ceola more help than he needed as he climbed into the passenger seat. She leaned unnecessarily close to fasten his seat belt for him, before pressing a folded square of paper into his hand. "If you have any problems at all, Detective, just give us a call," she said. Her beaming smile faded into cool politeness when her gaze connected with Selena's.

What was on the paper? A prescription? Directions for aftercare? Or Merry Sunshine's phone number?

Selena pulled onto Twenty-first Street and stopped at a red light before glancing at her passenger. The swelling around his eye made her wince in sympathy, an emotion she tried to keep under control as she dryly commented, "Looks like you didn't duck in time."

"It's hard to duck when you have three-hundred-some pounds on top of you."

"How did someone who weighs three-hundred-some pounds catch you to land on top of you? I've seen you run. You're faster than that."

"I had two guns, a canister of pepper spray, and two other detectives. I wasn't expecting trouble."

"That's the first rule of living," she said. "*Always* expect trouble."

His head was tilted back against the headrest. He slowly rolled it to the side so he could see her. "Do you?"

"Yes."

"Do you usually get it?"

She thought of her mother and stepfather, of the people they'd sold her to and the people *they'd* sold her to, of that Ocho Rios alley, of William and of Greg Marland, with whom her date two years ago had ended so disastrously, and felt the bitterness creep into her smile. "Often enough. Do you need to stop anywhere before we go home?"

"The drugstore, if you don't mind. They gave me a prescription to get filled." He glanced around, then looked chagrined. "There's one back at Utica Square. Sorry. I should have said something . . ."

"Not a problem." As they approached Woodward Park, she shifted into the right lane and swung the T-bird around in a tight U-turn.

Ceola closed his eyes—at least, the one that wasn't already swollen shut. "Well, there's a $117 fine," he said under his breath.

"It's okay. I know a cop," she said, flashing a faint smile. A few minutes later she pulled into a parking space in front of the pharmacy. When he started to unbuckle his seat belt, she held out her hand. "I'll get it."

"I don't mind."

"You look like hell. Stay there, and I'll get it."

He made no effort to hide his relief as he handed over the slip—not the same one the brunette had given him—then sank down in the seat again. "Thanks. Let me give you some money—"

Without waiting, she grabbed her purse and headed into the drugstore. She dropped the prescription at the pharmacy, then gazed out the window. Ceola was slumped in the seat, eyes closed, one hand raised to shield his face from the sun. Between the weariness in the position and the Technicolor bruising, he looked vulnerable. He *was* vulnerable, more so than he'd ever imagined. He expected danger from the criminals he dealt with every day, but he didn't have a clue that the biggest threat to his life right now was the woman he'd called when he needed help.

It was only fair, then, that he should be the biggest threat in her life. Killing a man in cold blood would be hard enough, but killing a man who made her feel safe at the same time he roused her own protective instincts . . .

The man behind the counter called that the prescription was ready, interrupting her thoughts. She paid, then, as she headed toward the exit, opened the slim bag, and removed the pill bottle. Percocet. Some part of her had hoped for an elephant-strength painkiller, something that would knock him out for the next few hours so she could take the opportunity to snoop. No such luck.

They were both silent during the ride and were back on Princeton Court in a matter of minutes. She parked next to the Corvette, got out, and started toward his house, then realized he wasn't following. She turned back. "Detective?"

Slowly he eased that one eye open.

"You're home. Do you need help?"

"No. No, thanks." He got out, then moved carefully as if trying to minimize the jostling effects of walking.

Part of her wanted to see him to the door, then beat a fast retreat. The other part knew that wasn't possible. This was her best chance to learn the code to his alarm, her best chance to get inside and look around without arousing suspicion. No matter how much she hated doing it, she couldn't pass up the opportunity.

Adjusting her pace to his, she accompanied him to the stoop and up the steps. After missing twice, he fit his key into the lock, opened the door, and punched in the alarm code. She managed to catch the first two numbers—seven and six—but he swayed unsteadily on his feet as he input the second two, blocking her view. She swore silently.

He didn't seem to notice the calico darting up the stairs or the black cat watching him balefully from the living-room door. The dog's excited barks registered, though, making him wince. "Thanks. If I can have the pills . . ."

She moved forward, forcing him to back away, and closed the door behind her. "Lie down. I'll get you a glass of water."

For a moment he looked as if he might argue, then he turned and walked into the living room. The black cat hissed at him before slinking up the stairs to the landing.

As she walked down the hall, Selena made a mental note of the motion detector high in the corner above the front door. There was another in the kitchen, and a quick glance through the double doors into the dining room showed a third. The dead bolt on the kitchen door was double-keyed, just like the front door.

Detective Ceola liked to feel secure. Of course, the man was a police officer. No doubt, he had more than his share of enemies. He'd certainly made a powerful one in William. For the time being, until she found some other way out, that made her his enemy, too.

She filled a glass with water from the sink and carried it and the pill bottle into the living room where Detective Ceola lay back on the couch, his feet propped up on the coffee table. "It's late. Have you eaten?"

"Not since breakfast."

"Here." She pressed the glass into his hand, then shook out two pills. "Take these, and I'll fix you something. You do keep food in the house, don't you?"

In spite of the stitches and bruising, he managed to look insulted. "Of course I do. I'm Italian."

She watched him swallow the pills before returning to the kitchen. Despite his boast, the refrigerator was half empty, and most of its containers held either condiments or leftovers of indeterminate age. The small pantry wasn't much more encouraging, with its selection of Hamburger Helper, rice, and canned soup. She decided on soup, and stretched onto her toes to check the offerings. Tomato, tomato, and . . . "Looks like tomato wins," she murmured.

After zapping the soup in the microwave, she located a small cookie sheet that would do as a serving tray, added the bowl, a napkin and spoon, and a sleeve of crackers from the pantry, then carried it all into the living room.

He was sitting up now, his loafers kicked off, his feet still propped on the table. She handed him the tray and sat down across from him. He crumbled a handful of crackers into the bowl, then fixed his gaze on her as he stirred the soup. "Why did you come to get me?"

"Because your nurse friend asked nicely."

"She's not my friend."

"She wanted to be."

His only response to that was a disinterested shrug. Selena had known more than her share of attractive men, but she'd never known one who didn't appear to care that women found him attractive. Would he care that *she* found him so?

"Maybe you should have taken her up on her offer to bring you home. I'm not very good at coddling."

His gaze was steady. "If I wanted coddling, I would've called my mother. She's very good at it, and she doesn't expect anything in return."

She let him eat a few more spoonfuls before asking her own question. "Why did you call me?"

She knew the answers he might give—she was close, she

was convenient, she was available. She was prepared to hear them. She *wasn't* prepared for the grin that was far more boyish than any grown man had a right to, or for the words he offered. "Because I wanted to see you."

I wanted to see you. She'd heard the words before and knew better than to read any real meaning into them. She'd learned not to read real meaning into anything most men said. Everyone had an ulterior motive for everything they said and did, and Detective Ceola was no different. *She* certainly wasn't.

Oh, but they were lovely words that she wanted to believe more than she could say.

"The way you look, you probably see either two of me or a very blurry vision of one."

He nodded, then winced. "I couldn't be lucky enough to see two. Jeez, my head hurts."

"Getting pounded into the floor will do that to you."

"You know that from experience?"

"I don't have to experience it to know it hurts." But she'd had plenty of experience. She'd been Rodrigo's favorite target for years, and had taken as many beatings from her surrogate parents as she'd dodged. Greg Marland had gotten in a few blows, as well, before she'd managed to grab that statue and leave him dying on the guesthouse floor.

Only William had never laid a hand on her in anger. No, his preferred punishment was far more subtle—looking at her in a certain way, speaking to her in a certain tone. For years it had bent her to his will in an instant. But where he had counted on it breaking her, instead it had merely taught her to give, then bounce back.

Ceola's big dark eyes were starting to droop. Rising from the chair, Selena took the tray from his lap and set it on the table, then lifted his legs onto the sofa.

"You don't have to . . ." His words were slurred, his breathing slow and heavy.

"The medicine will help you sleep. You should be comfortable." Guiding him with her hands rather than words, she pulled him forward, removed his suit coat, worked the shoulder holster free, then unbuttoned the shirt that was stained with his own blood. By the time she helped him lie back, he was more asleep than awake. When she covered him with the throw from the back of the chair, he sighed heavily and was out.

A good neighbor would go home now, checking back periodically. A friend would make herself at home in that easy chair and keep an eye on him.

She did neither.

With a deep breath, she crossed the short distance into the dining room. The blinds were closed, the curtains drawn, and she left them that way. She twisted the knob that lit the chandelier, then turned on the desk lamp. Papers covered the dining table, along with file folders, a few issues of magazines geared toward law-enforcement officers and a couple of forensic-science books.

Drawing out a chair, she sat down at the table, opened the nearest file folder, and found herself connecting with a blank, unseeing gaze. There was no question that the man in the close-up photo was dead. Though the camera angle didn't show the full extent of the damage, clearly a large portion of his head was missing.

Her first impulse was to drop the folder, jump up from the chair, and run away, but she forced herself to remain steady and calm. To breathe slowly in and slowly out. To look. She had seen dead people before, two of them up close and personal. Both had been the victims of intimately violent death, but they hadn't looked like this. They had appeared somewhat peaceful, as if they were merely sleeping. There was nothing peaceful about this man.

She stared at the photo, taking in the blood and tissue splatter, the gaping wound where his cheek and jaw should have been, the subsequent distortion of his other features. She looked until she could do so as calmly and dispassionately as she imagined Detective Ceola did. Only then did she go on to the next photo, and the next, until finally she reached the notes underneath.

Ceola's handwriting was far too elegant for a cop, though exactly what one might expect from a rigid Catholic-school upbringing. The man in the photos was a drug dealer who had been murdered a few weeks previously. His body had been found in an abandoned building in east Tulsa, with very little evidence to process. It appeared to be one in a series of murders committed by a man who left calling cards that suggested a religious/vengeance motive, though Detective Ceola seemed to hold the minority opinion that the killer was another drug dealer looking to expand his share of the market.

William was a drug dealer. In their early years together, he'd never mentioned the nature of his work. All she'd known then was that he had a great deal of money and didn't mind spending it on her. She had been in college before she'd begun to suspect that his business was less than legal, a fact he'd confirmed when he'd offered her a job upon her graduation.

She shouldn't have been surprised. She had been raised by people who'd forced her to steal. But she had been surprised, nonetheless. William—elegant, sophisticated, her savior—was no different from those people, just more successful.

Was that why he wanted Ceola dead? Because he was

killing off his competitors and feared Ceola's trail would lead back to him?

Selena read every scrap of paper on the table, examined every photo, and even scanned the pages in the forensic books that Ceola had flagged, but she found no mention of William's name. Not in the notes. Not on the "Known Associates" list for each victim. Not in the meandering theories Ceola had penned on a legal pad.

Frustration surged anew at William's refusal to share details with her. How could she find anything when she didn't know what she was looking for? Was this a test to measure her resourcefulness? Or merely a demonstration of his power, that he could force her to such an impossible undertaking?

The sofa creaked as Ceola changed positions. She looked but found no sign of the black attaché he normally carried. That left the computer. She moved to the desk, plugged the power strip into the wall, and turned it on, but when her finger touched the power button for the CPU, she didn't push it. Instead she walked into the living room.

If possible, Ceola looked even worse than before. His eye was puffier and surrounded by a rainbow of dark hues. The black of the sutures and the red line of inflammation that backed them stood out in stark contrast against his olive skin. He looked tired. Defenseless.

She could take the forty cal from the holster on the coffee table, aim at the smooth, undamaged skin of his left temple, and pull the trigger. Douse everything in the dining-room office with gasoline, light a match, and walk away. That easily, her job could be done. The method wasn't quite what William had instructed—he wanted the evidence first, then the murder—but the end result would be the same.

That easily . . . except she couldn't force her feet to move from the doorway. She couldn't stop hugging herself—holding herself together—long enough to pick up the gun.

Most murders were the desperate acts of desperate people. She wasn't desperate enough.

Yet.

With long strides, she walked out the door and across the lawn, letting herself into her own house and shutting off the alarm before starting toward the kitchen. She hadn't taken more than a few steps, though, before she stopped, senses on alert. Something was wrong, different. She was sure of it, though a cautious walk through the first floor revealed nothing out of the ordinary. The locks on the kitchen and sunroom doors were secured, the windows undisturbed. Still, she felt . . . something.

She stood in the middle of the kitchen, listening, breathing, concentrating. There were no unusual noises—just the tinkle of chimes from outside as a light breeze stirred them, and the ticking of the clock near the door. The glass of tea she'd been drinking when the call had come from the hospital stood in the same place on the island, its ice long melted, and the phone book was still next to it, the cover showing a view of the downtown Tulsa skyline at sunset. Beside that was a notepad, bearing the name of the gym she'd chosen, and an ink pen, ready to write the address of the firing range she . . .

Slowly she reached out, her fingertips grazing the thick book. She'd been looking for a shooting range—had had the phone book open to the business listings when she'd answered the hospital's call—and she didn't remember taking the time to close it. She couldn't swear that she hadn't. After all, she had been concerned about Detective Ceola's injuries. But she didn't *think* she'd bothered.

Unease pricking her spine, she walked slowly upstairs,

looked in the bathroom, every bedroom, and every closet, and found no sign of an intruder. The Beretta was still in the nightstand drawer, at least until she took it in hand. The forty cal was still on the top shelf in the closet, and the dagger was tucked between towels in the hall linen closet. Her emergency stash—new ID, cash—was untouched in its hiding place.

After inspecting the house outside, she returned to the kitchen. Though she would have a difficult time convincing anyone that her security had been breached, she was sure of it herself. Someone had let himself in, walked through her rooms, disturbed her peace, and then let himself out again.

The *who* was fairly obvious—one of William's people. No run-of-the-mill burglar was going to break in, then leave without taking anything. And entry had been gained with a key—the only way the double-keyed dead bolts could be locked again—which, no doubt, William had obtained from the real-estate agent. As for the *why* . . . to remind her to be careful? To keep tabs on her? To warn her how easily he could get to her?

She reached for the phone, then drew back. Calling him would accomplish nothing. He would admit or deny it, whichever suited his purpose. More important, he would know that he'd succeeded in rattling her, which was most likely his primary purpose. He liked keeping people off balance. That was why he'd insisted they have dinner at the guesthouse the night before. He had taken some perverse pleasure in making her sit and eat fifteen feet from where she'd killed a man . . . just as she had taken pleasure in hiding her discomfort from him. He'd wanted upset and distress, but she'd saved them for later, when she was alone. She had maintained her composure.

She wasn't about to jeopardize it now.

8

"Daddy, read me a story."

James Tranh looked up from tying his running shoes to find four-year-old Jesse holding a book and wearing a hopeful grin. Most days he arranged his schedule so he could be home until Jesse went to bed. Having dinner together, reading stories, tucking him in—they were all an important part of the family routine.

And family was important. He'd learned that after leaving most of his behind when he'd escaped Vietnam nearly thirty years ago. His mother, grandmother, and two sisters had begun the journey with him. Only one sister and his grandmother had completed it. They'd worked hard, made a new home in Los Angeles, and saved every penny to bring his father over to join them.

But his father had died before they'd had a chance.

"Sorry, buddy," he said, swinging Jesse up onto his shoulders. "I've got to get to work. Mom will read to you tonight, okay?"

Jesse's sigh collapsed his entire little body until he draped over James's head like a rag doll. "Okay . . . *this* time. But tomorrow I get *two* stories. Deal?"

"It's a deal." James swung him upside down and set him on the floor, then walked down the hall to the kitchen. Jesse hitched a ride on his leg.

His wife was standing at the stove, fixing Jesse's favorite

dinner of beef stir-fry over crispy noodles. She tilted her cheek for James's kiss, then shifted the baby on her hip so he could kiss Maya, as well. "Why are you going in so early?"

"So I can support you in the manner you've become accustomed to."

Nancy's delicate little face screwed into a pout, just like Maya's before she burst into tears. "I don't like this, Jimmy. Why can't you take a few weeks off? Give the police time to catch this crazy."

"The police have been looking for him for two months. Do you know how broke we can be in two months?"

She swatted at him. "As tight as you are, you could quit working for three years before you ran out of money."

He grinned. "The word is *frugal,* and I'm proud of it." In Vietnam, his family had been poor, and in California, it had taken years for things to get better. Now he had a $150,000 house in a nice midtown neighborhood, and his van shared garage space with Nancy's BMW. He'd bought a cottage in a retirement village in south Tulsa for his grandmother, and a restaurant for his sister to run. Their lives were good . . . but he worried about the vigilante killer.

Not that James shared anything more than a common business interest with the dead men. Unlike them, he knew how to be discreet. He'd never been arrested, never flashed big wads of cash. He didn't drink or party or sample his own goods.

For him, the drug business *was* strictly a business, not a way of life.

Nancy's worried look drew his attention back to her. "This vigilante—"

"—doesn't know I exist. I'm careful. You know that. Besides"—he planted his feet wide apart and his fists on his hips—"I'm Superman. Bullets bounce off me."

Nancy giggled as she always did. "Super*chump* is more like it. Go on. The sooner you get out of here, the sooner you can come back."

He kissed her again, on the mouth this time, thrusting his tongue inside. They'd been married eight years, and just a kiss could still make him hard.

"I'll be up when you get home," she said with a soft sigh.

"So will I," he said. After kissing Jesse and Maya, he took his keys from the hook near the garage door and left.

The restaurant was located on Memorial between Sixty-first and Seventy-first, a congested area he would avoid forever if it were possible. Since he put in an appearance there every day, it wasn't.

He was sitting at the stoplight at Yale and the bypass when the cell phone rang. It was strictly a business phone. The people who mattered knew how to reach him at home, the restaurant, or on his other cell phone. The people who didn't matter . . . well, didn't.

He checked the caller ID, saw that the local number was a pay phone, and decided against answering it. As he turned into the restaurant parking lot ten minutes later, the same number called again. Twenty minutes and two calls later, he finally answered.

"Mr. Tranh, you're a difficult man to reach." The well-educated male voice lacked the local accent and seemed vaguely familiar. Someone he'd done business with in the past, or maybe one of the restaurant's regulars?

"Who is this?"

"I'm the solution to your problems."

Just his luck—a salesman. "Sorry. I don't have any problems."

"So it would appear. You've done well for yourself in your adopted country. A lovely home, a beautiful wife, two wonderful children. Jesse and . . . Maya, isn't it? Named for your mother, My."

Though his office off the restaurant kitchen was a cool sixty-eight degrees, sweat popped out on James's forehead. His fingers clutching the phone tightly, he demanded, "Who are you, and what do you want?"

"As I said, I'm the solution to your problems. I want to meet to discuss how we can help each other. Deal?"

The echo of Jesse's earlier words—*But tomorrow I get two stories. Deal?*—made James's blood run cold. "I can't talk right now. I'm not alone," he lied. "Call me in a few hours, okay, and we'll discuss it then."

"Then it's a deal. We'll hammer out the details later. And Mr. Tranh? Don't fuck with me. You won't like the results."

James continued to hold the phone to his ear long after the line had gone dead. The man's tone hadn't changed at all—had remained genial and cultured through the vulgarity.

Maybe that was why James felt so threatened.

A sharp slap echoed through the night. "I swear, that mosquito nailed me on the ass. You can stay out here and commune with nature all you want, but *I'm* going inside."

Damon watched as Lucia stood, unmindful of her nudity, and strolled across the grass to the patio. The sway of her black hair, the curve of her hips, and the seductive grace of her movements were enough to make him hard again, as if they hadn't just indulged in amazingly hot sex for the past hour or more. He could go months without, if the situation warranted it—and had, until meeting Lucia. The problem with that was he then tended to get obsessive about it, to feel the need to make up for lost time.

That was why he'd spent the better part of the past week with her. Why he thought about her even when he wasn't with her. Why, after coming three times tonight, he could go inside and fuck her another three times before he got close to being satisfied.

He had plans for her, even though he hadn't yet decided how he could best use her. Was it enough to just screw her every which way—to dirty the pampered-darling image clung to by those who loved her? Even if no one else ever found out, *he* would know, and that, he'd learned from William, could be enough.

Or was it better to use her to throw a kink into William's careful plans for Selena? Killing her would send a powerful message, and would be so easy. But what a loss, he thought as a light came on in her bedroom.

She stood at the window, beautiful, delicate, managing to look demure despite the fact that she was buck naked. She was brushing her hair, a sensual act in itself, made more so by the fact that she *was* naked, bright lights all around her, and an illicit Peeping-Tom feel to the whole scene. His gaze shifted from her hands to her face, her expression dreamy and provocative, to her breasts, rising and falling with each stroke of the brush, and his cock swelled to life. First, though, there was something he had to do.

He reached for his clothes, neatly folded next to the careless tangle of hers, found his cell phone, and dialed a number stored in memory.

Twelve miles away, the phone rang three times before a husky voice answered, "Hello."

Two syllables, no more, yet they told him so much. She'd been asleep, or nearly so, which meant she was in bed, and she was wary, wondering who would call her this late at night, who would even have this number. William did, of course, but he would have called her on her cell phone rather than the land line. She knew he didn't run his empire alone, but he'd always kept his lackeys from her. Damon and the trusted few who reported to him weren't good enough to make her acquaintance, though the old man fully expected them to one day take orders from her.

The odds of that happening were somewhere between nil and none.

"Hello?" There was less sleep in her voice this time, more wariness.

He lowered his voice, masking it. "Hello, Selena. I stopped by to see you this afternoon, but I guess I missed you."

The silence on the line was palpable. Did her breathing quicken a bit, her heart rate increase? Probably. She had such hang-ups about personal safety. She was easy to tweak. "Who are you?"

"No one you know . . . yet. But we'll remedy that soon."

"I don't think so. I'm not looking to make any new acquaintances." That was her cool, superior tone, designed to keep most people at arm's length. But he wasn't most people. He knew too much about her—her fears, her desires, her secrets. He knew how the rejections she'd endured had scarred her, and how William's twisted manipulations had shaped her.

He could even relate to her, because William had manipulated him even longer. Other than that, though, he had no real feelings for her. Even his resentment that she was William's chosen heir was directed at William rather than her. In fact, if not for William, Selena wouldn't even register in Damon's life.

Her voice penetrated his thoughts and his fingers clenched around the phone. "If you have nothing else to say, I'm hanging up now." She sounded bored, though he knew she was anything but.

"We'll have plenty of time to talk later," he responded smoothly. "Sleep tight, Selena. Don't let the bedbugs bite." With a laugh that sounded uncannily like William at his most treacherous—as it should, since that was where he'd learned it—he hung up, gathered his and Lucia's clothes, wadded up the comforter they had fucked on, and headed for the house.

Sleep tight. Don't let the bedbugs bite.

When she'd lived with the woman who'd repeated those words to her, Selena had had far more pressing concerns than bedbugs. The woman had gone by many names, but her real name, or perhaps merely the name she'd liked best, was Dorotea. She hadn't been the motherly type, though she'd claimed Selena as her own anytime she was questioned. With her fair skin and red hair, and her even fairer-skinned husband, Philip, she was a poor candidate to produce a half-Latina, half-black child, but nothing had swayed her from the lie.

As mother figures went, she hadn't been bad. She hadn't hated Selena as her real mother had, or been jealous of her, as her second mother had. She hadn't beaten her, starved her, or sold her services by the hour. In Selena's world, that had constituted "good."

She rolled onto her side, facing the window, and slid her hand under the pillow until she could feel the reassuringly solid mass of the forty cal. The night was quiet. No lights shone where they shouldn't, no dogs barked, no cars idled on a street where all the residents were in bed. For the moment, all was safe in her world . . . but safety, as she'd been reminded yet again, was an illusion. She'd felt safe that night two years ago with Greg Marland. She'd felt safe the night she'd nearly died in a garbage-strewn alley.

She'd relived that night often enough in nightmares and in quiet times. The night she'd made a mistake that could have been fatal. The night her entire life had changed. The night she'd met William.

Just a little loosening of her control, and she was four-teen again—tall, gangly, forever outgrowing the second-hand clothes Dorotea provided her. That night she'd worn a brightly colored skirt that barely reached her knees and a white blouse stretched tight across her chest. Her dirty white sneakers were worn through over her little toes, but made running easy if it became necessary. She was so good at what she did that it rarely was.

It was nearing two A.M. on a Sunday morning, but you couldn't tell it by the activity on the streets. Revelers still wandered from bar to bar, diners sought late-night meals at busy restaurants, and drug dealers and prostitutes sold their wares on corners and in alleyways. No one noticed a scrawny kid who moved swiftly and silently through the shadows. She liked to think she excelled at becoming invis-ible, but the truth was, she was an urchin, a street rat, un-worthy of anyone's attention.

She roamed the city at all hours, but night was her favorite. Tourists were easy then—tired, intoxicated on booze, drugs, or plain good times. Bump-and-runs were simple when your mark could hardly stand on his own feet. She'd pocketed a good haul, close to six hundred dollars, and was on her way home when she spotted a mark too tempting to ignore. A fat Latino staggered out of a bar, clutching a wad of cash in one hand, while the owner of the bar stood in the doorway, yelling insults and threats after him.

She was through for the day, she reminded herself. She was tired. Best to go home and leave him to the mercy of someone else.

But the roll of money kept drawing her gaze, even after he shoved it into his coat pocket. As drunk as he was, he probably wouldn't notice a thing. Even if he did, as fat as he was, there was no way he could catch her. She would be safe at home, counting her prize, before he'd wheezed two blocks.

He lurched to the opposite side of the street, and she followed. When an alley opened a few feet ahead of him, she began walking faster. Just a foot behind him, she deliberately stumbled, crashing into him with enough force to make him stumble, as well. She neatly transferred the money from his pocket to hers, all the while apologizing profusely in Spanish. With the cash safe in her possession, she disentangled herself and turned smoothly into the alley, grinning at her easy snatch.

Then a hand yanked her hair hard enough to bring tears to her eyes, and she was slammed facefirst into the faded brick wall. Pain swelled through her, and she tasted blood where she'd split her lip, felt it drip from her nose. She blinked, trying to catch her breath, to force the tears from her eyes so she could see.

All she could see, though, was the brick biting into her skin as a smelly, soft body pushed against her from behind. Sour breath brushed her cheek when the mark pressed his face near hers. "You thieving whore! You think I'm stupid enough to fall for your trick? Nobody steals from me, and sure as hell not some dirty little street trash!"

Every breath she took reeked of sweat, stale smoke,

booze, and her own blood. She breathed through her mouth to settle the roiling of her stomach. If she could wiggle free, get even the smallest of head starts . . . Then she felt his hands on her, searching for his cash, and she stopped breathing, stopped thinking completely. "Please," she whispered as his dirty hands pawed across her breasts and down her stomach. "No . . ."

Just when she was certain she was going to be sick, he located the roll of money and pocketed it. Before she could fully appreciate the relief that his hands were no longer touching her, he yanked the backpack from her shoulders. All too aware of the consequences if she went home empty-handed, she spun around and grabbed for it. "No, that's mine! Give it back!"

He answered her demand with a slap across her face. She stumbled several feet before hitting the ground, the wall at her back, too stunned and too hurt to move.

He looked inside the bag, then grinned broadly. "Now it's mine, you little bastard. To make up for the trouble you've caused me."

Fear trembled through her. Dorotea understood that sometimes things went wrong, but Philip didn't, and Dorotea wouldn't lift a hand to protect Selena from his rage. She had to get that bag back or there would be no place to sleep, nothing to eat, no home to go to, until she'd made up her losses. If she lunged at him, kicked him, gouged at his face and his eyes, surely desperation would give her enough of an advantage . . .

The mark's drunken gaze moved over her as he licked his lips, and her blood went cold. Men had looked at her like that before. Philip looked at her like that on occasion, always around the time he began discussing whether she would be of more use to them as a prostitute than a thief.

"I'm thinkin' I need a little more than money for my trouble," he said, his breath coming harder as he reached down to rub his crotch.

Heart pounding so violently it hurt, she looked desperately for an escape. She wasn't sure she could get to her feet without help, wasn't sure she could run once she made it up. She could scream, but no one would come to her aid. Even the stupidest of tourists knew to avoid the alleys in this part of town.

Still grinning, he moved nearer, and she kicked, her foot sinking into the flab of his belly. She got little more than a grunt for her effort, and he struck back with his own kick. She crumpled into a ball, hugging her middle where the pain was worst, and whimpered, "P-please . . . h-h-help . . ."

Bending, he grabbed a handful of her hair, hauled her to her feet, and propped her against the wall. His beefy hands ripped open her blouse, exposing her to the hot night air. While one hand groped her breast, he slid the other to the hem of her skirt, yanking it toward her waist.

Then he stopped. He gave a harsh grunt, and his eyes widened an instant before he sank to the ground, unmoving. She stared at him, too dazed to understand, until she saw the red spreading over the back of his jacket and the ivory knife handle protruding there.

The trembling started inside and worked its way out. Her legs gave way, and she slid to the ground again, huddling as far from the mark as she could. She heard footsteps but couldn't move, couldn't jump and run away, couldn't scream or do anything but shake.

Shoes stopped near the body, and long slender fingers slid the knife from his back and wiped it clean on the dead man's jacket. The newcomer came a few steps closer, and those same fingers reached toward her—clean, uncalloused, with manicured nails—but when she shrank back, they stopped short. Instead, the man crouched, then ducked his head so they were on the same level.

"It's all right," William said in the kindest, most reassuring voice she'd ever heard. "He'll never hurt you again. No one will ever hurt you again."

Eyes wide, fingertips still resting on the pistol, Selena stared into the darkness. William's promise had been the sweetest words she'd ever heard, even if they hadn't been true. Greg Marland had hurt her physically, and William himself had hurt her in so many little ways. How much more pain was he willing to cause before this whole mess was over?

She was afraid she would soon find out.

"Do you feel as shitty as you look?"

Tony would have glared at Simmons if every movement hadn't hurt. Instead, he eased into his chair, removed an aspirin bottle from the desk drawer, and washed down two tablets with a swallow of Coke. "Don't fuck with me," he said at last, fixing his one good eye on him. "I'll have to hurt you if you do."

"Christ, Chee, why aren't you home in bed?" That came from Lieutenant Nicholson, their supervisor. He'd been a cop a lot of years, was the son of a cop and the father of three cops, and Tony's Uncle Vince's best friend. No one teased him about that the way they did about the chief, though. Nicholson didn't cut anybody any slack. Family, friend, or fuckup—he treated them all the same.

"I feel fine," Tony said, straightening in his chair, ignoring his body's protests.

"Yeah, right. You get any finer, we're gonna find you

stretched out on a slab in the M.E.'s office. You have clearance to be back here today?"

"Yeah, Chee, where's your note from Mommy?"

Below the desk and out of the lieutenant's line of sight, Tony flipped off Darnell Garry. "The ER doc said as long as I didn't have any problems last night, it'd be okay to work today."

Nicholson grunted, then directed his next words to Simmons. "Keep an eye on him." Then his gaze narrowed on Simmons's own bruise. "And learn to duck, for Christ's sake."

"The guy broke a fucking chair over my fucking head! I didn't have time to duck!" Simmons made a disbelieving face as the lieutenant walked away. "Jeez, I can't believe the sympathy I've gotten. Let someone break a fucking chair over their heads and see if I give a shit."

Yeah, yeah, Tony thought, pretty damned unsympathetic himself. "What did you and Collins find out from Spradlin?"

"He says only him, Samuels, and Cousin Lewis knew the code to the gate. No one else ever went out there, and everybody who ever met Lewis wanted him dead. He thinks it's cops doing the killing—make a phone call, set up a meet, then blow 'em away. Crazy fucker."

" 'Make a phone call'?" Tony repeated. "Did Dwayne get a phone call setting up a meeting?"

Simmons shrugged. "Pretty boy sent over Samuels's phone records in case you want to match 'em to what we've already got. I put 'em on your desk."

Tony opened the folder that topped everything else on his desk. He'd barely had time to register the sheer volume of numbers when Simmons's voice turned wheedling.

"After we finished with Spradlin, I went by the hospital

to see if you needed a ride home, and they said you left with a woman. An island-girl woman, by the description. You get lucky and forget to tell your partner about it?"

"Yeah, I got lucky. I survived Albert Spradlin. Let the son of a bitch slam you onto concrete, throw himself on top of you, and pound your face in, and maybe I'll be more sympathetic about him breaking an old chair over your head."

Simmons wagged one finger in the air. "Don't try to avoid the subject. I'm a detective. I'm trained to get answers. Who was she and why was she picking you up at the hospital?"

Darnell Garry was actively listening in, and so was Jeff Watson, one desk over. Had Tony's personal life become so pathetic that the mere mention of a woman was enough to make everyone around take notice?

He scowled at all three of them. "She's my neighbor, and she was . . . being neighborly."

"You got an island-girl neighbor and didn't tell us?"

Simmons's description of Selena was more accurate than he knew. All the things Tony associated with island getaways—hot days, steamy nights, sensual rhythms, the seduction of the sun, the mind, the body, and the spirit—were all things he now associated with her.

"Aw, I know that look. I vote we move the weekly poker game to Chee's house tonight, so we can all get a look at this neighbor," Watson said.

Tony scowled again. He had such lousy luck at cards that he'd dealt himself out of their regular game years ago. And as for whatever *look* he'd been wearing, hell, it couldn't have been that bad . . . could it?

"Trash your own house," he muttered. "Besides, what would your wives think?"

"Suz and I have an agreement," Simmons said. "I'm allowed to look all I want, but if I try anything else, she gets to remove vital parts of my anatomy."

"Like you know what to do with them, anyway," Garry jeered.

With a grunt, Tony tuned them out. If any woman could change Suz's policy, it was Selena. Just looking at her could be dangerous to a man's state of mind. He was living proof. He had awakened that morning from dreams of her soft voice and softer touches, of her perfume in the air, so subtle he couldn't be sure it was really there. He'd walked out the door without first shutting off the alarm, then had needed a moment to clear his head enough to remember why his Impala wasn't parked in its usual spot.

He deliberately shifted his attention back to the cellphone records. They were listed by date and time, with the most recent at the bottom. He started there and worked his way back before stopping at a familiar number. The prefix was downtown, and the number rang in on the phones on his desk and every other desk in the room.

Why had Dwayne Samuels called the Detective Division only hours before his death? Looking for Tony? To the best of his knowledge, he was the only one who'd had a working relationship with Dwayne, though he would have to ask around to be sure. Had Dwayne had information on the case to pass along? Had he been contacted by the vigilante, or heard something about him?

"Anybody take a call Monday morning from Dwayne Samuels?" he called out.

"I was in court," Watson replied.

"I was with you," Simmons said.

Tony glanced around. Lieutenant Nicholson had left,

and except for Darnell Garry's, the rest of the desks were empty. "Garry?"

With the phone propped between his shoulder and ear, Garry covered the mouthpiece with his hand. "I was in, but I can't honestly say. If I did, it wasn't interesting enough to remember."

Tony couldn't argue with that. A lot of people who called the Detective Division weren't exactly talkative, and that went double for confidential informants. C.I.s, as a general rule, were a tad paranoid. "The call came in at eleven-thirty-two. Does that help?"

Garry shook his head. "If he left a message, I left it on whoever's desk. If he didn't leave one . . ." He finished with a shrug.

No message, likely no name. Too damn bad, Tony thought as he scanned the rest of the calls on Samuels's records, adding those identified as coming from pay phones to the list he'd compiled from the previous victims' records.

Pay phones were popular with criminals. Drop in your thirty-five cents, make your call, and take care of business with no billing records, no caller ID listing showing your name, nothing beyond fingerprints or an eyewitness to tie you to that phone. The fingerprints would be taken care of by the next person to use the phone, and as for an eyewitness . . . who paid attention to anyone using a pay phone?

From his bottom drawer he took out the locator for pay phones in the city, made available by telephone company security. Once he'd identified each phone, he studied the list. The calls from Dwayne's business associates were spread out across the city, with a concentration in west and southwest Tulsa—to be expected for someone who operated in the county west of town.

Cross-referencing his records with the other victims', Tony didn't find any numbers that appeared on all the lists. More than a dozen numbers showed up twice, and one appeared on five lists—including Grover Washington's and Dwayne Samuels's. The phone came back to an address at Fourth and Denver—only a block or so away from the police station.

"You're gonna what?" Simmons asked when Tony told him where he was going. "It's a pay phone, for God's sake. Do you know how many people use pay phones every day—especially *those* pay phones? A lot. And you think you're gonna get anything usable off it?"

"Probably not, but who knows? We're due for a break."

"I think you already got your break—in your skull—and your brains leaked out. You never get nothin' off a pay phone but germs."

"It can't hurt to try, can it?"

"Just don't expect me to tag along. If I want to beat my head against a wall, I can do it right here in the air-conditioning."

"Aw, Frankie, I don't expect anything of you. I'll see you later." Tony left the office, took the stairs to the forensics lab, and located Marla inputting information into the computer.

She glanced up when he stopped beside her desk, made a sympathetic face, and continued typing. "How do you feel?"

"I'm fine." Just a little bruised and battered, and his head hurt like a son of a bitch. "Can you lift some prints for me?"

"Sure. Let me drop everything and get my gear," she said, not lifting her gaze from the computer screen. "I live to do your dirty work."

"I can get someone else . . ."

"And settle for second best? Give me a few minutes."

He found an empty counter to lean against and closed his eyes. Sounds drifted down the hall—voices, machines, music playing faintly—but the only disturbance in the office was the rapid *click-click* of the keyboard. The room was cool, the relative peace soothing enough to offset the antiseptic odor. More than a few minutes of it, and he would doze off where he stood.

"There." Rubber wheels rolled across the floor as Marla pushed back from the computer and stood up. "Whose prints are you hoping to find, and on what?"

"The vigilante's would be nice, on a phone."

She looked at him. "I don't suppose it's a cell phone you've got tucked into your pocket."

"Would I carry evidence in my pocket?"

"So where is the phone?"

"About a block from here."

Her expression turned comical. "A pay phone? You don't get anything from a pay phone, not unless the call was made within the last thirty minutes or so. When do you think he used it?"

He knew when, right down to the hour and minute, but if he answered truthfully, she would blow him off. The odds of lifting anything usable from more than a week ago were virtually nonexistent. So he lied. "Monday."

"Three days ago?" She looked as skeptical as she sounded, even as she took a camera case from a nearby cabinet and handed it to him. After slinging the strap of a thin leather briefcase over her shoulder, she headed toward the door. "Talk about your long shots. But if it could pan out for anyone, it would be you. You do have the damnedest luck."

He followed her down the hall toward the garage. "I'm not feeling too lucky here lately. I've got a killer with nine victims and counting, and not one damn clue."

"I don't know. You've got a beautiful neighbor who picked you up at the hospital yesterday and, presumably, spent the rest of the day pampering you."

He didn't ask how she knew—gossip traveled fast in the department—and didn't point out that opening a can of soup and helping him off with his jacket hardly counted as pampering. But it was a start.

Marla unlocked the van she normally used and took out the fingerprint kit. He extended a hand to take the case, about the size of a large tackle box, but she shook her head and led the way to the intersection. "Where exactly is this pay phone?"

He gestured across the street, and her blue eyes widened. "The bus station? Jeez, Tony, are you nuts?"

"Remember? I have the damnedest luck."

The Denver Avenue Station was relatively new, its style sort of Neo–Art Deco. The terminal was round, with glass brick, and the benches scattered around the ten bays were made of green pipe. There were two pay phones outside, one backing each of the route/schedule kiosks and both lacking visible numbers. Tony punched the number they wanted into his cell phone and hit SEND. Almost immediately, the phone to their right began to ring.

Marla set the kit and the attaché in front of the phone, gave it the once-over, and scowled. "I understand the last two victims were killed with a shotgun instead of a .45," she remarked as she pulled on a pair of latex gloves, then selected a brush and white powder. Tony took out the .35 millimeter camera with a close-up lens while she dusted the handset, then snapped a shot of the partial palmprint she'd raised before she lifted it and transferred it to a mounting card. "Do you think your shooter changed his method on purpose, or did someone see the chance to take care of a problem and use the calling cards to point a finger at the vigilante?"

"In a perfect world no one else would know about the calling cards." Unfortunately, the relative who'd found the first victim's body, a God-fearing woman, had told anyone who would listen about the bloodstained card calling for repentance, including reporters from the *World* and channels two, six, eight, and Fox.

"In a perfect world there would be no drug dealers for the vigilante to kill—and no jobs for you and me. What would you do then?" She studied the side of the phone box, then dismissed it as useless. Their killer could have pressed both hands flat against the roughly textured surface, and she wouldn't be able to raise so much as a single whorl. Instead, she turned her attention to the smooth silver surface along the top, trading the light powder for black. "You going to get a wiretap order?"

"As soon as I get back and talk to Nicholson." With a pen register to track the numbers to which outgoing calls were made, and a wiretap to record the calls, maybe they could identify the vigilante's next victim before he became a victim.

"Just think, if this were New York City, you could do like the detectives on *Law & Order* and say, 'Get me the LUDs for this number,' and not have to bother writing up a wiretap request and walking it through the system."

"But this isn't New York City, and the phone company doesn't track Local Usage Details, even though they can. They don't want to make it too easy on us."

She finished up the last print, then stepped back to

study the phone. "I think that's pretty much it. We've got two partial palms, a heel, and three fingers. I'll run them through NCIC and see what we get, but don't hold your breath."

She slid the prints inside the briefcase, removed a small spray bottle and a handful of paper towels from the kit, and wiped the residual powder from the phone's surfaces. "That's the cleanest this sucker's been since they installed it," she said as she peeled off her gloves and wiped her damp hands on another towel. "Any other fun little jobs you'd like me to do? Maybe print the urinals inside?"

"This will do for now. I appreciate it."

"Not as much as you will when I decide to call in your debt. Don't worry." She gave him a sly smile. "I won't ruin you for other women."

There wasn't much chance of that, he admitted. But Selena ruining him for other women . . . *that* was a distinct possibility.

Selena left the gym shortly after twelve, gear bag slung over one shoulder, and headed for her car. Her muscles were warm and loose, still tingling from her workout. She'd gone through a series of weight-training exercises, then worked in a little full-contact sparring with a set of walking, talking muscles that answered to the name of Rocky. By the time they'd called it quits, she'd been battered but not beaten, and Rocky hadn't been quite so brash. Learning that size and gender weren't everything was a lesson he'd needed.

Remembering that cunning, agility, and determination couldn't always defeat size and gender was a reminder *she'd* needed.

She tossed her bag in the passenger seat, put the convertible's top down so her hair, still damp from her shower, could dry, then headed toward the nearest grocery store. If she was in the habit of lying to herself, she would pretend she needed a few things for her own meals. Truth was, she had everything she needed for the evening meal at home . . . as long as she was cooking for just one. But since she was giving serious consideration to sharing with her neighbor tonight . . .

She was picking through a bin of yellow and red peppers when a cart in need of oiling squeaked its way into the produce section. A glance into the mirror behind the vegetables showed an empty cart and the lower half of a well-dressed man. A familiar voice said, "Excuse me, miss. How do I know if a cantaloupe is ripe?"

Her gaze flickered to William. Elegantly dressed and suavely handsome, he looked as out of place in the produce section as she felt whenever allowed into his world.

After taking a covert look around, she smiled blandly. "The best way is to sniff it. If it smells like cantaloupe, it's ready."

A silver-haired woman dressed in an outfit thirty years too young for her sashayed up, reached between them for a red pepper, gave him a dazzling smile, then sashayed away. William watched her with apparent appreciation while muttering, "Old crone."

Though her smile remained in place, the muscles in Selena's jaw tightened. "What a coincidence, running into you here. Having me followed?"

His only response was a smile of his own. "You look lovely, as usual. The healthy glow that comes from a work-out suits you."

Oh yes, there was no *chance* to this meeting. "Do you distrust everyone who works for you, Uncle, or just me?"

"I've always kept tabs on you, Selena. It's part of my responsibilities—watching over you, keeping you safe, providing guidance. Besides, this is your first job for me. Naturally, I want to make certain all goes well."

"My *only* job for you, remember?" That was the deal he'd offered. *Do this for me, and I'll never ask for anything else. Together we'll destroy every bit of evidence linking you to Greg Marland's death. Our business will be finished.* As if she were foolish enough to believe him.

He picked up a cantaloupe, sniffed it, then returned it to the pile. "How is your neighbor? I hear he had a small disagreement with a suspect yesterday."

She didn't ask how he knew. It was advantageous to a man in his position to know everything, and to that end, William had sources everywhere. "He went to work this morning. He seemed fine." She had watched him leave, dressed in a dark suit, as usual, moving stiffly and looking the worse for wear. Since his police car was elsewhere, he'd driven the 'Vette, the engine growling with that low-throated rumble men equated with power.

There was something damned appealing about the man, black eye, stitches, and all, in a vintage 'Vette, top down, on a cool summer dawn.

William's long, slender fingers scooped up another cantaloupe. "Have you slept with him yet?"

The casual question sent a shiver whispering down her spine. For William, sex was probably just one more tool. Even the wariest of cops would relax his guard around his lover. But how cold-blooded did a woman have to be to use the intimacy of sex to kill a man? Colder than she was.

Not that she wasn't tempted by the idea of intimacy with him. Under different circumstances . . . but circumstances *weren't* different.

She managed to keep her voice calm when she responded. "As you mentioned, he had a disagreement with a suspect. I imagine he'll be out of commission for a while."

"It takes far more than a black eye to put a man out of commission for a woman like you."

A woman like you. It could be a sweet compliment or a stinging insult. It was impossible to tell from his tone which he'd intended. "Tell me, William, after I seduce my way into Detective Ceola's bed, is there anyone else you would like to pimp me to for a few hours?"

Though he continued the charade of searching for a ripe melon, his eyes turned cold. "Those people who pretended to be your parents would have turned you into a whore by your fifteenth birthday if I hadn't intervened. I saved your life, Selena. I gave you a life worth living. I made you what you are. Don't disappoint me by forgetting all that you owe me."

"How could I ever forget?" She'd meant to keep the words inside, but they came out anyway, harsh and bitter.

The stare he directed her way should have made her shudder—would have in the past. But she merely looked at him, her breathing even, no sign of the tension knotted inside her.

Looking grim and displeased, William asked, "Has he asked you out?"

"No."

"Make him do it. Go out with him. Go to bed with him. Find out what he knows, then kill him. You have no choice, Selena. It's his life . . . or yours."

She nudged her cart a few inches with her hip and began selecting jalapeños. "I don't need the reminder—"

Some sixth sense made her look up. The empty shopping cart still stood nearby, but William was gone. With a glance around, she spotted him, striding toward the exit, tall, dapper, striking.

You have no choice. It's his life . . . or yours.

He was wrong. She had other choices. She just had to make the right one—the one she could live with.

9

After work, Tony drove across town to his parents' house, parking in the driveway behind Julie's car. The grass needed cutting, he saw when he got out. Anna's flower beds were rapidly being overtaken by weeds, and there was a small cedar growing in the gutter over the garage. Well, hell, he didn't have anything planned for Saturday.

Anna opened the door before the doorbell's echo had faded. In place of a greeting, she took hold of his chin, then turned his face for a better look. "Isn't that a beautiful shiner?" she asked dryly before presenting her cheek for his kiss. She smelled of perfume and cookies and bedtime stories, and made him nostalgic for childhood, when there wasn't anything her hugs couldn't make better.

"Come on in. You're letting out the cold."

He obeyed, and she locked the dead bolt behind him, pocketing the key. "How's Dad?"

Her only response was a shrug before she started back to the kitchen.

"How are you?"

She smiled at him over her shoulder. "I'm fine. I'd ask you, but the answer's pretty clear on your face. You know, you're my middle child, and I've always loved you best"— she disregarded his snort—"but, son, why don't you get a job where people don't consider it their duty to beat you up?"

"It's not like it's a regular thing," he protested, then changed the subject. "Why don't you find a good lawn service to handle the yard?"

She tweaked his ear before turning her attention back to the sauce on the stove. "Your brothers will take care of it."

"When?"

She waved a hand in the air. "They're busy, you know."

Paying customers came first—that was the business's motto, and they always had enough paying customers to keep them busy. Nick's and J.J.'s own yards would look like hell if their wives didn't nag regularly, and Dom and Matt chose to live in an apartment where mowing wasn't a consideration. That left him. "I'll come over Saturday."

Anna offered a token argument. "You don't need to."

"I know." Leaning against the counter, he shifted his gaze to the window over the sink. Julie was sitting in a chaise longue, and Joe was standing in the middle of the yard, squirting her youngest two children with the hose. The kids were squealing and running circles around him, making him laugh that full, deep laugh Tony remembered so well. "They're having fun."

The spoon Anna had been using clattered against the ceramic rest before falling to the stove top. When he turned, her arms were folded tightly across her middle, hands clenched into fists. "He asked me who the kids were four times in the space of an hour. His own grandbabies!"

"Mom . . ." What could he say? *He can't help it*? She knew that better than any of them. *Be patient*? She'd already shown the patience of a saint. *Everything will be okay*? It wouldn't. Not ever.

She stood there, her face pale, lips thin, the usual light in her eyes dull and bitter, and he realized for the first time how much his father's illness had affected her. Maybe Lucia was right. Maybe this was too much for Anna to handle alone. Granted, Julie came over almost every day, the others stopped in at least once a week, and Tony swore he would start coming by more than his usual twice a week. But the bulk of the responsibility rested on their mother's shoulders, and right now those shoulders were looking pretty insubstantial.

Before he could come up with anything, Anna forced a smile and patted his hand. "Never mind me. I didn't sleep well last night. Will you stay for dinner?"

"I . . . can't. I have plans," he lied. If he stayed, he would feel honor-bound to bring up Lucia's assisted-living idea, and he didn't know—didn't want to know—if he would be strong enough.

"Dare I hope that these plans involve a woman?"

An image of Selena came to mind, sitting in his living room, a cool look on her lovely face. Maybe sympathy could get him a few more hours of her time this evening or, hell, maybe he could just ask her out. "Hope away."

"Oh, good! Bring her with you Saturday. I'll fix your grandmother's linguine alla marinara and we'll chat while you cut the grass."

He tried to imagine Selena chatting over linguine with Anna. Selena was so exotic, and pudgy, motherly Anna was about as far from exotic as a person could get.

"I'll find out if she's busy," he hedged. If Selena turned down his invitation, he might have to consider the idea that she wasn't attracted to him at all—not something his ego wanted to know, to say nothing of his libido. "I'm gonna say hello to Dad and Julie, then head on home."

As he stepped out into the muggy heat, he removed his jacket, then loosened his tie. "Hey, Dad, Jules, kiddos."

His nephews shouted hello in unison, but Joe's only response was an absent nod, stranger to polite stranger.

Julie came to stand beside him, sliding her arm around his waist and resting her head on his shoulder before squinting up at him. "Cool stitches. Two more than last time. You ever get tired of having a target painted on your back? Though, in this case, it looks like the bull's-eye was on your nose."

"I'm a sucker for pain." He nodded toward Joe. "Where is he today?"

"About twenty-five years in the past. He thinks we're the nice family who moved into the Howards' house down the block. He's invited the boys to play with Dom when he gets home from preschool."

"Damn. I wish . . ." Instead of finishing, he pressed a kiss to her forehead. "I've got to go. Thanks."

"For what?"

He gestured toward his father, crouching in the yard now and watching the kids play.

"Hey, he took care of us. How could I not help Mom take care of him? You'd do it if you had the time."

"I'll make the time. See you later."

On the way home he considered how he could rearrange his schedule. He could cut back on his self-imposed overtime and give his mother a break a couple evenings a week. It wasn't much, but he imagined every little bit would help.

While locking Joe away somewhere wouldn't.

The first thing he saw when he turned into the cul-de-sac was a tall, slender figure pushing a lawn mower across his front yard. By the time he pulled into his driveway, Selena was pushing the mower back toward him from the far edge of the lawn. Her own yard was already cut, making his look shaggier in comparison. Sweat glistened on her arms and legs and soaked her tank top where it clung to her breasts and middle. The sight made his breath catch and his blood drain lower.

He got out of the car, gathered his briefcase and coat, then collected the mail from the box before meeting her at the edge of the driveway. As she released the handle on the mower, the engine cut off, leaving in its wake a quiet so strong it echoed. "You don't have to do this."

Her smile was cool and elegant despite her sweaty state. "I know. I like mowing. It's instant gratification."

Oh, honey, I can show you instant gratification. He swallowed, difficult with an already-dry mouth, and hoped the hard-on he was getting just looking at her wasn't too noticeable. "I, uh, really appreciate it, but, uh, I'm already in your debt. . . ."

"Who's keeping track?" She raised one damp hand in a subtle gesture toward his face. "How do you feel?"

"Better than I look, which is life as usual."

"You look fine."

No, *she* looked fine. Amazingly beautiful. Sensual. Sexual. Combustible. Lethal.

Death by Selena. What a way to go.

He casually shifted so that he held his coat in front of him. "I can finish up here."

"By the time you change clothes, I'll be done. Then . . ." For the first time since he'd met her, she looked insecure. Her dark chocolate gaze flitted to his, then away, and her fingers knotted around the mower handle. "After I clean up, I thought I would get some dinner. Maybe you . . . I wouldn't mind having company."

It wasn't the most flattering invitation he'd ever received, but, hey, he wasn't proud. He would take her any way he could get her. "What a coincidence. I wouldn't mind being company. You have anything particular in mind?"

"You can choose," she replied with a shrug.

"Around seven?"

She smiled faintly. "I'll see you then." She started the mower with one pull, then turned to cut another swath along the length of the property. He watched her a moment before climbing the steps to the door. Maybe Marla had been right. He really did have the damnedest luck.

Damon was annoyed as hell when he let himself into William's study. He crossed to his usual spot in front of the desk in three strides and bluntly asked, "What do you want?"

William slowly swiveled his chair around to face him. Damon knew the admonishments he was about to offer— knock before you enter, wait for an invitation, watch your tone, watch your attitude—and didn't care. He'd heard them all before. But when William spoke, he didn't bother with admonishments. "Apparently I disturbed you."

Hell, yeah, getting a royal summons right in the middle of the best fuckin' blow job he'd ever had, had disturbed him. And Lucia, damn her selfish little heart, had refused to finish. The mood was broken, she'd said. *Go on, do whatever you have to do, and we'll try again later.* Bitch.

"I spoke to Selena today," William announced. That was all he said, forcing Damon to at least pretend he gave a damn.

"How is she?"

"She was impudent. She accused me of distrusting her, of having her followed."

Damon couldn't resist pointing out the obvious. "You

told me to assign someone to follow her. You did it because you don't trust her."

William directed a dangerous gaze his way. "And now *you're* being impudent."

Closing his eyes, Damon drew a deep breath. What he was, was off balance. Too little blood flow to his brain was making him reckless, and *reckless* never paid off with a man like William. "I'm sorry," he said, hoping he looked and sounded humble enough to satisfy the boss. "I was . . . in the middle of something—"

William dismissed him with a wave that expressed zero interest in what he'd interrupted. "She looked me in the eye and called me by my name."

That caught Damon's attention. Once he'd suggested that perhaps he should call William "Uncle" to explain the unusual alliance between a teenage boy and a stranger nearly three times his age, and he had been quickly and harshly rejected. A few years later the old man had proudly announced that he'd taken in a half-black, half–Puerto Rican orphan who would now call him "Uncle." The bastard.

"So you think Selena is developing a backbone." It was damn well past time, though who was Damon to judge? It had taken him twenty years with William to decide he was through playing the role of good and loyal servant.

"I think she's testing her limits, like a child. She's pushing to see how far she *can* push." William paused, then formed his next words precisely. "I want you to push back."

"How hard?"

He gestured negligently. "Remind her who's in control. Frighten her. But don't hurt her. And don't let her recognize you."

Damon smiled faintly. With the exception of Bryan Hayes, he'd never let anyone recognize him unless it served his purposes. And Hayes had simply gotten a lucky break. His idiot friend, Tommy Howard, number three on the hit list, had asked him to wait outside their meeting place, as if some fucking loser outside the building could save Howard's life inside. Damon hadn't been expecting surveillance, and he damn well hadn't expected Hayes to follow him back to the estate, then attempt to blackmail William. But like his friend Tommy, Bryan wasn't a problem anymore.

"Do you still have the key to Selena's house that Christine Evans gave you?"

Damon nodded. He'd used it to gain access to the house the day before, though William would shit if he knew. He had walked through the rooms, studied the paintings in the sunroom, located the hiding places for her three weapons, then closed the phone book on the kitchen island. Such a little thing, but he'd known it would be enough to rattle her.

"Use it. Help her to understand who's in charge here. And do it tonight." Turning away, William dismissed him without another word.

Damon left, taking the stairs two at a time and exiting the back door. He would deliver the message to Selena, all right. And someday, in the not-too-distant future, he would deliver his own message to William.

Though Selena had had every intention of cooking dinner at home, seven o'clock found her standing in front of the bathroom's full-length mirror. Dressed in crimson and blue silk, hair cascading down her back, the fragrance of jasmine mixed with passionflower on her skin, she looked . . .

Like an island girl, Tony's voice whispered in her mind. All she needed was a flower in her hair, a little island music, stars to dance under, and a man to dance for . . .

The ringing of the doorbell drew her from the sensual haze of her thoughts. She took a shawl of fringed and embroidered silk from the closet shelf, picked up her straw handbag, and silently chanted to herself to stay calm as she made her way down the stairs.

Tony had shaved and changed into jeans and a polo shirt the color of creamy butter. From the left, undamaged side, he looked downright handsome. When he smiled, he was gorgeous from both sides. "You look incredible."

She hesitated. She normally accepted compliments easily, largely because she didn't believe most of them. This one felt different—charming and sweet and real. Because she wanted it to be? "Thank you," she murmured. After setting the alarm, she stepped onto the stoop to lock up, then turned to find him much too close. *Go to bed with him,* William had ordered. That could well be the easiest thing she'd ever done in her life.

And the hardest.

He offered to put the top up on the 'Vette. She politely refused, instead gathering her hair in one hand to protect it from the wind. They talked little on the way to the restaurant, where they were seated side by side at one end of the sushi bar.

The chef, a lovely young woman with multiple piercings, greeted Tony by name and took their order. Selena idly watched her, all too aware that Tony was watching *her.* She was accustomed to receiving interested looks from men. She wasn't accustomed to reacting—to her skin growing warm, her breath becoming more shallow, a tingling of anticipation spreading through her.

Finally, she faced him, finding his expression part curiosity and part pure male attraction. "They seem to keep you busy at work."

He shrugged. "Homicide's a growth industry."

"What is your caseload like?"

"Normally, it's not too bad, but lately we've had a string of related murders. Right now our guy's got nine kills to his credit, so it's keeping us busy."

"Do you have a suspect?" When he shook his head, she lent a sympathetic tone. "It must be tough. Like making sense of a puzzle without all the pieces."

"It doesn't help that all the victims were bad guys themselves. Half the department and most of the city don't want us to catch the guy. They like that he's cleaning up the streets at no cost to the public."

"You don't share that opinion?"

He gave another shrug. "It doesn't matter what kind of crooks these guys are. It doesn't give someone the right to kill them in cold blood."

"The media say the killer is a vigilante." She'd learned that from his notes—had learned, too, that he doubted that theory. "Do you agree?"

For a long moment he merely looked at her, until the chef interrupted to hand him a scallop-shaped plate with the first part of their order. As he set it between them, he said mildly, "I spend my entire day and a good part of my night focused on nothing but this case. I'd really like to take a break from it, if you don't mind."

Selena picked up her chopsticks, breaking the slender pieces apart. "You must get that a lot—people wanting to know about your work."

He dipped a piece of squid in soy sauce, then ate it before replying. "People are curious. Hell, I'm curious. That's why I became a cop."

"Of course, having a father who was a cop didn't influence you at all."

"Maybe a little." He grinned. "What about you? Who influenced you to become an artist?"

She was so unaccustomed to answering personal questions that she didn't have a ready answer. "No one in particular," she said at last. "A few of my art instructors encouraged me, but most people thought it was a risky way to earn a living."

"What people? Your parents?"

"No. They were already gone." Not a lie. *Gone* meant no longer in her life. She couldn't help it if he translated it to *dead.* "My uncle paid for my education. He wanted a degree he could use."

"You mean, a degree *you* could use."

She considered it a moment, then gave him a sidelong look. "No. I don't."

"So he's not happy you're in the art business."

"Not particularly. He keeps trying to recruit me into his business."

"Which is?"

The drug trade wouldn't go over well with him, she was sure, and *import/export* seemed too clichéd. "Shipping," she said. There was enough truth to it to satisfy her, but not enough to rouse his suspicions.

"Sounds . . . interesting."

For the first time in too long, she laughed. "I can tell you really think so. I bet other careers interest you only to the degree they become involved with your police work. You're a born cop."

"What can I say? I bleed TPD tan and green."

The chef handed them each a dish before moving down the counter to wait on new customers. Hers held a roll made of sticky rice, asparagus, raw tuna, cream cheese, and spicy sauce, wrapped in seaweed and cut into six pieces. Each piece was a mouthful, but she savored the first bite—the difference in textures, the mingling of flavors, the tang of the sauce—going so far as to close her eyes briefly in appreciation.

When she opened them again, Tony was watching her, a heated, hungry look in his own eyes. "Good?" he asked hoarsely.

Afraid her voice would sound just as raw, she nodded.

"Try this." He scooped up a piece of his roll, balancing it precariously between the slender chopsticks, and lifted it to her mouth. There was something intimate about the gesture, something curiously sweet that made her chest tighten and forced her gaze to drop away and focus instead on the bite of food he offered.

He was still watching her when she dared to look his way again. "Wonderful," she murmured, and wondered exactly what she was referring to.

By the time the final course arrived—chilled orange halves topped with cherries—Selena was feeling quite possibly as normal as any other woman out to dinner with a handsome man. It was a state she'd known rarely in her life. Given a chance, she could learn to crave it.

When they left the restaurant, Tony rested his hand at the small of her back as they crossed the parking lot to his car. The air had cooled only a few degrees, and hung heavy and sultry. It was a perfect evening for . . . how had he put it? *Relaxing under an old paddle fan and sleeping in a four-poster bed surrounded by filmy netting, with the doors open to let in the ocean breezes.* For dancing under the stars and living—and loving—to the rhythm of the islands.

And not a bad night at all for a drive in a Corvette with the top down and a handsome man behind the wheel.

When they got home, Tony walked her to the door. She unlocked it, then faced him again. His expression was easy to read, even in the dim light—interest, awareness, attraction. If she gave him the slightest encouragement, he would kiss her. She could see he wanted to, could admit that deep down inside she wanted him to. Just a kiss . . . but could she risk it?

He reached out to tuck a loose strand of hair behind her ear, his fingers warm against her skin. She resisted the urge to rub against them, like a cat against a soothing caress. "Thank you for dinner." His voice was soft, husky.

"That's supposed to be my line. After all, you paid."

"Yeah, but you suggested it." The faint sound of a dog's bark drew his gaze to his house. When he looked back, he was grinning. "How about doing it again tomorrow? I know a place that makes the best barbecued pork sandwiches anywhere."

Common sense insisted she turn him down, but the prospect of spending another evening alone with him was too pleasurable to refuse. "All right." This time her own voice was warm and husky.

"All right," he echoed. He hesitated a moment—now the kiss?—then squeezed her hand lightly and walked away.

Disappointment washed over her as she went inside and locked the door. It was for the best. She had enough danger in her life without adding a relationship with him to the mix. She couldn't let herself get involved.

But she would have, a little voice inside her whispered. Tonight she would have risked a kiss . . . and a whole lot more.

William sat at his desk, a leather-bound journal open in front of him, a fountain pen in hand, but he wasn't writing. Instead, his thoughts had drifted fourteen years into the past, to that fateful November trip to Ocho Rios. His business had been in its early years then, and he had been refining the techniques for living two lives: the public one—the easy, respectable one—and the secret one that excited and challenged him. Back then, he had welcomed all challenges, so when a problem had arisen with his Jamaican supplier, he'd traveled south to deal with it himself.

Instead of his usual souvenir—an antique, some local art, a pretty piece of jewelry—he'd brought back Selena. Acquired her, molded her, shaped her, *created* her. Because he could. Because it pleased him. Because it gave him someone to pass his business on to.

The business was important to him, more so than anything else. It gave him a sense of power and satisfaction that a more traditional life could never deliver. It ruled his thoughts, his goals, his ambitions. He loved the risks, the thrills, the danger. He loved proving time and again how good he was, and especially how much power he had over the lives of others.

He still recalled his discovery of that risk, that power. The hot, muggy air, the dirty odor of the river nearby, the delicate scent of jasmine. More than twenty-five years later, the slightest whiff of jasmine brought it all back in stark relief.

There had been no moon or stars in the sky that night, hidden by clouds heavy with rain. The promise of a downpour had been a fitting accompaniment to the two voices weeping inside the small house, one for what she had done, the other for what she had lost.

Don't let me go to jail! That had been his sister's command—her plea. Because he loved her, and because he'd been raised to believe that duty to family came first, he'd done all he could to ensure Kathryn's safety. He'd finished what she started, disposed of the body, and taken care of the witness—tasks that had taken the rest of the rain-washed night—and he'd steeled himself for the steep price this particular family obligation would cost him. After all, he was an honest man, law-abiding. He would suffer the consequences.

To his great surprise, there had been no consequences. He'd felt some guilt, but not as much as he'd expected. As the days became months and his secret went undetected, he'd found himself relishing the memories. He, who had never done anything worse than cheat on his taxes, had turned a moment of passion into the perfect murder. To this day, only two people knew what had happened that stormy summer night, and only he knew everything.

It had given him a sense of achievement, the power to take one life to save another. But he'd also wanted the danger, the euphoria, the challenge of something few people ever mastered. And so had begun his descent.

But personal honor still guided him. He didn't target the innocent. He didn't steal from poor widows or tolerate attacks upon young women, and no one in his employ dared to hurt a child. His punishments were directed against those who deserved them.

Did Selena deserve punishment? a little voice asked.

He wasn't punishing her, and someday she would see that. He merely expected repayment for all he'd done for her. It had taken him twenty years to build his empire, and he was offering it to her, free and clear.

And, by God, she *would* take it.

After getting ready for bed, Selena settled in at the kitchen table, gazing out the window as the computer booted up. No lights shone from Tony's house. Was he working at his own computer on the far side of the house, or had he already gone to bed? Was he immersed in the lives and deaths of his drug dealers, or did he spare a thought or two for her?

She would like to say she couldn't remember when she'd enjoyed an evening more, but it would be a lie. It had been two years ago, when Greg Marland had wined and dined her . . . before he'd tried to rape her. Before she'd killed him. That had been her last date, the last time she'd trusted a man enough to spend time alone with him.

She trusted Tony enough to spend time alone with him . . . and William expected her to kill him, too.

A shudder ripped through her, easing only when a *beep* from the computer demanded her attention. The information she'd provided the investigative website was sketchy; so was the information she got in return. No credit cards in the name of William Davis came back to the Riverside address. No bank records. No utility accounts. The name was too common, the biographical details too incomplete, to come up with a Social Security number or a birthdate.

The only information of any substance was the property tax data for the estate. It was deeded to DoubleD, Incorporated, which was owned by another company, also owned by someone else, and so on. Once the investigators managed to find their way through the corporate maze to the true owner, they would send her a supplemental report.

If she knew William, they would get lost in that maze and never find their way out again. No doubt, all those corporations were shams. Not one of them was going to lead to him. He was too damned good at keeping secrets.

After shutting off the computer and the lights, she went upstairs to bed. Sleep came easily . . . and so did awareness sometime later. The bedside clock showed that it was one-twenty-eight, and the house was so still that she could hear the faintest whisper of movement outside her bedroom door. Slowing her breaths, she slid her hand beneath the pillow to the pistol there, then eased onto her back, her eyes closed.

Once, when she was alone in the locker room, Montoya had shut off the lights, then lunged for her. That time she'd gotten the worst of it. The darkness had disoriented her, had fed her panic and tripled her heart rate. Now she used the lack of sight to heighten her other senses. The movement was footsteps, soft and careful. She felt the subtle shift in the air when the bedroom door swung open, heard the tiny *whoosh* it created, smelled expensive cologne. She tracked the intruder's movements and sensed the deepening of shadows when he stopped between the bed and the window, blocking the pale light from the street lamp. Her heart was thudding, the adrenaline soaring through her veins, screaming at her to *do something!* But she remained motionless, her breathing deep and steady, feeling him draw nearer, nearer, until his hand, clad in leather, clamped over her mouth.

Swinging her right arm around, she brought up the muzzle of the forty cal so that a scant inch separated it from the intruder's forehead. He froze, tension streaking through him and vibrating the air between them. Then he laughed. "If you were going to shoot me, you would've done it by now. You wouldn't have hesitated and given me the chance to do this—" With his other hand, he knocked the weapon away. It landed without a sound on the mattress, just out of her reach.

Grasping his wrist, she bent it back in a wrist lock, forced his hand away from her mouth, and, at the same time, took advantage of his momentary surprise to maneuver one knee up. She planted her foot in the middle of his chest and shoved hard enough to send him stumbling backward. The wall behind him stopped his fall as she scrambled off the bed on the opposite side, then hastily searched the tangled covers for the pistol. She'd just found it when he lunged onto the mattress and grabbed her hand in a brutal grip.

"Son of a bitch!" he grunted, clawing at her fingers to free the gun.

She held on tightly, Montoya's voice echoing in her head. *Use whatever you can; outwit him, outlast him, fight dirty, and never give up.* Ducking her head, she clamped her teeth onto the meaty part of the man's hand and brought a bellow of pain from him. He let go of the gun to smack her across the face with the back of his uninjured hand, the force throwing her to the floor. She cracked one hip on the wood planks and banged the back of her head against the dresser, her vision blurring as bright points of light danced across the darkness.

Never give up, Montoya whispered, taunted.

The man, all shadows, was cradling his hand, swearing, arrogant enough to think that because she was down, she was out. She eased to her knees, none too steady, then to her feet, drew a deep breath, and lashed out with a side kick, her foot connecting solidly with his jaw. He went down hard, crashing against the night table and shattering the beaded lamp.

"You crazy fucking bitch!" He lay there a moment, breathing heavily.

His voice was muffled by the balaclava that covered his head and all of his face except his eyes, but even so it was familiar. Someone she knew? Someone she'd met since coming to Tulsa? Or someone . . . merely someone she'd spoken to on the phone. The man who'd called the night before, who had broken into her house yesterday afternoon, who most likely worked for William.

"What do you want?" she demanded, her breaths rasping as loudly as his.

"Do you know how easily I could have killed you?"

"As easily as I could kill you now." She'd lost the gun once again when he'd backhanded her, but she didn't need a gun to kill. A marble-and-bronze statue had done the job the first time. A well-placed kick or chop could do it now. "Did William send you?"

He struggled to his feet, then shook his head as if to clear it. "I don't know anyone named William."

"Right. Tell him I got his message."

"I don't know what you're talking about." When he took a few steps toward the door, she took a few away. It was a bad move on her part, though, because at the last instant he pivoted, grabbed her by the throat, and shoved her against the wall next to the window, pinning her there with his body. Her lungs emptied of air and she couldn't squeeze a breath past his grip, couldn't manage even the smallest of kicks, couldn't do anything but pry at his hand as the need for oxygen burned through her.

Fight dirty, Montoya reminded her. *An eye for an eye,* William added. Blindly she grabbed at the man's face, scratching, gouging. The balaclava came away, and he swore viciously as the street lamp dimly illuminated one side of his face.

"Oh, God." Selena thought she'd whispered the plea in her head, but heard her voice, tiny and trembling. "Oh, God, oh, God, oh, God."

Releasing her, he grabbed the balaclava, spun, and thudded away. She didn't snatch up the gun and run after him, didn't do anything but sink to the floor and gulp in oxygen to ease the panic racing through her.

It *wasn't* Greg Marland. He was dead. *She* had killed him. Had cracked his skull with the statue that sat on the sofa table in William's guesthouse. Had splattered his blood on her hands, face, and torn clothes. Had left him crumpled and dead or dying while she panicked and called William. He was *dead.* William had told her. She'd seen it for herself.

As her heart rate slowed and her alarm subsided, she worked to calmly explain away the panic. It was just the stress of being back in Tulsa, or a delayed reaction to Tuesday evening's dinner in the guesthouse. It was only logical that the first genuine assault she'd encountered since Marland had attacked her would remind her of him.

Greg Marland was dead, which made him the least of her problems. This man had been sent by William. He suspected he couldn't trust her, suspected he'd lost some of his control over her, and so he'd sent her a warning. It would appeal to his perverse nature to send that warning via a man who resembled the ghost that haunted her.

She didn't know how long she sat there, huddled on the floor. When the air-conditioning sent a chill through her entire body and her hip throbbed too much to ignore, she forced herself to her feet, located the forty cal where it had slid under the bed, then crawled between the covers.

Regularly through the years William had boasted about all he'd done for her—how he'd saved her life, how he'd given her a new life, how he'd turned her into an educated, intelligent, capable woman.

She had no argument with him taking all the credit. He deserved it. He *had* made her what she was.

A woman who hated him with every fiber of her being.

10

Leaving Simmons to his own devices Friday morning, Tony paid a visit to the David L. Moss Criminal Justice Center. He went in through the main entrance, then walked to the alcove where banks of lock boxes lined the walls. After securing both his service weapon and the .9 millimeter Smith & Wesson he carried for backup, along with the extra cartridges and his canister of pepper spray, he headed down the hall and requested an interview with Albert Spradlin.

He was seated in a small conference room when Spradlin was escorted in, wearing the standard jumpsuit, along with handcuffs and leg irons. The greasy-haired bastard grinned when he saw the results of his handiwork.

"Sit," the guard directed, and Spradlin willingly slid into the seat across from Tony. He waited until the guard was gone to speak.

"You're fuckin' lucky I didn't put you in the hospital."

"You're fuckin' lucky I didn't put you in the morgue," Tony replied.

"Big talk from a little guy," Spradlin taunted.

"A little guy who carries a damn big gun," he reminded him. "I want to talk about Dwayne."

"I know my rights. I don't gotta talk to you without my lawyer present."

"You're right. And I don't have to help you."

Spradlin studied him with beady eyes. "Help me how?"

"You're going back to prison, Bucky, you know that. Detective Collins has already filed an application to revoke your parole. I can't do anything about that . . . but I *can* do something about those felony assault charges you're facing. I can talk to the DA. Tell him you're cooperating with us on a multiple homicide. Ask him to go easy on you. Maybe even drop the charges. All you've got to do is tell me everything you know that might help us catch this guy."

Bucky leaned forward. "How do I know you'll do what you say?"

"You'll have to trust me. Dwayne did."

"Yeah, well, Dwayne's dead. That's not much of a recommendation, is it?"

Tony didn't respond, but merely waited, his gaze fixed on Spradlin. The man glared back, shifted uneasily in his seat, then blew out a rush of air. "What do you want to know?"

"Dwayne made a call to the police station the day he died. What was it about?"

Spradlin shrugged. "I don't know. I hadn't seen him since Saturday."

"Do you know who he was calling?"

"Nope."

"Had he had any trouble with anyone recently?"

Spradlin shrugged again.

"You told Detectives Simmons and Collins something about the killer making a phone call, setting up a meet, and killing his targets. Did you hear that's been happening?"

For a long time Spradlin did nothing but stare at him. Tony said mildly, "If you want me to talk to the DA . . ."

"Guy in a bar told me them last three that was killed got a call from some guy wanting to discuss business with them just before they died. Dwayne got a call like that, too. Fucker said he was friends with this guy named Arias I knew down in McAlester."

"What was he in for?"

"Drugs. Murder. He's still there."

"What's his first name?"

"Jose. Jorge. Somethin' Mexican."

"Did you check with Arias to see if he'd referred someone to Dwayne?"

"Him and me ain't buddies. We just knew each other in the system. I ain't had no contact with no one down there since I got out."

Why bother? Tony thought. Spradlin had probably known he would be going back before long. "Did Dwayne agree to meet with this guy?"

"Said he hadn't decided, and then he didn't mention it again."

Tony gazed into the distance. Odds were pretty good that Mr. Arias didn't have a clue he'd supposedly put together a joint business venture, though Tony would make a call to McAlester to confirm that. He would bet the elusive Marcell Napier didn't know anything about the call to Grover, either. Which told him what?

That the vigilante likely wasn't a vigilante. He knew who the major players in the drug trade were. Knew who they associated with. Knew names to drop that were likely to inspire some measure of trust.

Not things an avenging civilian would know. In fact, only two types of people knew that kind of stuff: criminals . . . and cops.

"So . . . you gonna talk to the DA?" Spradlin asked.

Tony refocused his gaze on the man. "I said I would. Is there anything else?"

When Spradlin shook his head, Tony signaled the guard they were through. He left the conference room, retrieved his weapons from the lock box, and returned to his car, where he sat for a moment, making notes of the conversation.

Criminals and cops. They seemed polar opposites, but in truth they went hand in hand. Without one, there would be no need for the other. Of course cops would know the sort of stuff the vigilante knew—as a rule, cops knew even more about crime and how to commit it than the criminals. But if their killer was a cop . . .

Jeez, all he'd ever wanted to be was a cop, like his dad, his uncles, and Henry. If he had to start investigating his fellow officers now . . .

His jaw clenched, he started the engine and pulled out of the parking lot. If he had to investigate his fellow officers, he would do it, and if one of them was guilty, he would damn well see that he paid for it. That was his job.

He grabbed one of the reserved parking spaces in the Civic Center lot and was on the phone to McAlester less than five minutes later. It took a while, but eventually he hung up with the confirmation he'd expected. Juan Arias knew nothing about any business deal or meeting, had never heard of Dwayne Samuels, hadn't known Spradlin was working for him, and for damn sure never would have sent any business Bucky's way.

"So what now?" Simmons asked after Tony filled him in on everything. "Please don't say we gotta go looking for that car again. We've done more knock-and-talks on that alone than I've done in the past year on everything else combined."

"That's because you're lazy, Frankie. Remember, most crimes are solved by the soles . . . the soles of your feet."

Advice from a detective they'd both worked with, now retired.

"Yeah, well, too bad my feet get dragged along with yours."

"Hey, you don't want to follow up on the car right now, we won't," Tony said as they headed out the office door and toward the elevator. "We can go to Lewis McElroy's funeral instead and stand out in the hot sun for a few hours before we try to interview his mama."

"Bullshit. Darnell's already there. He don't need our help. Besides, I've done enough funerals for a while."

They took the elevator to the garage level, where they ran into Henry and one of his deputy chiefs. "How are things going, Detectives?" Henry asked as they stepped off the elevator.

When Simmons remained uncharacteristically silent, Tony replied, "We're keeping busy."

"I imagine so. If you get too busy, you can probably give up a case or two."

Tony forced a smile. "We'll never be that busy, sir."

Forcing a smile of his own, Henry stepped into the elevator where the deputy chief waited.

Simmons remained silent until they were pulling out of the parking lot. "Chief still wanting to pull you off the Hayes case?"

Tony grunted.

"Any other detective currently working nine homicides, in addition to his old cases, would be happy to give one up. Not that it matters to me either way. You want to add to our workload, hey, I'm there. I'm happy to follow wherever you lead. It don't make me no never-mind. I'm—" Simmons broke off as the radio crackled, dispatching units to a shots-fired call. The address was in north Tulsa. "That sounds familiar. Weren't we over there just the other day? Doin' a knock-and-talk or—no, your C.I., ol' Javier, lives in that area, doesn't he?"

Not just in the area, Tony thought grimly as he switched on the siren and the Kojak light, but at that address.

"Damn," Simmons muttered. "I hope it didn't just become ten."

When he picked up Selena for dinner that evening, Tony looked as if he'd had one lousy day. He'd commented on the bruise darkening her cheek—*Working out again?*—and she had lied and said yes, followed by a suggestion that they forget the date, or stay home and order pizza. He'd politely declined, and by the time they'd completed the half-hour drive west to the small town of Cleveland, he'd obviously put his troubles aside, at least for a time.

She wasn't sure exactly what she'd expected the place that made the best barbecued pork sandwiches around to look like—a log cabin, maybe, with country decor and an acrid tinge from the smoker out back. The Dari Diner was old-fashioned, all right—a drive-in with a half-dozen parking spaces underneath an awning and hard plastic booths inside to seat maybe thirty.

"How did you discover this place?" she asked as she slid onto a bench in the corner booth.

"Cops know all the good places to eat."

"All the good out-of-town places?"

"You bet. There used to be this place in Okmulgee, down south of Tulsa, that had the best hamburgers. When Dad was still in Patrol, sometimes one of the guys would take orders, then drive down and pick them up."

"And their supervisors didn't frown on that?"

"Only if they got left out." Stripping his straw, he stuck it into his drink, then wadded the wrapper in a neat ball. "Truthfully, Simmons grew up here. He turned me on to this."

"Simmons . . . is he your partner?"

"We don't generally work with partners, but when you've got nine homicides—" His eyes darkened, his mouth flattening. "Make that ten . . ."

Ten murders. More people than populated her life on a regular basis. The tenth, she suspected, had happened in the past twenty-four hours and was the reason for his subdued manner.

"Still no suspects?"

He made an obnoxious sound. "Only enough to fill a phone book."

"How do you go about weeding them out?"

"You question everybody who might have a reason to want them dead—family, business associates, competitors, enemies. Most of them, of course, don't like cops, and plenty of them had reasons for wanting these particular guys dead, so they're not real cooperative. It's tedious work, and sometimes it gets you nowhere."

"If it's a vigilante—" She broke off when he scowied. "You don't buy that theory. Why not?"

"It's been two months since the first murder, and it's no harder to buy meth or crack or heroin in Tulsa today than it was before. That means somebody's picking up the slack, which means somebody's now supplying the markets that those guys supplied."

"And making the money they made."

He nodded. "I just don't think it's about justice."

"The tenth one . . . it happened today?"

He nodded grimly. "The guy was one of my informants.

I think the killer paid him to give me bad information about last week's triple homicide, and I . . . I let him know I thought he was lying. I don't know if he went to the killer and told him I was suspicious, or if the guy just figured out on his own that Javier wasn't credible, but . . . he was found this afternoon with a bullet in his head."

Offering comfort was foreign to Selena, but she made the effort anyway, and found it was surprisingly easy. She covered his hand with hers, gave his fingers a squeeze. "It wasn't your fault."

He rubbed his thumb back and forth over the sensitive skin between her thumb and forefinger. "I've known since Monday that Javier lied, but so much has happened this week that I didn't find the time to follow up on it. If I had, maybe he wouldn't be dead."

"Or maybe he would have died sooner. He had choices, Tony. He made the wrong one, and it cost him. You can't take responsibility for that." Just as *she'd* made wrong choices and paid for them, starting with stealing from that drunk in Ocho Rios. Giving William her trust, affection, and loyalty. Making excuses for him, remaining blind to the darker aspects of his character, letting him manipulate and threaten her. He couldn't take all the credit for what she'd become. She was responsible, too, for wanting the wrong things, making the wrong decisions.

"You look blue. Are you speaking from experience?"

Before she could answer, the waitress delivered their order. Selena neatly folded back the paper sandwich wrapper, then took a bite. "You're right. This is the best barbecued pork sandwich I've ever had."

"Not that you're a connoisseur of barbecued pork," he added as he finished squirting out packages of catsup for his fries.

She admitted as much with a shrug. "Though pork was a mainstay of our diet growing up, barbecue wasn't. But this is delicious."

"What other mainstays did you have?"

She tore off a piece of bun and nibbled it while considering an answer. Fear, isolation, punishment, abuse—those had all been an everyday part of her first nine years. Confusion. Anger with her mother for not loving and protecting her, and with herself for not being lovable. Bitterness. Bewilderment.

And the one thing that had seen her through—determination. To survive. To escape to a better life than the one her mother and Rodrigo had denied her.

When she didn't respond, Tony asked another question. "What was your life like when you were ten?"

Better than when I was nine and not as good as when I was fifteen. But that answer would merely lead to more questions she couldn't answer satisfactorily. "Typical. I was living in Jamaica then, going to school and playing with friends." She'd been receiving daily lessons in the fine arts of begging, lying, cheating, and stealing, and the *friends* had been partners in crime or targets. Even then she'd wanted another life so desperately she could hardly bear it.

"Why did you come to the U.S.?"

That was an easy lie, one William had come up with fourteen years previously. "My parents died, and my uncle wanted me educated in this country."

As he dug into the second of his two sandwiches, Tony studied her. She'd eaten the bulk of her meal and was now just picking at what was left, spending far more time coating the fries in catsup than eating them. Her expression was serene, the lines of her face relaxed, but the look in her eyes . . . She was blue again. Was she thinking about her parents? Or those wrong choices she'd made?

It would be more polite to let the subject drop, but he didn't. "How did your parents die?"

With precise movements, she gathered the sandwich wrapper and dirty napkins, balled them up inside a clean napkin, then squeezed it tightly between her hands. "In a car crash."

Not an unusual way to die. When he'd been assigned to Traffic, he'd worked more than his share of fatalities. Most Tulsa drivers were inattentive, otherwise occupied, and drove too fast. "You weren't with them?"

That brought her gaze to his. For a long moment, she just looked, as if she might find something in his face to answer the debate going on inside her. Abruptly she shrugged and offered a tight little smile. "No. They sent me to live with someone else when I was nine. I hadn't seen them since."

"Why?"

"Why hadn't I seen them?"

"Why did they send you to live with someone else?"

Another of those long looks, then . . . "My mother was Puerto Rican. Her husband was also Puerto Rican."

And Selena's father was black. Undeniably, couldn't-pass-her-off-as-anything-else black.

Seeing the understanding cross his face, she smiled again, a smile that was meant to be cool and unaffected, that in fact was cool and bitter enough to hurt. "Rodrigo, her husband, didn't like being responsible for another man's bastard, especially a nigger bastard. Sending me elsewhere was better for everyone."

Definitely better for Rodrigo and his wife, and probably better for Selena, though also probably too little, too late. A bigoted son of a bitch could do a hell of a lot of damage to a defenseless kid in nine years, and her mother couldn't have been any help. Any woman who, when forced to choose between her husband and her little girl, chose the husband, couldn't have been much of a mother in the first place.

"I'm sorry." The words were inadequate, but hell, what else could he offer? Going to Puerto Rico to kick Rodrigo's sorry ass was out of the question, since the bastard was dead.

She inhaled, straightening her shoulders, literally shaking off the memories. "It's in the past," she said, her tone lighter. "It doesn't matter."

He knew better than that. He'd worked enough child-abuse cases to know that it always mattered.

And it helped explain her aloofness. When the people closest to you betrayed you, it must seem safer to keep everyone else at a distance. After all, if you never let anyone get close enough to hurt you, then you couldn't get hurt.

Too bad the theory didn't work so well in practice.

The restaurant door swung open, admitting a large group of laughing teenagers. Taking that as a sign, Tony polished off the last of his sandwich, added his trash to the tray with Selena's, and followed her to the door. "Are you in a hurry to get home?" he asked as they walked to the 'Vette.

"No. Not at all."

"Good. We'll take the scenic route back." He was mostly joking. There wasn't a whole lot that was scenic between Cleveland and Tulsa. Once you'd seen one rolling hill covered with trees, you'd pretty much seen them all. But he knew a place that was sort of along the way, and it was scenic enough to suit him.

He took a two-lane road out of town that meandered

more or less eastward, passing woods, farms, and pastures, and skirting the edges of Keystone Lake. They didn't talk much—one of the drawbacks of a convertible—but that was all right. When they got there, they would have all the quiet they could ever need.

Tony turned off the highway onto a county road for a few miles, then left that for a dirt road that wound through the woods and blocked out the setting sun as thoroughly as turning off a light. After a time, he made one more turn, this time onto a road barely wide enough for one car. Grass grew on either side of the tire ruts and rustled against the underside of the 'Vette.

They came to a rusted gate, propped open as it had always been and bearing a sign that stated No Trespassing, Hunting, or Fishing.

He felt Selena's gaze and glanced her way. "This property belongs to my Uncle John. The whole family has a standing invitation to use it, though the only time the women come is when Uncle Pete brings his RV. Otherwise, it's just the men and occasionally the kids. We bring sleeping bags, pitch a tent, forgo little things like shaving and showering, eat nothing but sandwiches and chips, and drink nothing but beer."

"Sounds . . ." Unable to find the appropriate word, she settled for wrinkling her nose. It expressed a lot for such a delicate little gesture, and made him laugh.

The lane widened into a clearing about fifty feet from the shore. When he shut off the engine, the quiet seemed to rush over them, then the night noises became noticeable. Insects buzzed, crickets and tree frogs chirped, and a few birds sang. Off in the distance a boat roared past on the lake, and, closer, the water lapped against the shore.

He grabbed a jacket from the trunk, then met Selena at

the passenger side of the car. She looked out of place, but not uncomfortable. The last woman he'd brought here for a family cookout a few summers ago had spent so much time worrying about bugs and spiders that neither of them had had any fun. Selena didn't seem at all worried . . . but she did look entirely too well dressed to be wandering around the lake at night.

He was about to suggest they put off the visit until she was appropriately dressed when she moved away from the car. "Can we walk down to the water?"

"Sure."

The sun was setting, but enough light remained to see the path. It ended at a small beach, built by his dad and uncles when he was a kid and maintained now by the next generation.

She stepped out of her shoes and, for a moment, just wiggled her toes in the sand that still held the day's heat. When she started to lower herself to the ground, he stopped her. "You can sit on this."

She glanced at the jacket he offered, then sat down with a smile. "You must know some prissy women."

"My share."

"Well, I'm not one of them." Drawing her knees up, she wrapped her arms around them and gazed out over the water. "You don't strike me as the prissy type."

"We all make mistakes." Tossing the jacket aside, he sat down next to her. "Haven't you ever been suckered by a pretty face or pretty words?"

She tilted her head to the side to study him. "I can't imagine the woman who could sucker you."

"Hey, I'm a man. Of course I can be suckered."

For a long time she did nothing but stare at him. Then she kissed him.

It wasn't a tentative, exploring first-kiss sort of kiss. It was hot and hungry and demanding, as if she'd just discovered he had something she needed desperately. She twisted around, sliding her hands into his hair, sliding her tongue into his mouth, and bore him down onto the sand, her breasts pressed into his chest, her body heated and soft against his.

It took him a moment to react—not his fault, since his swelling cock robbed his brain of the blood needed to function. He caught her wrists and guided her hands down to his chest, then rolled with her, pinning her on the warm sand. Her muscles tightened, as if her natural instinct for self-preservation had kicked in, then he thrust his tongue in her mouth and she relaxed, then stiffened again in an entirely different way.

With a helpless moan, she pulled his shirt up and over his head, greedily biting his lip before kissing him again. Her fingers swiftly and surely unclipped the holster from the small of his back and tossed it and the pistol aside, then began unfastening the button-fly of his shorts. She got distracted after undoing only a few buttons, and instead drew a long, strained groan from him with one slow, talented caress.

"I—aw, jeez—I can't—" Panting, he unwrapped her fingers from his hard-on and pressed her hand to the sand. Immediately she reached for him with her free hand, and he did the same with it. His blood was pounding and his temperature had redlined and he couldn't even see straight, but damn it to hell, he had no problem with thinking straight. "We can't . . . I don't have any condoms."

She smiled the sweetest, loveliest, wickedest smile and freed one hand to remove the purse slung bandolier-style around her neck. It was a tiny thing, big enough for a lipstick, a key, and some cash. "I do."

And a condom. The plastic crinkled as she drew it out.

The sudden tensing of her muscles was the only warning he received before she flipped him onto his back, then rolled over to straddle him. With her hips rubbing hot and steady over his erection, he was at her mercy.

Her blouse was sleeveless, fitted, and pale blue. She unbuttoned it and let it fall to the ground, revealing breasts large enough to fill his hands, nipples hard and swollen, and skin that same smooth coffee-and-cream all over. As she sat on his cock with nothing but a few layers of material between them, she reached back to pull the band from her hair, then combed the braid loose. With curls falling down her back, moonlight gleaming on her skin, and wooden beads around her throat, she looked like some primitive goddess—earthy, sensual, greedy—and she was killing him with every move, every look, every breath.

He'd never been so willing to be anyone's sacrifice.

Her skirt fastened on the side from waist to hip, then fell open the rest of the way down. She undid the large wood buttons, swept it aside, then bent to press a line of kisses to his rib cage. Her hair made his skin ripple as it swayed with each kiss, across his ribs, down his belly. When she mouthed his cock through the denim, he damn near came. His vision went dark and sweat popped out along his forehead. He wanted to be inside her—without the damn condom—wanted it *now*, all night, forever.

"Fuck me, Selena," he gritted out, everything in him so tight and hard he might explode.

"Such language." She made a *tsk*ing sound as she laid the condom packet on the ground between them, slid out of her panties, then lay back on the sand, incredibly, beautifully naked. "You fuck me, Tony."

The vulgarity coming from a woman he hadn't heard swear before made him even harder and hotter. He kicked off the rest of his clothes, rolled the condom into place, and lowered himself onto her. He fucked her until they were both trembling and hurting, until their skin was damp with sweat and their breaths came in rugged, ragged gasps, until every sensation was a raw scrape, as much pain as pleasure. He fucked her long and hard, coming more times than the condom was good for and feeling her match him orgasm for orgasm.

The last one drained him. He sank to the sand beside her, struggling for one deep breath, able to hear little over the pounding of his heart. But he was aware of her. Every nerve, every muscle, was attuned to her softness and heat against him.

When he managed to open his eyes, she was looking at him, solemn and innocent and sensual. "I thought your father didn't tolerate swearing in front of women."

"He'll never know unless you tell."

"I won't tell on one condition." Rolling onto her side, she combed her fingers through his hair, then let her palm rest against his cheek as she brushed her mouth across his. "Take me home, Tony," she murmured, "and fuck me again."

When William had suggested that she sleep with Tony, Selena had been hurt at the proof that he thought nothing of prostituting her for his own gain. In the dawn stillness Saturday morning, she was feeling pain of a different sort—tenderness between her thighs and around her nipples.

Tony was a passionate lover who gave as good as he got—maybe even better. She couldn't recall the last time she'd felt so thoroughly satiated. Maybe never.

He was still asleep, lying on his side facing her. He'd pushed the covers down past his waist, giving her the chance to admire what circumstances and need had denied her the night before. His chest was smooth, nicely muscled, not like Montoya's, less defined but more appealing. There was a faint bruise on his ribs—left over from his run-in with the guy who'd given him the black eye or a souvenir of last night's run-in with *her*? "Fierce" wasn't her normal operating method, but last night hadn't been exactly normal. She had never wanted a man the way she'd wanted him, had never felt that need to possess, to claim and own.

She considered easing the covers away so she could see what she'd only felt the night before—his flat belly, his lean hips, his long, muscular legs, and his long, strong—

Before the word even formed in her mind, she noticed the swelling that raised the sheet, and that quickly, the mere consideration became a temptation almost too strong to resist. She was managing, though, until a sleepy, husky voice murmured, "You keep looking at me like that, and you're gonna have to do something about this." Reaching down, he adjusted his erection, an image that sent a tingle straight through her, then he opened his eyes. "This is a pleasant surprise."

"Waking up with an erection?"

"Nah, I have those all the time. I meant waking up with *you*. I half expected to find out it had all been one truly erotic dream."

"I'm nobody's dream," she said, hoping he didn't notice the wistfulness that seemed so obvious to her.

"You've been in my dreams practically since we met."

He yawned, stretched, then rolled onto his stomach, pillowing his head on one arm. "Do you always wake up so early?"

"Always."

"Why?"

She could give a dozen answers that didn't come near the truth, or no answer at all. When she opened her mouth, though, the truth surprised her and slipped out. "Habit. Rodrigo, my mother's husband, liked to drink late into the night, then stumble back to consciousness somewhere around noon. Every hour I was up and about before that was an hour when I wasn't his target."

Tony's expression didn't change, but his eyes darkened a few shades. "He beat you." He said it flatly, the lack of emotion somehow conveying great emotion.

"Often enough." The desire to brush it off, leave the bed, and get started on the day was strong. Confiding in anyone was difficult. Doing so with no clothes, no attitude, to hide behind, she felt as vulnerable as the little girl Rodrigo had abused. But she forced herself to remain where she was, to continue breathing slowly, steadily, to meet Tony's gaze.

"How often?"

"The serious beatings didn't happen more than once or twice a month." Unless she'd gotten in Rodrigo's way, or things weren't going as he wanted, or someone had taunted him about the black brat her mother tried to pass off as his.

Apparently, her dismissive tone didn't set well with Tony. His jaw tightened, and his voice was hostile as he asked, "And what about the funny beatings? How often did they happen?"

She sat up, stuffing pillows behind her back, tucking the sheet beneath her arms. "I'm not being flippant, Tony. When you routinely get beaten until you're afraid you're going to die, getting backhanded across the room or shoved off the porch doesn't seem such a big deal. I can't remember a single day that he didn't hit me, but he only tried to do serious damage once—"

"Or twice."

"—a month."

Now he was scowling at her. "Why didn't your mother leave him?"

"He was her husband."

"You were her daughter."

"She needed him."

"You needed her."

"I didn't matter." The words were out before she realized it. She would have taken them back if she could, no matter that they were true. She *hadn't* mattered, not to her mother or anyone else. If Rodrigo *had* killed her, no one would have cared, except possibly the other kids, since he would have needed a new outlet for his rage. She had been dispensable to her family and everyone in her life since then, including William.

Including Tony?

As if he read the thought, he slid his arm around her waist and pulled her down onto the bed, sliding her body half under his. "She should have protected you," he said fiercely, his nose inches from hers. "She should have killed the bastard. You were the *only* one that mattered. You *are* the only one . . ." His words ended in a harsh kiss that took her breath away and spread quivering, tingling heat all through her body.

He left her only long enough to retrieve a condom from the night table, then they fucked again. Such a lovely, coarse, great-sex word, she thought drowsily when it was over, when they were sprawled across the bed again instead of across each other, when the air that surrounded them was heavy, charged, and smelled of lust and intimacy and satisfaction.

She was lying sideways across the bed, her hair hanging over the edge, her eyes half closed as the ceiling fan cooled the sweat that dampened her body. "What's on your schedule today? Detective work?"

"Huh-uh. I've got to do a few things over at my mom's." Beside her, he opened one eye to peer at her. She pretended not to notice. "Mom's making linguine for lunch, and you're invited."

Amazing how quickly her stomach could tie itself in knots. She hid the anxiety with a smile, though, as if the words she was about to say didn't sting. "What? You Ceola kids have a standing invitation to bring all strays and sex partners along when you visit?"

His gaze narrowed. "No. I told her I had plans with you Thursday night, and she said, 'Oh, good, bring her with you Saturday. I'll fix linguine and we'll chat while you cut the grass.'"

There was no reason for the rush of pleasure that tried to break free. So he'd told his mother he was seeing someone. Big deal. It was a sure bet he hadn't told her Selena was just visiting and not about to stick around.

Frowning, she faced him. "What plans? I didn't invite you out Thursday until *after* you left your mother's."

"I was planning to ask you, but you beat me to it. You were just more eager." He said the last words with a grin, though, that made objection impossible. "So how about it? Lunch and chitchat with my folks? You won't really have to say much. Mom's a big talker. So is Dad . . . though these days he might be living in another decade inside his head."

She touched his hand, just briefly, when his expression

turned grim. "I'll think about it. Right now I need a shower and clean clothes. What time are you leaving?"

"Around eight-thirty."

"I'll let you know." She stood and looked around, locating her skirt half under the bed. After buttoning it around her waist, she found her blouse hanging from the dresser, and one sandal in the middle of the floor, the other in the doorway. The only thing she couldn't find was her panties, and they—

"When you threw them aside last night, they landed in the lake, remember?"

Her skin flushed. She did, indeed, remember. It was the first time she'd ever lost her underwear on a date. She wasn't convinced it would be the last.

Fully dressed—more or less—she stood at the foot of the bed. Tony was still lying there, all brown skin and muscle, looking lazy and relaxed and too handsome for her own good. "I—" Couldn't think of a thing to say. *Thanks? Sorry? Forgive me? Help me?* "I, uh, will let you know."

He let her get as far as the door before he spoke. "It won't make a difference."

"What won't?"

"Whether you go. Whether they like you. Whether they care about your race. It won't make a difference to me."

He believed that. She wasn't so sure, but then, she'd had experience with the situation.

But she didn't point that out—or that, in the long run, it *didn't* matter, because she wasn't staying and he wasn't leaving and the odds that he would survive her or forgive her were too minuscule to calculate. Instead she smiled, said, "I'll be back soon," and wiggled her fingers in a wave before going.

At the front door, she reached for the knob, then stopped. "Tony? What about the alarm?"

"The code's seven-six-nine-nine," he called down the stairs.

Her stomach knotted again, and her hand trembled as she punched in the numbers. *Ask and ye shall receive . . .*

Inside her own house, she headed upstairs to the bathroom. After her shower, she squirted a dollop of lotion into her palm and let her thoughts drift back to one of the happier times in her life, when she was sixteen and living at her Swiss boarding school, where she'd made her first black friend ever. J'niece had taught her that the right emollients would banish the ashy skin tone that plagued her. Had told her all about wigs and weaves and sleep-pretty pillows to protect both hair and styles. Had shown her how wrapping her hair in silk scarves at night would prevent breakage.

Even though Selena's own hair wasn't so coarse as to require the scarves or pillows, for a time she'd used one or the other regularly. It had made her feel closer to the father she'd never known and the big, loving extended family he surely must have had—the family she'd been convinced would have loved her if they'd only known she existed.

J'niece had made her appreciate her own café-au-lait skin, though she'd also envied her friend's darker skin. There was no question J'niece was black, no doubt she belonged in the black community, while Selena had never belonged anywhere. Too black for the Latin community, too Latina for the black community, and too much of both for the white.

And Tony said it didn't make a difference.

And even seemed to believe it.

Before she could consider how much *she* wanted to believe it, the cell phone rang. She stood motionless, one foot propped on the mattress, and watched it as if merely staring would tell her who it was and what he wanted.

Of course, she *knew* who it was, and what he wanted. Since she wanted nothing to do with him or his demands at the moment, she returned to lotioning up. A moment later the ringing started again, and a few moments later, once more. Finally she answered.

"What are you doing?" William demanded without a greeting.

"I just got out of the shower. Did you call earlier?"

"This is my third time. I want to see you this morning. Meet me at—"

"No."

The silence on the phone was sharp with danger. She swallowed hard. Never in fourteen years had she flatly refused one of his demands. Even turning down his job offers had been handled more delicately, dancing around the issue, delaying, making excuses. But never had she simply, plainly said "No."

Maybe if she had, she wouldn't be in this position.

"What did you say?" His words were pure ice, cold enough to burn, sharp enough to scrape her nerves raw. That voice meant disaster, but before it had always been directed at others, never her. That was the voice for warnings and threats that would soon be made good. People died after hearing that voice.

Instead of answering, she changed the subject. "I got your message Thursday night. Next time, try picking up a phone. It's easier on the hired help."

"I don't know—"

"Please show me enough respect not to lie."

There was a brief silence, followed by a chuckle. "You left some vicious bruises on his hand."

"I could have killed him."

"He could have killed you, if that had been his directive."

"But then who would kill Detective Ceola?" she asked sweetly. With her next words, though, her voice was as icy as William's had been. "You brought me here to eliminate a problem from your life. That's not going to happen if you keep interfering."

"I brought you here to obey my orders. To do what I instruct in the manner I instruct you to do it. If you're going to work for me"—her derisive snort interrupted his speech for only an instant—"you'll have to learn who's boss. Now . . . I want to see you this morning—"

"I have plans with Detective Ceola this morning."

"Cancel them."

"No."

The silence this time was longer, and tense enough that she fancied she could hear the connection humming with it.

Finally he asked, "What are these plans?"

"We're going to his parents' house—"

"No."

"But—"

"I said no, damn it! Stay away from his family, Selena. That's an order."

"Why?"

"Because I said so. Do you require any further reason than that?" He waited a moment for her response, but when none came, he sighed heavily. "Sometimes you disappoint me, Selena. That you can question my judgment after all I've done for you . . . all I've given you . . . What kind of thanks is that? I treat you like a daughter, but no beloved daughter would disappoint her father like this."

In a gentler tone, he continued. "Forget meeting with me. Tell Detective Ceola you can't go with him this morning. Give him any excuse you want. Just send him off with a kiss and a smile, and then use the time to search his house. What about the code to the alarm system? Have you learned it yet?"

"Yes, this morning."

William chuckled. "See? For the pleasure of having you in his bed, he was willing to compromise his own security. Now, when you kill him, he'll have no one to blame but himself. Renege on the invitation to visit his parents, then do a thorough search of his house while he's gone. I'll expect a report as soon as you're finished."

"Yes, Uncle," she said dutifully, because it was what he expected. "What if he comes home before I'm finished?"

"You're proving to be very resourceful, Selena. If he comes back early, you can handle it."

She was more resourceful than he knew. But he would find that out soon enough.

"Give me a call when you're finished with your search. And, Selena . . . don't disappoint me again."

11

"I don't understand the game you're playing with her."

After hanging up the phone, William turned his attention to Damon, who was standing in front of a display case and fingering the premier example of his netsuke collection. The jade figurine was small, intricately carved, and centuries old. For generations it had belonged to the same family, passed down from father to son. William had once tried to purchase it, but the then-current owner had laughed at his offer. *You'll have to pry it from my cold dead hands,* he'd said in a parody of a bad movie.

As you wish, William had replied, and shot him in the center of the forehead.

Truthfully, he'd intended to kill the man anyway—it was the only way to take over his Asian supply lines—but the story sounded so much better without that little detail.

Removing the figurine from Damon's hand, he returned it to its place in the cabinet and closed the glass door. "You don't have to understand anything but what I tell you."

"You tell her to spend time with Ceola, then when she tries, you stop her. Why?"

William smiled. "Because I can." He allowed the reply to achieve its full impact, then relented and explained. "The invitation this morning was to visit his parents. Despite everything, Selena still maintains this damnable sentimentality when it comes to family. If she sees Detective Ceola as the good son, the adored brother, the favorite uncle, she'll begin to question the need to eliminate him. Better that she think of him only as a neighbor, a police officer, a man alone."

"A lover," Damon said dryly, turning the last word into a mockery.

William fingered a cigar without lighting it. One of Damon's flunkies had been watching Princeton Court the night before—most nights, in fact, since Selena's arrival—and had reported that she'd spent the night with Detective Ceola. "The words *Selena* and *love,* or any variation thereof, don't belong in the same sentence. She's merely doing what I instructed her to do."

"If you're so sure of that, why did you send me to see her the other night?" Damon emphasized the question with a glance at his hand, still bruised and swollen from her bite.

There was the problem: No matter how much he wanted to trust Selena, he could never be totally sure of her. He'd spent fourteen years shaping her already-damaged psyche to his needs. Even longer than that, he'd watched her and plotted how he would approach her, how he would control her, and for a time he had succeeded beautifully. He'd been able to predict her response to any situation with near-perfect accuracy . . . until it was time for her to repay his efforts by coming to work for him. She thought she had the right to turn him down. She thought she owed him nothing but love.

She owed him far more than she knew. He had literally given her life, and such a debt couldn't be repaid with simple affection. But it could be repaid by Ceola's death at her hand, for then William would have the leverage he needed to own her, heart and soul. She would never refuse him anything again.

A simple plan with two major drawbacks. First, Ceola had to die. He hadn't yet put together everything he knew, but he would, and then it would be too late. Second, Selena had to kill him. When William had brought her to Tulsa, he'd been as sure as he ever could be that she would do exactly what he told her. Each conversation with her, though, raised little alarms. He knew too well that small problems, left unchecked, could grow into big ones, and Selena on anyone's side but his own could be a big one indeed.

But he had no intention of confiding his doubts to Damon. His assistant already nurtured a jealousy of Selena and wouldn't hesitate to take advantage of any weakness. If she showed herself untrustworthy . . . that would be soon enough to let Damon deal with her.

"Your visit to her house was merely a reminder who was in control," he said in response to Damon's question. "Even you require chastisements from time to time, and you've been playing this game far longer than she has. Don't worry. Selena will prove herself."

One way or the other. Depending on which way she chose, she would fulfill her obligations to him . . . or she would die. It would be a terrible waste, one he would regret deeply, but it would be for the greater good.

His good. In the end, that was all that mattered.

Tony had showered, dressed, fed the dog and the cats, emptied the litter box, and had a cup of instant coffee by the time eight-thirty rolled around. He stood at the kitchen island, watching the clock, giving Selena a few minutes longer—eight-thirty-two, eight-thirty-four, eight-thirty-six—before finally grabbing his keys and heading for the front door. Just as he twisted the knob, the bell rang.

Part of her hair was pulled back and secured with a big wooden hair clamp, leaving the rest curling down her back. She wore pants that ended halfway between her ankles and knees, and her blouse was sleeveless with a little stand-up collar. She looked incredible, and unsure as hell.

"I was just on my way to coax you out of the house."

Hands clasped around the narrow strap of her purse, she smiled hesitantly. "No coaxing needed."

He was pretty sure that wasn't true. She'd probably used the entire time she'd been gone to give herself a big enough pep talk to make it this far. While part of her wanted to go with him, another part really wasn't up to being disappointed. To make certain that didn't happen, he'd called his mom to give her a heads-up, but the line had been busy. His folks were the only people he knew who didn't have Call Waiting. His mother refused to put one call on hold simply to answer another. If the second caller had something important to say, he would call back.

Unfortunately, he was going to walk into her house with his *something important,* and she was going to have to deal with it without notice.

He grabbed the ball cap and sunglasses he'd left on the hall table, then locked up before walking with Selena to the car, staying a few steps behind so he could covertly admire the way she moved.

"If you keep looking at me that way . . ." Her words trailed off in a sensual promise, magnified when she looked over her shoulder and gave him a knowing smile.

"I'd be happy to do something about it when we get back," he replied. "Actually . . ." He backed her against the passenger door, moving forward until their bodies touched and he could smell all the scents of her—the exotic flower-tinged perfume, a hint of cocoa butter that reminded him of hot summer days at the lake, something he could define only as tropical in her hair. "I'd be *really* happy to do something now"—he brushed his mouth across hers—"but Mom's a real stickler for doing what you say you'll do . . . and you don't want to miss her linguine . . . and there's a tree growing in her gutters. . . ."

Selena laughed—not exactly the reaction he'd been looking for, but gratifying just the same—and gave him a quick smack on the lips. "Come on. I want to see this gutter-growing tree."

They made fair time on the drive across town. Tony parked in the driveway behind his mother's car, got out, and headed toward the side of the house. Realizing belatedly that Selena had, naturally, started toward the front door, he backtracked, caught her arm, and pulled her with him. "They'll be out back having coffee." Holding her hand, he led her through the gate into the backyard, where stepping stones gave way to a brick path, and around the back corner of the house.

Nick's twin daughters were the first to spot them. Five years old and identical right down to the space between their lower front teeth, they left their toys in the grass and launched themselves at Tony, forcing him to let go of Selena to catch them. "Uncle Tony, Uncle Tony!" they clamored. "Nonna says we can help you cut the grass!"

"Gee, thanks, Nonna," he replied, giving his mother a wry look.

Sitting at the patio table in the shade, Anna shrugged as if to say *Better you than me.* "The only other choice was to let them help me weed the flower beds, and you know what happened the last time I got help with that."

Yeah, without telling her, they'd "weeded" a hundred dollars' worth of flowers she'd just planted. It took a lot to get her irate with her grandkids, but they'd succeeded that day.

Still lugging the kids, he stopped between his parents' chairs. "Hey, Dad."

For a moment, Joe remained motionless, gazing out across the yard, then abruptly he looked up, eyes wide. "Oh, sorry, I was just thinking about work. You must be—" As he got to his feet, confusion crossed his face, then he grinned and shrugged. "Anna told me we were having company this morning, but I have to admit, I wasn't paying much attention. I'm Joe Ceola."

Tony looked at the hand he offered before reluctantly taking it. "I'm Tony."

"You're new to the neighborhood, aren't you? Anna and I just moved in a few months ago. You've got cute kids. Anna and I are planning to have at least six." Joe grinned again and said in a conspiratorial tone, "She wants three, and I want nine, so I figure we'll split the difference. Are these your only two?"

"Uh, yeah," Tony said with a glance at his mother. She was deliberately not watching.

"Grandpa's wanderin' again," the twin on Tony's left said. "He thinks I'm a boy."

"That's 'cause you look like a boy," her sister pointed out.

"Do not. If I look like a boy, then you do, too, 'cause you look just like me."

"Huh—"

"Hey," Tony interrupted, setting them both down. "Go play."

Obediently they ran back to the toys they'd left in the

yard, and he turned to introduce Selena. She was hanging back, and came forward only when he held out his hand. "Mom, Dad, this is Selena McCaffrey. Selena, my parents, Anna and Joe, and those are my nieces, Kara and Sara."

Anna swung her gaze around, and her eyes widened with surprise. She covered it fairly well, he thought, but he had no doubt Selena had seen it.

Anna set her coffee down, stood, and wiped her hands on her pants before taking the few steps necessary to offer her hand. "It's a pleasure to meet you, Selena. Tony's told us virtually nothing about you. I'm looking forward to getting acquainted."

"It's nice to meet you, Mrs. Ceola, Mr. Ceola."

Anna pulled out the third chair at the table. "Have a seat and I'll get you some breakfast. Do you prefer coffee or juice? Oh, never mind, I'll just bring both. Make yourself comfortable and I'll be right back. Tony, will you help me, please?"

The look Selena gave him as she reluctantly moved to the chair wasn't desperate enough to be labeled "panic," but it was close. He gave her a reassuring smile, then followed Anna into the kitchen. His mother had taken a tray from the pantry and was piling it with sticky buns, still warm from the oven, a bowl of fruit salad, and dishes. She didn't speak until she began taking coffee cups and juice glasses from the cabinet. "She's a lovely girl."

"Yes, she is."

"But she's . . ."

He waited, but when she didn't go on, he agreed. "Yes, she is."

"You know I'm not prejudiced, Tony. I believe everyone should be judged on who they are and nothing else—

except maybe your father's hateful old grandmother. Who she was, was a bigot, pure and simple. But I'm not."

He took a carton of orange juice from the refrigerator while she poured coffee into a thermal carafe. After snitching a chunk of cantaloupe from the salad bowl, he ate it, then licked the juice from his fingers. "You always told us the color of a person's skin doesn't matter."

"Yes, I did, and I meant it." Finally she looked at him. "But I was talking about friends, not girlfriends. Not potential wives. I don't want any half-black grandbabies, Tony."

"Just like Nonna Ceola didn't want any southern Italian blood flowing through her great-grandbabies. But when she got that, she loved them anyway." Not that he and Selena were anywhere near thinking about kids. Hell, she wasn't even thinking about staying in Tulsa.

"I'm sure she's a nice girl, but—"

"She's a very nice woman. She's smart and serious and talented and generous. If you quit worrying about her race and went out there and talked to her, you would probably like her a lot."

Anna stopped working to gaze out the window at Selena, sitting primly at the little table, listening to Joe talk. Her legs were crossed, her hands folded in her lap. She looked comfortable, but Tony could see the occasional twitch of a muscle in her jaw, the tightening, then easing, of her fingers against one another, and the unnaturally straight way she held herself.

He wasn't sure when his mother had shifted her gaze from Selena to him—long enough to see things he should probably be keeping to himself. "*You* like her a lot."

"Yes, I do." More than was smart under the circumstances.

"Hmm" was all she said. It could mean anything from

Then I'll like her, too to *I'll pray to the Virgin for that to change.* "Bring the drinks, would you? If you're going to get the yard done before lunch, you need to get started."

He held the door for her, then went back to get the juice and coffee. Outside he set them on a nearby redwood table, topped off his parents' coffee and poured juice for Selena and himself, then pulled up a chair in front of the plate his mother had loaded for him.

They ate in silence for a time, broken only by the twins' chatter twenty feet away, until Joe set his coffee down, focused his gaze on Selena, and asked, "Are these your only children?"

"Yes, they are," she lied easily.

Joe looked from Kara and Sara to her, then to Tony. "They take after your husband. Not that that's a bad thing for the boy, but it's a shame the girl doesn't look like you. You're very pretty, you know."

She smiled graciously. "Thank you."

"You're new to the neighborhood, aren't you?" he asked again. "Anna and I just moved in recently ourselves, and we're never gonna move again, are we? We're gonna grow old and die right here. This is *home.*"

Anna made a choked sound before mumbling some excuse and rushing into the house. Tony stared at what was left of the roll on his plate, his fingers clenching the fork as if it were fused to his palm. He should stay there and watch his father, or go inside and check on his mother, but he couldn't let go of the fork, couldn't give his brain the command to come up with something rational to say—as if Joe would know the difference.

Then he felt a warm touch on his arm. He shook his head to clear the buzzing, as Selena stood up. "Why don't you two chat? I'll see if Anna needs any help inside."

Checking on Anna was his responsibility, but like a coward, he was more than happy to leave it to her. He would be happiest if he could just walk away and leave everything to someone else—if he could live in some fantasy world, like Joe, where everything was the way it should be, where his father was healthy and normal, where his mother's life was going exactly the way it was supposed to.

The door had just closed behind Selena when his father broke the silence. "So . . . Anna tells me you're new to the neighborhood. You and your wife will like it here. We sure do. Do you have any kids?"

The house was relatively quiet and smelled of citrus and polish and something fabulously aromatic cooking in the kitchen. Selena hesitated, wondering what had possessed her to come inside. Anna Ceola was obviously upset, and with very good reason. What did Selena know about calming distraught mothers? She wasn't even supposed to *be* there. If William found out . . .

When William found out, he would be furious. And she couldn't care less.

A faint sniffle came from the far end of the house, drawing her down a long hallway lined with family photographs. She wished for time to study each one, to locate Tony in them, but that was easier said than done. Each Ceola brother looked like the others, particularly in their younger days. The only one she could be sure was him was a photograph in which he stood with his father, both in their police-department uniforms. They were flanked by two more Ceolas also in uniform—his uncles, she assumed. Tony looked so young, no more than twenty-two, and Joe looked so vital.

"That was when he graduated from the academy." Still sniffling, Anna appeared in the next doorway, a stack of neatly folded towels in her arms. "Joe was so proud of him. He never pressured any of the boys to become cops, but he was thrilled that Tony chose to."

"Were you thrilled?"

"I would have been happier if he'd gotten a job bagging groceries at Albertson's. It can be bad enough having a husband on the job. You don't want your child doing it, too."

Together they looked at the photograph, as if looking negated the need for conversation, but finally Selena took a step back. "I . . . I'm sorry about your husband."

Anna smoothed a work-roughened hand over the top towel and exhaled heavily. "He always said that about the house—this is home, we're never going to move again, we're going to grow old and die here. Now there are days when he doesn't know where he is. He can't go out by himself anymore because he forgets which house is ours." Her voice grew tighter, thick with tears. "Our five-year-old grandchildren have to watch him the way they watch their little brother, and tattle on him when he does something he's not supposed to. I hate this. I *hate* it!"

"I'm sorry." Such inadequate words, but they were the best Selena could offer.

"We all are." Then, in an obvious effort to lighten the mood, Anna asked, "How did you and Tony meet?"

"We're neighbors."

"And you've been dating . . . ?"

Did two dinners and some incredible sex constitute dating? Selena wondered. Probably not to a mother. "We've been out a few times," she hedged.

" 'A few times,' and he's bringing you home to meet his parents." Anna's gaze slid from her to the photographs again, this time to wedding portraits of her two oldest sons. Was she imagining how a photo of Tony and Selena would fit in there with his brothers and their fair-skinned brides? Her sigh suggested so.

"Don't worry, Mrs. Ceola. We're *just* dating. There's still time for Tony to find a nice Italian Catholic girl who will fit in as if she were made for this family."

For a moment Anna looked stricken, as if she'd just realized that not only was Selena a different race, but quite possibly a different faith. Though a blush tinged her cheeks, it couldn't keep the hopefulness from her voice. "Are *you* Catholic?"

Selena shrugged. Luisa and Rodrigo had shepherded their brood to mass every Sunday, but she felt no connection to the church. Once, too young to know better, she'd made the mistake of asking the priest to intercede with Rodrigo for her. She wasn't sure what he'd said to Rodrigo, but she'd gotten the worst beating of her life as a result, and when she'd gone to mass the following Sunday with two black eyes and a broken arm—only the most visible of her injuries—the priest had refused to even look at her.

"I'm only in town temporarily. Tony knows that. When my business is finished here, I'm going home to Florida." It surprised her how difficult it was to be so dismissive, to keep her voice in a neutral, polite range. "I probably won't ever come back."

She expected the information to relieve Anna's concerns, but the woman seemed even more anxious. She took Selena's hand in her own, clasping it tightly. Her hands were warm, soft, gentle in their grip. Mother's hands, skilled at comforting, patting, soothing. "My son is a good man, Selena. He's honorable and decent and kind and fair and loyal and loving. Please . . . don't break his heart."

Don't break his heart. As if she could, she thought, even as regret surged through her. It was his *life* that was in danger. William was a powerful man who usually got what he wanted, and what he wanted was Tony dead. If she didn't kill him, someone else would.

Unless she stopped them.

William pulled his car behind the cover of a van parked two houses away from the Ceola house and tugged the ball cap lower over his forehead. A blue sedan was parked in the driveway, with Detective Ceola's Corvette behind it. The scene in the front yard was about as homey as could be—Anna on her knees weeding the flower bed, Joe sitting on the porch steps with the newspaper open but unread, and a pair of twins racing around the yard with more energy than any ten kids needed. Detective Ceola stood on the top step of a ladder in the driveway, cleaning the gutter. Just another middle-class Saturday.

Tension he'd hardly been aware of eased from his muscles. He'd known Selena wouldn't come. After all, he'd told her not to, hadn't he? And she virtually always did what she was told. That meant she was back on Princeton Court, searching the detective's house, just as he had instructed her.

Satisfied that there was no reason to spy from afar, he was reaching to turn the key when the Ceolas' front door opened and a slender figure stepped out, balancing an armful of water bottles. Selena came down the steps, handing out the drinks, carrying the last two bottles to the ladder in the driveway. Detective Ceola pulled an eighteen-inch cedar from the gutter and dangled it in front of her, making her laugh as she stretched onto her toes to hand him a bottle of water.

"Goddammit to hell!" He slammed one fist against the steering wheel hard enough to make it throb. "I warned her—I *ordered* her—'Yes, Uncle,' " he mimicked furiously. " 'All right, Uncle. Whatever you say.' " And then she'd hung up the phone and done exactly what he'd ordered her not to. She'd *lied* to him. The ungrateful, deceitful, little—

Abruptly he became aware of a man who was pushing a mower back and forth across his yard watching him. Gritting his teeth, he drew a calming breath. Though her betrayal was no great surprise, he didn't want to believe it. Perhaps Detective Ceola hadn't been so easily put off. Perhaps he had refused to take no for an answer. Wasn't his doggedness one of his greatest failings?

He would give her the benefit of the doubt—*once*, William decided as he swung the car into a tight U-turn. He would assume that Ceola had left her with no choice but to accompany him. But the next doubt, the next betrayal . . .

Damn her to hell, the next time he would have no choice but to make certain it was the last.

"What are your plans for today?"

Damon stretched his arms above his head before glancing at the bedside clock. It was noon, and he'd just spent a nice two hours in bed with Lucia. Much as she enjoyed sex, though, she was also eager to move on to whatever came next. She wasn't the type to laze around until the mood hit to do it again. Now she wanted lunch. Next she would want to go somewhere, do something.

"I don't have any until tonight. Then I have to work."

She pouted prettily as she ran her fingers through her

thick black hair and matched her voice to her expression. "You always have to work."

" 'Always'? I got called in once."

"And you can't go out tonight. And you had to work Thursday night."

Had to get his ass kicked Thursday night, he silently corrected her, and by a girl, no less. It hadn't been one of his finer moments.

She turned onto her side to face him, leaning on one elbow. The position pushed her breasts together into full, rounded mounds, the sheet barely covering her nipples. If she took one good breath, it would slide away, and the question of what they would do next would be answered.

When his gaze returned to her face, she was smiling smugly. "Tell me what kind of work you do, and I'll let you see them," she said in a tempting, sultry voice.

He turned onto his back and gazed at the ceiling, adopting a careless attitude even though the sheet was tenting over his swelling cock. "I've seen 'em before. I'll see 'em again."

"Don't be so sure of that." He could tell without looking that she was pouting again, her lower lip stuck out, her eyes cast down. She was quite likely the sexiest woman he'd ever known—innocent and wicked, adorable and wanton, nasty and lusty and sweet. She was the only woman who'd tempted him in a long time. Not to change—he was too old for that. But to stick around. To try a real relationship. To put his plans to take over William's business on the back burner for a while . . . just long enough to get Lucia out of his system. However long that might take.

She sat up and stretched, arching her back to show her breasts at their fullest, then slipped into a silk robe that barely covered her ass and went to sit in front of the old-fashioned dressing table against the wall. "I wonder sometimes if you even have a job," she remarked as she picked up the brush there.

"You think I get by on good looks alone?" He sat up, too, stuffing the pillows behind his back so he could watch her.

"I wonder if maybe you aren't married. If that's why you're so secretive."

"Nope, no wife." He had no plans to marry. A wife was just excess baggage, and once he'd taken over the business, he would have no time or space for baggage. Besides, what man wanted to have sex with the same woman year after year? How boring would that be?

Not that he'd even thought about boredom with Lucia.

She stopped brushing her hair and met his gaze in the mirror. "Then why all the secrets?"

"I have no secrets."

"Except where you work. What you do. Where you live." She looked so serious—Lucia, who was never serious about anything except the quality and quantity of her own pleasure.

Rising from the bed, he went to stand behind her. "I work for a businessman here in town. I do whatever he tells me to. Run errands. Make phone calls." *Take care of a few dope dealers.* "I keep odd hours because he keeps odd hours. When you have the kind of money he has, you can do that. And I live . . ." He picked up a tube of fuck-me-red lipstick from the marble tabletop, leaned forward, and scrawled his address across the mirror. It didn't matter if she knew. If necessary, he could pack up and move out in under an hour, and leave nothing behind that anyone could use to find him again.

Something flashed in her eyes—relief? gratitude?—then she took the tube from him and applied its rich color to her lips, making a kissy face at the mirror, before offering him a catlike smile. "Sounds like a girlie job."

"Say what you want. I'm secure in my manhood." For emphasis he rubbed every inch of his hard-on against her. When her eyes went hazy and the tip of her tongue appeared between her lips, he backed off and returned to the bed. "What are *your* plans for today?"

After making an obscene gesture in his direction, she replied, "My mother always fixes a big lunch on Saturday for anyone who wants to drop by."

Though her manner was casual, the look in her eyes was anything but. He ignored it, though, while he considered whether there was anything to be gained by meeting Mom and Dad. For one thing, brother Tony would be there. It would be an easy introduction, one that wouldn't rouse any suspicion in the good detective. He could charm the man as easily as he'd charmed Lucia, could become his newest best buddy and have easy access if Selena failed to carry out her assignment. William would be impressed with how easily and efficiently Damon handled it for him.

But on the down side, Selena would likely be there, as well. And William would be watching. It wasn't yet time to let William know that he'd hooked up with Detective Ceola's baby sister.

After his phone conversation with Selena that morning, the old man had acted so damn confident that she would do exactly what he said. When he had suddenly dismissed Damon for the rest of the day without explanation, though, Damon had known the truth: William wanted to check up on her. Damon never would have believed her capable of it, but maybe this time the old man had pushed her too far. Hadn't he finally pushed Damon too far?

"I take it by your silence that you're not interested in dining at Chez Ceola."

"Sorry, babe," he said without a hint of remorse.

"Okay, scratch lunch at Mom's." Her tone was so accepting that he knew she hadn't thought for a moment he would agree. "How about lunch at Abuelo's, then a movie? I'll even let you choose some mucho-macho bang-bang-shoot-'em-up."

If staying in bed wasn't in the running, a dark movie theater on a hot afternoon seemed the best alternative. "Sounds good. Just let me jump in the shower."

The phone call James Tranh had been waiting three days for—and hoping wouldn't come—came Saturday evening as he walked into the restaurant. Weekends meant busy nights, with a crowd waiting in the lobby for tables to come available. He hadn't even had the chance to say hello to his sister, who was too busy juggling reservations and walk-ins to do more than nod when he passed.

Once again caller ID displayed a pay-phone number. He let it go to voice mail, but knew from the knot in his gut that instead of leaving a message, the bastard would call right back, and keep calling until James answered.

Sure enough, the phone began ringing again as he cut through the kitchen. Most of his staff was Vietnamese, and that was the language they spoke while working. Between the sounds and the aromas of the traditional dishes, he could almost believe he was home again. And he was. Home these days—for the rest of his days—was the restaurant and Tulsa and his family, and damned if he was going to let anyone take that away from him.

Once he was in his office with the door closed, he answered the cell phone. For a moment, there was annoyed silence, then the voice. "You need to do something about this habit of not answering your phone, Mr. Tranh. It's very rude."

"I was busy. This was the first chance I got."

"Likely story."

"Saturday night is our busiest night," James retorted. "If you've ever been here, you would know."

"I've been to your restaurant a number of times," the man said. "Enough to know that Saturday nights are indeed busy. Enough to know, as well, that your sister shoulders most of the restaurant's responsibilities."

The last time they'd talked, the guy had made James sweat. This time a chill spread down his spine. This man who called himself *the solution* to James's problems might be another dealer wanting to go into business together . . . or could just as easily be the vigilante.

"I want to meet with you tonight."

"I just told you, Saturday night's our busiest—"

"You can come to me, or I can come to the restaurant . . . unless you prefer we meet at your house after the restaurant closes tonight. That might prove upsetting to Nancy and the children, but it's your choice."

"I really can't—"

"Afford to piss me off." Just like the last time the guy had slipped into vulgarity, his voice remained cool and composed as he said again, "It's your choice, James."

"Okay." He dragged his fingers through his hair. "Where do you want to meet?" No way was he inviting the bastard into his house, and he didn't want him at the restaurant, either. He did his best to keep his two businesses as separate as possible. The restaurant provided basic support to his family, his sister, and their grandmother. Cops would bend over backward to make the case that one was part of the other, so they could seize everything in an asset hearing, and what would happen to his family then?

"There's a warehouse downtown just off 244 and Denver with a mural of a horse painted on the side. You can't miss it. Be there in two hours—alone. And Mr. Tranh? Don't try to warn your family. One of my men is watching your house. He knows Nancy's routine. If she does anything out of the ordinary, he'll have no choice but to take action."

The line went dead, leaving only the heavy rush of James's own breath echoing in his ears. Slowly he set the phone down, unlocked the bottom desk drawer, and removed the Glock from underneath the folders at the back. He added an extra clip, hesitated, then picked up the phone again and dialed 911.

His fingertip hovered over the SEND button. Calling the police just might be the stupidest move he'd ever made. Why didn't he just walk into 600 Civic Center with his hands in the air and say, "Arrest me, I'm a drug dealer"? The result would be the same—the end of life as he knew it.

But not calling the police could be the end of life, period. Regardless of who the bastard was or what his goal was, one thing didn't change—he'd threatened James's family. Nobody did that and walked away.

Resolutely he pressed the SEND button, listened to it ring, heard the operator pick up, then swallowed hard. "I need—I need to talk to one of the detectives working those drug murders. I think the vigilante's planning to kill me."

12

Usually when Tony got called in on his time off, he wasn't doing anything important—watching television, reading, already working, or sleeping. This time it didn't *look* as if he were doing anything important—sitting on the back steps scratching Mutt and watching Selena grill lobster tails and shrimp—but it was something he would really rather keep doing.

Regretfully, he went inside to grab the phone that hung next to the kitchen door. It was Simmons at the other end. "Today's our lucky day, Chee. You ever hear of James Tranh? Owns a restaurant out by Woodland Hills that serves pretty good food—I've been there a few times—and also represents the Vietnamese in our local drug network?"

"The name sounds familiar," Tony replied, though it had been a long time since he'd worked Narcotics. "What about him? He dead?"

"Not yet, and he's hoping to stay that way. He got a call he thinks is the vigilante. Guy calls him from a pay phone, tells him he's the solution to his problems, throws in a threat or two against Tranh's family, and sets up a meet for tonight. Tells him to come alone to an empty warehouse downtown. Tranh likes being among the living, so he calls us." Simmons snorted. "Damn drug dealers. Any other time, they'd shoot us in the back without blinking an eye, but someone tries to shoot *them*, and we're the first people they call."

"You talk to the guy?"

"Yep. Just got off."

"And he sounds legit?" It didn't escape Tony's notice that the vigilante might find a certain satisfaction in setting up and taking out the detectives trying to stop him in the same way he'd killed eight of his ten victims. Tony loved his job, but damned if he wanted to die for it.

"What he sounds is scared. My gut says yeah, he's legit. He wants to meet with you and me at that pool hall over on Memorial—you know the one. Says he can't go to the station. The guy says he's watching Tranh's family. He's afraid they might be watching him, too."

"You said the guy called from a pay phone. Did you get the number for CSU?"

"Yeah. It's at River Parks. Someone's on their way over now to print it. I also called the ADA to get an okay to wire Tranh if we need to."

"Jeez, Frankie, you really can do your job. And here you've hidden it so well all this time."

"Fuck you, Chee. Kiss your little island girl and haul your ass out here, and come loaded for bear."

"I'm on my way."

After hanging up, he went outside to the grill, sliding his arms around Selena's waist from behind. "I have to go."

"Your vigilante strike again?"

"Not yet, but he might. I'll be back as soon as I can."

She smiled dryly. "Mutt and I will try to leave some dinner for you."

He nuzzled her neck before releasing her and going inside. After changing into jeans and running shoes, he grabbed his badge and weapon and headed for the driveway. There he transferred his Second Chance bulletproof vest and raid jacket, along with his handheld radio and shotgun, from the Impala's trunk to the 'Vette. He'd rather take the Impala, but if the vigilante did have someone watching Tranh, it would be better not to advertise police presence with a vehicle that was clearly an unmarked cop car.

Simmons was just getting out of his car when Tony pulled up and parked in front of the pool hall. The place didn't fit the smoky, dingy hole-in-the-basement image summoned by the name. It was spacious, well-lit, and sold seven-buck drinks to a white-collar clientele. James Tranh fit right in, except for the fact that he was nervous as hell. He had a table to himself in the corner farthest from the door, but he was far more interested in what was going on around him than what was on the table.

They approached the table as if they were meeting a buddy for drinks and a few games. Tony took a cue from the rack nearby. "James? I'm Detective Ceola and this is Detective Simmons. How about a game while we talk?"

"Are you kidding? I don't play pool."

"Lucky for you, neither does he," Simmons said with a nod in Tony's direction.

Tony gave him a "screw you" look. He was better at pool than poker, which wasn't saying much. "I found better ways to spend my formative years," he said evenly as he racked the balls, then stepped back and gestured for Tranh to break.

Simmons walked around the table to stand near the guy. "Because we don't want to draw attention by taking notes, I have a tape recorder in my pocket. Stick close to me so it can pick you up over the noise."

Tranh's gaze shifted anxiously from Simmons to his shirt pocket to Tony, then around the room. "I'm not sure I should be talking to you at all."

"Hey, *you* called us," Simmons replied. "We didn't come

looking for you. You want our help, you talk to us. You don't want it, we'll be happy to go back to what we were doing."

Still looking uneasy, Tranh bent over the table. His break was lousy enough to make Tony look competent in comparison. "I want my family safe. If anything happens to them . . ."

"We'll keep them safe," Tony said. "What makes you think this guy is the vigilante?"

"He called out of the blue—said he was the solution to my problems. I told him I don't have any problems, but he called again. Said he wanted to meet and discuss ways we could help each other. I'm not interested in a partner, and I'm damn sure not interested in meeting some stranger in an empty warehouse late on a Saturday night, not with some nutcase out there killing people."

Tony moved around the table to sink a ball, then studied the balls remaining. "Did you tell him you weren't interested?"

"No. He brought my family into it. He's been coming to the restaurant, he knows where I live, he's having my wife and kids watched. He threatened them."

"Exactly what did he say?"

Impatiently Tranh repeated the conversation in detail while Tony pretended to concentrate on the game. Just his luck, he was playing better than he ever had when there was money or pride riding on the outcome.

"Okay. First, we're gonna get some undercovers to check out your neighborhood. Does your wife have a cell phone?" Tony waited for Tranh's nod, then searched his pockets for paper. The best he could come up with was a business card from his wallet. He snagged a pen from a passing waitress, then handed both across the table. "Write down her name, cell number, and address, and make, model, and color of her car. License number, too, if you know it. Another detective will call her and tell her to take the kids and leave. The undercovers will follow her, and if anyone else is following her, they'll pick him up."

"What if they lose her in traffic?"

"They won't. They'll be on the phone with her the whole time, telling her exactly where to go."

When Tranh finished writing the information on the card, he offered it to Tony, who nodded to Frank. He took it, pulled out his cell phone, and stepped away a few feet to make the call.

"This bastard said that if she does anything out of the ordinary, he'll have no choice but to take action. Leaving the house with the kids this late on a Saturday night is damn sure out of the ordinary. What if—"

Tony interrupted. " 'What if' nothing. Look, the guy is supposedly watching your house. That means he's got to be close, and unless you just got a new neighbor, he's got to be outside, either sitting in a parked car, driving back and forth, or walking up and down the street. For the house to be visible to him, he's going to be visible to us. He's not going to get a chance to do anything but go to jail. Your wife and kids will be safe. I promise."

For several moments, Tranh looked conflicted, as if he knew better than to take the word of a cop, but the truth was, he had no choice. If the man who'd called him *was* the vigilante, trusting the cops was the only thing that would save his life.

Finally he nodded. "What about the meeting? Will you have cops there, too?"

"You're not going."

The panic came back. "But—"

"We'll already have your family in custody. There's no way we're gonna send you into what is very likely an ambush."

"You could go in now, before he gets there, then arrest him when he shows."

"It's not like TV," Tony said patiently. "If he wants you there at ten o'clock, he's either already there or has somebody there. He's not careless, not with ten murders to his credit. He's not going to walk in blind."

"So he just walks away? What's to stop him from going after my family tomorrow or the next day? They can't *live* in police custody! I can't count on cops always being around until this guy's caught! You just said yourself, he's killed *ten* people!"

"We'll take care of you." Also unlike TV, police protection for a private citizen wasn't easy to pull off, particularly when the department had suffered so many years of budget cuts. But Tony could pull some strings for the family of an informant willing to set himself up as a target. He could go to the chief, if that was what it took. Being his godson had to be good for something besides a hard time in the Detective Division.

Simmons came back to the pool table. "We've got cars on their way to the Tranh house, Watson's already on the phone with Mrs. Tranh, and there are cars headed downtown to check out the warehouse. That leaves us to set down somewhere with Mr. Tranh."

"Why don't you do that? I'm going downtown." On the way he could call Henry and bring him up-to-date on what was happening.

"Why don't we turn him over to Uniform Division East and I'll go with you."

"You take care of that, then meet me at the warehouse." Tony didn't have an address for the place, but like the caller had said, you couldn't miss it. Three stories tall, brick, empty for longer than he could remember, it was just waiting for a buyer to come along and demolish it. In the meantime, some budding artist had painted a twenty-by-forty-foot mural on one side, of a horse running wild on the prairie. It wasn't a neon sign with an arrow saying *This is it,* but it was close.

Tony sank the last ball, then returned the cue to the rack. "Which vehicle out there is yours?"

"The silver van," Tranh replied. "Parked next to a lamppost."

"Go out, get in it, and drive to the police station on East Eleventh between Garnett and Mingo. Simmons will be right behind you in a red Honda. I'll watch until you're gone." If anyone in the pool hall or the parking lot showed any interest in Tranh's leaving, Tony could check it out, though instinct told him there wouldn't be anyone watching. The threat against his family was enough to control him, and the vigilante knew it.

As Tranh walked away, Simmons scowled. "Don't go get yourself killed before I get downtown."

Tony grinned. "Aw, Frankie, I didn't know you cared."

"Damn right I care. Something happens to you, they're gonna pair me up with Darnell Garry and those damn pine-tree air fresheners of his." He gave a doleful shake of his head. "I freakin' *hate* the smell of pine."

The air in the warehouse was stifling, despite the fact that every one of the forty-eight windows was broken out. Damon sat on his motorcycle in the dark of the northwest corner, a scoped Remington 700 rifle balanced across his knees. He'd been there since seven o'clock—an hour before William had made the call to Tranh—and he felt it in the sweat that dampened his skin and the ache in his butt from sitting so long. He didn't get up and walk around to stretch, though. He figured Tranh for the wary sort who would hope to gain some kind of advantage by showing up early.

Hey, if he wanted to die at nine o'clock instead of ten, it was no skin off Damon's nose.

On the north edge of downtown, the area was pretty quiet, except for the interstate a few hundred yards away. For a while he'd counted cars passing on the street to the west, but they'd come so few and far between that he kept losing count. Then he'd amused himself by thinking about Lucia. He'd left her naked except for that little silk robe again, sitting in the middle of the bed with one of those pouts she wore so well. She'd made him promise to come back when he got off work, and he'd said he would, without really intending to. After three hours or so in the warehouse, he was going to need a cold shower, a stiff drink, and a good night's sleep. But when he got a hard-on just thinking about her in that little robe, he thought maybe he would keep his promise.

He watched out the nearest window as a car drove by, then blew out his breath. He would give a lot for a bottle of cold water, a candy bar, or even a pack of gum, but he never ate or drank on a job. William had ridden him for years about that. Everybody brings something to a crime scene, and everybody takes something away, he said every so often, as if Damon needed a reminder. *Yeah, I've seen* C.S.I., *too,* he'd wanted to snap back.

But if he overlooked the sanctimonious arrogance in William's delivery, it was a good reminder. Everyone *did* pick up and leave behind microscopic spores and shit. Except him. He couldn't help taking some stuff with him—dirt, gravel, blood, brain matter—but he was as sure as a man could be that he didn't leave anything behind. No fibers—

leather didn't shed like other fabrics. No hairs, not with his motorcycle helmet fitting so snugly. No chewing gum. No wrappers or fingerprints. No brass unless he wanted to screw with the cops. Nothing but the *Repent* cards.

He was good, and he was careful. That was why he hadn't been caught.

Another car drove past on Denver, followed within a minute by one more. Both turned onto the narrow street that ran along the front of the warehouse. Tranh coming early and hoping to sneak in a pal? Damon didn't mind that, either. He could kill two as easily as one.

As the sound of another car approached, he pressed the button to illuminate the face of his watch. Another hour.

He'd just snuffed out the faint glow when a thud floated through the front windows. A car door closing. It was followed by another. The little bastard *had* brought a friend.

Damon shifted on the seat, then hefted the rifle. It was a good little weapon, but if he had to ditch it, it wouldn't be of any use to the cops. The serial number was long gone, and there wasn't so much as a single ridge of a fingerprint anywhere on it. He'd never touched either the gun or the ammo without gloves.

He imagined he heard the murmur of voices out front, but couldn't be sure it wasn't in his head. In the cavernous space, with so much silence all around, small noises seemed magnified and nonexistent noises seemed real. Then came a different kind of thud that was all too real—a foot tripping over one of the loose bricks scattered outside.

It was time to get this show on the road. The rifle was loaded, the *Repent* cards were in his pocket, and the Ducati was ready to prove what a fine Italian machine was capable of. Dressed all in black—leather pants, jacket, gloves, and helmet with a dark-tinted full-face shield—he didn't even have to worry about any witnesses outside. Any description they could provide the cops would be worse than useless.

From nearby came the scrape of boot on concrete. Someone was sneaking around the back of the building. At the same time, the front door creaked, then opened slowly. In the glow from the street lamp, he could make out a bulky figure wearing a flak jacket and helmet and carrying a big-ass gun. His senses went on high alert. These fuckers weren't Tranh and a couple of his trusted associates—they were goddamn cops. The fucking gook had ratted them out to the cops, who thought they had him trapped. They were in for one hell of a surprise.

He waited until four of them had slipped inside, then started the Ducati with a mighty roar. By the time the startled cops directed a flashlight his way, he was already halfway across the warehouse, aiming for the door, not caring whether he took out a cop or two, as well.

The cops inside scattered like chickens. The ones outside dived out of the way, too—harder for them, since they were standing on high concrete steps. The Ducati soared over the steps, hit the ground with a hard bounce, then went into a skid as Damon maneuvered a tight turn onto Denver. Within six seconds, the speedometer had hit a hundred ten miles an hour and was still climbing, leaving a bunch of pissed-off, incompetent fuckers scrambling behind him.

Bent low over the bike, he gave a rebel yell that went unheard over the powerful growl of the engine. He was not only good, he was the goddamn best!

Checking the rearview mirror, he saw cops scrambling all around the warehouse door, like ants that didn't know what hit them. He was laughing, feeling that exuberant rush that was better than sex.

Then the bullet hit him.

• • •

The ringing of the cell phone was an unpleasant interruption to Puccini's *La Bohème*. With Antonio Pappano conducting the Philharmonia Orchestra, it was one of William's favorites. Annoyed, he muted the sound, then reached for the phone and answered with a cold "Hello."

"Uh, Mr. Davis, this is, uh, Potter. I know we're not supposed to bother you, but, uh—"

William broke in impatiently. "Please do try to complete one sentence without saying 'uh.' Now what do you want?"

"Well, uh—sorry. Mr. Long's not answering his phone, but he said I should let him know immediately if the Tranh woman left the house, and she did."

Despite the silence, the lights on the stereo continued to flash, soaring when the music did, drifting back down on cue. William was missing his favorite part, but sometimes, he thought philosophically, business had to take precedence over everything—even Puccini.

A glance at his wristwatch showed that it was a few minutes after nine. Where could Nancy Tranh be going? To the grocery store, perhaps; even experienced mothers ran out of diapers and formula at inconvenient times. Or she could be taking the children to visit their father and aunt at the restaurant—in itself not unusual, though the timing was. She liked having her children in bed on schedule.

Or her husband might be trying to fuck with him. William had warned him of the consequences, but perhaps Mr. Tranh hadn't taken him seriously.

"Mr. Davis?" Potter sounded antsy, and why shouldn't he? Damon was the only one he ever dealt with. Having to report to the real boss was far outside his comfort zone. "What do you want me to do?"

"Where are you now?"

"We just turned off Yale onto Fifty-first. We're heading east."

East to Memorial, then south—that was the route to the restaurant. It could be perfectly innocent. "Continue to follow—"

"Holy shit!" There was a thud as Mr. Potter apparently dropped the phone, followed by distant curses and the squeal of brakes. Wonderful. The incompetent fool must have been paying too much attention to his nerves and not enough to traffic.

After a moment of rattling and bumping, Potter shrieked into the phone. "It's the cops, Mr. Davis, they're everywhere! What do I do?"

In the background came several commanding voices. "Put your hands on the steering wheel! Get your hands where we can see them!"

Heaving an exasperated sigh, William used his free hand to rub the tension between his eyes. "I suggest you do as they say, Mr. Potter. Don't say a word. I'll handle everything."

He hung up, used the remote to unmute the stereo, then went to the vault in the north wall. The door was securely locked at all times and no one knew the code but him. Inside were his most valued acquisitions, along with his vanity—records every cop in the country would love to get his hands on. He knew documenting his activities was foolish, but he was also certain no one would ever lay eyes on the records while he lived, and after he was dead . . . was it too much to want recognition for all he'd accomplished?

Ignoring everything else, he pulled an aluminum carrying case from a shelf. He didn't bother to check inside. No one had touched it but him, so everything was exactly as it should be. He didn't tolerate incompetence in himself. He was getting damned tired of accepting it in others.

He didn't pass any of the staff as he left the house and saw only one of his security guards on the way to the garage. He waved, and the fellow snapped to, then gave a hesitant wave in response. Inside the garage, he bypassed the Cadillac he normally drove for the seldom-used Mercedes, backed out, then headed for the back gate.

This wasn't the way he'd intended to spend his Saturday evening. He paid people very well to handle whatever problems arose, not to dump them in his lap, and he resented that, at least with Mr. Potter, he wasn't getting his money's worth.

But that was all right. He would take care of Mr. Potter. The man wouldn't disappoint anyone ever again.

Crouched in the bushes outside the gate, Selena watched as the Mercedes drove through. She had been able to keep her morning conversation with William out of her mind most of the day, but once Tony had left her to go to work, it was all she could think of. Too restless to wait with nothing to do, she'd decided it was as good a time as any to snoop around again. Now she debated returning to her car and following William, but since the lemon-yellow T-Bird was the very definition of conspicuous, she opted for sticking to her plan.

She had come prepared to scale the iron fence again, but when the gods offered small favors, she was happy to accept. She slipped through the gate as it swung shut, then set off for the garage at an easy trot. The lush grass muffled her footsteps, and the dark clouds scudding across the sky offered some protection from the nearly full moon. A storm was moving in, hopefully one of those full-blown thunderstorms Oklahoma was known for. With William gone, a little lightning and rain would likely keep his security guards safe and dry in the guard shack.

The wind quickened as she reached the protective cover of the garage, bringing with it the unpleasant odors from the refinery across the river. How William must hate having his precious air tainted. How it must annoy him that even he wasn't powerful enough to go up against and defeat the oil company.

She crept to the front of the garage, then darted into the shadows of a row of crepe myrtles, mercilessly pruned to form a hedge. The first raindrops fell as lightning split the sky directly overhead. The air sizzled with the electric charge, while the brilliance momentarily robbed her of her night vision. She rubbed her eyes, drew a breath, then dashed across the open lawn surrounding the pool. As another bolt of lightning flashed, she leaped the low hedge of azaleas that edged the patio, then ducked against the side of the house, out of sight of all windows.

There were four pairs of French doors across the back of the house, with twice that many floor-to-ceiling windows. A second-floor balcony shaded part of the patio, with its overhanging roof providing cover for the same number of windows and doors. On the third floor there were only windows.

Drawing a small collapsible grappling hook from her backpack, she moved to the south end of the house. It took two swings, standing in the rain, to anchor the hook over the solid concrete balustrade, where it caught with a clunk that was satisfyingly solid. No one else could have possibly heard it over the downpour, but she tensed anyway, listening for some hint that she'd been discovered.

When no sign came, she pulled on a pair of gloves, then started up the knotted rope. The climbing wasn't particularly difficult, though the rain stung her face and the wind made the rope sway. She was almost within reach of the balcony when an explosion sounded nearby, sending bright light and showers of sparks into the night sky. A line transformer had blown, she realized, as the lights in the house flickered, then went off.

She shimmied up the last few feet of rope, hauled herself over the railing, then pressed her face to the glass of the first door. The booming thunder vibrated the glass against her skin, and the subsequent lightning allowed her to see into a bedroom done in pastel shades, lovely and feminine, the perfect place for a visiting niece who was like a daughter. The room appeared unoccupied, awaiting a guest who would never come. William was a sociable man, but had too many secrets to be *that* sociable.

Gathering up the grappling hook and rope, she tucked them against the building between glass doors, kicked off her shoes, removed a towel from the backpack, and dried herself as best she could. Wet rubber soles tended to squeak loudly on wood and tile floors, and she didn't intend to leave so much as one drop of rainwater to indicate that she'd been there.

That done, she took out the lock picks from the backpack, knelt on the stone, and went to work. She was far more accomplished at picking pockets than locks, but even for her, this lock wasn't much of a challenge. William's arrogance at work again. He thought no one would get past his twelve-foot fence, electronic gate, armed security guards, and burglar alarm. He was probably right about the alarm. That was why she'd tucked a pistol into the holster clipped to the back of her pants. She didn't particularly want to threaten an elderly couple who had the misfortune to work for the wrong man, but she would do what she had to. That was a lesson life—and William—had taught her quite well.

When the lock *click*ed open, she put away the tools, drew the .40 caliber pistol, took a deep breath, then turned the doorknob.

The house was quiet. There were no flashing lights, no sirens, no electronic voice warning, "Intrusion! Intrusion!" Of course, William wouldn't tolerate such a display. He would opt for a silent alarm, one that increased the odds of catching anyone foolish enough to break in.

Guided by instinct, caution, and flashes of lightning, she stole across the room. Easing the bedroom door open, she saw no sign of movement, heard no thundering rush of security. Five closed doorways greeted her, three in back and two in front, with the massive main staircase in the front middle and the smaller servants' stairs at the rear. A dim yellow glow came from that way, along with a murmur of voices. She took the stairs one cautious step at a time until she was halfway to the kitchen and the voices became clearer. One belonged to a woman—presumably Sonja—and was clear, while the other sounded tinny and was full of static.

"I told you, it's the storm," Sonja yelled, as if shouting could compensate for the fact that the intercom, probably wired into the same battery backup as the alarm, was affected by the weather. "This stupid system goes haywire when the weather's bad. I've been complaining about it for weeks now."

There was a garbled transmission, followed by Sonja's "I can't hear you," then another burst of static. The housekeeper yelled impatiently, "Just stay where you are! I won't have you tracking rain into my house! I'm turning the darn thing off until the storm passes!" Footsteps sounded as she turned away. "Lord have mercy, those men are dumber than dirt, and the boss lets 'em carry guns. It's a wonder they don't shoot each . . ."

The words faded away as the footsteps did. Another gift from the gods, Selena thought, tucking the pistol into her waistband as she double-timed it back upstairs. A quick shine of the penlight she'd brought showed five of the six second-floor rooms were bedrooms, the front one belonging to William. The sixth room was a study, luxuriously furnished and smelling of fine cigars, old wood, and power. She stood for a moment on the marble tile and shone the light around the room. Serpentine marble fireplace. Rich dark paneling with elaborately carved moldings. An antique desk. A Monet print hanging above the fire—

Hardly aware she was moving, she walked closer, stretching onto her toes to study the piece. Good God, it wasn't a print, but was either the real thing or the most accomplished forgery she'd ever seen. He *owned* a Monet. He belittled and dismissed her own artistic interests, while he was greeted by a Monet every time he came into this room. And he'd never even offered to let her see it.

That made her feel more cheated than any of the other dozens of slights he'd given her. Of course he knew how dearly she would love a private showing of a Monet, which was precisely why he hadn't offered. Just as he'd known since they'd met that an invitation to visit him in his home would have meant the world to her. Just as he'd known how high her expectations were when he had invited her to Tulsa two years ago, and then he'd forbidden her access to the house and refused to spend time with her. He derived a sense of power from denying her things that were important to her. Even when she wasn't aware of the extent of his manipulation—who knew what other treasures were in the house?—he still found a perverse pleasure in it.

Pushing away the bitterness, she returned to her survey of the room. There was a display case filled with jade figurines. Bookshelves loaded with old, leather-bound volumes. A Remington bronze. A collection of Native American beadwork. The Monet aside, the value of the art in this one room reached easily into seven figures—and this was but one room in a house of at least ten. She'd known selling drugs could be a very profitable enterprise, but she'd had no idea just *how* profitable. No wonder William was willing to blackmail, threaten, and murder to maintain his foothold in the business.

Not even for ten times what he made would she get into it. She would go back to being hungry, sleeping on the floor, and picking pockets in Jamaica first.

A search of the desk revealed nothing—no locked drawers, nothing to suggest other names William used, nothing of a personal nature at all. There were no file cabinets to rifle through, no drawers elsewhere in the room, but closer inspection revealed a door in the far wall. It had been designed to look like nothing more than another section of paneling; only the small keypad mounted in the chair rail and out of sight behind a carved mahogany table gave it away.

She crouched in front of the pad, where a light glowed red, indicating the lock had a battery backup of its own. If she'd known in advance that she would come up against such a lock, she could have come prepared with equipment to electronically decipher the code and open the door in seconds. She could come back in a few days, armed to make the most of her exploration. But what were the odds of another storm, another transformer blowing, William going out again, to allow her undetected access to the house?

Hoping it wasn't the type of lock that allowed only a few

tries before locking her out, she raised one steady finger to the pad and put in the month, date, and the last two digits of what she knew as William's birth date. Nothing happened. She tried the month and date, the month and year, with the same result. She was about to give up when one final combination came to mind.

She'd never known her exact birth date. It had never been a cause for celebration in Rodrigo's house. She thought she was nine when Rodrigo had sold her, which would make her twenty-eight now, but that could be a year or two off in either direction.

But she'd needed a birth date for the false papers William acquired to bring her to the U.S., so he'd chosen one for her—the date they'd met. It was only logical, he'd said, since it had, indeed, been the day her life began. She typed in the numbers—eleven twenty-seven. Nothing happened. She added the year. Still nothing.

She hadn't realized that she was hoping, however faintly, until the disappointment settled in her stomach. She was a fool to think she might be important enough to him to merit an association with his secret code.

At a loss, she left the study, passed the main stairs, and slipped into William's bedroom. Like the study, it was beautifully furnished, with another Monet above the fireplace and another Remington on a small marble-topped table. She gave the Tiffany glassware little more than a glance, didn't waste even a moment coveting the series of framed sketches, but searched the room quickly, efficiently, futilely.

She was finishing up in the closet, easily the size of two bedrooms in her Princeton Court house, taking in William's familiar scent with every breath, when her gaze fell on an object tucked on the shelf above his dress shirts. Everything else in the closet was precisely placed—shirts grouped by color and fabric, ties by color and pattern, suits by color and weight. But the flat black-and-silver object was crooked, as if it had been placed there hastily, as if it didn't belong.

She wrapped her fingers around it and found that the black was fabric, rather coarse and glued to stiff cardboard. It was a hinged picture frame, she realized as she took it down, opening it to reveal two eight-by-ten photographs framed in silver.

The picture on the left was of a young woman, leaning against a massive white pillar with a house—*this* house— behind her. She was pretty, blonde, wearing an indulgent smile and an outfit that dated some twenty-five or thirty years ago.

The opposite photo showed two men, both wearing Tulsa Police Department uniforms. The man on the left, smiling urbanely and looking every bit as handsome as he was today, was William, and the man on the right—

She blinked, and her stomach clenched. It was Tony, but not—younger than he was now, though the photo must have been at least thirty years old. Not quite as handsome, the smile not quite as charming . . .

Because it wasn't Tony. It was his father.

William and Joe Ceola. Looking for all the world like best buddies.

13

Oblivious to the storm crashing around him, William crouched on a rooftop a few blocks from the correctional center on Denver, his gaze locked on the street below. The officers who had arrested Mr. Potter would transport him to the jail, where he would be booked, fingerprinted, and photographed, then interrogated regarding his interest in James Tranh's family. William was ninety percent sure he could trust Damon and Selena to keep their mouths shut if they ever got caught, but he had no such faith in any of the underlings he employed. That was why he intended to deal with this problem before it became a bigger one.

He had listened to the police scanner he kept for just such purposes and found out which unit was transporting the prisoner. Now all he had to do was wait, and not even for long, because at that moment the police car appeared around the corner a few blocks south, followed by two unmarked cars. He watched through the rifle scope, picking out a fresh-faced patrol officer behind the wheel, an undercover officer beside him, and the harmless-looking Mr. Potter in the backseat. He had a round face, wore glasses, and would be pegged for an accountant or insurance salesman long before *hired gun* ever came to mind.

The traffic light half a block to the north turned red as the car approached. Through the rear window, William sighted on the spot where Mr. Potter's hair was thinnest, then squeezed off a shot.

One perfect shot. That was all it took, and Mr. Potter was a problem no more.

He quickly broke down the rifle, returned it to its case, then headed across the rooftop. It was a five-foot drop to the next building's roof, then a hustle down two flights of rusty stairs, another drop, and into the Mercedes. He slid out of his raincoat, jerked the waterproof hat from his head, and stuffed both in the back floorboard, dried his face and hands with a towel, and dropped that in back, too, then drove calmly out of the alley to the west.

Sirens were wailing by the time he reached the street. If one of the officers on the scene was thinking straight—not likely to be the kid driving the marked unit—the first thing they would do was set up a perimeter, stopping all traffic leaving the area. It wouldn't take them long to figure out where the shot had come from, and to begin a search there, but they wouldn't find anything. The rain was already washing away every sign that he'd been there.

He hadn't gone more than two blocks when a police car pulled across the intersection ahead, lights flashing, and an officer got out. Wearing a yellow slicker over his uniform, he signaled the car ahead of William to stop, bent at the driver's window, and talked for a moment or two before waving him on. His fingers tightening around the wheel, William eased the Mercedes forward, rolled down his window, and greeted the officer with a smile. "It's a sorry evening to be out, isn't it?"

"Yes, sir," the grave-faced man replied. "Can I see your license and registration?"

William handed over his license, but didn't bother to

retrieve the registration. The officer looked at the license, bent down to look at him, then swallowed. "Sorry, sir. I . . ."

"Don't apologize, Officer," William said genially as he returned the license to his wallet. "You're just doing your job. Have a good evening."

Humming softly to himself, he drove away from the intersection. Away from suspicion.

Tony felt like shit.

The damn motorcycle had sounded like a couple of eighteen-wheelers coming through the warehouse door. He'd dived for the ground and landed hard, wrenching his knee and scraping his face on one hell of a rough brick, an instant before a Fugitive Apprehension guy in full body armor landed on top of him and knocked the last bit of air from his lungs. As if that hadn't been enough, the vigilante had gotten away without leaving so much as a tire track behind, and the weather had turned ugly. At times the rain came down so hard that visibility was limited to a few yards, and the lightning was striking too close for comfort.

The only good news was that the Tranhs were safe and the guy following Mrs. Tranh had been taken down.

The bad news was someone had blown off the back of his head at a stoplight two blocks from the jail.

Simmons leaned against the wall and gazed at the patrol unit's shattered back window for a time before finally glancing at Tony. "You ever think about changing jobs?"

"More every day."

"I ain't ever gonna get dry. My shoes are ruined. It's four hours past dinnertime. It's my day off. There's lightning hitting all around, and freakin' tornadoes touching down everywhere. This is *not* a night to be out looking for a killer who's already long gone."

Tony couldn't think of anything to add to that list, so he didn't.

"When can we call it a night?"

Most of the other officers on the scene already had. The M.E.'s investigator had pronounced the man dead, then carted his body off for autopsy. A tow truck was hooking up the patrol car as they watched. The area had been thoroughly searched, but they'd turned up nothing of any value. The Tranhs had been interviewed and come up with nothing new. They might as well call it a night before a twister swept down out of the black sky and carried them away. It would be the perfect ending to a perfectly lousy night's work.

But even on that thought, he didn't move away from the building or the awning that provided little shelter from the rain, and neither did Simmons.

"You have any thoughts on the vigilante you wanna share?" Simmons asked.

"He's not a vigilante."

"You've always believed that. I've always believed you were wrong."

"A vigilante is trying to right a wrong that the justice system can't or won't fix. This guy threatened Tranh's wife and kids. That doesn't fit."

"You think vigilantes are all misguided good guys? That they have morals or ethics about which laws they'll break and which ones they won't?" Simmons made a disgusted sound. "The guy is killing people in cold blood, Chee."

"He's killing drug dealers. That's wrong, but understandable. But killing a woman, a four-year-old, and a baby? No way. Half the people in the city think he ought to get a medal for cleaning up the streets. How quickly would that change if he murdered a baby?"

"So he didn't intend to carry out the threat against the Tranhs. He was just using them as leverage."

"Then why have someone watching them?"

"Shit, I don't know."

The tow-truck driver finished up, climbed in, and drove away, his lights flashing yellow in the rain. Tony watched as he turned at the next corner, then asked, "Does it strike you as odd that the day Dwayne Samuels calls the station out of the blue is also the day someone kills him?"

"Not particularly. The vigilante called Tranh, set up a meet, and planned to kill him that night, but Tranh called us instead. Maybe it was the same with Samuels, only the vigilante got to him before we could."

"Don't you think if Dwayne thought he was the next target, he would have made more of an effort than just one call? Don't you think he would have been anyplace other than the lab if he knew a killer was looking for him?"

Simmons shrugged. "Who knows how these guys think, Chee? Hell, all of 'em have fried half their brain cells and some of 'em have fried all of 'em."

"Not Dwayne. He manufactured the stuff and sold it, but he didn't use it."

"You believe that?"

"He was my informant for three years. Yeah, I believe it."

"So what're you saying?"

"Just . . . I think the timing's odd. Like . . . maybe Dwayne had something to tell us and the vigilante knew it."

"And how could the vigilante know?"

"The call came into the Detective Division," Tony said with a shrug.

For a moment Simmons just stared at him. "Jesus Christ, Chee, do you know what you're saying?"

He knew too damn well. "Look, I don't like it any better than you, but think about it. If the vigilante is just a fed-up citizen, how has he been able to pull off ten damn-near-perfect murders? People aren't that smart about murder. They screw up. They leave clues—but not this guy. How'd he know to pick Javier to give me a false description?"

"Javier was a dirtbag. Everyone knew he ratted people out."

"He was *my* informant. How did the vigilante know that?"

Simmons shrugged uneasily. "Lucky guess."

"How did he know to drop Juan Arias's name with Dwayne? How many average citizens knew that Dwayne's cook did time with Arias down in McAlester?"

"Okay, so maybe he's not a vigilante. That doesn't make him a cop. The bad guys know about snitches, they know who works for who and who's served time with who."

"How would a bad guy know his accomplice had been arrested? How would he know he could take him out here? There were two cars of undercovers right behind the marked unit, and all of us from the warehouse were here within a minute. How did anyone without a badge get out of here?"

Simmons dragged his fingers through his hair, then shook his head. "You're crazy. A cop wouldn't do that."

"Oh, come on. Cops and corruption go hand in hand."

"Not here. Not *our* cops. We know these guys. Some of 'em are assholes, sure, but they're *our* assholes. They wouldn't—they couldn't—"

Tony didn't say anything. Hell, he wanted to agree with him. He wanted to believe they were all honest and moral and upright. But the truth was, given the right motivation, *anyone* was capable of taking another life.

"So you've given up on the idea that it's another drug dealer taking over the market."

"Not necessarily."

He wouldn't have thought Simmons could turn any paler. "Holy shit, Chee, you think one of our fellow cops is not only a multiple murderer but a major drug dealer, as well? Goddamn, son . . . Have you talked to anyone about this?"

"Just you, so far." If things were different, he would have gone to his father for advice, but that wasn't possible. Same with his uncles—investigating cops was the sort of thing that engendered hostility among the ranks. If he was wrong, he didn't want to have dragged Uncle John or Uncle Vince into it. As for Henry . . . sooner or later he would have to talk to him. Having a murdering, drug-dealing cop on his payroll wouldn't reflect well on the chief. He needed to know before it went much further.

"Why me?"

Because he wanted to be sure whomever he confided in couldn't possibly be involved. At the moment, he could narrow that down to only four people—John, Vince, Henry, and Simmons. Frankie won by default.

Tony scowled at him. "What the hell do you mean, why you?"

"Why did you decide to tell me? Why not Garry or Watson or Collins? Hell, why not Lieutenant Nicholson?"

"Because you're a royal pain in the ass, but you're *my* pain in the ass."

Unexpectedly, Simmons grinned and made a kissing gesture. "I love you, too, Chee." Then he went totally serious again. "Maybe the vigilante had a scanner, and that's how he knew his partner got popped."

"Potter got arrested while the vigilante was still at the warehouse. You think he was sitting there in the dark, waiting for Tranh to walk in so he could blow him away, and listening to a scanner?"

"Maybe that wasn't the vigilante. Maybe both him and Potter work for the vigilante."

"Maybe. Probably." The time frame was pretty tight—from the time of the arrest to the time the motorcycle crashed through the doors to the time Potter was killed. It was very likely there had been a third person someplace else, pulling the strings—maybe pulling the trigger. "But a scanner wouldn't have told him to be at that intersection at that time to take out the prisoner. A scanner wouldn't have helped him get out of downtown without being stopped. The perimeter was up in a matter of minutes. They questioned everyone, searched vehicles, and found nothing. Maybe because the guy they were looking for was right there with them, pretending to be looking, too. It makes sense, Frankie."

"It doesn't make any sense," Simmons disagreed. "A cop, for Christ's sake—!"

They fell silent for a time. The rain turned into a torrent again, and the thunder reverberated against the ground. Water streamed along the sidewalk, flowing over and around Tony's shoes, but he was already so wet he couldn't feel it.

Simmons heaved a sigh. "I hope your brothers can make room for me at the lawn service when our asses get fired. Suz'll kill me, and I'll probably never get laid again. Holy shit, Chee, you're gonna be the death of me." Clapping Tony on the back, he moved out of the shelter. "Come on, son.

It's late, I'm tired, and if I don't get dry soon, I'm gonna grow gills. Let's talk about it Monday."

"Yeah, sure." Tony unlocked the 'Vette, grimacing when he squished as he slid inside. He wouldn't object to a warm shower, a cold beer, and a little food—or hell, just skip all that and go straight to bed with Selena.

He slid the key into the ignition, turned it . . . and got nothing. He tried again with the same results, smacked the steering wheel with one hand, then got out. Simmons pulled alongside and stopped, rolling down the passenger window. "The damn thing won't start. Can you give me a ride?"

Simmons gave a shake of his head. "I don't know why you don't sell that piece of junk to your brothers and be done with it. Come on, get in."

"Yeah, yeah," Tony muttered as Simmons made a U-turn on the deserted street. He remained silent until they reached Twenty-first Street, when he abruptly asked, "Drop me off at Henry's, would you?"

Simmons gave him a long look, then made a right turn from the left-turn lane. "You sure you want to do this now?"

"No." Truth was, he didn't want to do it at all. There was no good time to break the kind of suspicions he had. But if the department was facing a problem of that magnitude, Henry deserved to know. Besides, he was a damn good cop himself. Maybe he could help Tony figure out what the hell was going on.

After a few blocks, Simmons said, "I can talk to the chief with you."

Tony glanced at him, little more than a sodden shadow in the driver's seat. Frankie hadn't been kidding earlier when he'd talked about getting fired. Cops stood together.

They didn't turn on their own, not without indisputable proof. This could be a career-ending move. "Let's just keep it my neck on the line for the time being, okay?"

"I don't mind—"

"I know. Thanks, but no."

William knew Joe Ceola, had once been friends with him, and yet had ordered the death of Joe's son.

Selena had thought nothing he did could shock her, but this did. Hands shaking, she returned the picture frame to the shelf, then headed for the guest room and the balcony where she'd left her belongings. She stuffed everything into the backpack except the shoes, gathered it all to her chest, and slipped back inside. With the alarm off, there was no need to make a clandestine escape down the rope.

Moving silently, she went downstairs into the kitchen, through a utility room, and out the back door. The landscape, so impressively manicured, took on an eerie feel in the storm—pitch-dark one moment, the next moment wind-whipped trees looming up in the lightning and leaves and debris littering the grass. Stopping in the shadows where the north wing joined the main house, she shoved her feet into her shoes, then headed to the corner nearest the rear gate.

She'd taken one step around the corner when a flash of headlights broke through the night. Retreating once again, she crouched against the house's foundation, hoping she blended into the shadows, and watched as William's Mercedes drew to a halt on the parking court that fronted the garage. A motorcycle was already parked there, its driver taking shelter in the overhang of the garage roof.

As William got out of the car, engine still running,

headlights on, the man pushed away from the garage and stepped into the rain to meet him. He wasn't tall—under six feet—but muscular, and even though he clutched his right hand to his upper left arm, his movements were controlled, taut, power waiting to be unleashed. If she got close enough, she would see a nasty bruise on his hand; if she let herself, she could remember the feel of his hand across her face.

"I was expecting a quiet Saturday night at home, and instead I had to go out to take care of your Mr. Potter. What the hell went wrong?" William demanded, his voice cutting through the rain.

"You tell me," the other man replied. "The cops came to the warehouse instead of Tranh, and they fucking shot me."

Selena smiled. Too bad the wound was to his arm instead of his heart.

William swore viciously, but the rumbling thunder blocked his words. Frustrated, she watched them gesture, each clearly upset. Then William's voice rose again. ". . . discuss how Mr. Tranh will pay."

"Yeah. Sure." Moving closer to the car, the man bent to take a look at his arm in the headlights' bright glare. When he turned for a better view, the beam lit up his face like a spotlight.

Selena stared. Oh, God, it couldn't be . . . it wasn't possible!

But it was. The harsh light left no room for doubt. His hair color might have changed, as well as the style, but his nose, the shape of his eyes, the full set of his mouth . . . it was the friendly stranger who'd befriended her two years ago while jogging. The charming date who'd flattered and seduced her all through dinner. The angry man who'd tried to rape her when she'd rebuffed his advances.

The dead man who had made this whole blackmail scheme possible for William.

Greg Marland.

The two men exchanged a few more words before William shut off the Mercedes' engine, then started toward the guesthouse with Marland a few steps behind. As her heart thudded, the scene blurred, meshing with a similar scene two years ago. That night had been sultry and calm, and she'd led the way, unlocked the door, invited him inside. That night she'd killed him . . . and yet here he was, walking inside again.

Her shoulders sagging, Selena clamped one hand over her mouth. The urge to crawl off and empty her stomach was almost as strong as the rage slowly building. The worst night of her life, the guilt, the regret, the blame, the remorse that she'd lived with for two years . . . Dear God, she'd believed she had *killed* a man! And it had all been part of William's plan to bend her to his will.

Marland wasn't dead. William had lied. Had set her up. Had concocted this whole elaborate plan. Had let her believe she was a *murderer.* Had deliberately let her suffer, had fed her guilt and shame, while waiting for the chance to use her nonexistent crime against her. Oh, Christ . . .

Scrambling to her knees, she crawled a few feet away and vomited into the grass. When her stomach was empty and hollowness had started spreading through her, she got to her feet, stumbled across the parking court to the safety of the garage, then set out at a run for the gate. Her feet automatically lifted and fell, setting her usual pace, keeping rhythm with the words echoing over and over in her brain. *William lied. Marland's not dead. William lied.*

Mr. Tranh would pay, William had decreed. In his world, someone else always paid. He committed the crimes, but others died, got shot, suffered. But no more. No damn more.

Anger pounded through her with every step, knotting in her chest until she could barely breathe, feeding her hatred. She ran through the neighborhood, then turned south on Riverside, her lungs bursting, her muscles tight and burning. Staggering to a stop, she bent over, fists knotted on her thighs, and sucked in a harsh breath. She wanted to scream, to break something, to hurt someone—to hurt William. How dare he put her through two years of hell because it suited his needs? How could he care so goddamn little for her? How could he—

"Are you all right?"

Slowly she raised her head to find one of William's guards watching her cautiously from twenty feet away. Looking past him, she saw that she'd stopped just short of the estate's driveway. The big gate was open, and a second guard stood just outside, also watching.

Breathing shallowly, she straightened, her gaze locked on that open gate. William was inside. Greg Marland was inside. All she had to do was get past these two guards, hardly even a nuisance, and she could walk into the guesthouse and kill them both. It would be so easy . . . so satisfying.

"You picked a hell of a night for a jog," the guard said. He looked ridiculously young, and the uniform and gun belt did nothing to age him. One punch, and he'd be unconscious for the next thirty minutes. Plenty of time to do what she wanted.

She walked toward him, her first steps stiff. She hadn't known disillusionment and rage could be as crippling as a real physical ailment, but her head throbbed and her body ached. Her very *soul* ached.

The storm had let up, the thunder more distant, the rain

a light sprinkle. Lightning illuminated the sky to the east as the cell moved in that direction, and to the west, as another one moved in, but for the moment the weather was calm.

More than she could say for herself.

When she was only five feet away—too close for the guard's safety—she stopped. "I'd like to see Mr. Davis."

"There's no Mr. Davis here."

A wind gusted out of nowhere, whipping her hair against her face and plastering her clothes to her skin. She combed her hair back even as she shook her head. "I saw him. Tall, gray hair, early sixties, distinguished?"

His gaze shifted over her. When it returned to her face, the friendly concern was gone. "I'd like to see some ID."

She glanced down to see what her wet clothes had revealed—a narrow bulge at her waist and an inch or so of the switchblade's bone handle gleaming against her middle. She tugged the clinging shirt away from her skin, then down over the knife. "I don't have it with me."

"What's in the backpack?"

"A towel. Dry clothes. A bottle of water." And a grappling hook and burglary tools. Fortunately, the forty cal was still in the back of her waistband, out of sight.

"How about you hand it over and let me see for myself?"

This was a stupid move, a voice in the still-rational part of her mind whispered. She should either put him and his partner out of commission or back off and get out before they called the police.

She hesitated too long. His partner stepped forward, gun drawn, and Baby-face reached for her backpack. Rain trickled down her spine and her face was hot with the sheer recklessness she'd displayed. If the guard found the pistol—and how could he not?—he would call the police, and if they arrested her, sooner or later they would discover that Selena McCaffrey didn't exist. She would face prison and/or deportation, and she would lose *everything*.

And she would *tell* everything.

She backed away and injected a conciliatory tone into her voice. "Look, I just wanted to talk to Mr. Davis. Obviously, that's a problem for you, so I'll go. I'll call him later."

"Hold it right there," the guard ordered, but she kept moving backward. When she'd put about ten feet between them, she spun around and headed away, but the guard lunged, catching hold of the backpack despite her best efforts to wrench free.

"Gun!" the other guard yelled, and Baby-face abruptly let go of her, sending her stumbling. When she caught her balance, both men were pointing their weapons at her.

Oh, God, she'd done it now.

His movements edgy, Baby-face gestured toward the iron gate. "Over there. Put your hands above your head and spread your legs."

She eyed the distance between her and the street. She could make a run for it. Odds were that the guards wouldn't shoot, or would shoot wildly, but with the streetlights out, she wouldn't make much of a target. But it was a dead certainty they would call the police. It would be easier to plead that she hadn't done anything wrong if she hadn't run.

Cautiously she moved the few yards to the gate and wrapped her fingers around the wet bars, holding so tightly the pads went numb. *Why* hadn't she just gone home? She could have confronted William the next day, could have broken in again if necessary. Now she was in serious trouble.

"You watch her," Baby-face said. "I'll search her." He was

starting to pat her down when Selena heard two car doors slam, followed by a familiar voice.

"Trust me, partner, you don't want to do that." *Tony.*

"The hell I don't. She's got a gun," the guard said resentfully. The fabric of her pants was pulled taut, then relaxed, as he jerked the holstered .40 free and, presumably, held it up for emphasis. "Who the hell are you guys?"

The responding voice spoke with a definite Oklahoma twang. "I'm Detective Frank Simmons, TPD, and that's Detective Anthony Ceola, golden boy of the Homicide Division. Son of the legendary Sergeant Joe Ceola. Godson of the chief himself. And do you know who she is? His girlfriend. Yep, that's right. Do you know how bad it would look . . ." His words trailed off to an indistinguishable murmur as he led the guard away to give her and Tony some privacy.

She couldn't look at him. Couldn't speak. Couldn't move. Could hardly breathe. She wished she could just sink into the sodden ground and disappear from sight.

After what seemed like hours, he came closer. His voice was low, his tone mild, as he said, "If you keep standing there like that, I'm going to give in to temptation and search you myself, and then I'm going to have one hell of an erection."

She lifted one hand, then the other, and clasped her aching fingers together. Biting the inside of her lip, she finally faced him. "What are you doing here?"

"I asked Frankie to drop me off. I wanted to talk to Henry about something. Here's a little tip, sweetheart—when you walk up to the gate of the house belonging to the chief of police, *don't* let the guards see your pistol. In fact, don't be carrying a pistol. Best tip of all—leave the weapons at home and call his favorite godson to go with you. What are you doing here, anyway?"

All the air disappeared from her body in a whoosh. She stared at him, wide-eyed, aware in some very small part of her that still functioned that she very well might pass out if she didn't catch a breath, but her brain refused to send the command. *The chief of police? William? Tony's godfather?*

Oh, God, oh, God, oh, God.

"Selena?" His voice came from far away, barely penetrating the buzz in her head. He lifted her hair off her neck, then wiped the rain from her face. "Are you okay?"

As her body began to tremble, she brushed him away and took a few steps backward. She didn't want him to feel how badly she was shaking, didn't want to arouse his suspicions or to make him rethink his decision to intervene. Summoning a smile, she folded her arms across her middle, hiding her clenched fists from view. "I'm—I'm fine. Are they g-going to call the—the police?"

He grinned. "Honey, we *are* the police. Frankie will persuade them to let us handle it."

She glanced past him to the detective, one arm around Baby-face's shoulders, gesturing jovially with the other. The guard's expression was serious; his nods of agreement, eager.

"So . . . what's your interest in Uncle Henry's house?"

"No interest," she lied. "I didn't even know . . . I was out jogging and got caught in the storm. I was on my way back to the car when I stopped to catch my breath and the guard got suspicious. I wasn't doing anything, but he wanted to search my backpack and then he saw the gun . . ." She shuddered at the thought of how close she'd come to getting hauled off to jail . . . or was it how close she'd come to cold-blooded murder?

"Security guards get a little overzealous sometimes." Tony gently brushed a curl from her face. "You okay now?"

She nodded as Simmons joined them. The guards, she saw, had returned inside the gate but continued to watch them. "I still have the magic touch," Simmons boasted as he offered her her pistol. "I convinced the kid it wasn't in his best interests to haul in the chief's godson's girlfriend in handcuffs."

Casually sliding his arm around her, Tony performed the introductions. "Selena McCaffrey, Frank Simmons."

Selena smiled weakly, nodded, and said, "Hi. Th-thanks."

He responded with his own nod and a grunt, then spoke to Tony. "Can I go now? I'd like to get home while Suz still remembers what I look like."

"Yeah, go ahead. I'll catch a ride with Selena." Tony extended his hand to the big man. "Thanks, Frankie."

"Hey, just remember this when I'm askin' your brothers for a job." With another nod, he returned to the car parked in the driveway, backed out, and drove away.

"Where's your car?"

Selena had to give the answer a moment's thought. "It's . . . over there." She gestured toward the lot across the street and down a few hundred yards, where the Thunderbird was the only vehicle parked. When Tony clasped her hand in his and started in that direction, she dragged her feet. "I thought you needed to talk to . . ." She couldn't say it. *The police chief. Uncle Henry. Your godfather.* The words simply wouldn't come.

"I'll hook up with him tomorrow. Right now you need to get home. You've had enough excitement for one evening."

Excitement? Hardly. Mind-numbing shock was more like it. When they got to her car, she couldn't think what to do, other than offer the keys to Tony. When she merely stood by the door, he opened it and helped her inside. When her fingers fumbled over the seat belt, he fastened it for her.

She stared out the window as he left the parking lot. The rain was picking up, and the wind buffeted the small car. The frequency and intensity of the lightning increased, and the thunder seemed a constant rumble, but all that registered only vaguely with her. All she could think about was William.

He was the chief of police. Had likely been a cop all the years she'd known him. Was Tony's godfather. He'd been there when Tony was born, had been part of his life as he grew up. He was a beloved member of the Ceola family . . . and he wanted his godson dead.

If she'd harbored even the faintest hope, after recognizing Greg Marland, of escaping this mess without someone dying, it was gone now.

And if she'd harbored even the faintest hope that Tony would believe everything she could tell him, it was gone now, too. He loved Wil—Henry, while he loved only sex with her. He had a history with Henry, while he was merely having an affair with her. He would never believe his godfather was a cold-blooded killer, and he would hate her for proving it to him. But she wouldn't care if he hated her for as long as he lived.

Just as long as he did live.

When they reached Princeton Court, Tony parked in his driveway, shut off the engine, then looked at Selena. She was staring blankly, as she'd done all the way home, unaware that they were here. Was it the run-in with the security guards that had shaken her so badly, the threat of arrest when she'd done nothing wrong, or both of those combined with getting caught in the storms?

He climbed out and circled to the passenger door, unhooking her seat belt, pulling her out and through the rain to the stoop. Once inside, he headed straight upstairs, tugging her along, and into the bathroom. By the time they'd changed into dry clothes, she was looking a little better. He caught the ends of the towel she was using to blot her hair and pulled her close. "You okay?"

Her smile was wan. "Apparently I'm doing better than you." She reached toward the raw scrape across his cheek, but stopped short of touching it. "Have you ever considered finding a new line of work?"

He pressed a kiss to her palm. "I've just taken a few hard knocks here lately. It doesn't happen all the time. In fact, the last time was more than two years ago."

"Hmm . . . once in two years. Now twice in four days. That doesn't sound good. Is it safe to hope that this time the guy responsible looks worse?"

He snorted. "He was on a racing bike and must've been doing eighty or more. He was long gone before I even got up off the ground."

"I take it you foiled his nefarious plan?" she asked with a smile that didn't touch her eyes.

"Yes and no. He didn't get to kill the drug dealer he'd targeted for tonight. He *did* kill one of his own people, though—the guy who'd been watching the dealer's family. While he was in police custody, no less."

As he spoke, thunder shook the house, and the power flickered off. When it came back, mere seconds later, Selena's eyes were wide and her hands trembled in his. "It's okay," he said. "If it gets worse, we'll head for the basement. We'll be safe there."

The smile she gave him was sickly. "We may not be safe anywhere."

He never would have figured that, living in hurricane country, she would be afraid of storms, but he reassured her anyway. "Trust me—the basement's safe in a storm. I even keep it clean for just that purpose."

She looked as if she wasn't the least bit convinced, but before she could argue, the blast of a siren split the air, making her jump. "What the—!"

"Did I forget to mention that the tornado siren for this area is at the end of the block?" He went into the bedroom and turned on the television in time to hear the meteorologist say, "—a funnel on the ground in the area of Twenty-first and Peoria and traveling east-southeast. If you're in that area, go to your safe place now."

Stopping at the bathroom again, Tony grabbed their shoes, then pulled Selena down the stairs and along the hall to the basement door. There he gave a sharp whistle for Mutt, who came running and trotted right down the stairs. He'd learned from the last tornado that hit the area how impossible it was to force the two cats to go someplace they didn't want to; it was safer all around to let them fend for themselves. Selena looked as if she'd rather fend for herself, too, hanging back ten feet. "Come on, darlin'."

"I—I can't."

"You have to."

Wearing nothing but an old T-shirt of his and hugging her arms to her chest, she looked as vulnerable as a woman could get. Slowly he moved toward her. "Don't tell me one of your rotten parents used to punish you by locking you in a small dark space."

She tried to smile, but the quivering of her lips made it less than successful. "Rodrigo. How did you guess?"

Son of a bitch! If the worthless bastard wasn't already dead, he would hunt him down and kill him. Controlling his anger, he said lightly, "Hey, the basement's not that small, and we can do all kinds of fun things in the dark. Hell, we can do 'em with the lights on if it makes you more comfortable."

As if on cue, the power flickered, surged, then went off. He fumbled for the flashlight that hung inside the door, clicked on the beam, then went to her. "Come on. I'll hold you the whole time, I promise." He gave her a grin and a wink. "I'll be your safe place."

She let him guide her to the doorway before her feet started dragging. He shone the light down the stairs and around the room. "See? There's nothing to be scared of." The space *was* small, but it was relatively empty. A set of steel shelves held his tools, a few boxes of Christmas decorations filled one corner, and there was a rollaway bed, complete with bedding in a zippered bag. Other than an oil lamp and an old comforter folded into a bed for Mutt, that was it.

The storm had intensified even more, and Tony could swear he heard the freight-train sound everyone associated with tornadoes, even over the damn siren. Leaving her no choice, he moved her onto the steps, slammed the door behind him, then forced her to the bottom. He left her long enough to light the lamp, unfold the rollaway, shake out a sheet, and fit it over the mattress, then he brought her over to sit with him. After wrapping his arms around her, he softly asked, "You want to talk?"

She made a choking sound that might have been the beginning of a laugh or a sob. With no follow-up, it was impossible to guess which. She was usually so very calm, serene, and controlled. If he wasn't seeing it with his own eyes, it would be difficult for him to imagine her showing fear. She seemed impervious to such human frailty.

"I'm sorry," she said, her voice strained.

"There's nothing to be sorry about."

For a time she remained still and tense, lost inside herself. She broke the silence in a voice so soft he could barely hear it. "I told you, Rodrigo didn't like raising another man's child. Sometimes he hit me. Sometimes even that was too much bother, so he just locked me away in a closet under the stairs. It was small and cramped, but I could lie down if I curled up tight. Usually he left me there an hour or two, and it really wasn't so bad. As long as I was in there, he wasn't bothering me. But one day he locked me up and he . . . forgot about me. They left, and they didn't come back for hours—all day, all night, and part of the next day, with no light, no food, no water. I screamed until I lost my voice, and I beat on the door until my hands were bloody and raw. I thought . . ." Her voice dropped to a whisper. "I thought they'd left me there to die."

At least that explained her response to the incident with Henry's security guards. If she couldn't voluntarily walk into the basement, the prospect of a jail cell probably filled her with terror.

Tony cradled her close and stroked her hair. "If I could give you a different past, different memories, I would," he said at last. "You deserved better."

The breath she exhaled was warm against his throat. "Not long after that, I got it. The next time Rodrigo tried to put me in the closet, I got hysterical. For the first time ever, I fought back and did a good bit of damage. The next day he sent me away. But to this day, I don't do well in small dark places."

"Nah, you're doing fine." He kept his voice as soothing as his touch, as he rubbed and patted.

Before she could do more than smile weakly, a crash sounded out back, followed by the thud of something slamming into the house. The wind's roar turned deafening, and the house seemed to literally sway above them as the light fixture hanging from the ceiling swung from side to side.

Within seconds, the noise level went from teeth-jarring to relatively calm. The house settled back in with a shudder, the siren faded away, and the rain diminished from torrential to what sounded like a sprinkle.

"Is that it?" Selena asked.

"I think so. For that one, at least. Want to walk outside with me?"

"Yes." She wiggled free and shoved her feet into her wet shoes while he put on his own. Holding tightly to his hand, she climbed the stairs one step behind him.

The first thing he noticed when they stepped out the front door was that the Impala was gone—not far, just ten or fifteen feet across the yard, though it appeared undamaged. The smaller T-Bird was exactly where he'd left it and intact. Branches, leaves, and flowers littered the street, two of Selena's lawn chairs leaned at an angle against the side of his house, explaining the earlier thud, and a half-dozen trees were down at the back edge of the yards.

"Part of my yard is gone," Selena said in amazement, pointing to a bare patch of earth. "It literally sucked the grass out of the ground."

All of her patio furniture was gone and, except for the two chairs next door, was nowhere in sight. Shingles were missing from both houses, and a strip of siding had been torn off the far side of the sunroom, but that seemed the extent of the structural damage.

Tony grinned as he helped her over a sycamore uprooted from next door and dropped in her front yard. "Well, we survived the first one okay."

She scowled down at him, her lips primly pursed. "The first one?"

"Where one tornado goes, others often follow." He lifted her down and held on when she would have stepped away. "But it doesn't matter if that's the only storm or if there are a dozen more. You'll be okay. We'll be okay together."

She simply looked at him, holding herself distant, then the tension abruptly drained from her. She leaned against him, her cheek pressed to his shoulder, one hand knotted in his shirt. "Thank you," she murmured, and brushed a kiss to his jaw.

And just like that, his lousy Saturday night became pretty damn good.

14

It was after 3 A.M. when William's quack doctor finally left the guesthouse. Damon locked the door behind him, then leaned against it, a sling holding his left arm close to his chest. The old man had needed a hand from Jose Cuervo to clean and pack the wound, which Damon could have done just as well himself, and in half the time. But at least the doc had had some pills—antibiotics to prevent infection and some little white marvels for the pain. Going into the kitchen, he washed down the antibiotics but left the pain pills where they sat.

Fucking William had let him into the guesthouse, shown him where the oil lamps and candles were stored, then disappeared into the main house. He hadn't even waited to get the doc's drunken opinion about the seriousness of the wound. Arrogant bastard didn't care whether Damon lived or died, as long as he didn't inconvenience *him* any more than necessary.

That was okay. Damon knew someone who *did* care. Retrieving the cell phone from his jacket pocket, he dialed her number. She answered on the fourth ring with a sleepy "Hello." "Christ, you sleep through tornadoes?" he asked.

There was a moment's rustling as Lucia resettled in the bed. "Tornadoes know better than to fuck with me. There hasn't been one anywhere close to the house. What about you?"

"What about me?"

"You wanna fuck with me?"

"I'd like nothing better, but . . ." He pushed aside one curtain to look at William's house. From this angle it was impossible to tell whether anyone was up and about over there. Both the old man's bedroom and study faced the front of the house, and the flicker of an oil lamp wouldn't carry far. But that was okay. Sooner or later the bastard would come around, and Damon would be ready.

"But . . . ?" Lucia prompted.

"But you'd have to come to me. I'm a little incapacitated. I could use some tender loving care."

"Poor baby. Lucky for you, I'm good at tender loving care. Are you at home?"

"No. I'm staying at the boss's guesthouse." He smiled as he gave her the address, told her to call him when she arrived at the rear gate, then disconnected. Lifting the curtain again, he gazed at the house. He hoped the old man got a good night's rest. He was going to need it to face tomorrow.

Rolling out of bed after only a few hours' sleep was tough, but Selena managed on the second try. The power had come back on sometime while they'd slept—the clock on the nightstand flashed in the dark—but she didn't need the lights to locate the T-shirt she'd discarded the night before. Sliding it over her head, she went downstairs and into the dining room, where she booted up the computer and signed online.

It was amazing the information you could find out about a man when you knew his real name. After an hour on the Internet, Selena had learned practically everything she'd wanted to know about her dear Uncle William . . . Henry.

For starters, there was absolutely no question that the

men were one and the same. She'd needed only one photograph to confirm it, and had stopped counting at ten. Handsome, urbane, aging gracefully through the years, Henry Daniels, respected police official, was most definitely William Davis, drug dealer and murderer.

His grandfather had made a half-dozen fortunes in Oklahoma's oil boom years and had built the house along the river to show it off. Henry was the older of two children; his younger sister was rarely mentioned in the articles. He had started his police career in Tulsa, had eventually moved on to Boston—where his mother's family was from—then to Philadelphia and Savannah, each time moving up through the ranks.

A few years earlier, he'd come full circle, hired to head the department where he'd started his career. His years with each department had been stellar. No one had anything negative to say about Henry Daniels. He was tough on crime and tougher on criminals. He'd married in Boston and divorced in Philadelphia two years before Selena had met him in that Jamaican alley. They'd had no children. He had been best man at Joe and Anna Ceola's wedding, and Joe had returned the favor at his own wedding. He'd cited the Ceolas as one big reason for taking the chief's job in Tulsa. They were *family*, he'd said on more than one occasion.

The son of a bitch didn't know the meaning of the word.

Selena wasn't sure which she was angrier about—that he had lied to her from the start, that he had lived this wonderful, respectable life while keeping her hidden away like a shameful secret, that he'd betrayed the faith and trust of countless people, that he'd made a mockery of the positions he'd held, or that he was committing the ultimate betrayal against Tony and his family. They loved him. They trusted him. They had been a part of his life for forty years . . . and this was how he intended to repay them.

By the time she quit, the sun had been up for a time and she'd read every highlight of Henry Daniels's life. Of course, there wasn't so much as a hint anywhere in there of her presence in that life.

She sat back in the chair, drawing her bare feet into the seat, and stared at the computer screen. She'd learned a lot about Henry, but nothing about William. Nothing to suggest that they were two sides of the same man. Nothing to tie the distinguished police chief to the consummate criminal.

Nothing to convince Tony to believe *her* when Henry was sure to tell a different story.

Her hands were clasped loosely around her ankles, her chin resting on her knees, as she tried to think. Give her a mugger on a dark street and she knew exactly what to do. Put a paintbrush in her hand and stand her in front of a blank canvas, and the next step came naturally. But gathering proof of a dark secret life that would stand up against the denials of a venerable man . . . she was totally at a loss.

She might not be able to prove the truth about him, but she could stop him. She could kill him.

Kill William. The thought robbed her of breath and left her unable even to tighten a muscle. After all he'd done for her, the life he'd given her, the advantages, the chances. The man who'd pretended to love her like a daughter, whom she had loved like a father.

Kill William. For everything he'd done to her, the life he threatened to take from her, the love he'd refused to give her, the perverse ways he'd manipulated her.

Kill him. To save Tony. To save herself.

If she had no other choice.

But she did have another choice right now—she could prove that Greg Marland was alive and well. That was a start.

A hiss from the fat black cat alerted her that Tony was awake an instant before the stairs creaked. She rose from the chair to meet him in the foyer. He wore jeans and a T-shirt, and was moving gingerly after last night's run-in with the vigilante. "What are you doing up?" she asked.

"I'm gonna check on Mom and Dad—make sure they didn't have any damage from the storm. Want to go with me?"

She shook her head. "I might go for a run before it gets too hot. How about we meet back here for an early lunch?"

Drawing her close, he kissed her on the mouth. "It's a date."

Smiling faintly, she let herself out. Next door she took her time dressing—in shorts and a jogging bra, followed by workout pants and a sleeveless top that allowed for easy movement. If she needed to convince Tony that she had, indeed, gone for a run, she wanted to be prepared. And if she ran into Greg Marland . . .

She clipped the forty cal at the small of her back. The .22 went into an ankle holster, the double-edged dagger in a Velcro strap around her right ankle, and the switchblade in its usual place. Once she'd slid extra clips for both guns into her pants pockets, she was ready to go. *Armed and dangerous,* she thought with a grim smile. The only way to be.

As she retrieved her digital camera from the closet, the rumble of the Impala's engine broke the quiet. She watched from the window as Tony drove out of sight, breathed deeply, and left the house.

Detouring around limbs and storm debris, she drove to William's neighborhood and parked in the Thirty-first Street River Parks lot, out of sight of his estate. If she'd known when she bought the Thunderbird that she would be doing covert surveillance on William's house, she would have opted for something nondescript.

If she'd known . . . Here she was, actually doing it, and it still sounded thoroughly ridiculous. She wasn't the covert type. The stuff she knew about weapons, knives, and alarms was to protect herself, not harm others. All she wanted was to paint her pictures, run her gallery, and feel safe for the rest of her life. Was that so much to ask?

No. "So much to ask" would be to paint her pictures, run her gallery, and make a home with Tony for the rest of her life. Maybe, God forbid, get married. Maybe even, in her wildest, most sacred and secret dreams, have babies with him.

That was too much. She would expect disappointment if she ever entertained such fanciful desires. But her own three wishes were nothing. She'd worked hard to achieve them . . . and William wanted to take them away simply because he could. Such a pitiful reason for manipulating and destroying people's lives.

Crossing Riverside Drive, she turned north on the trail, camera in hand, and walked past his house to the next street. She took a meandering route through the neighborhood until she finally reached the dead-end street one block east of his rear gate. Everything was still. No dogs barked. No birds sang. Other than the occasional sound of a car passing by on Riverside, there was no sign of life at all. Satisfied, she cut across the grass between two houses, then followed William's fence to the service entrance.

Staying well out of view of the camera, she ducked into the bushes. Unlike the neatly manicured gardens inside the fence, the plantings outside were allowed to grow more naturally—luckily for her, since sprawling azaleas and rhododendrons provided much better cover than the formal gardens.

She settled in to wait, unmindful of the water dripping from the bushes and seeping into her pants. The pistol provided a welcome pressure on the small of her back, and she held the camera loosely in both hands. She couldn't imagine William letting anyone, even his right-hand man, stay long at the estate. If Marland wasn't already gone, she wanted proof that he was alive and well. Proof of William's deception.

She'd learned during a second round of thunderstorms last night that Tony had been at the warehouse Marland had mentioned. She regretted she couldn't tell him what she knew: that it had been Marland on the racing bike who had caused Tony's latest injuries. That one wild shot had found its target. That the police chief had sent Marland there. That William had murdered one of his employees.

And the worst thing she knew: that Tony's godfather wanted him dead.

But if she could get proof, starting with Marland . . . maybe this would be one time William didn't get what he wanted, but instead got what he deserved.

Damon would have killed for a few more hours' sleep—and he had just the person in mind—but he dragged himself out of bed way too early Sunday morning. With some effort, he pulled on his boxers one-handed, then walked through the guesthouse to the front door. He knew who was ringing the damn bell. He'd been watching from the bedroom window as Henry crossed the patio.

He had expected a command via the intercom or Sonja to appear in Henry's study—a command he'd intended to ignore. He had thought he would have to lure Henry to the guesthouse instead, but here he was, meticulously dressed, shaved, and ready to face the day.

And why shouldn't he be? He hadn't spent hours roasting in that fucking warehouse last night. He hadn't had half the cops in Tulsa trying to take him out, and he for goddamn sure hadn't gotten shot.

When Damon undid the chain lock and opened the door, Henry was looking annoyed. "I was beginning to wonder if you'd died in there," he said, pushing past without an invitation and striding into the living room.

Wonder. Not *worry.* Not *fear.* Just fucking *you-don't-mean-a-damn-thing* wonder.

"So you finally decided to check on me." Damon's tone was sour as he headed for the kitchen.

"I knew you were in good hands with Dr. Adams."

The refrigerator had been empty when Damon had arrived the night before, but he'd remedied that with a second call to Lucia. Now he took one of the beers she'd brought, popped the top, and swigged a healthy swallow as he joined Henry in the living room. " 'Good hands'? With that old drunk?" He snorted. "He doesn't even have a license to practice anymore."

Henry gave him a narrow look, distaste appearing at the sight of the beer and intensifying as he took in Damon's dress, or lack of. He didn't ask about the beer, though, or order him to put on clothes. Instead, he stuck to the subject. "If you were unhappy with Dr. Adams's care, you could have gone to any of Tulsa's fine hospitals. Of course, they would have had a few questions for you, and would have been obligated to notify the authorities. And where would that have landed you?" Then he gestured toward the bandage. "It appears he did an adequate job."

Adequate—and that was good enough for the hired

help, Damon thought bitterly. Oh, but not for Henry. If he had a damn headache, he'd want the best neurologist in the state. Only the best for him.

He glanced at the dressing, too, and dismissed it. "That's not his work." Before Henry could ask the obvious question, Damon pointed with the bottle's neck. "What's that?"

The old man pulled a section of the Sunday *World* from under his arm and held it so Damon could see the headline: *Man Killed in Police Custody.* "We made the papers."

What was with this *we* crap? Damon didn't have anything to do with Potter's murder. He didn't like executing employees every time something went wrong, especially when the problem was no fault of theirs. It wasn't good for morale.

If the boss needed a scapegoat for last night's fuckup, he need look no further than himself. He was the one who'd decided to bring Tranh's family into it, who'd pushed Tranh so hard that Tranh had no choice but to push back.

Henry tossed the paper on the coffee table, steepled his fingers together, and studied him. "While you were waiting for me last night, did you come inside the house?" His expression was one of friendly curiosity, echoed in his voice, but it didn't fool Damon for a moment.

"No." He'd been soaking wet and bleeding, and had known Henry wouldn't appreciate either water or blood soiling his precious antiques. "Why do you ask?"

"Someone did. When I left you last night, the rear door was unlocked, and someone had tried to gain access to the vault."

"Maybe security came over to check the alarm. Sonja says it malfunctions during storms."

Henry considered the possibility that his security experts had forgotten to lock the door behind them, then nodded. "Perhaps. But they wouldn't have attempted to access the vault, and certainly neither Sonja nor Leonard would have, either."

Damon shrugged carelessly. "Hey, dust it for prints. You won't find mine."

Henry gave no response but gazed at the bronze-and-marble statue that had once cracked open Damon's skull. It pissed him off that the old man had not only kept it, but kept it on display like some damn trophy. "I wonder what Selena did last night while the good detective was trying to catch the vigilante."

The idea that Selena might have broken in amused Damon, especially since Henry considered her some sort of wild animal tamed only by him. With the right incentive, though, even the tamest of wild beasts would turn on its handler.

"Maybe she *was* here. The fence isn't electrified, the alarm malfunctions, and the guards don't patrol the grounds during storms. Could she have found anything of interest?"

"Of course not," Henry said scornfully. "The problem is that she would even try."

"She showed some initiative. So what?"

"I don't pay her to show initiative. I pay her to follow orders."

"You don't pay her at all," Damon pointed out, keeping his tone mild.

Henry's gaze turned cold and sharp. "She owes me her *life*." And he would take it if it suited him. "Why are you defending her? I thought you didn't like her."

Damon started to shrug, but the pain shooting through his arm stopped him. "I'm not defending her. I just think she must have a hell of a set of balls to come waltzing in here, especially after waiting so many years for an invitation that never came."

Taking a cigar and lighter from his jacket pocket, Henry lit up, then gestured, sending a plume of smoke swirling in the air. "Crudely put, but, yes, she must have. She spent yesterday with the Ceola family, in direct defiance of my orders."

"Yeah, that defiance seems to be going around," Damon murmured.

"What do you mean?"

The timing couldn't have been better if Damon had choreographed it. Henry's question had hardly faded when the soft slap of bare feet against wood sounded and Lucia came around the corner. She was wearing Damon's T-shirt, her hair was tangled, and she looked ripe and lush and very well-fucked. Her gaze locked on him first, but as she crossed to him, she saw Henry, too. She ignored him, though, until she'd stretched onto her toes and given Damon a long hot kiss. Then she hooked her arm around his good arm, smiled at the bastard, and said, "Uncle Henry. You look wonderful this morning."

Actually, he looked as if he was about to explode. His eyes had gone ice cold, and a vein throbbed in his temple. His mouth worked, but no words came out the first few tries. Finally, his muscles taut with the effort, he managed, "Lucia, princess. I—I never expected to see you here."

She smiled again, coyly this time, and snuggled closer to Damon, rubbing her breasts against his arm. "I know the whole family thinks I can't keep a secret, but they're wrong. Now that you know, though, I guess we won't have to worry about secrets anymore, will we, sweetie?"

"I need to talk to Damon alone," Henry said, still sounding strained.

"No problem. I've got to get dressed. I told Mom I'd help her take Daddy to church this morning." She kissed Damon again, wiggled her fingers in a wave to Henry, then disappeared back down the hall.

Damon had barely registered that Lucia was gone when Henry caught him around the throat and shoved him against the wall. "Don't . . . you . . . touch . . . her . . . again. How dare you? You don't deserve to breathe the same air she does!"

"She's a whore." Damon said the words with the deadly softness he'd learned from the master himself. "She puts on a good act, but, plain and simple, she's a whore."

His face turning purple, Henry squeezed tighter, cutting off Damon's air, but even one-handed, Damon had no trouble freeing himself. He bent the old man's arm back until it threatened to break, leaned close, and amended his last words. "She's *my* whore. And there's not a goddamn thing you can do about it."

"I'll tell her what you are!"

"And I'll tell her what *you* are. Who do you think she'll believe? Her stuffy old uncle? Or the man who fucks her senseless every night?"

Henry's breathing came faster, sharper, sounding as if he was about to have a damn heart attack. Damon wished he would, wished he would drop dead right here in the same room where *he* had almost died two years ago. Instead of becoming weaker, though, the old man suddenly regained control. His color returned to normal, his breathing slowed, and his voice became strong and threatening.

"I will kill you."

It wasn't an idle threat, or words spoken in anger soon to be forgotten. It was a promise, and Henry always carried out his promises. He *would* kill Damon . . . if Damon didn't kill him first.

"Go ahead and try, old man." He waited until Henry reached the door before he parodied a gun with his thumb and forefinger. "In the meantime . . . watch your back."

Henry gave him a deadly look before walking out.

Damon leaned against the wall again, rubbing his throat gingerly. For months he'd entertained the idea of removing Henry from the business and running it himself, but thinking about it was all he'd done. Until now.

He should feel excited. Elated. Hyped. Instead, he just had a knot in his gut. He'd always known he had what it took to take charge, just as he'd always known the only way to accomplish that was to kill Henry. But thinking about it and doing it . . . those were two very different things. After all, he owed the man a lot.

At the same time, Henry owed *him* a lot.

And it was time he took it.

Selena wasn't sure how long she'd been waiting before the gate slowly swung open and someone approached. It wasn't Marland's motorcycle, or one of William's cars, but two people on foot, talking as they walked. *Security guards making rounds?* she wondered, rising to a crouch for a better view, lifting the camera, and sighting through a break in the bushes.

No guards. It was Greg Marland and a pretty young woman. Selena snapped off photos, getting several close-ups of the woman, but mostly focusing on Marland, then lowered the camera as they came even with her hiding place. Barely breathing, she watched as they kissed. The woman tried to pin him down for later plans; he refused, insisting instead that he would call her. Finally, after another kiss, she sashayed to the little red sports car parked nearby, gave him a pouty look, then got in and drove away. Marland watched her go.

Did William know he'd brought a woman to stay at the guesthouse with him? He'd been upset with her two years ago for inviting Marland in—not because she could have been raped or worse, not because she'd been forced to kill the man, but because it had violated *his* privacy, caused problems for *him*.

What if all that had been an act? In truth, what problems had that night caused William? He'd had to get someone to clean the blood and dispose of the damaged rug. But the other hassles he'd claimed—disposing of Marland's body and the other evidence, covering up a murder—none of that had been necessary because the murder had never happened.

What if it had been a setup from the start? If William had instructed Marland to befriend her, take her out, assault her, all so he could blackmail her when the opportunity arose?

The thought made her sick. She closed her eyes tightly, swayed unsteadily, catching a branch to steady herself, and forced shallow, even breaths until the shakiness passed and her stomach settled. This was no time for weakn—

"You look a little green there, Selena. Or would you prefer Gabriela? That *was* the name you were using the first time we met."

Slowly she opened her eyes and found herself looking down the barrel of a .45. On the other end, Marland was looking grim, without a hint of the charm that had captivated her that first time. He backed away, then gestured for her to stand. She did so slowly.

"Which is it? Selena? Gabriela? Or something new?"

"Selena's fine. Are you still using Greg?"

"Actually, that was just for your benefit. You can call me Damon. Damon Long. Henry's right-hand man for the past twenty years." With his left arm in a sling, he sketched a parody of a bow. "Get your hands in the air and come on out of those bushes."

She obeyed, hands raised shoulder high. He backed up one step for every step she took forward; when she reached the driveway, he was well out of striking range. Stopping near the open gate, she faced him. "You look pretty substantial for a ghost."

"How long have you known I wasn't dead?"

"Since last night."

"So it was you who broke into the house."

She shrugged.

"It didn't sit well with Henry. Your being here today isn't going to sit well with him, either."

" 'Henry'?"

"Aw, come on. Surely you've figured out that William is really Henry Daniels, chief of police."

She responded with another shrug. "William or Henry, or whatever he wants to call himself, doesn't rule my life."

"Since when?"

Instead of answering, she considered her options. Running was out of the question; there was no cover near enough to be of any use. Disarming Long was a possibility, but a slim one. If she so much as twitched a muscle, he wouldn't hesitate to shoot her. That left cooperating for the moment and hoping for a better choice in the near future.

"Are you going to turn me over to him? Earn a few points for yourself?"

He gestured for her to turn around, then slowly approached. "Inside," he commanded. After they'd cleared the gate, he began talking in a conversational tone. "You're a problem, Selena. Always have been, always will be. Henry knows you went to the Ceolas' house yesterday, and he suspects that you broke in here last night. He doesn't trust you anymore, and you know what that means."

He would order her killed. She swallowed hard. "He's not going to turn the business over to you just because I'm out of the picture."

"I don't expect him to."

She didn't believe him. He'd worked half his life for William, had helped him build the business, had killed for him. That kind of service demanded reward, and most likely, in his mind, *she* was all that stood in the way of that reward.

As they approached the garage, she looked around. If only she could appeal to the security guards . . . though after last night's incident, the chances they would intervene on her behalf were nonexistent. She could make a break for it, using the garage as cover, get to the guesthouse, then make for the fence behind it. Scaling the fence without a rope would be a problem, but it was one she was willing to face.

Or she could make Long think she was going for the fence, and use the distraction to disarm him. She could make her captor the captive, and use him to get off the estate to safety.

As she drew even with the near corner of the garage, she gauged the distance between them the best she could without looking, then subtly lengthened her stride as she passed each of the doors. At the fourth, she lunged for the corner, reaching it as a bullet splintered the wood mere inches from her. She stopped short as the gun muzzle came in contact with the back of her head.

"It would be so easy to kill you, Selena," Long said softly. "And so easy to get away with it. Woman breaks into police chief's house, making threats, and security chief has to kill her. No one would care, except for your detective, and he won't be around long enough to raise a stink."

She stared at the fence, so far out of reach, as she slowed her breathing to normal.

"Put your hands on top of your head. If you move even your little finger, I'll pull the trigger. Now head for the house."

She did as he ordered, crossing the parking area, waiting at the back door for him to open it. Inside the cool, quiet house, he directed her up the servants' stairs and to William's study. The door was closed; he pushed it open, then motioned her inside, but she couldn't take that step, couldn't move at all. Someone was going to die in that room, and Long seemed pretty sure it would be her.

But he'd made the mistake of not searching her. He didn't know she was armed, didn't know she was just as willing to kill as he was. One way or another, this whole mess was going to end right here, right now.

Dear God, she hoped she survived it.

Only one tree at Anna and Joe's house had fallen in the storm, but that was one too many, Tony decided as he cut the last section of trunk into manageable pieces. He shut off the chain saw, stacked the wood at the curb, then straightened in time to see Lucia pull into the driveway.

She climbed out, took a good look at him, and grinned. "You must be slowing down in your old age."

"Screw you, brat. What're you doing, all dressed up?"

She struck a pose to show her red dress at its best, then came closer. "Mom and I are taking Daddy to church this morning."

"You in church? The walls will be trembling."

She reached out to swat him, then drew back, her face screwed up. "You're a mess. What have you been doing?"

"It's called 'work.' You should try it sometime."

"Hey, I work. I just prefer not to wallow in it."

She walked with him as he set the chain saw inside the garage, but when they reached the front door, she stopped him before he could open it. "Can I ask you something?"

"As long as it doesn't have to do with Mom, Dad, and nursing homes."

"It doesn't. And the places I suggested aren't nursing homes. They're assisted-living facilities, and—" When Tony scowled at her, she drew a breath, then started again. "It's about Damon."

When she didn't continue, he asked, "Who's that?"

"Damon Long." Her manner was expectant, as if the name was supposed to mean something.

"Who's that?" Tony repeated.

"My boyfriend. He's a cop."

"*You're* dating a cop?" What a joke. No way a lowly cop could ever afford to hang on to Lucia, not unless he was on the take.

"Yes, I'm dating a cop," she said impatiently. "I just want to know what you know about him."

"I don't know him. Never heard of him."

"Of course you know him. He was with you last night."

Tony stared at her. "What do you know about where I was last night?"

She picked a few dead leaves from the plant hanging

next to her, her gaze darting his way when she finally answered. "Damon's kind of, uh . . . private about things, so last night, I, uh . . . followed him when he went to work. And a while later, some other cops came, including you. That's why I assumed you knew him."

He didn't know every officer who'd been at the warehouse the night before, but he'd heard their names, and none of them was Damon Long.

"Even then I wasn't completely sure he was a cop, but after this morning . . . I mean, Uncle Henry knows him well enough to invite him to his house, so he *has* to be a cop, and he's probably working undercover, which would explain why he's so secretive, right?"

Tony stared at her, barely able to make sense of what she was saying. "Wait a minute. Back up. You followed your boyfriend last night. Where did he go?"

Lucia sighed impatiently. "To that building downtown that has the big horse painted on it. The same building you were at."

"Was he . . . ?" This couldn't be real. Lucia's lousy taste in men was legendary, but this was too much even for her. She *couldn't* be dating the vigilante killer.

He blew out his breath, then tried again. "Was he on a motorcycle?"

"Yes! A Ducati. That's an Italian racing bike. Cool, huh?" Without waiting for a response, she went on. "So you do know him. Not that I don't trust him, 'cause I do, but like I said, he's kind of secretive, and I just want to know—"

"And he was at Henry's this morning?"

She wasted a moment pouting over the interruption before explaining. "That's what I said, isn't it? Actually, he was there all night. He got hurt last night—like you—and

Uncle Henry let him stay in the guesthouse. He must be pretty high up if he reports to Uncle Henry at home, huh?"

What if the vigilante is a cop? It was a question that had been sneaking into Tony's thoughts for days now. He'd laid out an argument in favor of it to Simmons, had even intended to talk to Henry about it today, but he hadn't wanted to believe it. Cops were supposed to be decent, honorable, and law-abiding. They were supposed to hold themselves to a higher standard than regular citizens. They couldn't enforce the law for everyone else and twist, trample, and pervert it for their own benefit.

"You're sure he was at Henry's house?"

Her smile was too sexy by half for his kid sister. "Of course I'm sure. I spent half the night with him. He and Uncle Henry were talking business when I got up this morning."

Talking business . . . Tony dragged his fingers through his hair as he searched his memory for that phrase in connection with Henry. It came to him when he gazed into Lucia's familiar brown eyes, darkened with confusion at his behavior. *Joe.* Several weeks earlier he'd escaped Anna's watch and made it across town to Henry's house. A frequent guest in better times, he'd gotten past the guards with nothing more than a friendly hello, and the butler had let him in and sent him on up to the study without announcing him.

When Tony had gone to pick him up a short while later, Joe had been agitated and confused. *That's not Henry,* he'd insisted. *What is he doing in Henry's house, talking drug business with that man? What has he done with Henry?*

At the time, Tony had written it off as the disease talking. Obviously, Henry *was* Henry, there had been no one else around, and Henry's only connection to the drug business was in stopping it. Tony had been embarrassed for his father and upset that Joe couldn't recognize his friend, and he'd dismissed the entire incident. Henry had been eager to do the same.

Too eager?

Dear God, *Henry* couldn't be perverting the law for himself. He was the freakin' chief of police—Joe's goddamn best friend!

"Christ, Lucia . . ."

Her expression darkened. "You don't like Damon, do you? Why? What's the problem? I mean, yeah, he's kind of cocky, but so are you, and—"

Taking her by the shoulders, he gave her a gentle shake. "Listen to me—I've got to go, but I want you to stay here with Mom. Don't go anywhere, and don't talk to anybody, especially Henry and Damon. Promise me."

"But, Tony, what about church—"

He shook her harder. "Damn it, promise!"

"Okay, okay, I promise. But you have to tell me—"

Ignoring her, he opened the door and went inside. When he found Anna in the kitchen, he kissed her cheek. "I've got to go, Mom. Listen to me—you can't go to church this morning. Stay here, and don't let Lucia or Dad out of your sight until you hear from me, okay?"

Looking as confused as Lucia, Anna nodded.

Henry wasn't involved in the vigilante killings, Tony insisted as he backed out of the driveway. He could no more commit cold-blooded murder than Joe could. There must be a logical explanation. There were all those security guards at the estate, plus a full staff of gardeners. Maybe this Long guy was one of them, and that was why he'd gone there. Or maybe he had a legitimate job along with the illegitimate one, and that was what had taken him there—a delivery or a repair. It must be something like that.

Henry was a good man. He'd devoted his life to law enforcement. He'd been the best friend possible to Joe and Anna, and practically a second father to their kids. There was a reasonable explanation. All he had to do was go to Henry's and ask for it.

Then the two of them could get down to figuring out who the vigilante killer really was.

15

"What the—"

Damon interrupted William as he shoved Selena through the door into the study. "Look who I found sneaking around outside."

Slowly William rose from the desk, wearing a look that was part regret and part tautly controlled rage. Selena realized that she wasn't the only one in their relationship struggling between love and hate.

"Selena." Those few syllables were rife with disappointment. "I can't tell you how very sorry I am to see you here."

As she walked to a space in front of the desk, she glanced at Damon. What were the odds she could talk her way out of this? Claim that Damon had attempted to involve her in a conspiracy to seize control from him? That his right-hand man wanted him dead? Probably good enough that she would get them both killed instead of dying alone.

She smiled coolly. "Uncle— What do you prefer I call you? William or Henry?"

"Whichever is more comfortable for you."

She considered that, and decided on Henry. She felt less connected, less in debt, to Henry, and it had the advantage of being his real name. "Why are you sorry, *Uncle* Henry? You know I broke in here last night. You should have expected me to return."

"And why have you returned?"

She held up the small camera. "For proof."

"Of what?"

"That Greg Marland is alive and well. That you've blackmailed me with evidence of a crime that never happened." She hesitated, then deliberately added, "That William Davis is, in fact, the respectable Henry Daniels."

"You took a huge risk, coming back here."

"Everything in life comes with risks, Uncle."

"You want to be free of me badly enough to risk death?"

"I want to live my life as I see fit."

He considered that a moment, then dismissed it as meaningless. "What do you plan to do with this proof? Show it to Tony? Try to convince him that his beloved godfather—his mentor and friend—is a criminal mastermind?" He gave a rueful shake of his head. "Do you think he would believe you, Selena? Tony loves, admires, and trusts me. Does he love you? Trust you? Or merely use you for sex?"

She smiled thinly. She could always count on Henry to go straight to the heart of her insecurities. "Tony's a good detective. Sentimentality doesn't interfere with his work. No matter how much he loves you, if he has evidence that you've committed a crime, he *will* arrest you. You can't deny that. It's why you want him dead."

He acknowledged that with a nod. "I've worked too long and too hard to go to prison now. If I thought I could buy him off, I would . . . but of course, I can't. Unlike others I've worked with, his honor isn't for sale."

Taking a few steps to the right, Selena sat down in the chair there and crossed her legs. "You've been best friends with Joe Ceola for more than forty years. How can you even think about killing one of his children?"

"Joe's mind is gone. He won't even understand what's happened."

"But Anna will. The other children will."

"And, as their dear friend, I'll be there to help them cope with their grief."

Obviously, appealing to his own sentimentality was pointless—he had none. Selena changed the subject with a bold statement. "So you're the vigilante killer, righting wrongs outside the law. Pardon me if I fail to see the righteousness in what you've done."

"The religious motif was a nice touch, wasn't it?" Henry chuckled. "I wanted to expand my market, and the only way to do it was to remove the obstacles in my way. As for the vigilante idea . . . it was merely part of the challenge of dealing with the authorities. It's easy to kill five people using five different methods and get away with it. Damon and I have done that more times than I can count. The challenge is in tying them together, giving the authorities plenty to work with, and still staying a dozen steps ahead."

He talked as if it was a game—and to him, it was. Multiple murders for fun and ego gratification.

Some hint of dismay must have shown on her face because he gave her a chiding look. "Remember back in Jamaica, when you were earning your living stealing? You started out sneaking around, relying on someone else to create a diversion, taking only when you were assured of success. As you became more skilled, you created your own diversions, and before long, you had no need of them. You had developed your talents to the point that you could look your mark in the eye and take everything he had. Isn't that true?"

She responded with a shrug.

"It's exactly the same for me. You don't like to admit it, Selena, but we're very much two of a kind. We like challenges. We'll do whatever it takes to achieve our goals. We're fighters. And our own best interests are our only interests."

She wasted little time in taking offense at his comparison. Much as she hated to admit it, they *were* alike. She *was* a fighter, and she would do whatever it took to save Tony's life—even take Henry's.

"So what happens now?" She sat, hands folded in her lap, as if she hadn't just asked the question that very well might result in her death. In the silence that followed, a clock ticked somewhere, Damon shifted position, and a look of genuine regret came into Henry's eyes. His mouth thinned, and for a moment he looked so sorrowful that her heart practically stopped beating.

"I know you won't believe me, but this hurts me more than I can say. I've had such grand plans for you, practically from the moment I became aware of your existence. You chafed under the restrictions circumstances put on our relationship, but you truly have been family to me, more than you can ever know. But now—"

The buzz from the telephone behind his desk made Selena start. Calmly, as if he hadn't been discussing her impending death, Henry picked up the receiver and pressed the INTERCOM button. After speaking for a moment, he hung up and gestured to Damon. "I'm sorry, but I have an unexpected guest. We'll have to finish this later."

Before Selena could do more than blink, Damon had taken hold of her arm and was pulling her toward the vault. He pushed her inside, followed, and pulled the door shut behind him.

The room was the size of a small walk-in closet, with no windows and only the one exit, and being in there made the hairs on her nape stand on end. Drawers and shelves lined every inch of wall space except for one square where a small painting hung—a Picasso, stolen a few years earlier from a private collector who died trying to protect his property.

On the shelf beneath it was a Fabergé egg and an exquisite necklace of yellow diamonds.

She reverently touched the Picasso's frame. She'd thought William was driven by the desire for money and power, but that wasn't entirely true. Part of his need, perhaps the greater part, had to do with possession. He needed to *own* things—priceless art, rare gems, people. He had to keep these things hidden from everyone else, the way he'd kept her and Damon hidden, but he knew he had them, and that was enough.

In the corner behind her was an armoire, filled with jewelry boxes, presentation cases, and a row of leather-bound journals. Of course Henry would document his activities. It was part of his need, his arrogance. He believed he was safe in committing everything to paper because he was so good that no one would ever suspect him. For twenty years he'd been right.

Her hand trembling, she picked up the journal dated the year he'd acquired her. When she lifted the cover, the book fell open to a photograph attached to one page. It was dated April, and it was her, taken on a street in Ocho Rios where tourists were plentiful and no one paid attention to one shabby little native girl. She'd counted on that invisibility. It had made her very good at what she did. But . . .

She hadn't met him until November.

She was reaching out to touch the photo, to remove it from the page, when there was a whisper of movement, followed by her worst nightmare as the room plunged into darkness.

Tony sat in Henry's driveway, drumming his fingers on the steering wheel while waiting for the guard to call the house, then open the gate. For months the guards had automatically let him pass, but that had stopped . . . about the time of Joe's surprise visit, he realized. Because Joe had seen and heard things Henry needed kept secret?

After what seemed like forever, the gate started its slow swing open. "The staff has the day off, but the front door's unlocked," the guard said. "The chief says to come on up and join him in his study."

"Thanks." Tony followed the drive to its end on the north side of the house. He took the steps to the long porch two at a time, then let himself in the ornate door.

Henry liked to say that the house had been built to show off the main staircase, instead of the other way around. Twenty feet wide, with risers of marble and banisters of teak, stretching straight and true to the second floor, the staircase *was* grand. As many times as Tony had been there, it caught his attention every time. This time he hardly noticed it.

The door to the study was closed. Tony knocked, waited for an invitation, then walked in. Henry was seated behind his desk, the *World* open in front of him. The only other items on the desk were a leather pad and a crystal notepad-and-pen holder. Even the phone was relegated to a table beneath the tall windows. He smiled welcomingly, stood, and shook hands. Everything about him was so familiar. He couldn't possibly be keeping the kind of secrets Joe had hinted at. He just couldn't.

"This is a pleasant surprise. Have a seat." Henry gestured toward the leather chairs, and Tony chose one, catching the faint scent of perfume as the leather yielded beneath his weight. "Did you have any damage from the storms?"

"Not really. Some downed trees, a section of fence."

"How about your folks?"

"I stopped by there this morning. They're fine." Tony

took a deep breath, aiming for casual when he went on. "I talked to Lucia while I was there, and she brought up—"

"The assisted-living center." Henry gave a regretful shake of his head. "I know you hate the idea, Tony, but you've got to put aside emotion and look at it rationally. Joe's not going to get better. It's not fair of you to ask Anna to shoulder such an enormous burden. I know you wish for some miracle cure, but there is no cure, and the sooner you accept that, the better it will be for Anna."

Tony wasn't surprised by Henry's pitch on Lucia's behalf. She'd always been his favorite, and he babied her just like the rest of the family did. Hadn't she gone running to him for support and intervention after Tony's less-than-happy response to her first retirement-community suggestion? Henry had brought it up the day Joe had taken his joyride, when they'd met at the accident scene. *I was leaving a note at your desk when the call came in about Joe* he'd said, to explain the message form he'd dropped.

The message he'd returned to his pocket rather than give to Tony. The message that had had Tony's name across the top.

His skin prickling with apprehension, Tony closed his eyes and focused on the slip of paper. He'd seen it only for an instant, but that had been long enough to know some hand other than Henry's had written his name there. Henry's writing was like the man—bold, straightforward. The writing on the form had been a barely legible left-handed scrawl.

Darnell Garry was the only lefty in their squad, and the only one in the office the morning Dwayne Samuels had called—the same morning of Joe's accident. He couldn't remember the call, Darnell had said, but if Samuels had left a message, Darnell had left it on the appropriate desk.

Had Henry taken the message from Tony's desk? Had he known Dwayne had something to tell? He'd had access to the Known Associates lists for Grover Washington and Bucky Spradlin, and to informant information that linked Javier Perkins to Tony. He'd known Tony suspected there were problems with Javier's story.

He had known about the arrest of the vigilante's accomplice. Had the ability to find out where the unit transporting the accomplice to the jail was at any given time. Had the ability to pass through a police perimeter without so much as a blink. What officer was going to question the chief of police, for God's sake? The patrol officer who'd caught the suspicious persons report that had turned out to be Henry had been the butt of jokes for a week. No one wanted to find himself in the same position.

Tony's chest grew tight. That report had come in from Bryan Hayes's neighborhood around the time of his murder. And Henry had been there. Other cops had known about the operation last night—Lieutenant Nicholson, the division commander, every officer involved and his supervisor. Other cops could have passed through the downtown area without drawing questions or attention. Others would have known the patrol unit would most likely pass through that intersection.

But no one else, besides Darnell Garry, had known about the phone call from Dwayne, and Darnell had been at the warehouse with Tony at the time of the shooting. No one else but Frankie had known Tony's doubts about Javier.

And Lucia hadn't followed the killer from the warehouse to any other cop's house.

This was *Henry* he was talking about, for Christ's sake. Uncle Henry. Family. Tony had known him all his life. He was a good man, a good cop—had devoted his *life* to defeating the bad guys. Tough on crime and tougher on criminals. He couldn't . . . *couldn't* . . .

So there was no harm in asking. Henry would deny it, then laugh and say something about Tony remaining a little bit *too* emotionally detached from his cases. And then Tony could start looking for the real killer.

"I don't want to argue with you about Dad today," he said. "Can we talk about something else?"

Though he looked as if he did want to argue, after a moment, Henry nodded. "Do you have anything in particular in mind?"

"Yeah. The vigilante case."

"Do you have any theories?"

"I do." Tony took a deep breath, then said flatly, "I think the killer's a cop."

Henry's reaction was underwhelming. There was no surprise, no immediate denial, no anger. He just continued to toy with the pen for a moment before finally returning it to its holder and folding his hands on the desktop. "Based on what?"

Tony spoke slowly, putting his thoughts in order as he went. "Phone calls were made to five of the victims from a pay phone at the Denver Avenue bus station, a couple minutes' walk from the police station. But when the vigilante called James Tranh, he switched phones."

"Convenience?"

"Or he knew we had a wiretap order on the bus-station phone."

Henry wasn't impressed. "That's a stretch, Tony."

"The killer never leaves anything at the scene. No cigarette butts, no gum wrappers, no hair, no fibers, no nothing, and he polices his brass."

"Anyone who watches television knows to do that."

"Come on, Henry. You've been a cop a hell of a lot longer than me. How many damn-near perfect murders have you seen in that time?"

"Very few," he conceded. "People make mistakes. But most killings are crimes of passion. People in the grip of rage, jealousy, or vengeance rarely think clearly. Our vigilante is cold-blooded. He plans everything out. He has no emotional investment. He doesn't make mistakes. Is that all you have?"

Too restless to sit still, Tony stood and walked a slow circuit around the room, pretending interest in all the little things Henry filled his space with so he wouldn't have to make eye contact. "The vigilante has excellent intelligence—the kind cops would have."

"Finding drug dealers isn't exactly difficult, Tony."

"Not the nickel-and-dime guys, no. But their suppliers, guys like Tranh and Grover Washington—you don't just pick up the phone and call them, or get in your car and drive by their house. Dwayne Samuels lived out in the middle of nowhere, and he was paranoid about people coming out there. He had an electronic gate, alarms, motion detectors. Probably the only ones who knew how to find him were the guys who worked for him, his family, and the cops."

He glanced over his shoulder and saw Henry was waiting silently. His expression had begun to turn grim.

"He knew his accomplice had been arrested Saturday night. Knew Potter was in that particular unit and that he would be traveling that particular street to the jail. He knew in time to position himself on that rooftop, and he knew he didn't have to worry about getting picked up, even though cops were stopping people within minutes."

"Because he had a badge and a reason for being there."

Tony nodded, then took another deep breath. His hand was unsteady, so he wrapped his fingers around the cool, hard metal of a statue on a marble-topped table. "He also knew that Dwayne Samuels had some information for me."

"Samuels . . . victim number eight?"

Another nod. "Dwayne called the station looking for me the day he died. Darnell Garry took the message, but I never got it. Someone took it from my desk while I was out that morning—the morning Dad had his wreck. *You* were at my desk that morning. *You* had a message with my name on it in your pocket. Remember?"

In the silence that followed, Tony slowly turned to face Henry. Again, his response was underwhelming. He should have been shocked or angry, should have been quick to offer denials. Instead, he sat there in his leather chair, watching Tony with an oddly regretful look. Just that look was enough to tell him.

Jesus Christ.

"Perhaps you should be looking at Detective Garry." Too little, too late.

Numbly Tony shook his head. "Darnell was at the warehouse when the guy was killed."

"I was home."

"Can you prove it?"

Henry's smile was faintly amused. "No. More important, *you* can't prove I wasn't."

For the first time ever, Tony was glad Joe's mind was going. He loved Henry like a brother! He'd invited him into his home—had given him access to his *family,* for Christ's sake! To know how corrupt and twisted he'd become would have broken Joe's heart.

"I think I can," Tony said. "How hard do you think it will be to find the patrol or traffic cop who remembers stopping you downtown Saturday night?"

That brought a slight response—the tightening of his

jaw. Tony pushed ahead. "On top of that, I have a witness who places the man from the warehouse—the man on the Ducati—here at your house. Damon Long . . . that's his name, isn't it? And there's that visit Dad made here. He was convinced you were an impostor, a drug dealer, making plans with another man. That was Long, too, wasn't it?"

Rising from the chair, Henry walked to the intercom next to the door, pressed the CALL button, then returned to his seat. "I've always thought that if anyone could solve these murders, it would be you. Truthfully, though, I expected you to be dead long before you figured it out. You're more competent than even I believed, or perhaps Selena is merely less so."

"Selena—What— How—" The capacity for speech went right out of his head as the door opened and two armed thugs came in. Tony reached for the pistol clipped to his waistband in back, but the shorter of the men grabbed his arm, twisting it up around his shoulder blades. He landed one punch that didn't faze the bigger guy, and took one in the gut in return that made his legs buckle.

Henry steepled his hands together. "It's a good thing I had these two gentlemen standing by. I asked them here to deal with another small problem. Unfortunately, that problem just keeps multiplying." Turning his head, he called loudly, "Damon, come on out. Bring our other guest with you."

For a moment there was silence, broken only by the breathing from the two goons and the thudding of Tony's heart. Then, slowly, a door began to open in the wall. Jeez, he'd sat in this room dozens of times and had never known there was a door there. But hell, he'd sat with Henry hundreds of times and had never had a clue about the sick secrets he was hiding.

Now that he'd found out, damned if he intended to take them to his grave.

• • •

Henry's vault was so well constructed that not even the faintest ray of light leaked in around the door, but the voices from the outer room came through quite clearly. Selena stood frozen, barely able to think or breathe for the panic coursing through her. She had to get out of the room, had to breathe fresh air and see the light, had to face the danger.

But when she bolted, Damon grabbed her, his arm like a steel band beneath her breasts, his gun pressing against her and his other hand brutally covering her mouth. He held her so tightly that, for a moment, she was grateful; he was the only thing holding her together. But as she listened to the wariness and disillusionment in Tony's voice, the arrogance in Henry's, the panic receded. She was so damned tired of lies, betrayals, and disappointments, and damned if she would meekly take them anymore.

All those months of training kicked in. Montoya had never tolerated weakness in her. If she panicked, she got hurt. If she lost control, she got hurt. He'd pushed her, focused her, controlled her, and taught her to control herself. She closed her eyes, breathed, listened to his voice in her head, taunting, mocking, encouraging. With movements so restrained that she was hardly aware of them herself, she drew the switch-blade from her waistband, pressed the button that flicked it open, then sank it to the hilt in Damon's thigh.

Grinding out curses under his breath, he let go of her with one hand and reached for the knife. She grabbed hold of the wrist that covered her mouth, twisted it back, ducked, and came up free, then hit blindly, instinctively, with a heel-palm strike to his face, driving his nose upward with the force of the blow. Blood spurted, warm and plentiful, over her hand, but she ignored it. Getting a good grip on his hair, she cracked his head against the sharp corner of the cabinet behind him, felt his body buckle, then did it again for good measure.

"Damon," Henry called through the door. "Come on out. Bring our other guest with you."

She let go of him, and his body sagged backward, pushing the door open. He sank onto the floor, half in, half out, of the room, and lay motionless. As she wiped his blood on her pants, she debated her next move. Would it be wiser to stroll into the room for an open confrontation, or to make Henry send one of his flunkies after her?

Footsteps sounded outside, taking the choice from her. She pressed back into the shadows where the armoire met the wall. The figure that appeared in the doorway was huge—easily six foot six and three hundred fifty pounds—and he was carrying a big weapon, as well, holding it up to the right of his head. Grasping the open armoire door for balance, she waited until he was no more than a few feet away, then swung her left foot high into the air. It connected with his wrist, earning her a grunt of pain, and sent the pistol flying behind him.

The instant her foot touched the floor again, she slammed the armoire door into his body. This time he gave a howl and staggered back a step. She took advantage of his loss of balance with a sweep kick that caught him just below the knees and sent him tumbling backward. Damon's unconscious body behind him took care of the rest, sending him crashing to the floor, a big lump of tangled limbs, where he wisely remained.

From the outer room came an amused chuckle. "Bravo, Selena. I must admit that, in spite of all your training, I'd come to believe you didn't have it in you to actually hurt someone. Come out here, please, dear. I assure you, Mr. Ramey's associate won't walk into the same trap."

She unhooked the dagger from her ankle and slid it, sheath and all, into the back of her waistband, then drew the forty cal before she approached the door. Mr. Ramey was showing signs of life, groaning and shaking his head. He started to sit up as she stepped over Damon's body, but when she brought the pistol to aim on his forehead, he paled, choked into silence, and sank back to the floor.

She slipped past the hulk and moved toward Henry, sitting at his desk. Despite the pistol she held, he showed no fear. He'd intended to have her killed, but he still didn't believe she could hurt *him*. He still believed he was that important to her.

She eased between the desk and the credenza, passed behind the leather chair, and took up a position behind and to Henry's right. At the opposite end of the room, Tony was as motionless as Damon, held that way as much by shock as by the .45 pointed at his temple. He looked bewildered. Hurt. Betrayed. Henry was so very good at engendering those emotions in the people who loved him. Apparently, so was she.

Henry turned his chair to face her. "Holding a gun on me, Selena? After all I've done for you . . . all I've given you . . ?"

"All you've done," she repeated softly, then her voice strengthened. "*All* you've done? You've tried to control every choice I've ever made. You've manipulated me at every turn. You promised me the very things I wanted most, and then denied them because you could. You took advantage of my love and gratitude and tried to turn me into someone as cold and damaged and heartless as you!"

His gaze narrowed dangerously. "You can't blame me for that, Selena. You were damaged when I found you. Your own mother despised you for the color of your skin. Your own father wanted nothing to do with you. You'd been thrown away by three sets of parents by the time you were fourteen. No one wanted you but me. No one had any use for you but me . . . but now your usefulness has ended."

She waited for the desperate little girl inside her to react to his words, but nothing happened. There was no pain, no bitterness, no self-loathing for having proved herself unworthy. Coolly she smiled and waved the gun a time or two to catch his attention. "No, Uncle. *Your* usefulness to *me* has ended."

For the first time fear flickered through his eyes, lasting only an instant, but satisfying all the same. "You *can't* kill me," he boasted, and he sounded almost as if he believed it.

"Can't I? After all you've done?" She leaned a few inches closer, lowered her voice to a silky, soft imitation of Henry at his most dangerous. "You wanted to turn me into a murderer, Uncle. Well, guess what? You've succeeded."

"Not until someone lies dead by your hand." Henry gestured toward the vault door. "Damon will be conscious again in minutes, Mr. Ramey is merely letting his cowardice show, and obviously I'm still breathing." Then a sly look came into his eyes. "However, if you want a chance to redeem yourself, to prove yourself worthy . . ." He motioned elegantly in Tony's direction. "You can do so by carrying out the assignment I gave you. Kill him."

Selena looked from him to Tony, who returned her gaze. The bewilderment and hurt were gone from his eyes, replaced by bitter disdain. His mouth shifted, almost sneering before he looked away from her to Henry.

"Why are you doing this?" he asked. "You're supposed to be one of the good guys, remember? What the hell is so important you would betray everything you ever stood for?" He made an ineffective attempt to indicate the treasures in the room, stifled by the man with the gun. "For *money*?"

Henry gazed at the Monet. "That painting is worth

more than you'll ever make in your lifetime—and I've got a dozen more just as valuable. This desk—four years' salary for you. This rug—priceless. But, no, it's not about the money." With a genial smile, he amended that. "It's not *only* about the money. Money is good. I like living well. But I like other things more."

Such as power, Selena thought. Control over others' lives. Ownership of great treasures, whether artifacts, property, or people. The money was merely a bonus.

Tony prepared to ask the obvious question, but Henry brushed him off. "Analyzing one's self is tedious, particularly when you're not going to be around long enough to care." He directed his attention back to her. "Do you want that second chance, Selena? Do you want to prove that you aren't the biggest mistake I ever made?"

Mistake. She'd been called worse, but for much of her life that simple insult in that indifferent tone had been enough to break her heart. At the moment, though, she didn't care that he was disappointed. Didn't care whether he ever deemed her worthy. Didn't care, period.

But telling him so would only result in getting herself killed along with Tony. Achingly aware of him—of the chill and contempt emanating from him—she focused on Henry. "If I do your job, Uncle, what will I get?"

He smiled indulgently. Triumphantly. "What do you want?"

"That Monet. The Picasso. The Cézanne. Oh, and complete and total control of your business . . . without you."

His narrowing gaze was the only genuine response to her answer. He covered it with another of his charming smiles, as if he didn't believe for an instant that she was serious. "You can't live without me, Selena. Your heart and soul belong to me. Without me, you're nothing. Kill him.

We'll blame it on Damon—all the vigilante killings, all the drug deals. The investigation will be over, and you and I will be free to continue life as usual."

He was lying, just as he'd always lied. If she killed Tony, then Henry would kill her. If she didn't, Henry would kill them both. Nothing she did would change that . . . unless *she* killed *him*.

She looked at him, smugly confident, certain of his place in her life, sure that she would rather die herself than let him down again, then at Tony, whose expression made it clear that she would never again have a place in his life. He would never forgive her, but that was all right. She could live with his hatred. She could live with anything except his death.

The man who held him at gunpoint stood behind him, using him as a shield. He didn't mind killing for his boss, but apparently he wanted to diminish the odds of dying for him. The only way to get to the guy was through Tony. He was betting she wouldn't take that route.

Her fingers tightened around the pistol grips, squeezing so hard that the blood fled her fingertips. She lifted the gun, all too aware of its weight, its deadly power. At this distance, the steel-jacketed hollow-point bullet would tear through flesh and bone with equal ease. It would destroy everything it passed through—the heart, if she aimed high in the chest; the brain, if she went higher; the renal artery, if she opted for a lower shot.

She drew a perfect bead center mass. Tony stared at her, the look in his eyes unforgiving. As her finger tightened on the trigger, she shifted the angle of the gun up and to the right, then fired.

The force of the blast knocked Tony back into his captor and sent them both crashing into the wall before, with a faintly surprised look, he slumped to the floor. Stunned by her actions, the man with the .45 was slow to regain his balance. He was still leaning against the wall when her second shot tore into his chest.

By the time she swung the muzzle around to Henry, he had acquired a weapon of his own and was pointing it at her as he gracefully rose to his feet. "You've surprised me again, Selena. Now put the weapon down."

Her gun didn't waver. Just a little more pressure on the trigger, and his heart would cease to function. He would be dead before he hit the floor. "Why should I?"

"Because if you don't, I'm going to finish the job you started." He swung the gun toward Tony, sprawled face-down and bleeding on the priceless rug but clearly still breathing. "Put the gun down, or the next bullet will go into his brain."

She didn't move. Her pistol remained steady on Henry, the hammer back, her finger on the trigger. It would be so easy to drop him . . . but his own pistol was aimed, its hammer cocked, his own finger on the trigger. What were the odds he would lose consciousness before firing? Good . . . but not good enough.

She thought she heard a faint groan of protest from Tony when she eased her finger off the trigger, then raised both hands in the air. Stepping forward, she laid the gun on the end of the desk nearest her, then stepped back. She was vaguely aware of Mr. Ramey off to Henry's left, scrambling for his own weapon, and of Tony, still in a motionless heap, but she kept her gaze locked on Henry.

He leaned against the window casing at the far end of the desk, looking as casual as she'd ever seen him. Murder came so naturally to him. Human life had no value—not his godson's, not hers, none but his. Perhaps he hadn't denied her the love and intimacy she'd craved simply because he could, but because he'd had none to give.

"Selena," he said with patient disapproval. "You never give up your weapon, not as long as there's life in your body. That's a lesson you should have learned a long time ago. Sadly, now it's too late."

Not exactly. She'd given up two weapons—the pistol and the knife she'd left in Damon's leg. She still had two—and dwindling time in which to use them.

"I gave you everything," he went on. "I made you what you are, Selena. I gave you *life*. And now"—regret crept into his voice—"now I have to take it away."

The muscles in his hand flexed as he began to apply steady pressure to the trigger. She watched, her lungs growing tight from lack of air, waiting until the last instant to lunge, rolling across the desk, kicking for his gun hand but connecting with his ribs instead. The blow bent him double, but didn't stop him from bringing his own knee up into her midsection as she slid off the slick surface. The air rushed from her body with a grunt as she hit the marble floor, leaving her left knee throbbing. She gritted her teeth against the pain as she raised it to her chest, high enough to reach the .22 holstered at her ankle, but before she'd done more than clear the holster, a size fifteen boot, belonging to Mr. Ramey, kicked the gun out of her grip, making her fingers go numb in the process.

Henry bent down, grasped a handful of her shirt, and hauled her to her feet. "I should have left you in Jamaica to die. If I hadn't returned for you when I did, your parents would have whored you to any filthy lech with a few dollars in his pocket. You would have been dead before you were twenty, and would have saved me the trouble of killing you now."

For a moment she stood there, breathing heavily.

Henry's expression was smug. "I expected more of a fight from you, Selena. Once more you've disappointed me. I'm going to let you watch Tony die before I kill you. You'll go to your death knowing that you caused his death, as well."

"Bullshit," she whispered.

The congenial smile disappeared. "It's a simple lesson I've hammered in from the beginning. One would think you might have learned it by now. Vulgarity is so . . . well, vulgar in a woman."

"Fuck you," she retorted, shifting her weight slightly. The dagger sheathed in the small of her back bit into her skin, reminding her that she still had one chance. Tony still had one chance.

He released his grip on her, shoving her away. Catching her balance, she slowly straightened, then locked her gaze on Henry and forced short, steady breaths into her lungs. His aim shifted from Tony to her, and the hulk, she saw, had her in his sights, as well. She'd disarmed him once. If she could do it again . . .

She moved as if to favor her injured knee, drew the dagger, and threw it, end over end, at Henry. As soon as it left her fingertips, she used another sweep kick to bring Mr. Ramey to the floor. Henry's agonized cry barely penetrated her concentration as she struggled with the big man for control of his gun, a struggle that ended abruptly with a single shot.

The hulk froze, staring wide-eyed at his boss. She looked, too, and saw Henry looking wide-eyed himself. Blood ran from his right hand where the dagger had reached its target and, high on his chest, seeped in an ever-widening circle across his white shirt. Staring past them, he weakly, disbelievingly said, "T-Tony . . . you—you shot me. I can't believe . . . after all I've been to you . . ."

As if in slow motion, Henry staggered back, crashed against the window, then disappeared from sight.

Mr. Ramey's grip went slack on the gun. Selena pulled it free, then eased to her feet. At the far end of the room, Tony was on his feet, as well, his face ashen, his eyes dark and blank. With his gun hanging in his right hand, he limped past her on his way to the window. "If any of them moves, shoot 'im."

Those were his only words to her. He circled the desk, looked out the shattered window, then grimly went to the intercom and instructed the guards to call 911. He collected all the weapons except hers, leaving them on the desk. She didn't offer to help, didn't even move for fear it would make him look at her like that again—empty, lost. She didn't think she could bear that look again.

By the time the security guards rushed into the room, he was leaning against the desk, one hand pressed against his shoulder. Their guns were drawn, but they weren't sure who to point them at. "D-d-detective Ceola," the first one stammered. "What— Where's Ch-chief Daniels?"

"Out there." Tony gestured toward the window. "Handcuff him and him." He nodded at Damon and Mr. Ramey, then at the third man, gravely wounded. "And watch him. They're all under arrest."

Two guards moved to obey him; the third rushed to the window to look out. When he turned back, the color had drained from his face. "Oh, my God . . . is he dead?"

"I don't know."

One guard finished with Damon, then pointed at Selena. "What about her?"

Tony twisted on the desk to look at her. For the few seconds his gaze was on her, there was no emotion in it, not even pain. It was as if he was looking at nothing.

That was all right. She'd been less than nothing for the first fourteen years of her life. *Nothing* was a step up from that. She could live with it. She could live with anything.

When he turned away, he didn't even bother to speak. He just shook his head in the guard's direction, then grimaced again.

So that was that. It was finished. Henry, if he'd survived, and Damon would go to prison. So would the two thugs. Probably so would she. Shooting a police officer, conspiracy to commit murder, possession of illegal firearms . . . those were just a few of the charges she would face. And when she got out, she would probably be deported. No more art gallery, no more safe, secure island home . . . no more Tony.

But he was alive, and sooner or later, he would be well. Hadn't she insisted he could hate her for as long as he lived, as long as he *did* live?

Police cars began arriving at the estate, along with ambulances, TV news vans, and the crime-scene unit. Selena sat numbly out of the way, watching the paramedics work on and remove each victim in turn. They recovered Henry, still breathing, from the parapet four feet below the window and rushed him to the hospital with a flustered detective accompanying him on Tony's orders to guard him.

Tony refused their attention for his own wound while he talked with Frank Simmons, the blonde woman he'd gone jogging with a few Saturdays ago, and two men who looked so much like his father that they must be Uncles Vince and John. There was a Major Somebody making a lot of noise, while a Lieutenant Something-or-other tried to maintain control. For the most part, all of them ignored Selena, at least until the blonde came over and crouched in front of her. "I'm Marla Johnson. I'm from the crime lab," she said, her voice calm and soothing in contrast to the men's voices. "Are you okay?"

Selena nodded.

"I understand you're responsible for most of this."

She nodded again.

"I need to swab your hands for gunshot residue, okay?"

She nodded once more.

Marla opened the small kit, took out a handful of swabs, and began swiping them, one at a time, across Selena's palm, the back of her hand, and between the fingers. "I have to tell you, I like a woman who can hold her own against five men, though I suspect that shooting your boyfriend might be tough on the relationship."

"I needed him out of the way." Selena managed little more than a whisper, and it quavered. Funny. She wasn't a quavery sort of person.

"Well, I'd say you managed." After sliding the swabs into a glass tube and sealing it, Marla smiled. "There. Do the paramedics need to look you over?"

"I'm fine."

Marla gently touched the swelling on Selena's cheek and jaw. "You sure?"

Selena nodded.

"Okay. If you need anything, give me a holler. I'll be around awhile."

Selena nodded as Marla walked away, then raised her hands to cover her face. Catching sight of Damon's blood, she smiled bleakly, then lowered them again. It was Damon's blood on her hands two years ago that had set Henry's horrible plan in motion, and now there it was again.

After what seemed like an eternity, Frank Simmons approached, asking her to leave the room with him. With one last glance at Tony, she followed him downstairs to what had likely once been a gentlemen's parlor. She glanced around, noticing Henry's treasures but lacking even the faintest desire to examine them more closely. She just wanted it to be over. Wanted to be alone. To regret and mourn and find some way to survive. Henry's doubts aside, she *would* survive.

But she might never really live again.

Detective Simmons started by reading her her rights. Oh, yeah, she was going to jail. He questioned her relentlessly about her relationship with Henry, with Damon, with Tony, and she told him . . . not everything. Not how much she'd loved Henry, how desperately she'd craved his affection and approval. Not how much she'd hated him, how desperately she'd wanted to stop him. Not how desperately she'd wanted to keep Tony alive. But she told him enough that she couldn't be accused of withholding information, and it seemed to satisfy him, as much as anything about her could satisfy him. Putting the handcuffs on—that probably would. Hauling her off to jail—definitely. Seeing her locked away and out of Tony's life forever—absolutely.

At least he would get his wish on that last. No matter what else happened, she was out of Tony's life.

Finally he shut off his tape recorder and left her alone, with a fresh-faced young officer guarding the doorway. She waited, eyes closed, focusing on a safe place in her head, until footsteps on the stairs and raised voices shattered the calm she'd achieved.

"For Christ's sake, Tony, she *shot* two people, including you, and did some serious damage to two others!" Simmons said.

Tony's response was carefully enunciated, each word coldly empty of emotion. "Take her home."

"But—"

"Don't fuck with me, Frankie! I'm having a really shitty day. Just *take her home*."

"You're not thinking clearly. Maybe I should talk to the lieutenant or—"

The sound of scuffling feet was followed by a crash. "You don't fucking talk to anybody!" Tony said, the words ground out through clenched teeth. "This is my fucking case, and I'm fucking telling you to take her home *now*!"

"Okay, okay. It's okay." Simmons's tone was conciliatory. Apparently, he didn't want to be added to the list of walking wounded. "All right, Chee. I'll do it. Then I'll come back and we'll go to the hospital, okay? In case you haven't noticed, you've got a goddamn hole in your shoulder."

"Believe me, I noticed." Tony sounded exhausted. Emotionally, he probably was. He should already be at the hospital, cleaned up, medicated, and sleeping like a baby. "Don't bother coming back. I'll catch a ride with the last ambulance. Just don't let anyone call my family yet, okay? I want to talk to them myself."

"Okay. I'll, uh, take care of, uh, *her*. You take care of yourself." Simmons stepped into the doorway and watched, apparently, until Tony was out of sight. After speaking quietly to the officer posted outside the room, he beckoned her. "Come on. Let's go."

Feeling as exhausted as Tony had sounded, Selena crossed the room, then walked alongside Simmons to the door. The young cop followed on their heels. Selena didn't try to catch a glimpse of Tony. Nothing she could say could change the way he'd looked at her.

It was over.

16

She didn't even look to see if he was around.

That thought kept repeating in Tony's mind—while he finished up at the scene, once he'd finally accepted a ride to the hospital, after they'd fixed him up and stuck him in a room. He had a drain in his wound, a bandage, and an order for a painkiller, but he hadn't asked for it yet. The pain in his shoulder felt kind of good. It helped him keep all the other pains out of his thoughts.

His family had come and gone. So had Marla and his lieutenant and all three of the deputy chiefs. Simmons had stopped by on his way home, looking as beat as Tony felt. He'd delivered Selena safely home, he reported, defiantly adding that he'd left an officer watching her house.

Tony hadn't had any response to that. She and Henry and Damon Long were three of a kind—fake lives, fake people. The Selena he knew didn't really exist, just as the Henry he'd known had disappeared somewhere along the line. He'd fooled everyone so completely—no doubt part of his fun. He'd thought he would never get caught.

But he had.

The door made no noise when it opened. There was just a subtle change in the air, a whisper through the room. Tony glanced that way, then returned to staring at the ceiling. So much for the cop watching her house.

She came into the room, closing the door behind her,

and he wondered for one wild moment if she'd come to finish the job she'd started weeks ago. The thought must have shown on his face, because she lifted both arms away from her body. "I'm unarmed." Her smile was uneasy. "I haven't gone out without a weapon in two years. I feel naked."

Damned if his body didn't respond to that image. After all he'd been through, all he'd learned, sex should be the last thing on his mind, but he figured he would have to be impotent or dead to stop being turned on around her.

She came a few steps closer, a blur of motion and colors. "I know I'm the last person you want to see, but I wanted to—to apologize and to—to explain."

Explain. It sounded so innocent. How did you explain that you'd started an affair with someone for the sole purpose of getting close enough to kill him? That every word coming out of your mouth was a lie, that *you* were a lie? That you'd used him and betrayed him and intended to destroy him?

"Henry—or William Davis, as I knew him—once saved my life. I was fourteen and working the streets in Jamaica when I picked the wrong pocket and got caught. The man reclaimed his property, then beat me and tried to rape me. Henry stopped him. He—he killed him, and he kept me. He gave me a new name, called me his niece, and brought me to the States with him. He became my uncle, my father figure, my only family."

So the story about her parents dying in a car wreck was a lie. Surprise.

"Two years ago he invited me to visit him here in Tulsa. While I was here, I went out with a man named Greg Marland. When he assaulted me in Henry's guesthouse, I hit him with a statue. He was unconscious and there was blood everywhere, and Henry told me he was dead. I was hysterical. I wanted to call the police, but he said no, he would take care of everything. And he did. Two years later he blackmailed me into coming here, with the evidence of my crime and—and—"

Killing *him*. Tony still couldn't quite grasp it. His god-father had wanted him dead. And for what? To protect his business interests. What kind of crappy reason was that to die?

About as crappy as dying so Selena could protect her freedom.

"I didn't find out until last night that I hadn't killed any-one. Greg Marland, better known as Damon Long, is alive and well . . . at least, he was well until I stabbed him today. He's worked for Henry for years; it was all a sick plan to force me to do what Henry wanted."

She paused—giving him a chance to speak?—but he remained silent. When she finally went on, her voice was softer, huskier. "I know saying I'm sorry isn't enough. It's just words, and it can't begin to make up for what I've done, but . . . I am sorry."

So was he. Sorrier than he could say. Hell, he was the sorriest son of a bitch that ever lived.

"Tony?"

There were tears in her voice, but they didn't touch him. Tears were the one thing that left him immune, especially when they were lies. Just like her. Just like Henry. He continued to stare upward, seeing nothing but a blur, hearing nothing but a fake sniffle and a bogus sigh.

Without another word, she turned and left as quietly as she'd come. He remained in the same position for a long time, then finally uncurled his fingers from the fist they'd formed and pressed the nurse's call button.

"Can I help you?" a cheery voice asked.

"Yeah. I'll take that shot now."

• • •

Two days later Tony's shoulder still hurt like hell. He was supposed to be home in bed, taking the pills the doctor had given him and recuperating. But as soon as Julie had delivered him to the house, fussed over him a bit, then left, he'd gotten in his car and driven downtown. Now he leaned against the wall next to a two-way mirror that looked into the interrogation room next door.

Simmons sat in one chair, Garry in another. Tompkins, a detective from Narcotics, sat in the third chair, and the fourth . . . the fourth was the hot seat, and was occupied by Selena, or whomever the hell she really was. She was bruised and battered, and looked about like he felt—done in. In need of twenty-four hours of drug-induced oblivion.

They had been questioning her for hours, starting long before he'd arrived. Simmons had taken a break to fill him in on what they'd learned, which was exactly nothing. "How many freakin' times can she say, 'I don't know'?" he'd groused before returning to the interview.

Too many. To hear her tell it, William Davis was as much a mystery to her as he was to Tony, and *he'd* heard the name for the first time less than forty-eight hours ago.

After a few hundred more *I don't know*s, Simmons opened a file folder and removed a computer printout. "Since you insist you don't know nothin' about Uncle Bill, let's try a subject you *do* know. What's your name?"

She gazed at him a long time. Realizing he was holding his breath, Tony exhaled forcefully. Apparently, it was too much to hope that she'd been honest about such a basic thing.

"The name I use now is Selena McCaffrey," she said at last. "The name Henry gave me when he took me in was Gabriela Sanchez. My second set of foster parents called me

Rosa Jimenez, and my mother called me Amalia, though her husband preferred bastard." Her shrug was elegantly casual. "Take your pick."

"Where were you born?"

"Puerto Rico."

"Where in Puerto Rico?"

"I don't remember. I was very young."

Simmons scowled at both the answer and her thin smile. "When were you born?"

"I don't know."

"Oh, come on. How can you not know your own birth date?"

Easy enough when you'd been raised by a stepfather whose favorite pastime was beating the shit out of you—and Tony was convinced that, at least, was true. No doubt, her birthdays hadn't been cause for celebration in Rodrigo's household.

"What the hell are you doing here?"

Tony started. He hadn't heard the door open, and he damn sure hadn't heard Assistant District Attorney Matheny come in.

"I heard you got shot. Why aren't you in the hospital?"

He gestured to the sling that held his left arm immobilized against his chest. "I was. They discharged me."

"Then why the hell aren't you home in bed?"

He turned back to the mirror. "I've got too much to do." And too much to think about when he lay in bed.

Matheny reached past Tony to shut off the speaker. "Not on this case. Not anymore. The FBI's stepping in."

Even as he spoke, the door into the interrogation room opened. Lieutenant Nicholson stepped inside, followed by three agents from the Tulsa FBI office. At a nod from the lieutenant, the detectives filed out, with Nicholson bringing up the rear.

"What do they want?" Tony asked.

Matheny shrugged. "Daniels's drug operation is inter-state, probably international. It's their jurisdiction."

"But she doesn't know anything about that."

"So she says. They'll make it worth her while to remember."

A chill passed through Tony. Though he wouldn't wish anything bad on her, he didn't care what happened to her. He *didn't*. Still . . . "In what way?"

"She has a bogus driver's license, Social Security number, and passport. As far as anyone can tell, she entered the country illegally. She's in possession of two unregistered firearms, one of which has been illegally modified. She shot one of her accomplices, and she stabbed another. She was part of a conspiracy to murder a police officer, and she attempted to carry out that murder by shooting that police officer. I imagine with a little fancy footwork they'll even be able to tie her to those ten homicides you've been investigating. They've got enough to lock her up until she's old and gray, provided she doesn't get the death penalty instead. They'll make her an offer she can't refuse."

Lock her up. In a cell. She would make a deal with the devil himself to avoid that.

She *had* made a deal with the devil.

"She didn't try to kill me."

There was that damn shrug again. "Let her tell it to a jury."

Tony was finding it hard to breathe, and not because of the gunshot wound. All those hours he'd lain in the hospital with nothing to do but think and nothing to think about but her, he'd never imagined her in prison. Back in Florida, yes, painting her pictures, running her gallery, and even regretting everything that had happened. But arrested, convicted, incarcerated? She'd saved his *life*. Okay, so she'd done it by shooting him, but if she hadn't, one of Henry's goons—or Henry himself—would have done it, and they wouldn't have been nearly so careful about placing the shot.

He turned to face Matheny. "What do they want from her?"

"You know the drill better than me, Ceola. They probably want to turn her—make her a C.I. Get her to inform on all of Daniels's associates and partners in crime."

Put her in danger. Make her a target. Tony swallowed hard. She couldn't do it. She needed to go home to Key West. *He* needed her to go home. If he couldn't have her here with him—and there were no two ways about it: he couldn't. Even if she was willing to stay, he wasn't willing to let her. He couldn't look at her without remembering, couldn't trust her, couldn't forgive her. Not yet. Maybe not ever.

Grimly he shifted his attention back to the interview. Selena's spine was straight, her chin raised, but her gaze was fixed on the tabletop. She looked as cool and serene as ever, but he could see her hands in her lap, her fingers clenched so tightly that her knuckles turned white. Her responses were short, never more than a half-dozen words, and they drew no response from the agents.

He reached for the speaker switch, but Matheny stopped him. "This is between the feds and her, Chee."

Tony gazed down at the ADA's hand, blocking the switch, before looking him in the eye. "Don't fuck with me, Matheny."

Slowly the hand drew back and Tony turned on the speaker.

"—want to reconsider that decision, Ms. McCaffrey," the agent seated in the middle was saying. "Prison's a tough place. Stuck in a cell less than half the size of this room. Bars on every window—if you're lucky enough to see a window. I understand your stepfather used to lock you in a closet and leave you there for hours. But if you go to prison, that's all you're going to have, Selena. Small, dark, cramped spaces. Every miserable day for the rest of your life."

So it was true, Tony acknowledged. But who had told the feds? Obviously not Henry—he hadn't yet regained consciousness and the doctors weren't hopeful that he ever would. Probably Damon Long. He seemed the type to use any advantage he could.

When she spoke, her voice sounded tiny and frightened, but with a hint of strength. "I—I can't."

"At the very least, Selena, you face deportation."

"I can live with that."

The agent's voice sharpened. "At the very most, you'll get the death penalty. You can't live with that."

She didn't pale, her eyes didn't widen, she didn't catch her breath—no visible signs that the agent's shock tactics had worked. Because she'd heard that threat before? From Henry? *Two years later he blackmailed me into coming here, with the evidence of my crime . . .* For fourteen years, he had used her. What kind of damage did that do to a woman who desperately needed to believe someone could love her?

Tony could have loved her. If she'd trusted him, if she'd told him the truth . . . But honesty forced him to admit that if she'd told him the truth, he never would have believed her. He'd *known* Henry, had loved and trusted *him* too much to ever believe such stories.

If she'd told him the truth, he would have let her down—just like her mother. Rodrigo. Her foster parents. Just like Henry.

And that was a hard truth to accept.

Henry remained in a coma with little hope for survival and none for recovery. Damon Long was recuperating from a concussion and a broken nose, as well as nerve and muscle damage in his thigh, and the man Selena had shot was recovering, as well. Tony's sling was gone and, a week after the incident, he was back at work.

And outside of a handful of people, no one in the city of Tulsa knew what had really happened that day at the Daniels estate. The authorities had fed the media the version of events that best suited their needs—that Henry had walked in on a burglary in progress, and that only through a fortuitous visit by his godson had the chief's life been spared. People were mourning the terrible tragedy and hailing Tony as a hero, and the FBI planned to keep spouting that version as God's truth until they'd managed to bring down Henry's entire empire.

And they fully intended to do it with Selena's help. They thought she had only two choices—become a confidential informant, or face trial or deportation for her own crimes. They didn't realize she had a third option, one that had always been in the back of her mind while dealing with Henry: disappearing. A new name, a new place, a new life . . . that choice was looking better every day.

She'd gone so far as to reclaim the documentation for the new name—driver's license, birth certificate, Social Security card, and passport—from its hiding place. She'd crated up her canvasses for shipment to the gallery in care of Asha, with a note requesting that she store the unfinished self-portrait in the hopes that someday Selena could reclaim it. She'd packed a few outfits and squirreled away her emergency stash of cash. Once UPS picked up the crate, she would be ready to go. She was torn between hoping the familiar brown van would appear in her driveway at that very instant and wishing it would never come.

She'd started over before. It had always been easy, so why should this time be different? Why should she feel as if leaving Princeton Court and Tulsa could be the biggest mistake she might ever make? She had no choice. She couldn't accept the FBI's offer of immunity, and she couldn't calmly wait for them to lock her away. The idea of spending the rest of her life in prison terrified her . . . but not as much as letting Henry win disgusted her. She couldn't do it. Couldn't take over his business for any reason. Couldn't let him continue to control her. She'd fought him when he was alive and well, and she couldn't do any less now that he hovered on the brink of death.

The ring of the doorbell startled her. She jumped to her feet, looked out the sidelight, and saw the delivery truck parked behind the T-bird. Her hand trembled as she opened the door; her smile was unsteady as she greeted the driver. He collected her signature, loaded the crate onto a dolly, eased it down the steps and up the ramp into the back of the truck. She watched until he was gone, when she reluctantly turned back to pick up the sole bag in the foyer.

She had no doubt her house was under surveillance, just as she had no doubt she could easily lose the agent following her. She was dressed in capris, a T-shirt, and running shoes, and the clothing she was taking was packed in her gym bag. Anyone who knew anything about her would assume she was merely going to the gym to work out—and the FBI, she was sure, knew everything.

Except that Rocky, her sparring partner, had already shown her the rear exit at the gym. He'd agreed to loan her his vehicle, a pickup similar to thousands of other pickups on the Oklahoma highways, and to park it in the alley behind the gym. He was looking forward to stalling the agent as long as he could once the man's suspicions had been aroused. How could he do anything less, he'd teased, for the only girl who'd ever kicked his ass?

All she had to do was leave. Walk out the door. Say good-bye to Tulsa once and for all, knowing that this time, she really wouldn't ever return.

She picked up the bag. Opened the door. Stepped out into the blistering heat. It took several tries to get the key into the lock to secure it. Another couple tries to get her car unlocked. She'd tossed her bag on the passenger seat and was about to slide behind the wheel when a mournful sound stopped her. Mutt was standing at the fence in Tony's backyard, watching her, looking for all the world as if he understood she was leaving and never coming back. She walked back to the fence, crouched, and scratched between his ears. "Hey," she murmured. "Maybe you'll get a new neighbor with kids who will play with you. Or better yet, one with a pretty little female dog."

He closed his eyes and strained against the fence to get closer.

Abruptly her eyes grew damp and a lump formed in her throat. Getting teary over a dog because he was the only creature who had ever been sorry to see her go . . . how pathetic was that?

"I've got to go. You be a good boy," she whispered, "and—"

"What the hell are you doing?"

Tony's voice, sharp with suspicion and distrust, came from a few yards behind her. She balanced herself with one hand on the fence, took a deep breath, then eased to her feet before turning to face him. She was grateful for the dark glasses that covered her eyes, grateful that his own dark glasses kept her from seeing the hostility radiating from him. "I was petting your dog," she said, striving for even and cool. "Am I no longer allowed to do that?"

"What was that truck doing here?"

She glanced at her watch and saw it was nearly three-thirty. He must have come home shortly before the delivery van had arrived. It said something about her level of distraction that she'd missed that. "I'm sending some canvasses to the gallery."

"Why?"

"It's difficult to sell paintings that are in Tulsa at a gallery that's in Key West."

He didn't look as if he believed her. If she said it was a hot day, he would probably want to feel the sweat beaded on his forehead before accepting it as truth. "You've been here for weeks and suddenly you need to ship your canvasses?" He twisted to look through the windows into the sunroom. It was easy to see that all the canvasses were gone. Of course, he could have guessed that from the size of the crate.

When he faced her again, the skepticism was clear on his face. "Where are you going?"

"To the gym." She tried to smile but her mouth wouldn't cooperate. "I feel the need to hit something."

He wasn't amused. But that was all right. Neither was she.

She tried to think of something careless to say, but with every nerve in her body on edge, it was impossible. She settled for sidestepping him and starting toward her car. She'd left him some ten or twelve feet behind when he quietly spoke.

"You're leaving, aren't you?"

She stopped, turned, and managed a better smile. "I told you, I'm going to the gym."

"You sent your paintings home because you're not coming back. You're running away like a coward."

Stick to the lie, she counseled herself, but when she opened her mouth, something else spilled out. "A *coward*? Because I can't spend the rest of my life in a tiny, cramped prison cell?" Even saying the words aloud made her breath catch, made her chest tighten so that drawing in oxygen was impossible. "Because I don't want to surround myself with drug dealers and murderers? Because I'm sick to death of being used and manipulated and controlled for other people's benefit?"

"Hey, the choices were yours," he said, his tone short on sympathy. "When you found out Henry was a dope dealer, you could have cut him out of your life. Better yet, you could have turned him in to the cops. When he invited you to visit two years ago, you could have refused. When he asked you to kill a cop, you could have said no."

Incredulity drew her a few feet back toward him. "Cut him out of my life? He *saved* my life! He *killed* to protect me! He gave me food and shelter and an education and opportunities, and I owed him for that! He was all I had!"

"You owed him your gratitude, and that's all," he replied, displaying all that stubbornness Henry had hated in him. "You didn't owe him your life, and you damn sure didn't owe him your soul."

"I wouldn't even have had a life if not for him!"

He made a dismissive gesture with his right hand. "You survived fourteen years without him. You could have survived the next fourteen. Granted, it wouldn't have been so cushy. There wouldn't have been any fancy education or trips to Europe or a big old house in Key West, but at least you wouldn't have been living off the suffering and deaths of others. At least you wouldn't have been in a position where he could order you to kill someone."

The bitterness in her smile seeped through every part of her body, and made her movements stiff when she closed the distance between them. "It's so easy for you to talk. You never went hungry a day in your life. Your parents never dropped you off in town and warned you not to come home until you'd stolen at least five hundred dollars. You didn't fall asleep on a blanket on the floor every night just wishing that someone, anyone, would give a damn if you didn't wake up in the morning." The muscle in his jaw tightened, but before he could say anything, she went on. "That was my life, Tony, until Henry came into it."

She'd thought that taut muscle meant sympathy, but there was nothing but callous disregard in his voice. "So you had a lousy life when you were a kid. You're sorry, I'm sorry, everyone's sorry. But that doesn't excuse the lousy choices you made as an adult. He asked you to *kill* for him, for Christ's sake, and you said sure, not a problem!"

The unjustness of his words frustrated her. She had never intended to kill him! She had come to Tulsa looking for a way out, to save herself from a sin that would have destroyed her. She'd been willing to die so he could live, and all he cared about was that she'd pretended to agree to Henry's request in the first place. Her intent didn't matter; neither did her actions.

She stared at him, tears stinging her eyes. Then, folding her arms across her chest, she turned to leave. She paused only long enough to murmur "You don't understand, Tony. You can't."

He caught her wrist, yanking her to a halt. "Then explain, damn it! Make me understand how you can agree to murder someone you've never even met, how you can become friends with him and sleep with him, only so you can get close enough to kill him. Make me understand how you could be that twisted in your devotion to Henry!"

She tried to jerk free, but he only tightened his grip on her. "He was the only person in the world who thought *my* life was worth anything! He didn't look at me and see the results of an affair that was a mistake from the start. He didn't see another man's bastard or a punching bag or a thief with the potential to become a great whore. He saw a child who desperately needed someone, and he chose to *be* that someone. And I loved him for it!"

"And *I* loved *you*!"

For a moment Selena went utterly still. She couldn't think, breathe, move. Her wrist slid from his grasp, her arm limp. When she did manage a breath, it hurt. Swallowing left her throat raw and achy, and the tears that slid down her cheeks burned hot and salty. "D—don't . . ." She forced a swallow, then another breath, and her voice turned weak and pleading. "Don't say that. Please . . . nobody's ever said that . . ."

He looked as if he wanted to take back the words. She wished he could. She could live knowing that no one had ever loved her. She *had* lived with that for twenty-eight years. But to know that Tony *had* loved her, that he didn't now . . . She couldn't handle that.

But when he spoke, he didn't try to unsay the sentiment. He looked reluctant, unwilling, as if he had no choice but to follow through on what he'd started. His voice was low, his tone intense. "Then it's way past time someone did. I don't know how to get over being angry with you . . . but I do know that letting you go isn't the answer. I love you, Selena. I've tried real hard in the past week not to, but . . ."

She wanted to believe him, oh, God, more than she could say, but all she could do was shake her head in denial and all she could manage was a plaintive whisper. "Men like you don't fall in love with women like me."

He stepped closer and raised his right hand to catch a tear on her face. His touch was unsteady until the fingers came into contact with her skin, then they curved automatically to cup her cheek. "What do you mean, women like you? Beautiful women? Strong women? Sexy women?"

Desperation threaded through her—that he didn't love her, couldn't love her—along with fear . . . that he did. All her life she'd wanted it. Would she know what to do with it if she had it? "I—I shot you."

A hint of amusement was barely audible in his voice. "Yeah. I figure that ought to be good for getting my own way a few times, don't you? Starting now."

"Now?"

He tried to bring his other hand to her face but, with a grunt of pain, settled for resting it at her waist. "Don't go, Selena. We can work out the problems between us, but not if you run away. If you leave, you're just going to break both our hearts, and, honey, I'm not up to that right now."

Right now . . . but maybe he would be later. Maybe, if she stayed, if she let herself believe he really did care for her, in a few weeks or a few months he would decide that he *was* up to a broken heart, only it would be *her* heart. Could she let herself believe he loved her, only to find out that he didn't—or, worse, that he did, but not enough?

But what if he did love her enough, but she never knew because she didn't give them a chance to find out?

She raised her gaze to his. There was confusion in his dark eyes, and reluctance, and tenderness. It would be so much easier if she could look and see nothing but accepting, forgiving love . . . but her life had never been easy, had it?

"Do you know what you're asking?" she whispered.

He moved closer, until she could distinguish the heat radiating from his body from the afternoon sun, until she could catch a hint of his cologne, until she couldn't think about anything but how very much she wanted to be even closer. She wanted to crawl right inside him, become a part of him, trust her life and her heart to him forever.

"Yeah. I'm asking you to take a chance."

Everything comes with risks, she'd told Henry, and it was true. Living, dying, loving . . . all risks that she could take, or not.

She could run away, live more completely alone than she'd ever been, and never know exactly how much she'd lost. But that wouldn't be living—merely surviving.

Or she could stay. Face the consequences of her actions. Face the future and maybe even a shot at getting it all— even her wildest, most sacred and secret dream: Tony, love, marriage, and a family.

She laid one hand against his chest and felt his heartbeat, strong and steady. "I would have died for you."

"I know. But I just want you to live."

And the only way to do that was to take risks. She drew a deep breath and prepared to take the biggest risk of her life. "I love you, Tony."

He smiled, and it was like the sun rising after a long, dark night. She felt fearful and anxious and unsteady and off balance . . . and safe. *I'll be your safe place,* he'd promised the night of the tornado, and he'd kept his word. She'd never had a safe place before.

Wrapping her arms around his neck, she gave him her sexiest, sultriest smile. "I've had a really lousy week, Tony," she said, brushing her mouth along his jaw. "Make love with me."

With a laugh, he kissed her, then hustled her into the house.

About the Author

Rachel Butler lives in Oklahoma with her husband and son, where she is at work on her next novel of romantic suspense featuring Selena McCaffrey, *Deep Cover*, coming from Dell Books in Fall 2005.

They gave her the role of a killer.
And no one plays it better...

Don't miss the next thrilling novel
starring reluctant assassin Selena McCaffrey

Deep Cover
by
Rachel Butler

Coming in Fall 2005
from Dell Books

Read on for an exclusive sneak peek—and look
for your copy at your favorite bookseller.

DEEP COVER

They gave her the
role of a killer.
And no one plays
it better....

RACHEL BUTLER

Author of *The Assassin*

Deep Cover

On sale in Fall 2005

Selena McCaffrey had had one hell of a day.

A .45 gripped loosely in both hands, she sighted on a paper silhouette target seventy-five feet away. She'd emptied the last magazine center mass in the target's chest. This one was going into the head.

The day hadn't started badly. She'd gone for a run that morning, then put in a good six hours at the easel. Then she'd opened her door to find Special Agent King of the FBI on her stoop and everything had gone to hell.

Selena two-tapped the target—fired two shots in rapid succession—then did it again. The ground around her was littered with brass. The owner of the shooting range had left her alone to relieve her frustration. In the time she'd been there, the sun had set and the flood lamps had come on, but she still didn't feel much better.

It sounded so reasonable the way the FBI put it. She had an in—a fourteen-year pseudo-father/daughter relationship—with Henry Daniels, better known to her as

William Davis, a man who headed an extensive drug operation that stretched around the world. He had always intended for her to take over the business someday, and now that he was out of commission, the FBI was pressuring her to fulfill his wish—and, in the process, help them shut down the operation once and for all. If she cooperated, they would be willing to forget their list of charges against her. If she didn't. . . .

Sweat trickling down her spine, she fired the last of the bullets in the magazine and set the pistol on the table beside her. She pulled off the ear protectors and combed her fingers through her hair. Summer nights in Oklahoma weren't much different from back home in Key West— hot and muggy—though she missed the ocean breezes. In Tulsa the best they could offer was the Arkansas River, sluggish and brown, and the scents of the oil refinery on the west bank. But that was all right. She hadn't come for the weather, and she wasn't staying for it, either.

Clenching her jaw against the curses she wanted to shout into the night, she was reaching for the box of bullets when a puff of dust rose from the concrete only inches from her hand. She stared at it, and the small neat hole left behind, for the instant it took her brain to process the information—the same instant it took a second bullet to glance off the cement and ricochet into the night. Instinctively she dove to the ground, taking cover behind the nearest half-wall. From her position she could see her gun on the table—and fewer than ten

.rounds of ammo in the box beside it. She hadn't had a chance to reload, and the shooter probably knew that.

He couldn't have picked a better place for an attack to go unnoticed. The neighborhood was largely industrial, and the people who worked nearby were accustomed to gunfire. Even if anyone was around this late, they wouldn't think to call the police.

Another shot splintered the concrete above her head, showering fragments on her skin. She flinched, and the switchblade in her waistband dug into her skin. With the blade and her extensive martial arts training, she'd always felt confident wherever she'd gone, but neither was of any use against an attacker secreted in the darkness with what sounded like an AK. He could kill her, then disappear with no one the wiser.

Damned if she was going to die without a fight.

She shimmied on her belly along the length of the cinder-block wall, stirring up puffs of dust. When she reached the far end, she drew a deep breath, murmured a silent prayer as yet another shot rang out, then eased to a crouch. There was no sound—no heavy breathing, no fumbled reloading, no sirens racing to her assistance. Nothing but the thudding of her own heart.

One, two, three, she counted, then launched herself around the corner toward the table where her weapon lay. Bullets followed, biting into the ground, the cement, the wood posts that supported the overhanging roof. She hit the ground with a thud, rolling, reaching up to grab the pistol and the box of bullets. Weakening relief rushed over her when her blind groping located both. Holding tightly to her best chance to walk out of the range alive, she rolled again, came up onto her feet in one fluid movement, then dove once more for the cover of the cinder-block wall.

Her hands were steady as she fed the bullets into the empty clip. Once the final round was in place, she shoved it into the butt of the pistol, chambered a round, then pushed the remaining ammo into her pocket as she rose onto her knees.

The angle of the shots indicated they'd come from the same location, a spot high on the wooded hill to the south of the range. Presumably that meant there was only one shooter, and he had a bird's-eye view of the entire area. He knew she was alone, knew her odds of making it to the squat building that fronted the range or to her car in the parking lot beyond were minimal. He could pick her off like a sitting duck.

Selena was forty feet from the door, and the wall that shielded her was the last cover available. The door opened into a hallway that ran the length of the building. On the right at the back was the indoor range, used during the worst of Oklahoma's inhospitable summers and icy winters. At the front was the office and the armory, both heavily secured. She was a fast runner, but not fast enough, not with the shooter's vantage point and the flood lamps that turned darkness into day.

Unless he couldn't see her.

Sinking back against the wall, she sighted on the

nearest light and fired. The bulb exploded with a pop. Steeling herself against the panic that was just under the surface, she hit a second one, and a third, even as the shooter opened up on her protective cover with a hail of automatic weapon fire.

The instant the last lamp went out, cloaking the range in shadow, Selena surged to her feet and made a furious zig-zag dash for the door. Clods of dirt exploded around her and something hit her arm with enough force to send her staggering against the building. Biting her lip against the pain, she jerked the door open and raced down the dark hall. Wherever the assassin was parked, she had no doubt she could reach her Thunderbird seconds before he made his way down the hill. Seconds were all she needed . . . unless he had an accomplice waiting outside.

She didn't let the thought slow her. Gripping the pistol in one hand, she dug in her pocket for her keys with the other. As she burst outside, she unlocked the car with the remote, yanked the door open, and threw herself inside. The engine roared to life, and the tires squealed wildly as she backed up, then accelerated out of the empty parking lot, barely making the turn onto the street before pressing the gas pedal to the floor.

She'd gone two miles, the speedometer pushing eighty, before the adrenaline rush deserted her. Her foot eased up on the pedal at the same time her hands gripped the steering wheel tighter. The throbbing in her left arm was growing too strong to ignore. When she reached back with her right hand, her fingers came away sticky with blood.

In the last seconds her breathing had gone beyond rapid to nothing less than a pant, and her entire body was starting to shake. She turned off the street into a shopping center that was closed for the night, drove around one end to the back, and parked in the loading zone for a discount store, where tall walls shielded her on three sides. Pressing a tissue to the wound in her arm, she closed her eyes and forced herself to breathe, calmness and control in, fear and pain out. When the trembling had stopped, when her heart rate had returned to some semblance of normal, she reached for her cell phone and dialed one of only two numbers stored in it.

"Tony, this is Selena," she said when he answered, surprised by how calm she sounded. "I was wondering if you could come meet me. I think I've been shot."

Kathryn Daniels Hamilton nodded politely to the uniformed guards at the main gate of the estate, drove around to the back of the house, then went inside. Sonja, the Daniels family housekeeper since Kathryn was a girl, stood at the stove, and her husband, Cecil, the butler, sat at the nearby table, a newspaper open in front of him.

Ninety minutes earlier, Kathryn had been waiting in the reception area of the local FBI office, idly paging through a magazine in between glances at her watch. When Mr. King had called to set up this appointment, he had offered to meet her at the hospital or at the family's Riverside Drive estate, but she'd politely refused. She didn't want a stranger coming to Henry's hospital room, and she certainly didn't want to invite one into his home. That was reserved for family and friends, not glorified police officers.

A police officer himself, her brother didn't appreciate her opinion that policemen ranked with the hired help. One paid their salaries, and benefited from their particular skills when necessary, but one didn't socialize with them. After all, they were called public servants for a reason.

She'd always thought Henry had undercut his own potential significantly by choosing a career in law enforcement, no matter that he'd risen through the ranks to become chief of police. Business and politics—that was where the real money, power, and prestige lay. If he'd gone into either, he wouldn't be lying in a coma, wasting away before her very eyes.

Footsteps drew her out of her thoughts, and she watched a young woman pass by. The girl wore a slim, tropical-print silk skirt that reached almost to her ankles and was split on one side to mid-thigh. Kathryn didn't have to look any higher than her hands to see that she was black, or at least, half black—which was half too much, Kathryn thought as she returned her gaze to the magazine.

A moment later, more footsteps approached. "Mrs.

Hamilton? Special Agent King is ready for you," the receptionist said. "If you'll come this way . . ."

Now, Kathryn greeted Sonja and Cecil, brushed off Sonja's offer of coffee, and passed through the kitchen into the house proper.

She'd always loved this house—a beautiful white gem plunked down in the middle of a vast lawn, filled with beautiful things and, her grandmother had liked to say, beautiful people. Definitely privileged people, for all the good it had done them. Her father had grown up here, his every whim fulfilled, but it hadn't stopped him from dying of cancer before his forty-fifth birthday. She and Henry had been raised here as well, spoiled, yes, but nothing they'd been given—not wealth, not attention—could raise him from the hospital bed, where he lay dying before her very eyes.

She wandered through the rooms—the very formal living room called the white room, because everything in it was; the library filled with leather-bound first editions; the gentlemen's drawing room, where her grandfather had played poker with his cronies, betting oil wells and real estate; the ladies' drawing room where Grandmama had entertained their wives; the formal dining room that could seat thirty; the informal dining room that seated only ten. Every piece of furniture was antique, every slab of marble imported, every painting and knickknack and lamp worth a small fortune.

Kathryn had taken it all for granted when she was a child. All her friends had lived in beautiful homes, though none so beautiful as her own. She'd been the only one to have a Monet hanging on her bedroom wall, but then there had been a great master in every room; she'd paid them little attention. She had been in college before she'd realized that not everyone lived this way. A sorority house was as close as she'd ever come to seeing how the other half lived, and that had been more than enough for her.

Trailing her hand along the banister, she climbed the grand staircase to the second floor. Her meeting with the FBI had been far more unpleasant than she'd expected. She had thought they would ask a few questions about the men who'd harmed her brother, offer their sympathy, and leave her to visit the hospital.

As it turned out, *she* had been the one asking questions. They'd told her a fantastic tale . . . and had proof to support it. About how Henry, loving brother and highly regarded chief of police, was a drug dealer. How he'd suffered his injuries while trying to kill one of his own detectives and the young woman he'd referred to as his niece. How he'd lived a secret life, complete with a different identity, for twenty years. How the FBI now wanted to use his family home to destroy the business he'd worked so hard to build.

She hadn't been able to decide which part of the story stunned her most. In the time since, she'd figured it out: the niece.

Henry living a secret life as a drug dealer . . . it should shame her, but she could see that. He'd always looked for thrills and challenges; that was why he'd become a police officer in the first place. He'd been a master game player all his life. He loved competition, strategy, outsmarting, and outlasting everyone else. He loved pitting his skills against all comers, and he especially loved winning.

And he'd proven himself quite capable of looking the other way when a crime was committed, if the incentive was strong enough. She'd seen that for herself.

But the niece . . . the FBI agent had called her by various names—Gabriela Sanchez, Rosa Jimenez, Amalia Acostas, Selena McCaffrey. Henry had met her when she was fourteen, and claimed her for his own. He'd treated her like family—dressed her in the finest clothes, sent her to the best schools, filled her every need.

No matter how Kathryn tried, she simply couldn't imagine Henry taking someone else's child to raise. He'd been uncompromising when she'd told him she and Grant were adopting a child, and he'd never shown the least interest in Jefferson once the boy had joined the family. A simple legal process couldn't make a stranger family, he'd insisted. Blood mattered.

But then *he'd* taken in a stranger, and a fourteen-year-old girl at that. At least Jefferson had been a mere five years old when they'd adopted him. By fourteen, the damage caused by a child's upbringing was done; they were rebellious, troublesome, and not the least appealing. The only reasons she could think of for a man to take in a stranger's teenage daughter were too perverse to give voice to.

At the top of the stairs, she turned to the right and went to the one room she'd avoided since returning home—Henry's study. That was where the events that led to Henry's coma had taken place. The police had removed what they considered evidence, and Sonja had cleaned the room, then closed the door, and it had remained closed. Now, her hand trembling, Kathryn turned the knob to go inside.

It had been raining that day in Greenhill, when Kathryn received the call from a distraught Sonja saying that Henry had been gravely injured. Kathryn had hastily packed while Grant borrowed the use of a friend's jet for the trip to Tulsa. One of the deputy chiefs had picked her up at the airport and delivered her to the hospital, and he'd filled her in on what had happened.

A daytime burglary. The estate was encircled by a six-foot iron fence; there was an elaborate alarm system with panic buttons in every room; armed guards patrolled the grounds; and still the thugs had managed to find their way inside. It had been no secret that Henry was making a public appearance with the mayor that day—some sort of fundraiser that had received plenty of publicity beforehand—but he'd left early and surprised the burglars in the act. One of them had shot him, and the impact had knocked him through the window behind his desk. He'd fallen headfirst onto the parapet four feet below, and had been in a coma ever since.

That was the official version of events—what she'd

been told by the deputy chief, read in the paper, heard on the news.

Now the FBI was saying, no, sorry, it didn't happen that way at all.

The hand-knotted rug Grandpapa had brought back from Turkey was gone, leaving bare marble. There were dark spots on the wall near the vault door, and a large splatter at the far end of the room. Blood, her mind supplied, even though she didn't want to know. No one had died in this room, according to the authorities, but not for lack of trying. One of the thugs had been shot, another had suffered a concussion and a broken nose along with a stab wound, though the third had only bruises and contusions. The young detective credited in the media with saving Henry's life had, in fact, been the one to shoot him, and he'd been shot himself by Henry's other target that day. Selena, the girl he called niece.

Actually, someone *had* died that day, Kathryn thought as she forced herself to approach the windows and gaze down onto the narrow parapet. Sonja had brought in a crew to clean away the broken glass and blood, but it was still far too easy for Kathryn to imagine Henry lying there, dying. Machines kept his body functioning, but his spirit, his essence, was gone.

As a chill rushed over her, she hurried from the room, closing the door firmly behind her. She'd told Mr. King that she needed time to consider his request, to take in everything he'd told her, and he'd agreed none too graciously. He'd made it clear that she had little choice, that asking her permission was no more than a courtesy. He'd mentioned words like criminal enterprise, seizure, and forfeiture, and asked her to please give him an answer within the next day or so.

At the end of the corridor, she went into Henry's bedroom. Sonja continued to dust it every day, as if he was merely away on a trip and might return home at any moment. His toiletries still filled the bathroom, his clothes the closet. Kathryn pressed her face into a jacket, inhaling the familiar scent of him, and her breath caught on a sob. "Oh, Henry, you fool! Any man in the world would have been satisfied with what you had, but not you. No, you wanted more—more money, more power, more challenge, more excitement. And look where it got you."

Leaving the closet, she stopped in front of the portrait that hung in the sitting area between two love seats. Grandmama and Grandpapa were seated in the middle, Mother and Father stood behind them, and she and Henry flanked them. They'd been a beautiful family. Now they were all gone, or as good as.

On a small table beneath the painting stood two dozen or more framed photographs. Henry graduating from the academy. When he'd been promoted to detective. His first job as deputy chief. Receiving awards and commendations. Photo after photo of Henry in the highlights of his law-enforcement career.

"What about your other career?" she murmured as she studied his smiling face. "Nothing to commemorate earning your first million in drug money? No photograph marking your move from just another dealer to the big-time? Nothing to remind you of the first murder you committed in the name of the almighty dollar?"

She was about to turn away when a small frame caught her eye. It measured barely three inches tall and was easily overlooked among the larger, more prominently displayed photos. Her hand trembled when she reached for it—and with good reason, she soon realized.

The girl in the photo was in her teens, and she wore a school uniform along with an uneasy smile. Her skin was a creamy light brown, her hair black, and her features bore the obvious stamp of her African-American heritage . . . along with a familiarity that made Kathryn's heart clutch.

The frame fell from her unsteady grip, landing face up on the floor. Kathryn clapped one hand over her mouth and stared at it—at the lovely young girl she hadn't seen in twenty-eight years. The girl who had haunted her all those years. The girl she'd believed was dead.

She sank to her knees in front of the hearth and covered her face with both hands. "Damn you, Henry! Dear God, *what* have you done?"